OUTSTANDING PRAISE FOR THOMAS

"I CANNOT TELL YOU HOW GREAT AN ACHIEVEMENT I THINK IT TO BE. It is more than scholarship—though the scholarship of the years must have been immense. . . . The book is rich in texture, in imagination, in understanding of men in torment, and everything flows from this richness of mind." *—Theodore H. White*

SHELLEY MYDANS spent ten years researching Thomas. *She is also the author of* Open City, *a novel based on her experiences as a prisoner of the Japanese. She is married to the well-known photographer and author Carl Mydans. The Mydans live in Larchmont, New York, with their two children.*

"A more ambitious and more impressive work than all but a few historical novels. The narrative's wide panorama includes many interesting glimpses of the customs, manners and beliefs of the twelfth century. Mrs. Mydans has described sieges, sacks, tortures, diplomacy and high politics. But always Thomas Becket dominates her pages."
—Orville Prescott, The New York Times

Shelley Mydans

THOMAS

A Novel of the Life, Passion,
and Miracles of Becket

N·A·L SIGNET BOOKS

A Signet Book

Published by The New American Library

This is an authorized reprint of a hardcover edition published by Doubleday & Company, Inc.

FIRST PRINTING, FEBRUARY, 1967

The few fictional characters in this book (those of the family of the moneyer) are products of the author's imagination and are not related to actual persons living or dead; all others are historical figures taken from the records of their times.

Lines of verse adapted from *Medieval Latin Lyrics* by Helen Waddell are used with the permission of Constable & Company, Ltd.

Lines of verse adapted from *Medieval People* by Eileen Power are used with the permission of Barnes & Noble, Inc., and Methuen & Company, Ltd.

SIGNET TRADEMARK REG. U.S. PAT. OFF. AND FOREIGN COUNTRIES
REGISTERED TRADEMARK—MARCA REGISTRADA
HECHO EN CHICAGO, U.S.A.

SIGNET BOOKS are published by
The New American Library, Inc.
1301 Avenue of the Americas, New York, New York 10019

PRINTED IN THE UNITED STATES OF AMERICA

For CARL

AUTHOR'S NOTE

Nearly ten years ago, when we were living in London and our children were small, I sometimes read to them in the evenings from Charles Dickens' *A Child's History of England.* One night I came to this passage:

" 'I will make,' thought King Henry Second, 'this Chancellor of mine, Thomas à Becket, Archbishop of Canterbury. He will head the Church and, being devoted to me, will help me correct the Church.' Now Thomas à Becket was proud and loved to be famous. He was already famous for the pomp of his life, for his riches, his gold and silver plate, his waggons, horses and attendants. He could do no more in that way than he had done; and being tired of that kind of fame (which is a very poor one) he longed to have his name celebrated for something else. Nothing, he knew, would render him so famous in the world as the setting of his own utmost power and ability against the utmost power and ability of the king . . ."

I stopped. This was very colorful, but was it true? It seemed an odd motivation for one of the great dramas of history. "Just remember that Dickens had strong opinions," I said, "and he lived in his own times too. This is not necessarily the way things happened." We did not go any further with Dickens' version of history. "I think I will try to find out what did happen," I said.

I am not claiming that I have found out "the truth" or that I have fully digested or interpreted—or even read—all the facts about these fascinating men and their times. But I had the advantage of starting from a base of almost total ignorance and lack of prejudice. I had to spend several years wandering around in the twelfth century, reading somewhat haphazardly, peering at Norman architecture, pondering what I learned, before I got the feel of it.

This book falls into the category of novel, I suppose, partly because I invented most of the conversations (though some I took from the writings of those who claimed to have been there) and a few of the situations, especially in the early life, which is not so thoroughly recorded by contemporaries, and the characters of the family of the moneyer Elured Porre, although Elured himself has a place in the histories. (His name is recorded in a claim against the Crown.) But I have tried to be true to the facts—both large and small—as set forth in the original documents.

This original source material is surprisingly plentiful. On my very first visit to the British Museum I found, there in the open stacks of the Reading Room, seven volumes in the Rolls series of English history devoted to the "Materials for the History of Thomas Becket." Four of these volumes contain biographies written by men who knew Thomas or witnessed the murder; three are devoted to the letters exchanged by the principals in the quarrel. Luckily for me, because my Latin is rudimentary, this material had been edited and annotated in English by James Craigie Robertson, Canon of Canterbury, whose book *Becket, Archbishop of Canterbury,* though published in 1859, is so closely bound to its sources that I still find it the most valuable work on the subject.

These first biographers, seven of whom we know by name, were Churchmen writing at the time of the first great spate of miracles and were of course partial to Thomas' side of the story. But the chroniclers of that era were not always so, and in the centuries since then his reputation has had many ups and downs. For about three hundred years he was a most popular saint and colorful legends grew up about him: he was given an exotic background (his mother was said to have been a Saracen maiden who rescued his Crusader father from prison) and a pet name: Thomas à Becket. But after the Reformation he became something of a villain among Protestant writers, and even the Roman Catholics played him down.

Early in the nineteenth century he experienced a revival. A French historian, Augustin Thierry, suddenly (and erroneously) discovered him to be a Saxon hero battling his Norman overlord. And in England the Reverend R. H. Froude, writing somewhat more accurately, extolled him as a champion of the Church against secular oppression. (His brother, however, the historian J. A. Froude, could find almost nothing good to say about the archbishop in his *Life and Times of Thomas Becket,* while R. A. Thompson, whose *Thomas Becket, Martyr Patriot* was based on the same available information, could find nothing bad to say.)

Indeed, it seems that men cannot write about Thomas and Henry without taking sides. Tennyson, in his play *Becket,* took exception to Henry's sex life and Thomas came off well in contrast. Dickens, as we have seen, had little use for the saint. T. S. Eliot, in our own times, re-elevated him.

I am not going to list all the books I have consulted, but

if a reader would like to go into the subject further I can recommend *Thomas of London* by L. B. Radford for a history of Becket's early life, *Becket, Archbishop of Canterbury* by James Craigie Robertson, which I have mentioned before, especially for the details of the quarrel, and *St. Thomas of Canterbury, His Death and Miracles* by E. A. Abbot for a charming translation of the early miracles as recorded by Benedict, the monk of Canterbury who first collected them. The standard early work on the king is Lord Lyttelton's *Henry II,* and for an authoritative history of the period as a whole I used the modern (1951) textbook, *The Oxford History of England: From Domesday Book to Magna Carta* by A. L. Poole.

Sometimes when I went back to the book after leaving it for some months—or even years, as I once did—I wondered where I had come upon the alien rhythm in which I was writing and recently, on rereading St. Bernard's *On the Love of God* as translated into English in 1950, I was delighted to find what was evidently my unconscious source. The translator, a Religious of C.S.M.V., is obviously a scholar of unusual sensitivity and I am deeply indebted to her.

Other writers to whom I am indebted for their insight and sensitivity to the period are also—by happenstance, perhaps, or by some strange quality of our sex—all women. They are Helen Waddell, on whose *The Wandering Scholars* and *Medieval Latin Lyrics* I leaned very heavily, especially in the scenes set in Paris; Amy Kelly, whose scholarly biography, *Eleanor of Aquitaine and the Four Kings,* has more dramatic tension and vivid incident than most even first-rate novels; Lady Doris Mary Stenton, honorary secretary of the Pipe Roll Society, whose *English Society in the Early Middle Ages* is crammed with the sort of detail that brings past times to life; and Dr. Margaret Murray, whose anthropological studies, *The God of the Witches* and *The Divine King in England,* I used as a basis for the theme of the Old Religion in my book. The last time I was in England I went to call on Miss Murray not long after her hundredth birthday and shortly before she died. She was very wrinkled and small but her mind was alert and her eyes bright. She answered some questions for me that had not been answered in her books and it is on this conversation that I have based some of my suppositions—not, perhaps, an unquestionable source but one allowable, I hope, in a novel.

There are many other fine books on the period, of course, but the above mentioned are my favorites and my friends. It has been said that writing is a lonely job, but that is not so when the writer has such stimulating companions as these to work with. I was sorry to say goodbye to them when I finished the book.

I want to give my thanks also to Bernice Woll, who read the manuscript while it was in progress and whose perceptive intelligence and long experience in this field helped to bring it to its final shape, to Dr. Francis X. Connolly and especially Dr. Jeremiah O'Sullivan, both of Fordham University, who corrected my errors concerning Church practices in the twelfth century but should not be held to account for some of my opinions, to Dr. William Urry, Librarian of Canterbury Cathedral, who is so familiar with twelfth-century Canterbury as to know, among other things, the names and locations of nearly every householder in the city at that time and who shared his knowledge with me, to the Reverend Dr. N. W. Wallbank, rector of St. Bartholomew-the-Great in Smithfield, London, whose inspiration was given unawares but will last me far beyond this book, and of course to the editors at Doubleday, Anne Freedgood and, most warmly, Lee Barker, whose perception and enthusiasm kept me going all these years.

S.S.M.

Larchmont, New York
March 9, 1965

I

THE EMPIRE OF HENRY II OF ANJOU AND THE DOMINIONS OF LOUIS VII OF FRANCE

ENGLISH CHANNEL
Gravelines
Calais
Boulogne
Barfleur
Rouen
Caen
Falaise
NORMANDY
Amiens
Soissons
Compiègne
Rheims
Paris
BRITTANY
Rennes
MAINE
Le Mans
Montmirail
Sens
Pontigny
Orleans
Auxerre
Freteval
Blois
Vezelay
ANJOU
Nantes
Angers
Tours
Touraine
Bourges
Never
Poitiers
POITOU
FRANCE
Limoges
AQUITAINE
AUVERGNE
Bordeaux
Cahors
GASCONY
Toulouse
TOULOUSE
NAVARRE
ARAGON

BOOK ONE

MURDER AND MIRACLES

CHAPTER I

FOUR O'CLOCK had not long gone by, yet there was darkness over all the land. Black rain came in great gusts, driven before a wind that howled along the forest slopes from Harbledown. Wild forking rain stabbed the chalk downs beyond the river, and blind rain fell, heavy as a man in chains, from the black pit of heaven upon Canterbury below.

For six years the land had been harried. Fields lay untilled and the people in awe of something to come. Now at this hour of Vespers on the fifth day of Christmas in the year of Our Lord 1170, that which they had foreseen was done. And with that act the wind rose shrieking and the earth groaned.

Over the city the storm cracked and rolled so that the trees in the churchyards bent beneath it and in the turmoil bundles of thatch from the house roofs flew about wildly, this way and that. Lightning flashed. The golden turrets on the cathedral church leaped up and stood a moment, white against the sky, and nearby, just outside the monastery gates, the sign at the cordwainer's shop winked in the sudden glare. Then the wind took it as it swung, madly flapping in the dark again, and tore it from its joints and flung it down the lane until it crashed against the doorway of the moneysmithy and lay still.

Behind the door a boy named Viel lay shuddering on his bed. At this new sound above the storm he rose up on his knees.

"Father!" he called, his voice a whisper. "Father, there is someone at the door."

His father stood beside him, brought by the sound of knocking, the thud against the door, not by the child. He stepped up quickly to the latch—a little man, the latch as high as he—and lifted it and peered out through the crack. The boy crept up and stood behind his father, shivering.

There, in a flash of lightning, in the rain, he saw before him, phantomlike, as though they rose up from the mire of the lane, four giant horsemen riding the huge destriers men ride to war.

"Mother of God," he breathed. And in the next breath, "Father?" But neither heaven nor the silent man beside him answered.

The horses were black forms again, the men blurred humps astride them until the next flash showed them—riding single file, the nervous horses crowding each other and the men bent low, the hard cones of their helmets pointed against the rain. As the wind tossed their cloaks the boy could see the glint of wet chain mail, the iron hilts of swords. Then, in the darkness once again, they rode around the corner and were gone.

"What is it, Father? What will happen now?"

His father spoke at last. "No more, no more. It has been done," he said. Strange to hear mourning in that dry and bitter voice. Strange to hear woe—and under that, behind and through it, wonder, exhilaration almost, something of joy. "It has been done."

He pulled his cloak about his throat and bending almost double slipped through the door and ran out, skirting beneath the eaves, toward Burgate Street and the cathedral gates. The boy watched, wondering to see his father run so, in the rain and danger. He saw him dart across the lane while a white flick of lightning brought into relief his scurrying form against the shuttered shops and the queer hump that rose, lop-sided, horny, between his shoulder blades.

Rain made the horses fearful and the wide reins slippery under the gloved hand. The four knights bent against the wind and cursed, lifting their heads from time to time to search their way along the unfamiliar lanes and high streets of the city. They rode in darkness from the dark cathedral gate, four warriors as from battle and pursued by storm. Their soldiers had been left behind, within the monastery grounds. De Broc, their guide, their instrument, had gone ahead.

The horses picked their way out of the mud of Pillory Lane into the Highstreet where their great hoofs slipped and stumbled on the cobbles and the white rain, seen by lightning, struck and rebounded from the road like arrows.

The four knights halted, one behind the other, big men in their hauberks, their faces masked by the iron nasals of their helmets and their figures swollen by their wind-filled cloaks: four giant knights, four lords of standing in the court and loyal followers of King Henry II, four murderers.

Fitz Urse, riding in the lead, looked up and squinted through the rain. Across the narrow street he saw a church, St. Mary Fishman Church. He knew it. Ranulf de Broc's men had shown it to him when they came this way that afternoon. He nudged his horse to take the passageway that opened up beside it. And as the frightened animal, neck stretched, ears pricked, balked before plunging down into the mud and blackness, Fitz Urse felt Richard Brito push up close beside him and reach out and touch his arm.

Reginald Fitz Urse, Son of the Bear, well named, a rough and powerful man was one another man would choose to stand beside in battle, a man to follow when the fearful doubt comes creeping to a sobering mind. And Brito followed him and crowded close.

Fitz Urse felt Brito's hand, felt the trembling knee against his own, and smelled the wine that carried on the other's breath. He heard the Breton's voice, uncertain, "What lies ahead?"

"Mud and water," grunted Fitz Urse as he urged his horse forward.

But Brito kept beside him. "Which way to Watling Street?" His face came close as he ducked to avoid the eaves and swayed a little in the saddle. Fitz Urse did not answer. He turned to see if Tracy and Hugh de Morville had found the lane and kept with them.

William Tracy, riding bent behind them, glanced up to see their dark forms, close together, and observed the Breton's lurching form, was quick to understand. A man of action, Tracy, quick to hear a king's words spoken in anger, quick to interpret, quick to take the course laid out. He was a loyal man and what he did in loyalty could not be wrong. He raised his sleeve, less sodden than his glove, and wiped the water from his nose and smiled a small smile of disgust, just for himself.

Hugh de Morville saw Fitz Urse's signal and raised an answering hand, and they rode on. Hugh was their leader, though he rode last. He was a silent man and moved as though he bore a burden. His power came from his position; he was a man of standing. But there was something in his history that weighted him—the memory of his wife's cry like the cry of Potiphar: "Hugh de Morville, 'ware, beware! Beware of Leothwulf's drawn sword!" And Leothwulf, the boy, bound and lowered in the boiling oil and dying, placing the curse forever—that something never mentioned, as though forgotten by a silent, conscience-laden man.

They rode on, jostling together, through the crooked lane, past the dark houses, the stink of the empty fish market, past gardens and the small fields of the town, all beaten flat beneath the flail of rain.

When they reached Watling Street, Brito spoke again. "Reginald, for God's sake, where are the de Brocs? Where are their men?"

Fitz Urse looked at him, his dark face under the helmet split by the heavy nosepiece. "Ranulf's ahead," he said. "We meet at Ridingate. His brother and his men behind to keep the peace. Why, what's the matter?"

Brito recoiled, hacked out a laugh and spit the rain from his lips. "Water's the matter," he said, making light of it. They rode with their heads down again, but Fitz Urse heard him mutter curses on "this cursed wet land of England" and grunted at the note in his voice, but he said nothing.

At Ridingate Ranulf de Broc waited with a troop of men, taking shelter under the stone arch of the gate and beneath the overhang of old St. Edmund's Church nearby. Ranulf was jovial; this had been a day to make him glad. For six years he had had control of the archbishop's lands, to farm, to take the produce from, to loot. For six years Saltwood Castle had been his own from which to rule, an uncontested lord, from which to sally forth, he and his men, through the surrounding lands, even into the monastery of Christchurch, even into the palace of the archbishop which lay within its grounds. Then the upstart had come back again from quarreling with the king, to seek his lands, to take the people to his side, to quarrel with de Broc. But now no more.

Ranulf watched the four knights riding hunched and silent toward him. His men had lit the lantern in the gate. It swung and jerked upon its iron hook, casting a small glow, almost dying in the wind. Its light fell dimly over Ranulf's massive face, his brow in darkness, his mouth open as he laughed and filled his lungs. His yellow beard was dark with rain and when he closed his mouth he worked his jaw and bit the water that hung from the hair along his upper lip.

He shouted as the knights drew near and spoke in the rough Norman French that barons of England used. He would turn back and join the men who kept the watch at Christchurch. The monks who fled like beetles from the light would soon be creeping back. They might try to make a martyr out of the traitor there. "Why this haste for Saltwood?"

The knights sat in a row before him, eying him. At last de Morville as first of rank among them spoke. "Our job is done," he said.

But Ranulf would not be put down. No, wait; turn back, he urged. He could show them hospitality in the archbishop's palace, there was still treasure there, fine horses in the stables; they could help themselves. And to rouse, persuade them, he lifted his great fist and pulled the reins so that his horse stepped sideways and crowded theirs. "King's men!" he shouted, "Henry's men! This way!"

But the knights sat silent, blocking his path.

"I am for Saltwood," Hugh de Morville said at last. And turning to the others, "You?"

"For Saltwood," answered Fitz Urse and Tracy.

Ranulf laughed. "Richard Brito," he called, "are you King Henry's man to let his vengeance go half done and traitor priest have Christian burial in the king's own land?"

"I am for Saltwood," Brito muttered. He alone of the four felt de Broc's strength of person and quailed before it. "My sword is gone," he said as though in explanation.

The baron pushed his horse against the knight's. "That was a blow you dealt!" he said into his face.

"That was a blow," Brito repeated. "My sword snapped clean in two against the pavement."

Ranulf grinned. "Who would have thought a priest's head so hard a nut to crack, eh?"

The two laughed in each other's faces. The wind blew, and Ranulf shouted out above it, "We have taught them how to shave the crowns of clerks!" They roared. But Hugh de Morville, silent, unsmiling, pushed his mount past them. Fitz Urse and Tracy followed him.

"Richard, are you for Saltwood?" Fitz Urse asked as he brushed by.

Brito turned, still grinning. "We taught them how to shave the heads of clerks," he said. But his grin died even as he spoke and he lurched forward and clutched his comrade's arm. And suddenly his voice came groaning: "Reginald, that was a blow I struck. My sword leaped from my hand. I could not find it, there in the bloody church, and the monks' whisper, whisper in the dark. . . ."

"Silence, for God's sake!" Fitz Urse roared. "And be a man. What we have done we had to do. The king has had no peace for years. Now let us have some peace." He shook the hand away.

Brito drew back. "What we have done. . . ." he echoed.

But Fitz Urse raised his voice and shouted over him. "Now it is done, I tell you. Peace, for the love of God! I tell you it is done!"

Tracy and de Morville, riding ahead, turned at the shout, but no one spoke again. Fitz Urse rode after them and Brito followed.

In silence, panting, Ranulf watched them go.

And the four knights rode out from Ridingate and down the ancient causeway of Stonestreet, bound for Saltwood Castle and to send word across the Channel to the king in Normandy. Canterbury lay behind.

In the dark cathedral the corpse lay where it had fallen, in the north transept beside the bloody pillar, the feet pointing toward the open doorway to the cloister. From outside came the faintest glow from the wet pavement and the soft steady sound of the rain. An unseen wind pushed under the arched door and stirred the black and silent air, and on the little altar of St. Benedict the vespers light jumped at the touch of its breath and then sank back.

Far away in the heart of the cathedral the antependium of the high altar, heavy with gold and silver thread, sighed as it dragged its fringe across the marble. There was no other sound. And yet the great church sheltered many men. In cold stone corners they crouched in hiding—in the crypt below, in the turret stairway and the chapel of St. Blaize above, in the great empty nave, in the carved stalls of the choir and at every altar the monks knelt, clung, trembled and prayed. And from the west porch and in all the doorways the frightened citizens peered in, straining for a sign of movement, a rustle or a voice.

They had been gathering thus, the free men of Canterbury, since the baron's men from Saltwood had called on the city magistrates to muster men and arms against the archbishop. When the citizens refused, the soldiers had turned rough and ordered all indoors, never to stir whatever might be seen or heard. Yet through the darkening city and the storm, as the hour of Vespers came and went, men crept out from this house and that and ran for Christchurch monastery and the cathedral church.

Some had been witnesses to murder, kept back by the Lord de Morville and his men. But all they saw, across the nave and the black transept, were jumping shadows and the glint of crosier and of sword, and all they heard were echoes of an argument, of curses and the clang of steel on stone. A cry of victory. A final voice: "He wanted to be king and more than a king. Now, let him be the king!" Then silence, darkness. No one dared move.

At last came light. Osbert, the dead archbishop's chamberlain, had found a candle in the chapter house and now came gliding through the cloister to avoid the soldiers who still patrolled the grounds. At the north transept door he lit it and crossed to the pillar and placed it in the sconce.

There at his feet lay the body of his master. Still, composed, the long corpse stretched out on its side. The head was turned face up, as though a foot had thrust it, and the eyes stared upward into the darkness and the painted ceiling overhead. Across the nose, from the right temple to the left cheekbone, was one red gash, but otherwise the face was peaceful. And around the crown there lay a ring of mingled blood and brains, red and white like flowers.

Osbert crossed himself and knelt. He touched the body, touched the head. Then he felt around the dark periphery beyond the candle's glow, his fingers sticky in the cooling blood, until he found the severed scalp. With a long sobbing sigh he looked up and around him in the shadows but found no one to help. He glanced down on himself and with his trembling hands searched underneath his garments, tore a length from his own shirt, and with it loosely bound the mutilated head. Then he rose and went to seek the infirmarian.

From the doorways over across the church the citizens crept forward, one and then another, then the crowd. They came into the light around the corpse and there they knelt. Their hands reached out to touch the body, snatch a thread from the white pallium around the shoulders, dip into the blood upon the floor. Their heads bent down to kiss the garments and the hands.

Walter the hunchback, coming behind the others, saw the man in front of him fall on his knees and bending double kiss the embroidered sandal on the dead foot. He saw the corpse, the reaching hands, saw his friend Lambin, master of a royal mint, stretch out a finger to the bandaged scalp and bring it up to touch his own eyes, one and then the other. Walter also knelt. He felt for a dry place beneath his soaking skirts and tore a strip of hem from his short kirtle where it was dry. His hands were shaking, his whole crooked body trembling, as he leaned forward and reached out along the length of the long corpse until he felt the wet blood on the stones. He laid his bit of cloth there, patting it, until he felt it moisten under his fingertips. Then he drew back and rolled it into a spill and quickly thrust it down his neck, beneath his cloak.

There was a sound behind him of sandaled feet on the stone pavement. The monks came forward now, black-cowled and silent, and with wide arms drove the people from the church. Walter went with the others, crowding out the cloister door, and the monks closed and bolted it behind them.

Inside they turned upon the body of the slain and stood about it like dark birds, watching it, not quite entering the light, and waited. Dead by the sword he lay, within the sanctuary of the church, victim of murderers who might return. Some of the monks withdrew again, into the darkness.

Benedict the sub-prior came forward in the light. The duty fell on him, since Prior Odo was away. His face looked young and white as chalk, but when he spoke they did not question but went to and fro at his direction: the sacristan to the high altar to remove the Blessed Sacrament because the church was desecrated now, two more to grope down the dark stairway to the crypt to find a bier, Brother Ernold to the sacristy for a container, others to bring benches from the nave to place about the body to protect it. Brother Benedict himself bent down and took the sacred pallium from around the neck and folded it and put it to one side so that it might be given to the poor.

The Host was carried from the church, the hand-bier placed beside the corpse, the benches set about it. Ernold came from the sacristy, bearing a silver basin in his arms, and laid it on the floor beside the broken head. Then many hands, the black sleeves folded back, cupped and scooped the blood and brains from off the floor and spilled them in the bowl.

Gilfridus the infirmarian came walking swiftly, following Osbert, into the little squared-off place of death. He was a doctor, and with a doctor's face, unmoved, he looked down on the corpse. Then he pushed the others back and sat down on the floor and lifted the mutilated head into his lap. With thread and needle, swiftly, expertly, he sewed the severed scalp back into place.

All was done in silence except for Benedict's soft words directing them and now and then a sibilant escaping from their lips at prayer. The darkness ringing them breathed with the breath of many others, standing away, observing.

But when they lifted up the corpse, now straight and orderly, to place it on the bier, the monks cried out. For underneath it, now revealed, where it had been hidden by the fur-lined robe, there lay the broken blade, all blood-stained, of a sword.

Here was the symbol of the desecration of the church. And the monks looked from eye to eye and back again upon the body and the sword. This man before them, dead, their archbishop, their leader and their spiritual father—what was he now? A martyr as the common people thought? Killed in the cause of God and Church and to be reverenced? Or was he merely traitor to the king, he who deserted them for six long years, killed in a brawl of his own instigating? De Broc had shouted in the darkness when he left, he would return and feed the body to the pigs. Where should they hide it?

They looked at Benedict. His eyes were blank in his white face. A voice, a monk's, spoke from the darkness, phrasing the doubt that gathered in their minds: "He is no martyr; he is justly served."

They stood in silence, no one replied, until an old man walked into the pool of light: Robert of Merton, teacher, friend, confessor of the dead archbishop. His gentle, withered face was calm, abstracted, as though he had just left a peaceful place and still remembered it, but his eyes were shadowed when they looked down at his friend. Then he looked up at all their faces, doubt-ridden and dark-socketed under the wavering light, and spoke as teacher to a group of novices: " 'Do you see glory and yet not perceive it?' " Words from the office for the dead. Robert had found the ancient comfort in them once again as he knelt beside the little altar of St. Benedict and prayed that even now he might accept the will of God—even at this time, while the Devil's argument within the inner room, the confrontation by the pillar in the church, the deathblows and the final dying words still echoed in his ears.

Brother Benedict, who was a man to sift and test all words, said, "Show us the glory."

" 'There is one glory of the sun, another glory of the moon,' " said Robert, still in the words of Paul, " 'And yet another glory of the stars, for one star differs from another in its glory.' Come, take him up, and I will show you glory here."

Four monks bent down and took the handles of the bier. They followed Robert where he led them, up the steps and to the choir, leaving the broken sword, the costly fur-lined cloak, the folded pallium behind them on the bloody stones.

"Bring candles," Robert said, "and place him here before the altar where we may honor him."

They did as they were told, and knelt each one in his accustomed place as for a service.

Then Prior Robert stooped before the body of his friend.

He thrust his hand into the opening of the tunic and pulled forth a fold of cloth from that still breast, the rough and spiky cloth of a hair shirt. The dark, stained texture stood up stiffly in his fist and from its folds black specks of body lice ran out on the warm hand.

It was a proof. A monk said, "He was a saint indeed; we knew it not!"

Robert said nothing, holding the cold cloth in his hand. He knew, he sometimes glimpsed, what made a saint. He knew the many ways that men sought God, the many ways they failed, their sins, and he knew Thomas. "But if we seek thee, Lord, have we not found thee?" he said in his heart. "And may I not do this, for friendship, out of love?"

He nodded as they watched his face, his eyes. And they were swayed. Their voices rose in lamentation for the dead, in praise of this new martyr of the Church.

Walter the moneyer spoke to no one as he took the dark streets home. The soldiers of de Broc still loitered at Burgate, a mounted guard stood in the palace courtyard, and he was forced to make his way, hiding and darting, through the monastery precincts and out the postern gate and take the long way round, almost to Newingate, and up the Highstreet to the corner. As he ran he clutched the clothing at his breast, over the little roll of bloody rag beneath. The storm was almost over; only a little rain fell now. And when he turned the corner into Pillory Lane he looked up once, toward Christchurch, and saw the sky flush pink, then slowly deepen to a martyr's red, before he scurried to his door. He pushed through it and stumbled in the darkness to the corner where his wife lay rigid, staring her demon down. There he bent over her, still panting, fumbling for the holy relic in his breast.

On the very night of the murder a woman of Canterbury, Hawisa by name, who for three years had suffered from a nightly suffocation and oppression by a demon, was brought a piece of clothing dipped in the archbishop's blood. On seeing it she cried out that it should be boiled and that the water should be given her to drink. When this was done she was delivered of her demon and she rose up praising God and His new martyr of the Church, St. Thomas.

Thus was the first of all St. Thomas' miracles worked that first night, with all the children looking on, in a poor craftsman's house in Canterbury.

CHAPTER II

APRIL HAD COME with its sweet showers and the little birds sang loudly, for the dawn was clear. The earth smelled of the stirring root, the thawing clod. And up above, the turrets of the tall cathedral church stood out as black as twigs against a pale green sky.

Mary the nun of Barking made her way along the pebbled paths and high-walled walks, skirting the gleam of puddles, from the guest hall out beyond the Larder gate, past the monastic buildings, into the dark-roofed cloister. The rumbling voices of the monks at Lauds came from the chapter house—a drone, a monotone, for there could be no song or music while the church lay desecrate. She passed them, walking quietly, and entered the black doorway into the empty church. There, at the pillar whose white rounded trunk rose ghostly in the darkness, had her brother suffered death.

A glow of light beyond the transept showed her the stairway to the crypt. Softly she walked, her long lids covering her eyes, down the stone steps and under the low vaulting where the candles by the tomb, unwavering in the silent air, threw vault-shaped shadows on the painted walls.

The tomb was a gray marble coffin, low and long. The candles, of the finest wax, were golden-white, almost transparent, thick as a man's thigh, and stood tall in their wrought holders, tall as the thin and upright figure of the nun. They cast a pure light on the marble slab and on the covered chalice and the reliquary that had been placed on it: the cup that held the dried flakes of her brother's blood, the bowl that held his brains.

The old nun crossed herself. No one was there; Brother Benedict and all the monks had gone up to the chapter house for Lauds. She knelt. "In the name of the Father, and of the Son, and of the Holy Ghost . . ."

Mary of Barking, sister of Thomas, had not known her brother very well. They had been parted when they were still children and she had gone off full of expectations, riding pillion close behind her father's back, peering to see the wonders of the London streets as they rode all across the town and through the peaceful countryside to Barking Abbey where she had had her schooling and, in time, became a nun.

She had been forty years at Barking. Forty years. And not yet abbess, for the old abbess lived on, lingering. And then she had been wrenched from all she knew and all she hoped for when her brother the archbishop had fled England and defied the king, and all his relatives and friends had been plucked from their homes and sent in exile after him.

Now he was dead, some said a martyr's death, and she had come to kneel beside his tomb. She prayed for him, the brother whom she hardly knew: his soul's ascent; the growing glory of his name in which already miracles were worked; the downfall of his enemies; the sanction of the pope to call him saint, as many, in their eagerness, already did; for justice for herself who for her brother had borne exile cheerfully and but for him might well be abbess now, because of him should be. She was already fifty-six years old, all but the first ten of them spent in cloister and in the service of the Church, all but the last six serving Barking. . . .

The stones grew very hard beneath her knees, accustomed as she was to kneel, and the cold of the empty church, the towers of stone above her, pressed down and engulfed her, seeped through the many layers of her habit till her body shook. She rose and left the crypt and went to seek the comfort of a friend.

She had arrived at Christchurch only the week before and she had hoped that Prior Odo might assist her in the promotion that she longed for. But Odo, fearful of the king's wrath, had withdrawn from Canterbury even before the murder, and while the king's men prowled the countryside snarling like wild dogs when the martyr's name was glorified, would not return. She had tried Brother Benedict, who was sub-prior now, but Benedict's dark penetrating gaze lacked understanding. Then she had found one who did not judge, her brother's friend and old confessor, Robert, Prior of Merton.

She went to meet him now, in the guest hall garden where they always met just after Prime before they broke their fast. She saw him coming through the garden door, a small man, not over clean, with muddy sandals and the pelisse under his mantle spotted and wrinkled with long wear. Nevertheless, he walked serenely and his gnomelike face, tilted a little sideways, seemed to greet the morning as a friend. He held his head cocked thus because he always prayed—a little sidewise prayer that went from him to God continually. And his ear waited with delight to catch the answer.

Mary did not smile but offered him her thin, cold hands as he approached. "Benedicite," he said cheerfully, and they went to sit upon the bench that had been placed where the first morning sun would fall. Mary sat straight-backed with her knees together and her hands clasped tightly under the long sleeves of her habit. But in the dark, long-lidded eyes that searched his face there was a hidden warmth.

"What is the news today, dear friend?" she asked. "Are there more miracles? The people come?"

Prior Robert, knowing the reason, the ambition, behind her question, felt impatience twinge within him but with the help of God's word in his ear he warned himself: Judge not.

"Yes," he said, smiling to encourage her. "They come."

"The humble people come," said Mary. "Soon the world will come. My brother has been recognized by God. Bishops will kneel before him as I knelt this morning!"

Still Robert smiled, although his eyes had wandered off to where the cool, transparent morning air was flooding light upon the apple twigs.

"The Archbishop of York shall come himself to beg his mercy," Mary said. Then her face lighted. "They tell me that already Bishop Foliot suffers the torments of disease."

Robert brought his eyes to hers once more. "Let us not hope evil for one another," he reminded her.

Mary was rebuked. "I loved my brother; therefore I hate his enemies," she said.

"You loved your brother, and I loved him too. And yet we have not spoken of him," Robert said.

Mary was startled. "But I speak of him! Often. Always, since I have come!"

"Of the martyr, yes. Of the archbishop sometimes. Of what you want for him and for yourself. Not of the man." He smiled to take the sting out of the words. "Tell me of Thomas as you knew him. It will comfort me."

"As I knew him," Mary said. She paused in thought. "I knew him there in Pontigny when I was exiled and I came to show myself to him before I went to St. Remi. You were there. You saw how I came smiling, not as the others did."

"But you are speaking of yourself!" the prior said. "I thought that we might speak of Thomas."

Mary's hand went up across her eyes. "You ask a great

deal, Prior Robert. It is a long time since I have finished with remembering. . . ." Then with an effort she said, "He came to Barking once, when he was the king's chancellor."

"Ah?"

"Yes, he came once . . . Splendid he was, and with a noble train of men. He honored us greatly. And I was called from my duties to sit with him while all the great lords stood apart and the abbess left us to speak of old times together, just we two . . .

"He was kind and merry, remembering all, everything, between us." Mary was not aware her face had softened as she spoke, but Prior Robert saw. "We were very close as children, long ago."

"You played as children in your father's house?"

"Aye, I remember, long ago. The days were golden then . . .

"This I remember," and she turned to him, her face as young as he had ever seen it, "it was Michaelmas, oh many years ago. The fires were new-lit for winter on that day. And our father sat in the hall with his guests and we were in the solar off behind. Ah, Michaelmas . . . There would have been a folkmoot at that season, and extra guests, though I think my father was not alderman that year. . . .

"There was no need of a fire, understand. It was lit for sport because it was the time of year for it. But it was warm as I recall. Oh, I recall it now. That was the year the winter came so late and great gray spiders sat their webs in the garden long past their time.

"We were in the solar, Thomas and I, and Roheise in the crib, a baby still. And Thomas was all naked . . . because it was so warm, at Michaelmas. We laughed about it, and he ran and jumped about and kicked the rushes up and overturned the pot. Oh how we laughed!" She smiled and drew a breath. "He could not have been more than three or four," she said. "And I was six or seven. . . ."

Mary stopped talking with the smile still on her face, but she was not aware of it, nor quite aware when she began to speak again. "Mother came into the solar and reproved him and put his little shirt on him. She was not angry. Mother never scolded. But she told Thomas to remember that he was a man and to repent if ever he did wrong and ask Our Lady's help."

Robert smiled.

"And I must tell you," she went on, "what more my mother did. She took up Thomas from his knees and set him on her lap and told us of a dream she had when Thomas was a tiny child, only a few days old and newly baptized. She dreamed she saw a beautiful new cloth of gold folded on the cradle where he slept. She said she looked on it and loved it and had a longing to see all of it. She told Alfleda . . ."

The nun paused. "That was the maid who cared for us, we children, when we were small. Alfleda." She caught her breath. "I had forgotten her." She sat still, remembering a moment. Then she continued.

"My mother said, 'I told Alfleda: Take and unfold the cloth; I long to see how big and fair it is. Alfleda took it, but she said: Madam, there is no room within the chamber. Try again, I said, Go into the hall where there is ample space. And again she answered me: The hall will not hold all of it. Then go we to the garden, go we to the open fields! I cried. At that a voice spoke to me like the tolling of a bell. No use to try, it said. The cloth is broader than all England.'

"My mother's voice broke when she said this and I looked and saw that tears were on her cheeks. And seeing them Thomas wept too, although—as I remember—I did not. I was young them, in years and understanding. Six or seven. And Thomas that much younger. I think he only wept to see my mother's face. Such things as dreams were well beyond him yet."

Mary stopped speaking but her childhood lingered in her mind. This much she could remember of her brother: how he had lived his baby years in London, coddled, made much of, only son of a prosperous Norman merchant, lord of his sisters in the solar, petted by the maid Alfleda and fed by her on tales of ancient Saxon times, taught by his mother to love charity . . .

"My mother used to weigh him, when he was an infant, against the weight of folded garments or loaves of bread or other things to give to the poor," she told the prior.

She could remember this because she had been told of it, though she could never quite recall the scene herself. This she knew best, that she had loved her little brother. But they had parted early. She did not remember—she had never known—the workings of his fate, the play of circumstance on character, that brought the little naked shouting boy she loved so well, through all the winding years, to death in the black darkness of his own cathedral. . . .

How long was it since the old nun had thought of Cheapside and her father's house and of her brother Tom? She thought now, tucking her thin hands in the wide wool sleeves, slumping a little on the narrow bench, of how it was when all the world was full of boys and men. She thought how cold the men's cloaks were when they came in from out of doors in winter and how they smelled of horses when their cloaks dried out. And she remembered suddenly—a picture—Thomas' face: the dark eyes snapping and the thick hair falling on his forehead and around his ears, the skin almost transparent with the cold, the nose and cheeks stung red, and how he brought the cold of frost and winter skies into the solar and how he smiled and said—she heard the voice, a boy's voice, very sweet—that he had seen a man who could work magic, and, "God doesn't live in St. Mary Colechurch where you thought." Three years younger—six or seven he must have been—and trying to teach her and Alfleda something they didn't know. "He lives outside, near Smoothfield."

"Who told you?" That was her own voice.

"The magic man."

Thomas had been that afternoon—soon after Christmas it was, in the winter of 1125—out to the smooth field where in winter boys and men went skating on the frozen horse pond and where on Holy Days, sometimes, they set the dogs to fighting bears. He had gone with his father and two guests, two brothers, Churchmen from Boulogne, Baldwin and Eustace, who were in London for the first time.

Churchmen like these, and secular lords as well, were frequent visitors at his father's house. Gilbert Becket's hall was warm and welcoming, the life of London flowing in and out of it, and guests from far away were always coming. They made the merchant's house their stopping place in London because the food and wine were excellent, the company cheerful, and because good Norman French was always spoken there. They did not care that their host's rank was lower than their own, that he could claim no title or high family connections. Gilbert was a Norman like themselves, his wife Roheise a Norman too, and both were highly skilled in hospitality.

Gilbert planned a small diversion for his guests that winter afternoon and Thomas, for the first time, was allowed to come along. They rode through Cheapside and out Newgate, Thomas on the pillion seat behind his father, into the ward of Farringdon Without. They left their horses on the slope above the horse pond and walked down to see the skaters. Boys and even men had tied shin bones of animals to their shoes and pushed themselves with poles until they skimmed and looped and darted swift as birds.

Thomas wondered at them. This was something new to see! He was delighted; so were the Norman visitors. Such running on the ice was new to them as well. But Gilbert only smiled. "Never was there such a town as London for good sport," he said.

He pushed up, shouldering his way into the crowd that stood around the pond to watch, wanting to give his guests a better view. Most of the men there glanced around and saw that they were Churchmen and made room, but one among them stood his ground.

"Step on your own feet, noble lord," he growled.

Baldwin and Eustace opened their eyes wide at this. They did not understand the English but they heard the tone. Gilbert, however, was at home with every kind of man. "Aye, so I will, master porcupine," he said easily, and stepped beside him. He also spoke in English, badly accented but understandable.

Baldwin said testily, in French, "I do think, Gilbert Becket, you allow too much among your English peasantry."

"Yes, yes, perhaps I do," said Gilbert. "But this fellow is an outlander, I think. You will not find many men like him in London."

The man turned once again and scowled at them.

"I hope not to," said Baldwin sourly. "Let us move on."

They turned away and Gilbert, taking Baldwin's elbow, told him earnestly, "The men of London are not like other men. Here are we all brothers, Norman and English, side by side, all friendly."

"Is it so?" said Baldwin, unbelieving.

"Oh yes, we are together at our husting meetings and together in our sport. And as we live like this the feeling grows among us that we are one. Take my son Thomas here . . ."

Thomas, walking by Eustace just behind his father, pricked up his ears. "Tended by a Saxon maid and speaking her tongue with her," said Gilbert. "Learning his catechism from the English priest across the street. . . ."

Eustace spoke for the first time. "Surely you will not let him grow up so?" He had been captured by the boy.

"I know the worth of my own son," said Gilbert. "His French is pure, and he shall be sent to school to learn his Latin in a few years. We have our learned men here, also. Indeed, my lords, when you have come to know our city you will not be astonished at anything you see. London is older than Rome, you know, being founded in the ancient times by Brutus. And Londoners are ranked as barons—all men of standing, that is—by our ancient charter. Besides, our city is the home of every great lord in the land, you might say, since they live here as citizens while they attend the king when he holds court at Westminster."

Baldwin smiled at his host's earnestness. "You Londoners are proud, I'll grant you." But then he looked around him somewhat impatiently. His feet were growing cold.

"There is a church," said Gilbert hastily, "that I would have you see for your diversion. Let us walk faster. It will warm us. Then we can go home. There is a marvelous story connected with this church—just being built it is. Come, you will see."

They left the pond and walked back toward the city walls and soon, ahead of them, they saw the church—a shell, only the first stones in their places, rising from the frosty meadow, gleaming against the low gray sky. It was to be the priory church of a great house of Augustinian Canons and the architects and builders had been at work on it three years. Just now, this bitter afternoon, the masons had deserted it and it stood empty, silent, amid the blocks of stone, the hand carts and the wagons left on the frozen mud. Beyond its white stone arches and curving apse they could see smoke that rose up from a row of low thatched dormitories and, at a little distance toward the city, the hospital for the poor sick of London which had been dedicated, like the priory, to the apostle St. Bartholomew.

"The canon tells me," Gilbert said, "that he will build a fair large house of stone for his hospital as well—all in good time."

A man came toward them, thin and graceful in his canon's cloak, and with a long twisted face beneath his wide soft hat. "There is Canon Rahere coming now," Gilbert murmured, and explained to Baldwin that the stranger was a courtier of the king as well as a canon of St. Paul's Cathedral, "and now the founder of this priory, a most important man. . . ."

He raised his voice. "God be with you and your noble work, my lord."

Rahere recognized the merchant Gilbert, once an alderman and thus familiar to him at the hustings, and greeted him with courtly affability, welcoming the visitors, when Gilbert had presented them, to London and to St. Bartholomew's.

"Work has stopped, as you can see," he said, "but only for the moment. Soon we will hear the ring of chisels on the stones again. And meanwhile, I"—his face changed and the twisted mouth lifted a notch—"I cannot bear to leave it even for that moment."

"There is a marvelous story my lord Rahere tells," Gilbert said to his guests, "concerning this great church."

The canon broke in. "There are many marvels in the world which men will tell—but not so sure of proof as mine!"

Gilbert had heard the story many times but he was eager to impress his guests. "I had hoped, my lord, that you might show us. . . ."

"Yes?" said Rahere quickly. "Well, indeed, I do have here . . . ." He felt with one long hand into the furred sleeve of his cloak. But as he bent his head his glance brushed Thomas' solemn upturned face. He drew his hand forth empty, slowly opening the palm as though to study it. Then he thrust the other hand into the opposite sleeve. Again it came forth empty. He tried again, more quickly, and his hands flashed here and there, until, at last, he held out both hands to Thomas with the palms up, empty, and the sleeves pulled back. And there before their eyes, it seemed, a little parchment roll appeared in the right hand.

Thomas blushed red, not knowing whether he should laugh. The strange man sighed. "The king was wont to laugh at my small tricks," he said. "Even my jests amused him sometimes. Now my antics cannot bring a smile even to the face of a small child!" He spoke in a lugubrious voice, and yet his face was no more solemn than before. Gilbert laughed aloud.

Rahere looked up at him. "Aye," he said. "These are the tricks of the hand and the eye. You see they cling to me like a tiresome mistress. What have they to do with the marvels of God?"

He glanced again at Thomas. "Is this your son?" he asked.

"This is my son Thomas," Gilbert said formally, with pride.

Thomas bowed as he was taught to do, one foot behind the other. The canon bent and lifted him and sat him on the nearest stone. "Now, Thomas, I shall tell you something you can believe," he said in a changed quiet voice.

Thomas felt this curious man was cold, a little frightening, and yet it warmed him to be spoken to like this.

The men moved closer and Rahere related to them how, on the wreck of the White Ship these five years past and the great sorrow that had fallen on the court with the drowning of the king's son and heir—and with him many a flower of the court and dear friend also—he had vowed to go on a pilgrimage to please the king.

"You know the court . . ." He flattered Gilbert, for the merchant had not been at court. "The court is an unnumbered multitude striving to please one man. And I was likewise striving." The mouth twitched.

And thus, to please the king, the courtier had taken staff in hand and made the journey down toward Rome. But in that foul marshy region round about Tré Fontane the pestilence had taken him and he lay close to death for many months. And in his pain and fear he vowed, should God spare him, to build a hospital to help the poor of his great native city.

"It was the vow of a man in fear," he said. "Yet it was heard in heaven, for as I hung there between life and death a marvelous vision was vouchsafed me: I woke from fever and I saw a beast approaching me, a strong and terrible beast, a lion of great size, with eight clawed feet and wings like eagles' wings. He seized me in his talons and he took me up, out of my chamber, bore me through the air until we left the earth behind and soared among the stars. And there I felt it was the beast's intent to loose me. Looking down I saw a chasm, black and yawning, an unfathomable pit. My heart within my breast turned cold with mortal fear and I cried out for mercy.

"Then, even as the echo of my screams rang out among the stars, the figure of a man appeared beside me—a man but larger than a man, noble beyond describing, and clothed in gold.

"He spoke: 'I am Bartholomew, Apostle of Jesus Christ, come to succor thee in thine anguish.' And he stretched out his hand to me and I was saved.

"So was my vow solemnized. And in my gratitude I swore to build a church, as well as found my hospital, to glorify his name." He looked at Thomas. "Thus you see a silly man, changed by God."

Thomas stared silently into the long wry face.

"I have here," Rahere looked at the men, "the words that St. Bartholomew spoke, blessing his church."

He took the little roll which he still carried in his hand and opened it upon the stone, pressing it flat. The others came up close to look. Gilbert could not read it but the Churchmen could.

The world grew silent all about them as they bent. The little cries of men came floating to them from the horse pond down below. Then Rahere spoke the words for Thomas and his father. He did not need to read them, they were written on his heart:

"This spiritual house Almighty God shall inhabit, and hallow it, and glorify it; and His eyes shall be opened and His

ears intending on this house night and day; and the asker in it shall receive, the seeker shall find, the ringer or knocker shall enter. Truly every soul converted, penitent of his sins and in this house praying, in gracious heaven shall be heard. The seeker with perfect heart, from whatsoever tribulation, without doubt he shall find help."

He stopped. The final words rose up and faded in the air, and all were silent until Baldwin spoke. "Amen," he said.

Rahere straightened and put the little scroll away. "These are the words as St. Bartholomew spoke them," he said at last. "I read them to you because I know that you might doubt my story if I did not give you more proof than my own poor story telling.

"But hear me speak, and listen with your hearts and understanding. Do I speak such words as you have heard just now? No," a little smile came to the crooked mouth. "I speak with the tongue of a courtier. Surely, what you have just heard—that was the voice of a saint who lives with God."

In the narrow forecourt of the house in Cheapside the men dismounted and Thomas was lifted from his father's horse. He saw his mother standing in the doorway, a mantle round her shoulders, and ran to her while the men followed, stamping in the cold. She sheltered him next to her, under the cloak, while she greeted them. Then as the Churchmen climbed the wooden stairway to the hall she touched her husband's arm and drew him into the little chamber underneath the stairs.

"Gilbert, we have a noble guest," she whispered. "The Baron Richer l'Aigle and his men arrived not half an hour ago. I have made them welcome as I could."

"Good." Gilbert clapped his hands together. A guest was always welcome in his hall, and if he be a person of so high a standing as Lord Richer so much the better. "Have you anything for supper that will please him?"

"I sent Ebert to the cookshop, having so short a time for preparation."

"Good," Gilbert repeated, full of gusto. "What will he bring?"

"A chicken boiled with marrow bone," his wife said, "a meat pie, and the salt-beef seasoned as you like it." She smiled, knowing she would be praised, and Gilbert kissed her quickly and started up the stairs. Halfway he halted and leaned down to them. "Remind Ebert on his return," he said, "the baron likes the red wine of Touraine." Then he looked fondly for a moment at the faces of his wife and son. "Thomas behaved well today," he said and disappeared.

Thomas loved the praise. His mother, too, was pleased. "So you have been a good boy helping to entertain your father's guests. That makes me happy." And she took his hand and led him up the stairs.

The old familiar hall was warm, buzzing with people, flickering with light. All the candles had been lit and on the hearth the fire burned smoothly, eating at the logs. What smoke there was had risen to the rafters and hung high.

The sudden warmth made Thomas very sleepy. He saw Lord Richer in the chair and father bending over him . . . Alfleda in her new kirtle, the baby Agnes slung across her shoulder, and a jug in her other hand . . . the starling hopping in his cage . . . Mary standing with one foot on the other by the screen that shut the solar off . . . and many other things. But all were hazy. All the movement and the buzz of talk confused him and he blinked.

"Go into the solar and lie down," his mother said, amused to see him sleeping on his feet. He started forward, staggering on heavy legs across the hall, and Mary turned and followed him into the darkness of the little family room. "What was it like?" she asked. "What happened?" But Thomas could not say. His mind was crowded with the sights and sounds of all that he had seen that day—too many, far too many, to share with his sister.

"Nothing," he said. "I know where God lives. Out near Smoothfield where the big stones are."

"Who told you?"

"The magic man."

He had no more to tell her. Already life, experience, had come between them. And in the next fall Mary left the busy house on West Cheap never to return, never to know her little brother more.

* * *

"The latest is, the Archbishop of York has been suspended from the Church for his part in the murder." William Fitzstephen's ruddy, freckled face was eager as a boy's as he sat in the garden talking to the nun, for like a magpie he gathered bits of news and loved to show them off. He was a clerk; he had been a deacon and a judge for Thomas when he was archbishop. But more than that he was a man who loved to be where things were going on and to be first to tell the world of them. He had found Thomas' sister an eager listener.

She leaned forward. "And the other English bishops?" she inquired. "The Bishop of London?"

"I heard only of York," Fitzstephen said. But then he brightened, for he was a man who loved the color of the news more than the bare facts, and added, "But it is said in Rome His Holiness the Pope will excommunicate them all. On Maundy Thursday this will take place. . . ."

"What of the king?"

"The king? Well, I believe I told you that the Archbishop of Sens has put his lands in Normandy under an interdict. . . ."

Mary nodded.

"And that he sent a letter to the pope asking that the king be excommunicated too?"

"Yes, yes. What says His Holiness?"

"No word as yet. But they say he will not see the deputies the king has sent to plead his cause. They say he cannot even bear to hear King Henry's name."

Mary put her own long hands beside the coif over her ears as though she, like the pope, could not endure that name, and William, unkindly moved, said drily: "Some say that it is wrong to deal too harshly with the king. The Bishop of Rouen has gone to Rome to plead for him. Some say he is not guilty and that he deals too harshly with himself already. You know how long and hard he wept to hear of Thomas' death. I heard he would take nothing but a little almond milk for three days afterward. And for that long time—forty days it was—he would do nothing for the affairs of state or in his own defense. . . ."

"And now he sends to Rome to bribe the cardinals!" Mary broke in.

Fitzstephen stopped. "Of course. You may be right. You must be right, madame."

They sat in silence, Fitzstephen with his head bowed, showing his graying hair and freckled tonsure, until he had another thought. "Oh, I have better news," he said. "More miracles are worked! I have just come, only this morning, from the money-smithy. . . ."

But Mary would not be put off. "More miracles," she said. "Ever more miracles. Does the pope sanction them? Are we now free to pray to Thomas as one sanctified?"

"Not yet, Dame Mary," William said. "No word has come. It is not lawful; you know the pope's decree. We may not reverence a man as saint—no matter how many miracles are done by him—without the sanction of the Curia."

"And so we wait, and wait," said Mary bitterly. "And Brother Roger told me some of the monks are frightened lest the martyr grow impatient. Well," she sighed. "Well, tell me of your miracles."

William straightened and edged closer. "You know about the money-smithy down in Pillory Lane? There where the woman was delivered of her demon? People come there now to beg a drop of their miraculous water for their ills. I was there this morning. There was a boy who had a thorn implanted in his thumb. The water took it out. And then a man came in. . . ."

In Pillory Lane the house was in an uproar, people coming there from every part of town to borrow just a little of the water with the martyr's blood, or merely to step up and peer into it (they kept it in the pot where it was boiled) or to stare at the wife, Hawisa, whose demon had been driven off by it. She lay in bed. The smaller children played around her on the sheepskin covering. The neighbors and the visitors stooped by the fire or sat on the stools around the table in the center of the room—for that was all the house was, just one long room with a stone pillar to support the roof—and when there were no newcomers to prick their interest the grandmother, Wulviva of Hortone, retold the story of her daughter's miracle. This day the clerk Fitzstephen from the archbishop's palace was a visitor and she retold the tale for him.

Her son, Hawisa's brother, sat in one corner in a sort of shining silence as though he did not know he was afflicted (he was dumb), and in another sat the old man Elured Porre, the patriarch, he who had been a minter ever since the old King Henry's reign. He was the only one who knew the martyr in his lifetime, but he was old now, and no one listened to him when he spoke.

"I knew the archbishop, of course," he said. "A tall man."

No one listened.

"I said to him, 'Give me a penny. I am a beggar.' And he laughed at me." Elured laughed soundlessly, closing his eyes. No one took any notice of him. Who would have thought this withered old man propped on his stool in the corner had once ruled the household with a cutting tongue and that his slightly shaking hands once minted better pennies than any other moneyer in Canterbury, or in London either, for that matter.

"I told him, 'I am a beggar. Wash my feet.' Ayho, we laughed at that!

"That was a miracle if you want one. I struck a penny . . . no, that was another time. This time I thought, I'll put a knife into your back, scoundrel, taking a man's work from him!' Then when we laughed I dropped the knife. I didn't have a knife. I would have dropped it if I had had one. That was a man. I liked that man. . . ."

No one took any notice of him. They were grouped around Wulviva as she went on with her story of the demon and their miraculous water and they hung upon her words, watched her large gestures and her piercing eyes that went their separate ways—for never since her birth had the two looked at the same spot together—and listened to her strong compelling voice.

The father of the house, the hunchback Walter, came and went, a thin smile on his lips, into the forge to work and back again when someone new came through the little fore-court where the hand cart stood beside the smithy door. His boy Viel followed after him and it was he who saw his uncle coming—not his silent uncle, Almon, who lived with them, but his grandmother's cousin who lived in Certeham, Uncle Eilward, whom his father laughed at because he was so simple.

He came across the forecourt with his face aglow and his arms waving out before him and then stood inside the door-way smiling at them all. Wulviva was the first to speak, for she was always first to smell a miracle. "Another miracle?" she called out, turning her heavy body from the table where she sat.

Eilward lunged forward and the neighbors scraped their stools as they rose up and pushed one out for him.

"A miracle!" Eilward repeated, smiling up into the faces that surrounded him. "Another miracle. To me!" He was so pleased it brought tears to his eyes.

William Fitzstephen spoke as one of higher rank. "Tell us how it happened," he said crisply. "One, two, three. Exactly how it was. And no one else must talk." He looked around him warningly.

They waited until Eilward could collect himself. He thought a long time, smiling happily. At last he said, "It happened in the night. I had pain, a pain so terrible I thought I had gone mad."

"Where?" asked Fitzstephen. He wanted to know every-thing, exactly as it was, for he was keeping record of all the miracles he heard.

"Where?" echoed Eilward, "why in my house of course."

"The pain, the pain," Fitzstephen said impatiently.

"Oh, in my jaw, I aw," said Eilward, opening his mouth. There was a silence while Eilward's mouth hung open and he pointed in it to show them where the pain had been.

"And then?" Fitzstephen prodded.

"Why then I slept a little because it was the middle of the night you know. And that is when I saw the vision. A very tall man wearing a bright scarf. . . ."

"A miracle!" Wulviva shouted.

"Wait, wait, I have not finished," Eilward objected.

"What did he look like, this tall man?" Fitzstephen asked.

"He was very tall," Eilward said thoughtfully. "And he wore a bright scarf."

"Yes, tall, you told us that. But what about the face? Was there anything on the face that you remember?" Fitzstephen said.

"Yes," Eilward was eager to agree. "Yes, something on the face."

"What?"

"What?"

"What on the face? Any blood? Was there blood across the face?"

"Yes, blood," he nodded, watching Fitzstephen closely. "Blood on . . ." His eyes were fastened to Fitzstephen and his mouth hung slack. "Blood on his forehead."

Fitzstephen's hands were making marks across his own broad freckled face. "Yes, blood on the forehead. And? Where else?"

"Yes, on his cheek. Yes, on the eyebrow . . . right across your nose . . . to the other cheek?"

Fitzstephen straightened up. He looked around from face to face. "It is amazing," he said somberly. "Incredible. Even so was our lord Thomas in his death, a streak of blood across his face. I saw it. And even so has he been seen by all who have had visions of him since his death!"

Eilward smiled broadly, basking, but once again Wulviva called attention to herself. "I said it was a miracle!" she cried.

"Wait! There you go again!" Eilward said angrily. "I haven't told you what the vision said!"

They turned to him once more. "What did he say?"

"First *I* said," Eilward corrected them. "First *I* said, when I saw him, for he frightened me: 'Lord, who are you?' I said. *Then* he said, 'I am a clerk of Canterbury who was very close to the archbishop who was dead but lives.' "

"But lives!" Wulviva cried.

"But I said," Eilward went on stubbornly, " 'Do not say that to anyone. It is not safe.' And then he said—here is the part I best remember—'It is for them, my enemies, to tremble, not for me. See, I have here a letter from my lord the Pope saying that all the murderers shall suffer terribly and that de Broc shall go straight to the pit of hell.' And then he waved the scarf. . . ."

"It was his pallium," Fitzstephen put in quickly.

"And then he waved the scarf," Eilward repeated doggedly. "It was the letter from the pope you know, and brushed my cheek with it and fanned the air into my mouth . . . and there was no more pain. I woke up and the pain was gone!" He smiled, for he had finished, and because the pain was gone.

This was the latest miracle Fitzstephen told to Mary.

Its sequel was a tragedy that he had not yet learned. For after Eilward had told all the neighbors of his cure and then retold it to the monks at Christchurch, he had set off for Certeham with only Almon Drop the dumb man to accompany him.

Thus only Almon knew, and could not tell, how when they had approached the bridge he saw the horsemen there and knew them to be soldiers of de Broc and ran and hid himself and from his hiding place heard the rough questions and the voice of Eilward, full of his wonder, telling the story of his vision and his cure by the tall figure with the streak of blood across his face.

"Was it like this?" he heard the soldiers ask. "A stroke like this? A gash? A cut?" And at each word the horses' heavy feet upon the planks, the sound of blows, the screams. And then the wheeling of the horses and the words, "He's dead. Let's go." The clatter on the bridge and after that the galloping, dying away.

Almon waited for the dark to bring his cousin home, dragging the body with its head split open. But he had not tongue to tell, nor skill to write, what he had seen and heard.

CHAPTER III

JUST BEFORE EASTER of 1171, Prior Odo felt the time was ripe for his return to Canterbury. News of the miracles done in the dead archbishop's name had come to him not only from Christchurch—Benedict sent word of *those* by every messenger—but far afield in England and from abroad as well.

Not only were the poor and ignorant folk of Canterbury and its villages clamoring to tell the world about their miracles (no one but Benedict and some of the lesser monks would give much credence to the hysteria of common men) but now a noble lady, wife of a Sussex knight, hearing that miracles were worked, had prayed to the archbishop to regain her failing sight and had been cured. All over England such things happened, and as far away as in Jerusalem a holy monk who died on that same day the archbishop was murdered came—in a vision—to the abbot of his house and said that Thomas had been raised to equal rank in heaven with St. Peter himself. This last had been relayed to Odo by the Archbishop of Sens.

Thus, though the pope had not yet spoken, he felt it would be safe to venerate the martyr and let the pilgrims come to do him honor at his tomb.

He returned, then, to take up his duties in the great monastic house of Christchurch, early in Holy Week.

He found that all that Benedict had written him was true. In Canterbury men talked of little else but miracles, and daily pilgrims begged to be admitted to the tomb. It did not take the urgings of the brothers, or of the nun of Barking, to persuade him that this must be done. The time was ripe, and the decision was not so much his to make as his to acquiesce to.

"Good Friday, then," he said to Benedict's unspoken question. "Good Friday they shall be admitted—under your guidance."

The word was his to give; he gave it. Nevertheless he did

not want it said, just yet, that he had been there with them in the crypt. Better to wait and see.

"Under your guidance," he repeated. "Only a few. The better dressed among them." He turned away. "We do not want the mob."

Good Friday came, and Benedict spoke to the guard beside the gate and both together they peered through to see the pilgrims pressing close against the other side. One might have thought them foolish to crowd one another so, when all the rush market lay empty at their backs, but Benedict knew, and the guards knew, that the de Brocs still made their forays into the city, and instead they marveled that they had the courage to stand waiting there at all.

"Their faith has brought them and will protect them," the monk said solemnly. He put his face up to the crack again. Right in front of him he saw a shabby parish priest—one of the rustic kind—and next to him, clinging to him like a child to its mother's skirts, a brawny soldier with a swollen purple face and look of terror in his eyes. He saw a baby in its mother's arms. Some sort of freak? Its head was very large. Benedict shifted. Off to one side he saw a leper—man or woman he could not tell—and next to him a blind man, filthy, with his head bent down as though he searched the ground.

He did not see among them any of the well-dressed people Odo specified, but then, his view was limited. He stepped away and told the guard to lift the bar. He did so and the doors swung open, thrusting them back as all the pilgrims started forward and surged through together, crowding each other, with their mouths wide open and their eyes alight.

Benedict took one shocked look and without speaking turned and hurried back the way that he had come while they pushed at his heels. He heard a man call out behind him in a terrible loud voice, a groan that sounded like the bellow of a bull: "Oh Lord, Oh Holy Thomas, help me now!" And then the others all began to moan, to wail, to sob, to cry for help.

He hurried on, across the palace precincts, into the monastery grounds until he reached the entrance to the church. He thrust the doors apart and strode through, never looking back. He had not known that it would be like this. There was no order in this wild procession and it was useless even to try to speak to them. He led them rapidly across the transept and down the stairs into the crypt.

Here some held back, astonished and intimidated by the colors on the walls: the patterns studded with bright gold, the soft and feathery wings of painted angels and the flat and staring eyes of saints that watched them from above. But others pushed on past them and when they saw the tomb cried out afresh, so that their sounds re-echoed under the vaulted roof, and some fell down upon their knees and crawled while others ran ahead before they knelt.

Benedict stood back. A young girl paused beside him as though not knowing where to go. "Oh see what stones are here!" he heard her chirping voice. Then, as though taking heart, "St. Thomas guard me!" and "St. Thomas' name be praised!" She saw the tomb and trotted forward, still with her little cry.

He heard then the loud earnest voice of the broad woman from the money-smithy, she with the water that worked miracles. There was a young man with her, perhaps her son. Benedict heard her, urging, pleading with him: "Ask the holy martyr for your voice again. Ask that your tongue be loosened and explain your need of it. Tell him you might be parish priest some day—I'm sure of it—if you could only speak again. Singing's not necessary. Only the power of speech."

The young man did not seem to listen. His eyes were inward and his face was full of pain.

"Ask for the power of French as well," she raised her voice above the noises in the crypt. "English is not enough. You might as well be dumb if when the deacon comes to Certeham you cannot speak in French. Ask him, just ask him, Almon. He has done more for others." And she went forward and got down heavily upon her knees, pulling her son down with her. She clasped her hands and lifted up her broad and earnest face, all glistening with sweat. "Oh blessed saint in heaven give my son his voice," she called. Then rocking on her strong spread knees and lifting high her hands: "And French as well. Oh holy martyr, blessed Archbishop, French also! French as well!"

And so they knelt, the simple minded and the crippled and the ill, the demon-ridden—all those who suffered and were heavy laden—the pilgrims at the tomb. They were as unlike one another, in God's infinite variety, as one leaf differs from its brother though it hangs from the selfsame branch. These were the members of Prior Odo's mob.

One would have thought, to see them kneeling, rocking, rolling on the floor, to hear their frantic supplications and their weeping and their shouts, this was a madhouse rather than a spiritual house of God. And yet an ear intending on it might discern the overwhelming longing in the heart, the silent prayer: "Oh Lord, have mercy on me . . . that I might receive my sight."

The wailing stopped and all was quiet in the guest hall garden where Mary and the prior sat. William Fitzstephen had gone on to watch the pilgrims as they passed.

"What is it now?" the nun asked. "Why do their voices fade?"

"They have passed through the cloister," Prior Robert said. "They have gone into the church. The door is shut." Within himself, sitting so quietly, he said, "May the Lord hear them in their time of need."

Mary put one hand out and grasped the prior's wrist. "Prior Robert," she whispered, her hand tightening on his, "all the world, all the world will bow before my brother!"

Robert waited till her grip relaxed, then took her hand in his. "Dame Mary," he said softly, "men have bowed to him before. Who is served by this? What does it signify? Why, in my youth so long ago I once saw your own father bow before his son."

Mary raised her head and looked at him.

"Yes," he nodded, smiling a little, "when Thomas was a little boy, perhaps one year at Merton, and your father came—as fathers or their stewards always come to take their boys home after their winter schooling. . . . It was the ordered life, there at the priory . . ."

He spoke with a mild pleasure for he was a man more certain of eternity than time and did not find its passing painful . . . "And those were peaceful years, when the first Henry sat upon the throne and every man lived safe beside his neighbor. . . .

"I had been sent to fetch the scholar Thomas when his father came into the prior's guest room. I knew where to find him for I was young myself then, newly made a canon. And I found him, as I expected, with the other boys in the outer garden searching among the berry vines for the green fruit, like a flight of naughty blackbirds in their robes." He smiled. "Thomas was comely even then, already taller than his schoolmates, with his blithe face and the dark hair hanging like petals above his brow. And I was moved to love him; yes, he compelled it of us all, even that early.

"Yet I was stunned to see a father go down on his knee to greet his son. The prior was stunned too, for he rebuked him. 'Foolish man,' he said. 'Do you fall down at the feet of your own son? Surely it is more fit that he do thee that honor!' He spoke thus. I well remember it."

"And my father?" Mary asked.

"Your father answered that he knew what he was about. 'For,' he said—yes, I remember even now his very words—'this boy shall be great in the sight of the Lord.' "

"He spoke with the voice of prophecy, my own father!"

"Yes, thus he answered," Prior Robert nodded. "But when they had departed, your father and his son, our wise old prior taught me this out of his wisdom that I would like to share with you. He called me back and told me to listen as he spoke. 'You have seen,' he said, 'a man give honor to his son. But was he truly honored by this act? Honor, my son, is like love. Love comes from God, and all the love we have reflects but feebly back to Him. And so with honor, too. The world may bow, but honor is a gift that only God may give.

" 'And furthermore,' he said, 'I am distressed to think what thoughts such honoring may put into a young boy's head.' "

* * *

Thomas' heart was light as he rode home from Merton by his father's side. He was released from school, and furthermore he had done well in this first sally into the world outside his home. Learning by rote came quickly to him and his memory was stronger than the other boys', nor was he flogged so often. He had even earned the canons' praise. Thus he had found out, at the age of ten, that his place among his peers was at the top.

He took the knowledge with the humility of childhood; it was the way things were. And since he was accustomed from his infancy to praise, this fresh acclaim became him well.

His father's greeting of that morning and the prior's rebuke had made him blush, for he already knew, as certainly did the prior, that to flaunt custom in such a way, reversing the roles of father and son, was dangerous. More than that. He knew what the old prior did not know: his father's words and actions had come not so much from his convictions as from the teachings of his mother. They had been borrowed from her. He heard again his father's voice, "This boy shall be great in the eyes of God." His mother's words. And then the prior's stern rebuke, "Oh foolish man. . . ."

But he should know, thought Thomas in astonishment, that that was only Mother's doting, spoken out by Father, clumsily.

It was a sobering, almost frightening thing to see his father from the outside in this way and he looked quickly up at him as though to make amends for what he thought.

Gilbert rode beside him, in and out of the dappled light that filtered through the leaves, happy with the world and with his boy. Thomas had done well at school, learning his Latin, so the prior said. And now he rode beside his father, grown too big for riding pallion any more, a tall boy, good to look at. Gilbert smiled contentedly.

It was eighteen miles to London through the Surrey woodland and Thomas was not used to handling his own mount, so they went slowly, stopping to lunch on the smooth ground where the woods ended on the marshy floodplain of the Thames. Gilbert brought out bread and cheese and pickled herring from his wallet and the two sat silent while they ate. Under the wide pale sky the marsh birds called and far off, on the quiet river, little men in boats tended the brushwood weirs that stood out from the sandy isle of Battersea.

When they had eaten, Gilbert told his son of things at home: Roheise had grown quite big and helped her mother like a little woman, and Agnes toddled after, no longer a baby. At the summer carnival just past, the scholars of St. Paul's had won their game of ball with great distinction over the other schools. But the men of the cloth-dressers trade had drunk too much and caused a brawl over their game; one man had died of it and many more were injured. The Baron Richer l'Aigle had been a guest at Whitsuntide when he had come to Westminster for the king's ceremonial wearing-of-the-crown and would return again. He had asked most solicitously after Thomas.

This talk of home made Thomas eager to ride on. And when they traveled closer to the city, joining the highroad coming up from Kent with all its traffic flowing Londonward at close of day, his heart beat and he looked ahead as though to catch a glimpse of home across the reach. He saw the London Bridge at last and gave a shout and flapped his legs against his horse's sides.

The wooden causeway to the bridge was crowded and on the bridge itself the narrow lane between the stalls was packed, but when their horses stepped into the city on the other bank the crowd dispersed as each man went his own way through the town and now all was familiar: the river smells, the sound of water rushing down the conduits of the sloping streets, of hawkers' calls and cries of boatmen out upon the river, of barking dogs and, as they came past Dowgate, the creak of ships that rode the tide just off the landing place.

They passed the broad carved frontage of the Flemish merchants' hall and crossed the little Walbrook bridge into the ward of Vintry before they left the river bank to take the crooked street that led them northward to his father's house. Now they were almost home and Thomas was beside himself. "There's the cookshop!" he sang out. His father smiled. "There's the Jew's house!" Their pace was quicker now, and the streets quieter. "There's St. Mary Colechurch on the corner!" They rounded it. They were in Cheapside. The Vespers bells were ringing. Mother was at the gate. And they were home.

Word came to the merchant's house that they might expect the Baron Richer l'Aigle late in August as he had some business with the court. This caused a stir among the servants for Lord Richer was among the highest nobles of the land and held the Honor of Pevensey, that castle fortress on the Sussex coast which the Conqueror's own brother built upon the spot where William landed. The presence of the Lord of Pevensey reflected glory on them all.

Thomas was pleased as well. Lord Richer with his tall spare frame and laconic offhand way, his great name and his honors worn with poise, was his favorite among his father's guests. And when the day arrived he hung around the courtyard, hot and fly-bedeviled, waiting for the lord's arrival with his train, although he knew full well they could not ride the whole way up from Pevensey much before suppertime, even at the fast knights-pace the baron rode.

The sun had dropped behind the high square tower of St. Paul's across the rooftops and the shadow of the courtyard wall had crept almost to the stables when he heard the shouting in the streets as men and women scattered to make way for the tall quick-trotting horses of the baron's train. The groom ran to the gate, the servants gathered at the kitchen entrance to peer around the house, and Gilbert came downstairs to stand outside the doorway with his son. The baron and his men rode through the gate, their hoods thrown back, their harness jingling, the horses weary, throwing their legs a little, mouths open against the bit and breathing loud. They halted, and in the sudden silence Gilbert guided his son forward, his hand upon his shoulder, until the boy stood in the position of the host beside Lord Richer's mount.

Thomas felt the horse's flanks heave close beside him, smelling of sweat and lathered where the stirrups rubbed. But Lord Richer, as he swung down and away, seemed fresh and held himself with straight-backed ease. Save for one long dark patch of sweat which stained his jerkin—of which he seemed all unaware—one would have thought that he had ridden no farther than from Newgate down the street. He smiled and formally embraced his host and gave instructions, casually, about the horses before he sauntered into the house. Thus it was, thought Thomas, to be a great lord: above all weariness.

After supper Lord Richer called Thomas to him. The table had been cleared away and the baron sat in the only high-backed chair, sprawling as he leaned against it with his legs flung out, and yet not lounging but in every line correct.

"So you like my horse, young Thomas." Lord Richer's mouth moved and his eyes watched, but the rest of him was still. "Do you know horses as a young man should?"

Thomas was puzzled. He knew his father's horses by their names. Was this the way a young man should? He knew his mother's palfrey well; he had ridden her all the way from Merton. "I know Gray Mouse," he said.

"He knows Gray Mouse." Lord Richer raised his eyes to Gilbert, then looked again at Thomas. "So you are studying to be a clerk." There was a curious blank look in his face which Thomas could not read. Was this disapproval? "And learning Latin. That horse of mine you like so well has a Latin name. Anderida. Can you tell me what that means?"

"Anderida." Thomas' mind searched all the Latin verses he had learned. "No, sir," he said.

"Why, Anderida was a Roman fort. My castle Pevensey was built within its walls. Anderida they called it, in the Latin, when they put their bastions there." He looked at Gilbert, man to man. "They were good builders, too, those ancients," he told him. "Their outer walls still stand.

"So I have called my strong horse after that strong old fort," he said to Thomas, "in the Latin tongue."

Thomas understood. Latin was of service when it came to naming horses, a kind of plaything, used by clerks, perhaps, for other purposes, but otherwise of little use. Lord Richer neither read nor wrote; were these accomplishments indeed no more than little tricks for clerks to occupy themselves with? Thomas did not know. In all things he could wish himself to be exactly like Lord Richer. And yet the canons felt that learning Latin and the arts of grammar, rhetoric and dialectic were of the very first importance. And he had felt so too, at Merton.

"Your father tells me," Richer said, "that they hold the

horse fair on the edge of town tomorrow. Shall we ride out and see?"

"You may find it very hot on Smoothfield, my lord," Gilbert broke in. "And there is little shelter there."

The baron did not bother even to look up at his host. He spoke directly to the boy: "Thomas and I care nothing for hot or cold when there are horses to be seen and judged, eh, Tom?"

Thomas saw at once that this was rudeness, and he had not yet learned to differentiate between the rudeness of a lord and that of a common man. He stood tongue-tied, shaking his head, before the baron.

"Good," said Lord Richer, dismissing him. "Then after dinner we shall ride out and see the horses."

Thomas rode beside the Lord of Pevensey, very small on Gray Mouse beside the towering Anderida. Behind them rode the groom and two men of the baron's company. They passed the Smoothfield market where the country people gathered to buy swine and sheep and cows and docile horses for their carts. Lord Richer did not waste a glance on these. But on the trampled meadow of the horse-fair grounds he stopped, dismounted, and with his own hands helped Thomas slide down from the mare. Thomas did not need the help, but Richer was attentive. He led him, almost as a father might, his hand in gentle grip upon his neck, across the grass to where a crowd of quite a different sort—knights, earls and barons, as well as many citizens of rank—were looking at the horses.

At the first group he paused and bent to speak close beside Thomas' ear, letting his hand slide down the boyish shoulder and the arm. "These are palfreys, like your Gray Mouse, Tom," he said, pointing with his other hand at the small soft-gaited horses pacing before them. "Watch how they lift their feet, one side together."

Farther along, the sturdier horses, fit for squires to ride, were being trotted out, kicking the dust. And then the high-bred colts, unbroken, moving springily across the turf behind their handlers. Richer pointed out the best of each, still holding Thomas' arm.

But when the destriers, the costly horses that knights ride to war, were shown, Lord Richer straightened and forgot the boy. They were big animals with thick arching necks and heavy haunches, heavy in the legs. But for all their size and weight they skittered sideways like the colts, their nostrils flaring and ears quivering, when men crowded up to look.

Lord Richer watched them closely and found one to ask about and run his hands over, feeling the chest and legs.

Then suddenly a shout was raised and the men stopped their talking and looked around. A race was to be run between three of the fastest destriers, and now the slower horses were being led away, a path was being cleared to make a course. Lord Richer took a quick look at the three, each in its little knot of handlers. "The bay will win," he said in confidence to the old knight who stood beside him. But before a wager could be made he thought of Thomas and turned back to find him standing in the crowd.

The horses were lined up and boys were boosted to sit monkeylike upon their backs. Richer took Thomas by the elbows and lifted him so that he might see over the heads in front. They watched the horses toss their heads and sidle and kick up a screen of dust. Then at the shout of "Go!" they saw the handlers spring back, the horses plunge into a gallop while the boys astride them whipped at their sides.

Lord Richer, holding Thomas, tightened his arms as though he were excited as the boy. And Thomas, watching the horses stretch out in their stride, hearing the thud of hoofs against the ground, wished with his whole heart that he too, someday, might ride like wind and thunder over the earth mounted upon a destrier like these.

Lord Richer stayed another several days in London. During the daytime he was busy at the court in Westminster but he returned to Cheapside often. Several times he mentioned, lightly, that as he had no family of his own perhaps he would adopt the merchant's son. But though the offer pleased the father by its flattery, the jesting tones in which it was always made precluded serious discussion. He could do nothing more than laugh with a blush of pleasure in response.

"Thomas," said Richer, turning to the boy on the eve of his departure, "how would you like to come to Pevensey with me?"

Thomas smiled, his face full of the fresh eagerness of ten years old, but he remembered also that plans had been made for his return to Merton the next week. His eyes turned to his father's face in doubt; the baron noted it. "Next summer," he said quickly. He did not care to risk the indecision of a merchant torn between ambitions for his son. "Go to your monks and learn your Latin now. I dare say it will be most useful to you." He stood up.

Later, as the light was dying under the low ceiling of summer clouds, Lord Richer descended to the courtyard to see that all was ready for a dawn departure. His host went with him, and the two men stood together for a moment outside the stables.

"There are some things a boy should learn before he grows too old," the baron said. "His horses and his hawks, and how to conduct himself at court." He paused and stared at Gilbert, not really seeing him. "Hunting and hawking, providing knight's service for the king, attending his Great Councils, presiding over one's own court, these are the proper occupations of a man as I have learned them."

The merchant nodded in the twilight and held his tongue.

"I have at Pevensey," the lord continued, "several young men training up for knighthood. If you send Thomas to me for the summer months he shall not lack companionship."

Companionship, the father knew, far above his station. These "young men training up for knighthood" would be the sons of great baronial families like Lord Richer's own. Thomas could not hope to rise with them into the ranks of aristocracy. Yet what he learned with them would be of value to him, and Thomas was a boy worth teaching. The prior saw it, and now the baron saw it too. All saw the value of his son.

"We would be honored to send him to you," he said soberly.

"Nothing, it's nothing," the baron brushed away his thanks. "Surely I owe you something for your hospitality."

"Thank you, my lord," said Gilbert, standing back to let the baron pass before him toward the door.

Thus Thomas spent his growing years: from mid-September to the end of June among the canons in the thatched cloisters and wide rambling half-cleared acres of St. Mary's Priory at Merton; the summer months in the baronial hall and great walled bailey of Lord Richer's castle built on a flat gray neck of land that stretched out from the Sussex coast; and for a score of days between his journeyings to Pevensey or Merton he lived in London, ever more a stranger in his father's hall, wrenched with the emotions of arrivals and departures.

As the years of separation passed, his mother grew less close, increasingly intent on matters he knew nothing of, on shaping the younger girls for marriage, on duties in a household where he was but a guest, on devotions and secret charities now hidden even from her son. Always she greeted him at the door when he came home, exclaiming always at his size as he grew up to stand a head above her, weeping, always, at his departures, but they were strangers.

With his father he kept a closer contact for the two sat side by side at dinner now and Gilbert drew his son out with appropriate remarks to speak—with modesty, he early learned the worth of that—of his successes in the schoolroom or the tiltyard. And after dinner the father took his tall successful son into the city so that he might be seen by men of consequence and so that he might see, also, the lands and properties which Gilbert bought, for Gilbert did less of trading as the years went by and became instead a man of property, living on rents. And there were, as always, guests for Thomas to help entertain and plans for future entertainments wherein the father could instruct the son in the high art of hospitality.

In the first years it was to Merton that Thomas returned with the greatest pleasure. There his place was secure among the canons and the students, seemingly unchanging. When he was fourteen he took the tonsure with the other boys when the bishop came to administer this rite, although it was not planned that he should enter higher orders. His father thought a lifelong dedication to the Augustinian Order not fitting for his son. And Thomas, in most anguished adolescent prayer, discovered that he had not the selfless dedication to fit him for such a life. Yet when his crown was shaved he thought he felt the hand of God upon him and he vowed to follow all his life the rules of poverty, obedience and chastity. But from that year there was divergence in the aims—and thus a lessening of comradeship—between those of his friends destined to be Canons Regular within the Order and himself, a secular clerk. Sometimes thereafter he felt alone and very much apart within his circle of companions at the priory.

One confidant he had, not among boys of his own age but Canon Robert, whose duty was to supervise some of the scholars' lessons. He was a small young man, unprepossessing, shy. He had been taught in childhood that God gave to man the power of choice and that man, through his will and fortified by grace, might choose good over evil. But in his innocence, observing evil all around him as a child, he had concluded bitterly that few men had the will and God most frequently withheld His grace.

Then he had come to Merton, a frail frightened boy. And as he grew up there he was astonished, every time, to find how often men chose good. Now he was grown, and understood, forgave, and loved mankind. And yet there lingered in him that faint astonishment, a sense of gratitude, whenever he saw evil overcome. This made him shy of men.

It was a fragile bond between the bright successful student full of accomplishments and the small quiet man whose sober contemplation was surprised from time to time by happy, startled, inward thanks to God. It grew from something new in Thomas' life—something he had surmised, had glimpsed, but never fully recognized.

Thomas at fourteen had already learned to study faces and to judge men thereby, to a certain depth. Canon Robert's face, when he first judged it, left him with but a mild impression of reserve, self-abnegation. But there was something more. He looked up from his books to study it: a small-boned face with a broad forehead under a peaked hairline; so far a scholar's face. The lower half was disappointing: a tight mouth, withdrawn, above a jutting knob of chin. Thomas frowned, concentrating, and the canon glanced up, into his eyes.

There should have been a look of admonition or a reprimand; a student's mind should not stray from his work. Instead the canon smiled his brief, abstracted smile and then it was, through those mild violet eyes, that Thomas glimpsed a world he did not know—another life, a kingdom as it were, that "sea of endless light and bright eternity" men wrote about.

Robert, absorbed in contemplation, hardly aware that he had glanced up, looked down again upon his book. But Thomas sat wide-eyed in thought. He had seen other men at prayer; prayer was the center of his life, with study, here at Merton. He woke to prayer and fell asleep to prayer. But it had not achieved him this. For others, yes. For others, he saw now, he understood, it did.

At home in London, and at Pevensey, his father and his patron said that he would soon know all the canons had to teach him. He had not contradicted them. Now he perceived that there was something more to learn here at the priory other than what was taught by rote out of the books. But it was not the sort of thing, he realized, that he learned easily. How was it done?

Thomas sat frowning, head bent, cut off from the world. To learn such things might take a lifetime. Could he attempt it, living here quietly out of the world for his whole life—and risking failure in the end?

But the decision was not his to make. His father told

him, after the year was over and he went home in June: Thomas would not return to Merton any more.

CHAPTER IV

THOMAS MADE THE TRIP to Pevensey alone that summer of 1134, riding his father's horse and stopping overnight at Tonbridge Castle as Lord Richer had arranged, accompanied only by one groom. At fifteen he no longer needed to be dealt with as a child and the roads were peaceful under the stern rule of the old king. But he was tired as he approached the fort. The wind blew sharp against him from the ocean, filling his eyes and catching the breath out of his mouth, and far ahead the castle stood out lonely on its isthmus beyond the ditch and stretch of wall that cut it from the mainland. He had to pull himself together as he slowed his horse to walk across the bridge, for on the other side Lord Richer's guards were watching his approach, squatting in the lee of the old Roman bastion, squinting into the last long rays of the sun.

He held his back straight and his toes sharp pointed as he rode over the rattling planks and reined his horse before them. The sergeant, with some grunting, rose from the three-legged stool which he had tipped against the wall. "Well, Master Thomas," he said, walking toward him with a smile. "Welcome back. How are the roads from London?"

Thomas smiled down at him. This was the first step, always, into the world of Pevensey and the personality expected of him there, this greeting at the gate. Heretofore others had smoothed the transit for him. "The roads are peaceable," he said. "And all give way to me and my men." The groom behind him snorted and the sergeant laughed. But his eyes had traveled up to Thomas' head; he stared at the shorn circle of the tonsure.

"What's this, Tom. Have you been taking vows?" he said with no pretense at hiding his disapproval.

"I have vowed," said Thomas, forcing such lightness as he could into his voice, "with the help of one more powerful than I," he grinned, "to catch a hundred eels this summer."

He was referring to an incident of three years back when the big sergeant had volunteered to teach him to catch eels and the two had spent a morning sloshing in the ditch to no avail. It was the one point of personal contact that the two had. One of the guardsmen understood the jibe and laughed, and the sergeant screwed up his face ruefully as Thomas grinned again and rode on through the gate.

The men looked after him appraisingly. The boy was tired, that was obvious—perhaps too obvious—but he was game. The fact that they made no disparaging remarks—unusual for them when newcomers passed by—was as high compliment to Thomas as any praise from men of different station. They liked him, for he had been quicker than the other boys to learn the knack of getting on with men of all occupations. And Thomas, as he rode away, aware that they were watching, felt that their eyes were on his tonsure, but he knew not whether to be ashamed or proud. He did not even know exactly what it was he wanted them to think of him—except that they should like him.

The outer bailey court of Pevensey was large, ten acres of uneven, salt-encrusted ground enclosed by the old Roman wall. This time of evening it was quiet, all the worksheds and the long low barns deserted, horses in their stables, villeins in their huts—as though the sun in going down had drained the life from it.

Thomas rode in silence through the darkening, sea-filled air along the cobbled road. Ahead of him, beyond the spiky palisade that walled the inner bailey, rose the massive battlements and towers of the fort. The Norman keep stood clean-lined and uncompromising in the embrace of the old rounded bastions and the pink light glinted on the crenelated walls.

Thomas felt once again that quickening anticipation, blended of fear and pleasure, that he always felt when he approached Lord Richer's castle. That he was being tested here he knew, but for what purpose he could not be sure.

He rode unchallenged through the wooden gate and halted once again. Here in the inner bailey there was life. Miles Mauduit, his best friend at Pevensey, ran up to greet him shouting and announced, almost before Thomas could find his legs upon the ground, that his father—a chamberlain to King Henry, Thomas knew—had promised to buy him the heirship to the castle and the lands of Gifford with the little heiress Margaret. "If the king so wills of course," he laughed. "I think the king will give his grace to it. They say she's pretty," he added. "And some day I shall have an honor all my own!"

Thomas held out his hands but Miles brushed them aside and flung his arms about him. Then he stood back, laughing, flexing his knees in a peculiar way he had, especially before some test or tournament. The other boys revealed this same unrest and high expectancy as Thomas moved among them toward the keep. King Henry had announced a visit to the castle sometime this summer. He would stop here on his way from Winchester to his lands in Normandy across the Channel. This was important to these adolescent boys, not for the feasting or the sport that would attend the visit but because, although they were related—all but Thomas—to great baronial families or high officers in the king's court, not all of them were heirs. Most were younger sons, or bastards, without fixed inheritance, and their promotion lay in the king's favor or in the influence of courtiers close to him.

Thomas had known, of course—even at Merton such news was eagerly discussed—about the birth of the king's grandson, Henry, at Le Mans in March, and that the king would go to Normandy to see him. But in the priory such news had not the personal meaning that it had at Pevensey. He smiled and clapped his friends upon the back and promised them that they should all be earls. And then he went to find Lord Richer and announce his presence in the castle.

The hall at Pevensey was beautiful to Thomas' eyes, though as he entered now it seemed both dim and quiet. It was a huge room, massive and unadorned, a man's hall, roofed with heavy smoke-stained oak and floored with oak as well. The only light came from the narrow windows, and fell soft and slanting, funneled through twenty feet of wall.

The room was almost empty now. Only a few, some clerks and courtiers, lingered here after supper. The servingmen were finishing their evening's work, dismantling the supper tables, carrying benches to the windows, stacking the boards and trestles against the wall. They moved like shadows, and the dogs, still nosing in the rushes where the tables had been set, were almost lost in darkness. Only at the farthest end did any color show. There, where the wall was rounded like the apse of some great church, a row of rush lights burned. They spread a soft and flickering light on Richer l'Aigle's scarlet mantle and on the wimples of the ladies who had gathered there.

Richer was well aware the boy was in the hall even before Thomas had made his way down half the dusky length. He stood in conversation with his steward and his chaplain over a matter which had come before his honor court the week before. The chaplain was insisting that he read the tally over while the steward tried to cut him short. And the lord listened, with the lights behind him and his eyes upon the slender boy who came across the rush-strewn floor. He watched him briefly pause beneath a window where a game board had been set and two old friends were sitting down to play, again to let a servant carry a bench across his path and say a word to him, and yet again to pat and gently push aside the liam hound that came to smell his hand and lean against him. The Lady Juliana, wife of the steward, called to him from where she sat among the other ladies and Thomas turned and bowed and spoke an answer to her greeting, grave and flattering. And all the while the baron watched.

When Thomas stood before him, Lord Richer's eyes no longer held the look that had been in them. He bade him welcome formally as the boy knelt. Then, since Thomas had come late for supper and had not eaten on the road, he sent him to the kitchen for some food and turned again to listen to the chaplain as though that matter of his honor court compelled his full attention.

When Thomas came back carrying his cup of beer and slabs of bread and vension he found the boys had drifted in with darkness. More rushes had been lit and they were in their favorite corner nearest to the door. There they were not so much noticed by the clerks who huddled over their chess boards or vagrant knights searching about for resting places, and they were at the greatest distance from the lords and ladies by the dais at the far end. For pages the safe rule was: do your duty and then disappear.

They welcomed Thomas and made room for him and continued to talk earnestly, as all the court was talking, about the king and his grandson and heir.

"He should be brought to England for his nourishing," said Edric. Edric always made himself conspicuous by praising English things. He even wore his hair in the old Saxon way, down to his shoulders, although he was a Norman like the rest of them.

Miles laughed at him. " 'The proper cradle for a Norman king is Normandy,' " he quoted. "You heard the constable." Indeed, their arguments were only echoes of their elders' thoughts.

"What does Lord Richer say?" asked Thomas with his mouth full.

"Oh, he's concerned about succession to the throne if the

old king should die before the baby's old enough to rule; he doesn't care what happens so long as they both live. But he's afraid—I heard him say so to the constable . . ."

"But Empress Matilda would be queen if the old king should die," said Edric interrupting. "All the barons took an oath to that, so there's no question of succession."

Miles rolled his eyes at Thomas. "God's breath what innocence!" he said. And then to Edric: "I wouldn't give much for that oath now. Nobody takes it seriously since she remarried."

"An oath's an oath," said Edric stubbornly. "My father said so. And all the earls and barons swore that they would make Matilda queen whenever the king died." He saw Miles' smirk and burst out, "Oh you can laugh. You always laugh at me. That's all you know. Father was there; all the important lords were there. And they swore solemnly that since the prince had died in the White Ship and Empress Matilda was the only lawful child, then they would do as the king asked . . . "

"I wouldn't know about your father," Miles said scornfully. "But other people's fathers are more sensible. Listen, simpleton, Empress Matilda was a widow then. Do you think they would have sworn to make her queen of England if she had still been married to the German emperor?" He looked for confirmation at the other boys and they all shook their heads. "Well, then, isn't it just the same thing since she's married to the Count of Anjou? Do you think they're going to hand the throne of England to some dirty Angevin?"

Again the boys all shook their heads, but Edric said, "My father would. And anyway, if he's so dirty, what about his son? I guess you'd have to call the little prince an Angevin, wouldn't you?" he said triumphantly.

The other boys were torn between his logic and their loyalty to Miles, but Miles was unimpressed. "No, he's a Norman," he said.

Seeing his friend on shaky ground, Thomas took up the argument. He swallowed his last gulp of beer, put the empty cup down on the floor between his feet, and said with slow deliberation: "This is the logic of it, Edric: If a man's grandfather is Norman, and if his mother is a Norman too, then he is two-thirds Norman. And if he's reared in Normandy and speaks the Norman tongue, that's two more points for him. That makes him one and a third points Norman—even more Norman than you are, Edric, since you are only one. Therefore you have no argument. Prince Henry is a Norman and should be raised in Normandy. And one more item: he must grow to be a man before King Henry dies. Isn't that right, Miles?"

Miles snatched the empty cup up from the floor. "Long life to the king!" he shouted, jumping up.

Thomas sat laughing up at him, but in his heart he was uneasy that they should speak lightly of such solemn things. At Merton he had prayed that God protect the baby, Henry, born to be his king. He did not want Miles' laughter, or his own to besmirch that prayer. Taking the cup from Miles, he put it down beneath the bench once more and used this moment, with his head bent, close to his knees, to whisper hastily, "Almighty God, and King of Kings . . . ruler of princes . . . I humbly beseech thee, bless the baby, young Prince Henry . . . and forgive our trespasses."

He looked up smiling once again and said, "My eyes will not stay open any more; I have to go to sleep."

Thomas' tonsure caused less remark among his fellows in the hall than it had among the footsoldiers at the gate. Most of the boys had high connections in the Church, and their conception of a bishop, helmeted and wearing a cuirass over his robes, riding a destrier in preference to a mule, and holding baronial rights to strong-walled castles, was based upon their own acquaintanceship with high-born cousins. They took for granted without questioning that Thomas would rise in the Church as they rose in the service of the king.

But Thomas knew, as did Lord Richer, that his case was different. These boys with whom he learned to hunt and hawk, with whom he slept upon the rushes in the hall, with whom he served the baron wine at dinner, needed only a first slight boost of luck to rise to places of high title all their own. Thomas would require far more luck—some twist of fate entirely unforeseen—as well as all his charm and application. This they both knew, although they did not speak of it. To the baron it presented an interesting element of gamble as he toyed with the boy's future. And in Thomas, heart-set on excelling in all things, it bred an obdurate determination, centered on himself.

There was a little crooked dwarf the baron kept for his amusement—Valeran Fitz Pain, a long name for so small a man. He had an ugly body and a croaking voice, nor had he any talents such as turning somersaults or juggling with plates. One attribute he had: a piercing eye to single out the misfit or the lonely in a crowd. No matter with what desperate subterfuge a man or boy might try to camouflage those things that made him different from his fellows, Valeran saw straight through to where he suffered and there found opportunity for sport. The baron liked to laugh and Valeran provided laughter. This was the way he earned his keep; he was unfit for any other occupation.

Long ago, when Valeran first looked at Thomas, his eyes had glowed to see the way the boy sat slack-limbed on his palfrey, quivering with fatigue, as he rode through the inner gate that summer of his introduction to the castle. The dwarf stood on the steps and watched the way the boy's legs buckled under him when he slid to the ground. "Guard ho! Guard ho!" he called in his frog's voice, "Man the battlements! A strange knight enters through our gates!" Then he had scampered down the stairs and challenged Thomas to single combat.

In later summers he found cause for jesting in the fact that Thomas did not stay at Pevensey all year but "lay with monks" throughout the winter and came to the castle looking lean and spent. He gave a dissertation one day at dinner on the likenesses between this boy and a feather bed in that they both looked worn and flat after an active night, "abbots lie heavy, so I have been told," but were so easily puffed up. And for a while, when he was twelve years old, Thomas had had to smile down the nickname "feather bed."

Valeran might have found good fuel for laughter in the baron's eyes whenever they dwelt long upon the boy, but he was not kept to make sport of his lord. Instead, this year, he built his jokes upon the comic prospect of a tonsured Cheapside peddler genuflecting to fat housewives, calling his wares in learned accents: "Agnus Dei, buy my chamber pots."

Thomas had to strive to keep his temper while the table laughed, and Richer, through his laughter, watched him, gauging what he had learned of self-control. He saw the smile, the steady hands holding the ewer of wine, and he approved. But looking in the eyes he paused and withheld judgment, for there he saw not only pride, which he found good, but scorn and something of a promise that the jests would be remembered and repaid. The baron frowned. Boys under his roof must take hard lessons in the art of sportsmanship, in the hall as well as in the field. That Thomas' lessons were invariably harder than those of his fellows he understood. Indeed, it gave him an oblique pleasure. This boy must pass unscathed the hardest tests; he must be perfect.

So Thomas fought, under his tutelage, for perfection. Now he could manage the huge war horses that the baron rode, sitting high, knees straight, toes pointed in the long stirrups. He had learned to wear a heavy kite-shaped shield upon his left arm and carry in his right a long forked lance. And in the practice tourneys which the boys held out on the fields beyond the ditch he and his friend Miles Mauduit were the most successful in unhorsing their opponents.

By now he played a tolerable game of chess and in the hall his manners were all that could be wished. He seemed to have a way of speaking to this man or that so that each found a different way of praising him. One day Lord Richer, standing with his chaplain on the high castle steps, chanced to see Thomas as he came into the inner bailey with the other boys. As they strode forward, laughing, with their hoods thrown back, Thomas stood out tall among the group.

The chaplain murmured, unctuous in his learning, "A choice young man and goodly . . . and from his shoulders upward higher than any . . ."

The baron made no answer.

"The reference is to Saul," the chaplain prompted. "I thought it apt."

The baron turned and walked away, into the guard-room.

"Blockhead," the chaplain muttered as he turned after him. It was a pain to him to waste his learning on unlettered men. To converse with young Thomas, teaching him some snips of knowledge now and then, was a real pleasure. He knew not why he should not praise the boy before the baron.

But it was in the mews, where the lord kept his birds of prey for hawking, that Thomas was most successful, for he was fascinated by the sights and sounds of this most busy corner of the bailey. His love of hawks began when he was eleven years old, on his first visit to the mews, and Hugh the falconer had taught them, with elaborate patience, a little jingle.

"Now you repeat it after me," Hugh said when he had intoned it through, patently wishing he had not been given this task. "Take it line by line."

Thomas, to please him, ran through the verse as quickly as he could: "An eagle for an emperor," he said, "gyrfalcon for a king. Earls and other noble men should have a peregrine. Merlins are for ladies; their prey is the lark . . ." Hugh, unused to boys who studied, opened his eyes wide. "And for a priest," Thomas concluded, "a sparrow-hawk."

"Well, you've got that done," Hugh said. Usually he could

send such boys away to think about the verse and thus be rid of them for several days. Now he could only say, "Come back tomorrow and I'll teach you more." But Thomas did not recognize dismissal. He had heard a low-pitched whistling sound coming from a closed-up shed behind them. "Is that a hawk?" he asked. "Or is it just a falconer?"

"That's Bernard," Hugh said, "training a new peregrine."

"Talking to her?" Thomas persisted.

Hugh looked down at him and saw him clearly for the first time—not just another boy, but someone interested in his work. "Yes, talking to her you might say," he said. "This is the way it is." He eased himself onto a bench. "When you've caught a hawk she's lonely for her freedom, wants to fly away. You have to keep her in the dark so she won't bait."

"Bait?" Thomas asked.

"Try to fly away—and get caught in her jesses," Hugh explained. "Then when she's quiet you've got to coax her to take food. She's hungry, but she won't eat. Give her a piece of meat . . ." Hugh pinched his thumb and forefinger together. "And then you rub a feather on her legs." He waved his left hand gently back and forth under his right. "And when she takes the food . . ." He made a low whistle like the sound Thomas had heard within the shed. "She's got to know your call, you see. She's got to know that that means food. Otherwise, the baron takes her out for sport and once she's gone after her prey she won't come back."

"And when she's trained will she come back to your whistle?" Thomas asked.

Hugh laughed. "Oh well, there's more to it than that!" he said. "First the whistle till she eats. Then when she comes to you you can take the training hood off, let her see the light outside. Of course she's got to know the glove, so you can take her. Then the lure . . . Oh, no, there's more to it than that!" He looked at Thomas' earnest face, full of the intensity of learning, and said in a low voice, as though he were ashamed, "You've got to treat her right, you've got to feel the way she feels. A hawk's a living thing you know, she's wild, she's . . ." He could not find the word. "A hawk is beauty, that's what she is."

"Oh may I see her?" Thomas asked.

Hugh shook his head. "She can't bear strangers yet." He rose. "You run and play now. I have work to do." He looked down at Thomas. "You can come back," he said. "Come back when you want. You can tell anyone who asks I said you could."

And Thomas did. Whenever he was free—in the first summer and the summers afterward—he came back to the grassy plot among the sheds and cages of the mews where young hawks wheeled in the salt air above, trying their wings, and where the smell was strong of raw meat and of birds and leather trappings. He watched and listened and was useful, learning all he could, till, as the years went by, he grew to know the different hawks, their training and their modes of hunting, and how to handle them. And by the time he was sixteen he was addicted to the sport of falconry.

That year—the year he was sixteen—Thomas spent entirely at Pevensey, making only two short visits home, as he had done from Merton. Most of the older boys, the ones he had known best, were gone now. Miles Mauduit had been knighted and held a castle of his own within the honor of his father-in-law. There was a group of younger boys, new ones coming to the keep at Pevensey each year for nourishing in the arts of aristocracy, but Thomas, though he could command their services by right of his seniority, had little contact with them.

When the baron was in residence Thomas spent his time with him, hunting and hawking, an accepted member of his party. And when the lord was absent on tours of his other holdings or visits to the court Thomas rode out alone or trained a favorite hawk, or else he played a game of chess or talked of bookish matters with the chaplain. It was an easy life and Thomas might have stayed forever at the castle, he presumed, filling some indefinite post—helping with the book work of the clerks, perhaps, or simply for the baron's pleasure, as Valeran Fitz Pain was kept. But he was restless, his ambition pricking him. Only with Lord Richer did he forget the future in the excitement of each day's activity.

One summer day the two rode out to hawk alone, with just one dog and one fine peregrine. They rode at leisure, following and crisscrossing the wooded streams that ran through open meadows toward the sea, the baron not so keen as was his wont but sitting careless in the saddle, keeping the falcon hooded on his wrist and letting the dog run freely. He was content today to let the sport come where it may, and he talked softly as they went, his words compelling, of the pleasures of the hunt, the waiting for the quarry to break cover, and the chase. There was a vibrance in his voice that few had ever heard and he laughed softly more than was his habit, turning and looking often into the boy's face as they rode knee to knee. And Thomas rode—not ignorant, he knew there were such men. But still unwilling, at sixteen, to recognize the danger, still flattered that the baron chose his company, still innocent—beside Lord Richer, smiling, nodding, but never looking at his face.

They reached a reedy stretch along a millstream and the dog pointed. They reined and watched, the baron speaking quietly to the dog as he removed the falcon's hood and cast her off. She rose from the gauntlet, the bells tinkling on her legs, and climbed in sweeping, free-winged circles to her place of vantage in the sky. Then Richer gave a sharp command. The dog ran forward into the reedy growth, raising a frightened, rustling flight of grouse.

High overhead the peregrine chose her prey and dove, straight and swift as a falling plummet, down on the helpless bird. She made her strike and feathers sprinkled the blue sky, but she had missed her grip. The wounded bird swerved toward the nearest cover and the peregrine once more started her circling climb.

The baron pricked his horse into a gallop, keeping his eyes upon the spot of cover where the bird lay hidden, for they must flush it once again to serve the waiting falcon lest she fly after some other quarry and be lost. The stream now lay between them and their game, too deep and swift for fording, and they raced along the bank, searching for a crossing place, with the dog following. Where foliage grew high along the water's edge the baron laid his head along his horse's neck and plunged through. Thomas, following close into the slapping branches, pulled up his hood to cover his face and head and bent low in the saddle.

He did not see the clearing by the mill as quickly as the baron did, nor the little footbridge spanning the narrow race. And thus he overshot, and while the baron's horse was already stepping gingerly onto the other side, he was still pulling in his own horse, wheeling it, urging it all too hastily across the slippery plank. He saw the water racing under him and heard the slap and thunder of the mill wheel just below. His hand upon the rein betrayed excitement and the horse felt it, tried to back away, stepped into air and fell, hoofs clawing, into the stream below. Thomas was thrown clear but his hood hampered him, twisting across his face. He sank, rose to the surface, and the current snatched him.

The baron, riding on, turned to see if Thomas followed him. He had not marked the splash under the mill wheel's roar. Now he saw Thomas' horse, dripping and dark with water, heaving itself up the farther bank, the saddle empty. He turned, and with his face all made of iron and hand of iron on the reins, galloped across the shaking plank. But he was late. He saw the boy with his head hidden in the floating hood drawn in the clear swift waters of the race toward the great hammering paddles of the wheel.

He cupped his hands around his mouth and filled his lungs to shout to the oblivious miller within the millhouse: Stop the wheel! But even as he shouted the wheel stopped, and in the sudden silence the man appeared, shaking the flour from his apron.

The miller was astonished to see a horseman riding at him with his arm outstretched. But when he looked to where the man was pointing he acted with great speed and poise, grabbing a pole that stood beside the door and with it snaring the boy's floating clothes and drawing him to shore even before the baron could dismount and run to his side. Together they pulled Thomas onto the grass and tore the hood clear of his head. His face was white, his mouth was open, retching and gasping.

The baron smiled a thin smile and stepped back. "He'll be all right," he said.

The miller did not speak. He rolled the boy upon his face and pressed his large hands, hard and carefully, against his back until the water gushed out from the open mouth. Then he called over his shoulder to his wife.

Thomas, moaning on the grass, was conscious of the call. It was the first sound he heard after the roaring in his ears. He frowned under a flood of dizziness and pain, opening his eyes. All that he saw as he looked once again upon the world was silvery and gold: the fuzzy blades of grass before his face, a blurred expanse of apron flecked with chaff, the sunshine through translucent leaves beyond, all glowing as if in a sea of light—that sea of endless light and bright eternity that he had glimpsed before. Before. At Merton. That promised sea of light! A terror and a longing sprang up in his heart and he began to weep.

The miller's wife came running from the house and sank down on the ground beside him. She wiped the slime and water from his nose and mouth and Thomas looked up through his tears to see the baron's face, watching as from far off.

For a long moment the two looked, one standing, one upon the ground, a long inquiring look through that expanse of air. Then Thomas jerked away and rolled upon his knees and knelt with head bent over his clenched fists. He knew now, recognized, the life the baron offered. He knew where he had purposely not known before, because before he had not made a choice about his life and was content to drift. What he had seen there in the glimmering chaff, the clear translucent sky, threw light into the darkness of his future here at Pevensey—the safe life, but degrading. More than degrading, insult to all he was.

Shaken and sickened he knelt, as he had not knelt since he left Merton, curled in a shuddering ball, and felt the baron's eyes upon him and recoiled.

The miller and his wife drew back in deference and then looked to the baron. They were astonished to see his well-bred face all drawn up in disgust. He turned away and walked to where the boy's horse stood beside his own, cropping the grass, and felt along its legs, lifting its hoofs, to see if it had suffered any injury.

"Let the boy stay with us a little while," the miller said.

The baron straightened. With his back to them he lifted up his arms and let his hands rest on the saddle. At last he spoke. "Aye, let him stay," he said over his shoulder. "I do not need him."

Then he moved quickly, loosening the girth and lifting the wet saddle with its blanket to the ground and looping the reins over it. "He knows the way back to the castle when he wants to come," he said.

He took his own horse by the bridle, called to the dog where it lay panting on the grass, and gave one useless glance into the sky; the peregrine was gone. Then he swung into the saddle and rode off.

And Thomas, on his knees, heard the retreating hoofs, the arrogant *clip-clop* of them upon the bridge.

CHAPTER V

"I HAVE BEEN TOLD there was a miracle concerning a mill wheel," William Fitzstephen offered eagerly, "when he was saved from drowning . . ."

Brother Benedict, to whom he spoke, bent his head as though to examine the long-handled dipper that lay across his knees. He did not answer.

The two men sat in the dark crowded crypt at Canterbury;

it was soft summer of 1171. Thomas had been dead six months and in his name great miracles were done. The leprous and the dropsical were cured and men possessed were freed of demons. Candles were lighted most mysteriously, and barns and houses saved from fire, and ships upheld at sea. The blind saw and the deaf heard and the lame rose up from their beds and walked, all in his name.

Ever since Prior Odo had agreed to let the people come into the crypt the scene there—so wrote Benedict—was like the scene beside the pool of Bethesda. "Wonders, great miracles," he wrote, "daily occur." These were the words with which he introduced the catalogue of miracles he was compiling for the chapter of the monks at Christchurch. He and the young monk Roger had been deputed by Prior Odo to guard the sacred body and tend the pilgrims—and to collect, in the long-handled dipper, their offerings to the Church. Of his own will he had begun, after the first few days, to listen to the pilgrims' tales, sift them for truth, and then record them so that they might be read out in the Chapter House.

He sat now near the martyr's tomb, resting, and with him sat the clerk. William was also keeping an account of all the miracles he could get wind of, not only of the wonders done in Thomas' name after his death—these were becoming almost commonplace—but those that had occurred while he yet lived. He had in mind to write a life of Thomas, for he had known him well. But he had never witnessed, nor even could remember talk of, any truly miraculous incident that he could write about. So he had set himself to seek some out.

He spoke now, eagerly, his mobile hands gesturing before him and his freckled face alight. "The miracle occurred when he was but a boy," he said to Benedict. "The mill wheel stopped as by the hand of God, so I have heard, miraculously, just as our lord was being flung into its arms!"

Benedict watched him sideways, his chin down. In these last months of listening to tales of miracles he had become alert to innocent exaggeration or imposture. He said nothing.

The long procession of the pilgrims to the tomb moved quietly before them and the swish and echo of their footsteps mingled with the chant of plainsong, for the monks were singing in the Chapter House far off. Sometimes a cry or sounds of excited voices drifted down to them from the transepts of the church above where sick and weary travelers had spread themselves in every shrine and corner.

William dropped his voice a notch. "The miracle is well attested," he said in a half-whisper. "Master Grim of Cambridge tells of it quite positively. Thomas was hawking with a certain lord who was his companion in those days and his hawk, following a duck which was its prey, lit on the waters of a millrace and was drawn under. In plunged Thomas—giving no thought to his own safety—to save the hawk, and straightway was himself caught in the race. But even as the rushing torrent bore him to his death—suddenly the mill wheel stopped! And in the twinkling of an eye the water stopped its rushing and became as still as any silent pool." He paused, not long enough to give the monk an opening. "Nor did the current move again to turn the wheel till Thomas, as by an unseen hand, was lifted out unharmed!"

Again the monk gave him that sidewise glance. "A marvelous tale," he said. "But tell me, Master William, do you have witnesses?"

Fitzstephen drew back. "I had the story straight from William Grim," he said.

"And William Grim was there when this occurred—this mill wheel stopped so suddenly, and the water with it?"

A little frown tightened Fitzstephen's forehead. "You know as well as I do, Brother Benedict, that he first met the archbishop the very day that he was murdered. No, he was not there." He gave a little deprecatory shrug. "And no one else I know of—except that lord perhaps. He must be dead by now . . ." He paused. "Perhaps, as you say, I should scratch the story from my account. He sighed. "It is a pity, though. There are few miracles related of his boyhood. Indeed, of his entire lifetime—very few."

Benedict sat looking at him a long time. "I do not say the mill wheel did not stop," he said at last. "I asked you merely who was witness to it. Nor did I say that you should drop the story from your life of Thomas. God works many miracles, I know. I know it better than most men." He paused, his dark eyes searching William's face.

"But I confess," he said, "I must confess my incredulity, if incredulity's a fair name for the hesitation that I feel—not on my own account but for the reputation of our lord—each time I am confronted with a new marvel . . .

"Indeed, it is a habit with me now to question those who come to testify. For I cannot forget, although these simple people may, that there are evil men waiting to show us to the world as frauds and charlatans. You know as well as I do, Master William, that it is the poor and ignorant who come. They testify—we must remember this—they give their testimony to a hostile world. And it is for me to check them in their exuberance, lest the true wonders to which their simple hearts bear witness sink in a morass of half-truths and hysteria.

"Who is there but myself and young Brother Roger? What is there but our stubborn incredulity to guard the sacred reputation of our lord? Why, there came one this morning, a woman, claiming she had been blind for half her life and now restored. Stone blind before; now she saw as well as I —so she would have me think. I was to take her word for it. She had no witnesses. I tell you, Master William, she was of so mean appearance, so shifty and so short of temper, I confess I did mistrust her from the start."

"And she?" asked William eagerly.

Benedict smiled ruefully. "She gave me ugly words in answer to my questions and would not endure the slightest cross-examination. No, she called me hard of heart, wicked, unbelieving and unfit to attend the tomb of such a martyr— exactly as you would have labeled me just now, because of my unwelcome questioning about the mill wheel. Is it not so, my friend?"

William grinned foolishly under the earnest gaze and the monk rose and touched him quickly on the arm and turned away. He had seen a rush of sudden movement in St. Gabriel's Chapel across the crypt and sensed that he was needed. A woman, Serena of Yfeld, lay there dying, had lain there all day. Now her last breath was near. Her children, who had brought her here, were lifting her from the soft pallet lest, contrary to Christian custom, she should die upon a feather bed. Benedict had given them a thread out of the martyr's robe to place beneath her tongue and they had done so although Serena was steadfast in saying only "Thy will be done" instead of praying that her life be spared. Now she lay dying on the cold stone with her children all about her and the young Roger holding a cross for her to see. Benedict hoped that still the saint might intervene. Serena was a woman of pure faith. He crossed the line of pilgrims and made his way to her.

William sat staring after him, his sheepish grin fading to a look of contemplation. He knew the worth of the monk's argument, that formal recognition of the miracles was slow in coming and that as yet no dignitary of the land had followed in the footsteps of the poor to Canterbury. He knew that the de Brocs still menaced travelers who spoke of miracles and had accused the monks of using magic arts to implant devils in the pilgrims so that they might cast them out.

Indeed, at Eastertime, after the crypt had first been opened to the populace, Ranulf de Broc himself had come to Prior Odo and drawn his sword and threatened that he would carry off the body from the church. That night the monks, in secret, took the corpse out of its sepulcher and hid it in the dark behind the altar of the Virgin. Only the next day Crippled Richard, son of Einold, had discovered it. That was a curious miracle; William had witnessed it. Richard was hobbling past the altar where, unknown to him, the body lay when suddenly he cast away his staff and fell upon his face, then rose again, fell down again, and once again rose up and gathered all his strength and leaped upon the altar, agile as a boy. When he jumped down it was to stand upon the soles of his two feet like any healthy man.

William had run to him and asked him why it was he paused before this certain altar, why he had fallen there, why he had leaped on it. And Richard answered, "I was constrained to by the Mother of God."

Thus the monks knew they could not hide the body from the world. They put it back into its sepulcher and called the masons in to build a strong safeguarding wall around it. But for the pilgrims' sake they left small apertures through which petitioners might reach their heads to kiss the tomb. It was a curious fact, Fitzstephen noted, that some could put their heads through—easily—indeed, a wild man once had climbed right through—while others, though they were no larger, were unable to.

William, thinking these things, let his gaze fall on the little desk that Benedict used to keep his records on. He saw a pile of parchments weighted by the dipper Benedict had lain across them when he rose to go. William took them up and held them to the light to read. They were the miracles that Brother Benedict had written down that day: "Robert, a smith of Thanet, cured of a pain . . ." "Muriel of Canterbury, two years diseased . . ." The clerk's quick eyes raced over them. "Curbaran, a shoemaker of Dover, absolutely and incredibly simple enough . . ." His eye was caught and held. He lifted the parchment above the others and read on. "Simple enough to say the Lord's Prayer daily for the soul of the martyr, not knowing that he who prays for a martyr demeans the martyr, was visited in a dream by Thomas who directed him to dig in a certain place under a mill, and he did so and found a very thick and rusty *denarius* which he tried with his teeth and found to be gold. It was a coin of the Emperor Diocletian and worth some forty silver pieces . . ."

William stopped reading and smiled. He felt a glow of gratitude at the shoemaker's good fortune, simple though he was. Musing, he looked up; there was something more. Yes, gratitude for something more. He smiled again as realization struck him; gratitude for Brother Benedict. He shifted through the parchments and began to read again. "Mad Henry of Fordwich, dragged by his friends to the tomb . . ." Ah yes, he heard the wild commotion on the steps that morning . . .

A heavy woman stood in front of William. He looked up to see the matron from the money-smithy with her eye fastened upon him and in her hands a little package wrapped in linen cloth.

William smiled cautiously. Over the months Wulviva had become increasingly persistent in her visits to the tomb. The water which had cured her daughter had become quite famous; since then the monks had made great quantities themselves and with it cured a wide variety of ills—and yet her own son Almon remained dumb. Ever more frequently she came, with him or alone, bringing small offerings, pleading. Some of the monks had come to think of her as a reproach.

"Master William," she said when he looked up at her. "What do you think. Our Thomas' water's worked another miracle!" Pride and conspiracy rasped in her voice. She knew he liked to be the first to hear such stories. And William's face lit as it always lit when he heard promise of exotic news.

"I have a neighbor," she confided. "Blind, and now sees. He came today to beg a drop of our miraculous water and Walter gave it to him, though he holds it dear for his wife's sake—you know that miracle."

Fitzstephen nodded. "Of course," he said.

"The monks have writ it down," she said with satisfaction.

"But this blind man?"

"Walter brought the water and he put his finger in and with it wet his eyes—and straight away he wiped away the darkness! He had come guided, but he went home unguided. It was a miracle. Even Brother Benedict will say it was a miracle. And I was witness to it!" Another silent moment she held William with her gaze and then she let him loose.

William sighed and straightened. "Has the man come to the church?" he asked.

But she had turned away. Her purpose there was to see Brother Benedict. "Oh yes," she flung the answer over her shoulder. "He will come, with witnesses. It is a happy day for him." Despite her words her voice had lost its vibrance and she seemed to weigh the little package in her hands as though she found it heavy.

William watched her as she moved away from him without farewell. His heart was touched with pity for her—so immoderate in her enthusiasms, and so vulnerable to disappointment. And something of a pest.

He shrugged and once again picked up the parchments. "The boy Edric, ten years old," he read. "Fell asleep while praying near the tomb . . . suddenly confronted by the martyr in his dreams . . . 'Why do you lie on me? Go hence, I will do nothing for you . . .' " Again Fitzstephen raised his head, his face creased in a frown.

"Why some and why not others?" Thus he wondered, with his eyes blank and his lips drawn down.

In front of him he saw that Benedict was making his way crabwise across the crypt while Wulviva bumped beside him, talking in his ear. William could see the irritation in the monk's face and the strong resistance to the story he was being told as he came to the desk and snatched the dipper up. Wulviva put her little package in it and moved off, a sag to her broad shoulders.

William spoke his thoughts aloud. "Why some," he said. "And why not others?"

Benedict's eyes still held that look of stubborn incredulity. And then he nodded; he knew what William meant. Frail old Serena, of such tenacious and abiding faith, had died. And Almon with his inward seeing eye was dumb. And yet today that madman had been cured . . .

He stood in silence for a moment, then rebellion faded from his face and it was touched with the deep peace of resignation, of acceptance. "It is not for us to judge," he said. "Some find relief; for some there is no help. These things rest with God."

The two sat silent for a little longer, watching the pilgrims absently. And when Fitzstephen spoke again it was of those miraculous tales of long ago that he was gathering—the miracles of Thomas' lifetime.

"There was a miracle I've heard concerning some pontificals," he said doubtfully. "When he was a student in the schools of Paris. . . ."

CHAPTER VI

THOMAS HAD GONE to Paris in 1137, the summer of his eighteenth year. The incident concerning the miraculous pontificals occurred at the pre-Lenten "Parliament d'Amour" when he was twenty, just before his sad recall to home.

The tale was this: "*At that annual parley when the student clerics rose each one in turn to praise his ladylove in verse, Thomas the English remained dumb. And when they mocked him for it, calling him lifeless manikin, he only gently smiled and answered them: 'I serve Our Lady.' At this they mocked the more and threatened him, saying it will be worse for him if at the playmote the next morning he comes without some sample of fine needlework done by his fair beloved. Thomas goes home and prays, and in the night receives a marvelous tiny casket full of bishop's vestments, richly embroidered, with miter and with pastoral staff complete. With these he won the contest in the Virgin's name, whose champion he was.*"

That was the story. The truth was something different. Indeed, the incident was not one Thomas would himself have chosen to relate and might have been forgotten had his history turned out differently. For when he came to Paris, thoughts of bishoprics and martyrdom were far from him. He came as other men with eager minds came to the ancient Île de la Cité, drawn by the teachings of the schools of dialectics lately established there. And he had entered into student life as he went into all things: sharp-eyed and smiling, fiercely competitive, winning his way with a quick wit and laughing voice and holding it through hard work, some suffering, and stubborn pride.

He had come on foot from London, crossing the Channel in a fishing boat, tramping alone across the continent through the hot summer days, and by the time he reached the city in the Seine his white skin was well-blackened by the sun and he had gained immeasurably in confidence over the boy who had left Pevensey in sore bewilderment two years before.

The intervening years he spent in London, living once more in his father's hall and going each day to study in St. Paul's, the foremost of the London grammar schools. He had made good progress in his Latin, rhetoric and logic, and at home had learned to observe his family with a man's eye rather than a boy's. There was less entertaining now, and fewer guests. His mother, having loosed her hold on him and even on the younger girls, was fading from the busy world she once had known. His father, reaching for stature beyond that of merchant, gave up his trade entirely and now was finding it more risky than he had foreseen to live on rents from crowded wooden dwellings during those years when fire—along with the immoderate drinking of her citizens—was the acknowledged curse of London. Money was scarce; home life was quiet. Thomas found interests and pleasures elsewhere.

The canons of St. Paul's commended him for his hard application to his studies, the excellence of his memory. And on the holy days when boys from every London grammar school gathered to wage debates, exhibiting their knowledge and their skill in language, Thomas stood very high. These youthful wrestling bouts of wit, ostensibly for fun, made clear which boys might profit from a further education in the great schools of France and Italy. The canons recommended Paris and his father, proud of his son as always, gave him what money he could afford and sent him off.

Thus he reached Paris in late August a tall gaunt young figure, the adolescent awkwardness almost outgrown, sure of himself, or so he thought, in all contingencies after so many days of following foreign ways and nights of finding lodging in strange hostelries or among monks who knew him not. Many the time he had lost his way and had to double back, and many the night he slept in the barn of some kind farmer, eating for supper the bit of bread and cup of watered wine the farmer's wife set out for him, his tonsure and his destination being his passport to the world's hospitality.

At last, in the last light of a long shimmering summer afternoon he stood before the tower of the Porte de Paris looking beyond the great bridge and the crowded river to the city itself, the island in the Seine. Black shadow on rough masonry and slanting sunlight on hewn wood, roof piled over ragged roof, and shouldering above all the ramparts of the French king's ancient castle: this was the city.

Thomas loosed the pack strap from around his neck and let it fall, and with a widening smile of wonder and of challenge he looked up. The world was his this eighteenth summer of his life, and this was his new home in it.

He drew some glances, stopping as he did amid the traffic, but they were side-looks not so much of curiosity as recognition. A student's entry into Paris was a commonplace. The Paris townsfolk knew too well this hungry eager look, this wondering smile that soon enough would give way to the lifted brow and drooping mouth, the signs of overbearing intellect.

Oh, students were commonplace indeed to Paris. Menacing traffic they swung six abreast down streets not meant for more than a pair of horsemen; impudent to tradesmen trying to serve them honestly; breakers of sleep with their loud songs and brawling late at night, and, being tonsured clerks, beyond the reach of the king's justice. Each year the city trembled under the impact of them as they swept in from every land around, until the townspeople could best catalogue them by their most objectionable traits:

Normans, they said, were vain and boastful; Franks were foppish; Bretons were glib, Burgundians brutal and dull-witted. As for Italians, all who dealt with them knew the Sicilians to be cruel, the Romans slanderous, the Lombards vicious and avaricious both, as well as cowardly. Flemings were slothful, fickle, yielding as butter; Germans were foul-mouthed; English were drunkards. Indeed these last were worst of all, hiding their curled tails as they did beneath the fur-lined gowns they wore.

So did Parisians keep the tally on the foreign clerks, although in truth they had the help of educated wit thus to record the list. For there was mutual love between the city and the schools as well as mutual irritation.

Some thirty years before that August day when Thomas stood before the city gates, Paris had sheltered her first school of dialectics—that of the master, William of Champeaux, held in the crowded cloisters of the old basilica of Notre Dame. Ever since then these foreign students had poured in, lured by a call the townsfolk could not hear: the sweet and dangerous voice of Rationalism.

For more than a millennium men had lived by Faith. Now, in the springtime of this century, Reason bloomed once more and Understanding was a flower, as in the age of reasonable Greece, much to be sought. Daring men, scholars and Churchmen, tried to express in rational human thought the doctrines of the Church received of God. The science of philosophy must wed theology.

To others, more profound and cautious men, such union was unthinkable and dangerous. They spoke of heresy. Thus did the winds of controversy blow. And as dry leaves are sucked into the vortex of the rising whirlwind, students were drawn from every land into the heart of the scholastic world.

Some of them came with ravening hunger of the mind and stayed on, unsated, year after threadbare year, studying, writing, arguing late at night, gambling away their money, their garments, and at last their books, and finding solace finally in the more disreputable taverns or in the springtime on the roads of pilgrimage, sleeping with willing farm girls under a hedge, unkempt, wild, lost to the solid home or clerk's bench from which they came, scholars forever in the free air of France.

Others came more soberly to study dialectics and theology, to exercise already well-trained minds and seek advancement in the world. Thomas was one of these.

As he picked up his pack and wound his way past stalls and money-changers over the bridge, pushing and being pushed, he saw that flags flew from the turrets of the castle, blue and gold against the golden sky, stretched on the evening breezes from the river. Below, in the hot stinking streets, there yet remained this festive feeling, like the feeling of the snapping flags. He wondered at this as he kept on along the narrow lanes—dark tunnels where the second stories of the houses met above his head. The smells of cooking came from the black holes of the doorways, and the smells of pigs and chickens from the slime beneath his feet. He had been told to keep right, by the wall, if he would find the hostelries for English students and he came now into a little cobbled square crowded with people.

Those who came behind him pushed him into those before and he stood in the only place that he was able to—against the rough stone of a newbuilt church, his feet astride the gutter next the wall—while those in front of him leaned back upon him, stepped on his feet, and sent the smells of sweat and garlic upward into his nose. Yet they were friendly people, apologizing when they thrust an elbow inadvertently into his side or, turning to talk to one another, explored his ears with the long feathers of their hats. After a moment's hesitation he asked in his most courteous French why they were gathered here in this hot square. They turned to look at him and saw he was a stranger. Then many spoke at once, gesticulating with their hands, using an accent unfamiliar, so that he had to catch their meaning bit by bit. ". . . the old king dead." That he already knew. Louis the Fat, the Wide-awake, struggling in the heat of this unprecedented summer against his gross disease, had finally closed his eyes and died.

Thomas nodded in some uncertainty. "Young king married . . ." That also was well known. Even as the wise old king had labored against death the secret news was brought to him that his uneasy vassal to the south, the Duke of Aquitaine, Count of Poitou, had died on pilgrimage and thus left unprotected as his heir the young unmarried Duchess Eleanor. Her lands spread from the Loire almost as far south as the Pyrénées and from the Bay of Biscay to Auvergne, wider and richer than those of the King of France himself. Whoever of the lords of Western Europe could be the first to seize her hand would, by annexation of her patrimony to his own estate, raise his domain to preeminence over all rivals. Quickly King Louis sent his pliant second son, his heir already crowned Louis VII, on quick-march to Bordeaux where the girl duchess waited. Mild Louis, speeding from the bowstring of his dying father's will, reached his prize in mid-June and married her before the month was out. King Louis lived to hear the news and then laid his huge body on a carpet strewn with ashes and departed from this world. Thus the young couple had returned to Paris as the summer ended, King and Queen of France.

"The queen rides out . . ." The fat man's words were almost lost in a high silver trumpet blast, prolonged and beautiful above the rabble noise. The forerunners came shouting through the square, pushing the crowds back, and Thomas saw the parti-colored hoods of outriders as they jogged by and then the gilded top and painted velvet curtains of a litter.

The crowd was disappointed, for they had grown accustomed these past days to seeing both the king and queen well-mounted and more dashingly escorted. And Thomas also felt the lack of pageantry. The splendor of a royal court appealed to him. Two years ago in London he had seen the English court in its most lavish ceremonial parade when Stephen, Count of Blois, had himself crowned successor to his uncle Henry I.

For that old king had died, as Richer l'Aigle had dreaded that he might, while his grandson was yet an infant, two years old, playing with nursemaids in his mother's court. And despite the old king's wishes, despite the pledge that had been given him, the crown of England had been placed upon the head, not of his daughter Empress Matilda but of his sister's son, Stephen of Blois. There had been unease in England, but most Londoners loved Stephen, and so did Thomas, then. For he was young, and pageantry—so lacking in the later years of the old Henry—thrilled him. Stephen, at his Christmas coronation, had seemed the flower of knighthood riding so splendid on his black horse through the snow.

The present little cortege was no show at all. The queen seemed on some private visit and chose the cover of a litter rather than ride openly. Nevertheless, her presence touched off cheering. Thomas glimpsed the gaudy palanquin and, as the heavy curtains swung, the head of a young girl. She was turned from him; all he saw was the white floating corner of a wimple, a gleam of golden circlet, and an impression of a rounded brow and chin. Yet in that glimpse he sensed a warmth and vibrance.

Now she was gone. The crowd broke and thinned behind her and Thomas saw a young man stagger in her wake, then kiss his fingers, fling them to the sky, and fall back with a dying swoon into the arms of his two grinning friends. They were students like himself and when he could make his way to them he stopped them to ask directions.

Somewhat stiffly, he addressed them. They seemed to him to bear the mark of fellow-countrymen but they were older than he, their beards grown, a certain hardness in their eyes born of a knowledge of the world, and one had lost his teeth in some old wasting sickness or some brawl. He could not place them certainly, so he spoke to them in Latin, very politely, asking directions to the hostelry for English students which, so the canons of St. Paul's had told him, was provided by the bounty of the French king.

A quick look passed between the three, a hint of mockery, for this tall bony youngster with the courtly manner and the fierce black eyes, but they themselves had once known homesickness. They answered him in easy Norman French, accented as at home, and said that they would lead him to the hostel.

So they walked four abreast, rubbing the dirt of housefronts on their sleeves as they swung, arms locked, down the lanes, squeezing aside for men of rank, pushing along without regard for lesser citizens. The slowly cooling evening air was full of many sounds: the screech of housewives to their children and the squeal of unoiled wheels that was so similar; the grunt of pigs roused from their lounging places, the cluck of chickens; the sweet somber flow of plainsong when they passed a cloister door. To this the students added their own noise, their voices rising roughly as they tramped to the irregular rhythm of their song: the *Andacavas Abbas.*

Thomas was probably the only man in Paris who did not know the ballad—since he had arrived scarcely an hour earlier. They taught it to him, that rousing paean to the Abbot of Angers who drank his wine all times and seasons, out of gigantic pots and pans, until, as hides are dressed and tanned with myrrh, so was his skin made black and leathery with wine. It was a stirring song, its rhythm staggering, so that they walked like drunken men in keeping time to it. Thus they arrived at Thomas' hostelry, a narrow doorway in a narrow hall where young men came and went like bees into their hive.

Thomas' companions stopped their singing and let go his arms. They wished him well, patted his back and left him there. They were no longer novice "yellowbeaks" to stay in hostels, but rented chambers of their own: an attic room above a tanner's shop. But they were known here; several of the young men at the door looked after them with admiration as they departed. The story had been told of them that once in a winter of desperation, when they were down to one cloak between them in which to attend their lectures, they lured a neighbor's cat into their play at dice. The cat lost and was sent home with a note around his neck telling of his debt. The debt was paid, too, though the owner sent his own note asking that the cat be spared from further play because he could not count his throw.

Because of this and similar stories the three were much admired, and some of this admiration was transferred to Thomas, as he stood slipping off his pack before the door.

Thomas took up his life in Paris with the ease of youth. The hostel was a long dark very narrow dormitory room with crooked stairs and hall above, also for sleeping. Thomas had a wooden bed crammed in among the others and on the first night the students had accepted him and told him where to buy bedding and two new sheets—as he would find the white cloth helpful against lice—and the necessities of candles, all the waxed tablets he might need and stylus for his notes. Books he could rent. And there would be a senior student coming round to tell them of the various masters whose lectures he could hear, the fee for each, and where to register—though naturally if he had any sense he would choose Doctor Peter Abelard. They were all going to.

Most famous of all the men who studied and then taught

in Paris in those years of intellectual fire was Peter Abelard. His wit was sharp, able to move the minds of serious men to laughter, his character ambitious, and his mind far-ranging into the dangerous and unexplored. As a young student he outstudied and outargued his own master, William of Champeaux, and soon became a master on his own. He moved his school out of the crowded walks and courts of Notre Dame, across the little bridge of scholars onto the gentle slopes of Mont St. Geneviève. There students flocked to hear him lecture in the green orchards on the left bank of the Seine.

But he made many enemies, powerful and dedicated men, who feared the questions he put into malleable minds. He was accused of heresy, found guilty, forced to burn his books and live in exile from the centers of learning for many years. Now he had returned, old, battered, and again harassed, but not yet quite defeated. Once more across the Petit Pont his siren voice was heard inviting brash young men to measure God's intent against the fragile logic of the human mind. Thomas had heard of him of course. Even in London schoolboys knew the lyric songs the learned doctor wrote in those years of his passionate affair with the young lovely Heloise, the beauty of their melody enhanced by the dark scandal which surrounded them. He somewhat feared his teaching, yet he knew he should not miss the opportunity to hear his famed discourse.

Next day the senior student of whom the boys had spoken came to the hostel. He was John of Salisbury, quiet and grave, who had been studying at Paris several years, this last one under Abelard, and was known as a scholar and a gifted writer of Latin prose. He had the boys bring him a chair and table; he was a slight man and to sit behind a table gave him more authority than to stand up. Then, with his base established, he listened smilingly, a little absently, while the new students told him their backgrounds and their interests. To a group of them, including Thomas, he recommended Robert of Melun as a teacher and sobriety as a way of life.

A student laughed and John looked up. "You think my admonition to live soberly is out of place?"

Under the quiet look the youngster's laugh turned somewhat hollow but he answered bravely, "I think your choice of master out of place. I would choose Master Abelard."

John's face showed no expression. "Master Abelard has left," he said.

They did not believe him. Left for where? And why?

"That he is gone is quite enough to know," said John.

"So they have hounded him out again!" the brash young student shouted. "Who is it this time? The bishop? The metropolitan? Or was it the all-holy unforgiving Abbot of Clairvaux again?"

Thomas was shocked. No one had ever spoken thus before—as far as he had ever heard—about the Abbot Bernard of Clairvaux. Thomas had always heard that if saints walked the earth this man was surely one.

John brushed aside the question. "Therefore," he said, "those of you bent on study of dialectics may join yourselves to Master Robert, as I said, or Master Alberic if you prefer. I mentioned Master Robert because he comes from England."

"And what of Abelard?" the young man cried again.

"And *what* of Abelard?" asked John. "What will you have me say of him? That he is an illustrious teacher, better than any, admired by all who study with him? I will say that. And that he has departed all too hastily from Paris? That I will say. What more?"

"And we are not to have the privilege of hearing him!" The hothead turned aside and he and others formed a little group and stood apart, discussing the feasibility of following Peter Abelard wherever he had gone. Paris was not the only place of study in the world!

But Thomas would not be beguiled by talk like this. His journey to the schools had not been after some vague ideal nor yet to swallow discourse that might be critical. He came to study and to learn, to listen to advice and to advance himself.

"And you, sir," he spoke with great respect to John, though there could not be more than a few years between them, "Who will you join, now that Master Abelard is gone?"

"I have attached myself to Master Alberic of Rheims," John said. "Both he and Robert of Melun are good teachers, sharp of intellect—the one perhaps more subtle and profuse, the other lucid, brief, and to the point. Robert is more caustic in responses where Alberic may indicate that simple answers raise more serious questions. For you"—he looked up from the desk at Thomas and the years between them seemed to grow—"I would suggest Master Robert as being easier to follow."

Thomas, conscious of his youth, his newness, felt this was an insult. Yet it was true; he came to Paris to find answers rather than questions. He did not speak.

"There is a difference of flavor, only, between the two,"

John said placatingly. "Both are esteemed. You may choose English beer or French wine, as you will."

"I note you chose the wine," Thomas said bluntly. The senior student had an odd effect on him, making him awkward where with others he was smooth.

John's answer was to repeat the information he had come to give: the times and places of the lecture courses and the proper fees to pay. Then he arose to go. But as he passed by Thomas he looked up at him. He had a wide smooth brow and wide-set clear brown eyes, giving an air of deeper gravity than was, perhaps, indicative of his true character. "As for your beer and wine," he said with a small smile, "choose what you find best. I myself am a drinker of both." He looked back at the room where the young students hung in a bunch upon his sober words. "Nor do I abhor," he added, "anything—as long as it can make me truly drunk."

Thomas paid his fee and joined himself to Master Robert of Melun as he had been advised, and every day he and his comrades walked across the city and the Petit Pont to the hall which had been hired by the learned dialectician for his lectures. The boys sat on the wooden benches under the master's platform or, if they came late, upon the piled straw of the floor, and hung upon his words and memorized the rudiments of dialectic. Thomas remembered faithfully to hear Mass once a day and keep the vows that he had made at Merton.

Winter came early. And as the summer had been hot beyond men's memories, so were the dark months cold. Thomas put on his fur-lined robe under the scholar's hooded gown he was required to wear and wrote home for more money to buy himself strong leather hose and heavy gloves, for he was always cold. By day the streets were crackling with frost, the eaves were hung with icicles. By night the hostel stank—the doors and shutters sealed against the wind, the young men wrapped in all their clothes and stale bed coverings, their frosty breath soaked with the sour wine they drank for warmth. Shivering they sat upon their beds to study, shuffling their feet in dirty straw, their aching fingers cupped around the candle's glow.

To Thomas, used as a child to all the warmth and plenty of his father's hall, the lordly life at Pevensey, it was a gall to have to live thus as the poor boys lived who slept on naked straw and had to eke a living copying lessons or carrying holy water from the churches to stay in school at all. His heart went out to them as they stood shivering at the butcher's stall and haggled for a piece of tripe or sausage while next to them, soaking in the smells of the rotisserie, the servant of some lucky fellow ordered roast goose, mutton done in garlic sauce, or pork pie hot with pepper. He would have liked a heavy purse so that he might buy for them, and for himself, all that their stomachs craved. But he must make his money stretch and live on soggy pastries and roast eggs and buy the cheaper wines. It did not keep him warm.

Advent and Christmas and Epiphany came and went. Outside on deepest nights the icicles made eerie chimes and once or twice the gray wolves crept across the forest plains, through the lean suburbs into the cold black narrow streets. Thomas' breath hung in the air before him and he looked for spring.

With March the sap began to run, and blood to frozen fingertips. Within the lecture halls response was livelier to the master's sallies; students clapped and stamped upon the floor or hissed through their teeth at some disputed point. In streets now, going home, they sang. It was the time to play the tambourine, to follow pretty girls, to fall in love.

From Thomas' hostel came a plaintive song:

"If she whom I desire should stoop to love me
I would look down on Jove.
If for one night my lady would lie by me
And I kiss the mouth I love . . ."

Thomas pushed through the door and saw a group of students, most of his friends, crowded around a singer with a lute. He realized they must be making ready for the Parliament d'Amour. Lent was not far away.

"Innocent breasts, when I have looked upon them
Would that my hands were there . . ."

Serlon of Wilton sat with the lute across his knees, his eyes closed, singing. Thomas recognized him though he did not know him well; everyone knew him by his reputation. He had no true friends, only hangers-on. Serlon had been in the schools for many years and all of Paris talked about him for the scandalous life he led—and also for the quickness of his mind and searching intellect. A brilliant and dissolute man. The younger students, all of them yellowbeaks, were slumped around him on their beds, listening with weak smiles on their mouths.

"How I have craved, and dreaming thus upon them
Love wakened from despair."

Serlon broke off and put the lute aside. "That is enough. I must be gone," he said. Some of the boys jumped up as though to keep him.

"No, don't detain me." Serlon waved his hand. "Would you keep a lady waiting?" He looked around him with arched brows. "It would be nice, though, if I could buy her something—a small favor."

Some of the boys dug in their purses and the coins disappeared up Serlon's sleeve as though they burned his hands. He walked out, jaunty and disreputable, and Thomas noted as he brushed past him how the weary lines had settled on his face. He shrugged. The charity that he had sworn to did not reach as far as Serlon.

Warin, a thin young man from Winchester, a yellowbeak like Thomas and one of his close friends, had taken up the lute. He sat upon the bed, his pointed knees stuck out before him, and plucked the strings. Now he threw his head back as he had seen Serlon do and sang a wavering phrase, his Adam's apple moving to the tune.

"Patient have I been winter long," he sang in a high voice. "Now comes the wanton spring with song. Come, mistress mine . . ."

The others looked at him askance and someone groaned. Warin stopped and grinned, then plucked the strings again. "Thy virginity mocks my wooing; Thy simplicity is my undoing. Come . . ."

William Bigod, sitting next to him, grabbed at the lute. "The words aren't his," he said. "And anyway he has the tune all wrong."

"All right, you try," said Warin amicably.

Will took the lute and twanged it for a moment, frowning in fierce concentration. "This is the way it should go, it goes like this." He coughed. "Like this: 'Patient have I been winter long . . .' " His voice was very deep; the tune he sang was not at all like Warin's. He tried again.

"Patient have I been winter long . . . Patient . . ."

But the others had no patience. "Here, let me try." "Let Warin try again." "No. It's no good. You have to have your own words in the parliament." "Let Thomas try."

"Patient have I been winter long," Will rumbled once again.

"Let Tom try," Warin said. He put his hand across the lute strings but William clung to it.

Thomas laughed and shook his head. "I cannot make a rhyme."

"It doesn't matter; neither can Warin."

"I tell you it's no use," smiled Thomas. "Truly, I cannot make a rhyme. I can't take part."

"Sing one of mine."

Still Thomas shook his head. "I have no voice."

"He has a voice!" "He sings out like a rooster in the dawn. I've heard him!"

Thomas' smile was fading. "I will not take part," he said again. "Why practice?"

William looked up from his laborious plucking at the strings. "Why not take part?" he asked.

"He has no lady love," said Warin. "Tom is lady-shy."

"No more than you," said Thomas. "But if I sing . . ." They would not let him finish. They were laughing at him.

"What, has he got the unnatural vice?" asked William. His voice had not the lightness that the others' had. "Is that the reason?" He grinned round at the others. "That must be it."

The insult had no substance and the boys knew it—God knows they knew, in their cramped dormitory, which of them found their pleasure in other boys as well as they knew which ones snored, which young ones, sick for home and mother, sniffled beneath the covers in the dark, which were the ones most often driven to self-pleasure, and which light-minded ones sneaked out at night to gratify themselves with women. They knew that Thomas was as much a man as any, but they knew also that he had a temper and that Will had roused it. Thus they sat grinning up at him while his face went red.

Thomas, for all Lord Richer's training, could not hide his temper when he was made the butt of jokes and he was angry now. He reached for William, meaning to jerk him from the bed, but Will dodged back. He swung again, hit Warin in the face and knocked him to the floor.

It was a long fight but because it was within the hostel where all knew each other well and all were of one nationality, no knives or sticks were used and no one was seriously hurt. And afterward they all went to the Tavern of the Two Swords in the rue St. Jacques where all the students of the English nation went. They drew their wine and found a table.

Warin, sitting next to Thomas, winced as he swallowed because his mouth was hurt. He felt his lip and looked at Thomas. "What was it all about?" he asked.

The easiest, since the fight had ended amicably and they

were all together in the tavern and the wine not bad, would have been to let the subject go. For Thomas, ease of this sort was never possible. He said, "I tried to make the point—you would not hear me—that to sing of maids is unbecoming in a clerk."

Warin looked at him a long time and the friendly sparkle faded from his eyes. "To be a maid is unbecoming in a man," he said.

Thomas would have fought again but Warin was a thin frail boy, a good friend too. Instead he put his anger in his voice. "I took a vow of purity. And when I swore I did not do it lightly, with a smirk!"

It was a clumsy answer; there was no wit in it and with its implication of superior virtue sure to enrage the others rather than win them over. Thomas knew this. And what is more he knew quite well the way to please his fellows. Most of the time he practiced conscientiously those qualities that gathered others to him: wit and easy laughter in the summer months, fortitude in the dark days, and charity for those in need of it. He himself had need of their approval; his whole soul thrived on popularity. But even more than this he had a need to speak out in the cause of what he was convinced was right. It was a sort of curse with him; it made him appear ugly to his friends. And he was ugly now.

"Oh"—Warin's voice was high and quivering with sarcasm—"how praiseworthy it is to have such strength of will, how laudable to walk across the world in spring and never see the buds! It happens, Tom, that I am not as pure as you—I have the sin of gratitude. I can never see a flower or a bird, even a maiden with a flower face, but I thank God for it."

"It is said," said Thomas slowly, his face still glowering, "that the Abbot of Clairvaux once walked beside the waters of Lake Geneva and never raised his eyes to sky or mountain. Would you accuse the abbot of ingratitude to God?"

The others were all listening now, and Warin subtly shifted ground. If Thomas wanted to start formal argument, bringing in great authorities, he would quote Peter Abelard, the only source he knew to cite against the abbot. "I would say that God gave man eyes to see and hearts to feel. He gave the gift of mind, and of reason—just as he gave faith."

Thomas' eyes snapped for he knew that he had won this first point. "Let me remind you of the Abbot Bernard once again, Warin, since you have taken pains to remind me of Master Abelard: 'Is our faith a matter of private judgment? Is every man, in these great mysteries, to be allowed to think and speak whatever his tongue pleases?'" The others recognized the words—written by Bernard to the pope and much discussed in Paris. Thomas was claiming for his side the two great pillars of the Church who stood in mutual support of one another. There was no authority, not Aristotle nor the saints themselves, who could be used against them. They listened, downcast, for they all took Warin's side, while Thomas finished: " 'Is not, then, our hope baseless if our faith is subject to idle inquiry?"

He drank his wine. It was a victory but not a pleasing one. To be the first to cite the best authority, that was the way to win debate. Thomas had done it; Warin had not. As a result, though, they all resented him—and their original difference was unresolved.

Warin was silent for a moment. Then he said querulously, dropping all pretense of formal argument, "What has faith got to do with singing songs?"

"As we accept our faith," said Thomas, "we must accept our vows."

"I never took a vow not to sing songs," Will Bigod growled, his eyes fixed on his cup.

"You should have," someone said. But no one laughed.

"You took a vow of chastity," said Thomas stubbornly.

"Can't I be chaste," asked Warin with his thin voice rising on the question, "and still sing songs?"

Around the table all were silent, those who were chaste and those who were unchaste. They all knew what these spring-songs meant. Then Thomas answered, staring at his cup. "It's possible."

He knew that many students, chaste as himself, claimed as their own, composed love poems for, some lady of high birth whom they had glimpsed as she sat at a window or perhaps crossing a street with skirts so delicately lifted up and neck outstretched before her like a swan. It was, he knew, a novel and a fashionable thing to do, peculiarly French, thus to commit oneself to some fair matron-unattainable. But he himself had not the inclination for it, or perhaps not quite the ardent innocence required—as, it seemed, Warin had.

More frequently, he knew, when students sang of budding breasts they were the breasts of tavern women or of country girls—breasts they knew well and what the fondling of them did to a man. Thomas himself had known, those years in London, the feel of a maiden's mouth against his own and her soft body next to his all the night long—though he had never known this rapture without self-denial; he had kept the letter of his vow. And when they parted, he and those sweet and yielding girls, fumbling and whispering in the dawn, they were still virginal.

But the experience had left him with an understanding of himself; he was as easily roused as any other man. And when he came to Paris and saw temptation all about him he had resolved to keep himself from such temptations any more, to follow the example set by the more sober of his masters and the monks at Notre Dame. Thus he escaped the side glance from the wimple coyly twitched aside, the coarse words and suggestions of the prostitute, the downcast quivering eyelids of the milk-faced girl in church. In truth, he had not found it was so very hard to do if he was careful, strictly self-disciplined, and with God's help.

"Perhaps it's possible," he said once more. He sounded tired and old. "I see no reason to attempt it."

Thomas did not attend the Parliament d'Amour that year. He took his problem to John of Salisbury asking wise counsel: whether it was proper for clerks to sing of love and whether, if he thought not, scholars should hold a parley of this sort.

John's answer was a question: "In what way is it your concern?" And when he saw the flash of temper in Thomas' eyes he smiled and added, "I agree with you. But since I'm neither master of a school here nor yet a canon of the church, authority to censure fellow students was not given me. As for myself, if I decide that I love poetry more than I hate lascivious display—there will be some of each—why then I will attend. If I decide the other way, why I'll stay home.

"But as for you, Tom," John's clear eyes were slightly mocking, though he smiled, "why, I should say you ought to stay away—at least until you learn to bank those admirable fires of your righteous indignation."

It was the next year that the scandal which involved him broke at the parley. John was no longer there to be his friend and older brother; he had gone on to study and to teach at Chartres. And the story of Thomas' views on chastity—heightened and made ludicrous in the retelling—had gone the rounds till Serlon heard of it. Next year when the Parliament d'Amour came round he thought of it.

Serlon knew many ladies of high rank as well as whores and tavern women and the shy nieces of the canons who lived near the schools. That winter he had been kept warm by the dull wife of a city magistrate and when spring came he felt the need of laughter and fresh air. He decided to bring to the parliament, which he had won so often, a touch of the bizarre. Therefore he borrowed from the magistrate's wife a bishop's chasuble she was embroidering and polished up new verses, keeping them secret.

The place the students held their parley was on the left bank near the Petit Pont. They made a stage there, placing it aloft on stilts between two cypress trees and backing it with painted canvases tacked at the corners so that they would not fly away. The wind blew from the river and the hangings flapped and bellied and the stage swayed like some queer ship that might uproot her anchor any moment and sail away for Mont St. Geneviève.

The first contestant stood upon the stage, his long gown fluttering in the wind. He wore a strange embroidered collar that rested on his shoulders and hung down in pointed tufts on either arm. He was so conscious of this gaudy cowl made by some dull-eyed city girl, patting and arranging it, that it caused more comment than his song—for that was not worth comment of any sort.

The others stood below the stage on softly sloping ground where wet leaves glistened and the smell was strong of last year's foliage and fungus in the wood. The tiny pale-green shoots of spring were just appearing. The contestants and their various claques—for each had brought along a group of friends of his own nation—watched the stage and listened critically. It took a master singer or a verse of some distinction to keep them quiet. Otherwise they moved about and talked among themselves or even hooted at the stage to get the singer off.

Thomas stood among them in his double cloak. He had come only as a member of the English claque formed to support a student from his hostel—so he was prepared to say if any questioned him. He told himself it caused less comment that he came than if he stayed away. He was prepared never to speak again of the old argument if others were prepared to let it be.

The first poor specimen was hustled off and a Bavarian student took his place, stolid in bearing but with the freshness of the season caught in the skipping rhythm of his Latin verse. He sang without accompaniment:

"The earth lies open-breasted
In gentleness of spring,
Who lay so close and frozen
In winter's blustering.

Sweet it is to wander
In a place of trees,
Sweeter to pluck roses
And the fleur-de-lys.
But dalliance with a lovely lass
Far surpasses these.
If she for whom I travail
Should still be cold to me,
The birds sing unavailing,
'Tis winter still for me."

There was a roar of approval among the Germans. Their man had touched on all the popular themes: spring, the hope of dalliance, and of love spurned by chastity. Others who followed him kept to the same subjects. They praised their ladies' purity and swooned for love, each new contestant echoing the one before—till Serlon stepped upon the stage. Here was the master, and the audience stood still. He looked at them, his face quirked in a small contemptuous smile. And suddenly he played a strange and jarring chord and launched into a jesting song that mocked the lovesick verses that had gone before:

"I would have a man live in manly fashion.
Yes, I shall love, but given an equal passion.
I know not how to pray
In the old vulgar way.
Would she have me love her?
Then shall she first love me!"

He paused. They laughed uneasily and clapped their hands, but they were puzzled. Serlon looked at them. Then he began again:

"Alas, alas, what is it I have sung?
My song is all a lie, I am undone . . .
Worthy am I of all thy cruelty,
I do confess my guilt,
Then chide me as thou wilt—
But let thy chamber my tribunal be!"

This time they laughed more heartily and stamped and called for more while Serlon laughed with them. They liked his wit, but better his siren lyrics of seduction. They called for favorites. "Give us 'Who knows honey's sweet who tastes it not,'" one of his friends called out. But Serlon shook his head.

"I have a friend," he said, "who wrote a song but will not sing it. He is shy. They say he's chaste as Daphne. But you will see, he knows the pulse of love."

The audience fell quiet and Serlon took a pose familiar to them, with one knee thrust forward under the lute, his head thrown back and eyes half-closed, suggesting languor and the pangs of love. The song was subtle and his voice infused it with suggestion. He sang of sleep, of sleep like a soft breath from fields of ripening grain, like murmuring of shallow water over sand, like mill wheel turning, turning slowly round, the sleep that follows love. . . .

"After love's gentle commerce,
Languor, soft repose.
The brain swoons after such delights,
The eyelids close.
Oh sweet the passing o'er from love to sleep,
But sweeter the return from sleep to love.

Under the assenting trees
Where nightingales their questions cry
How good it is to lie at ease . . .
But better with a maid to lie
In the tall grass where scented herbs
Mingled with roses softly sigh
And after the exchange of love
Lure us to sleep. Our senses fly,
Instilled in lassitude.

Oh sweet the passing over from love to sleep,
But sweeter the return from sleep to love!"

A murmur of appreciation and recognition—not of the words but of their own dreams—ran through the students before they broke into applause. Thomas, among them, felt in himself the old ache and the swelling of desire. There in the softly springing grass, languorous, playing . . . time to depart and yet remaining . . . there lay the lure of flesh. He knew, he knew. He longed for it. And then into this dream—while he was open, vulnerable—came the joke.

Serlon, holding up his hands, cried, "Silence! Would you know the author's name? He must forgive me if I tell it: Thomas of London!"

Thomas felt his own name strike him like an arrow in the heart. The blood ebbed from his face, leaving him almost sightless while it pounded in his chest. He looked around him, blank, face grim, and saw the laughter: teeth, open mouths, the questioning eyes. For once he had no answer. He turned and with a long and furious stride walked from that place, his cloak pulled round him, never looking back.

CHAPTER VII

ON THE LAST DAY of the parliament, when the contestants brought their tokens, sewed by their ladies as they claimed, Serlon spread out in display the bishop's chasuble that he had borrowed, claiming again that he was Thomas' substitute. Even the students gasped—for it was Serlon's weakness that he carried things too far—and when word reached the masters, scandal broke.

Serlon took everything upon himself, absolving Thomas, and was contrite and did his penance. Because he was respected among his masters for his scholarship as he was known among the students for his songs, much was forgiven him. The incident was closed. And he and Thomas, brought together in the tavern, at last took pains to understand each other and each forgive the other for their differences, and learn from one another that each could laugh, and they were friends.

But his friendship did not grow, nor any other of Thomas' plans for his next years at Paris, for it was soon after this the message came for him, calling him home. His mother, so the letter read, lay dying, and his father needed him. He must return.

The messenger who brought the news brought also news of king and country—the sort that is more safely carried in the head than written down. He was an elderly clerk called Edmund Up, doorkeeper at St. Paul's, and he had come to Paris in the escort of a canon who was on business for the Church. Edmund had known Thomas as a boy and he spoke kindly to him concerning things at home while Thomas, holding the letter in his hand, sat silent on his bed.

What was written there was sad, he knew that, he had seen Thomas' father, he had been told. But what could not be written—that was a burden on the heart as well. They had better go and sit somewhere—Edmund rubbed a dry hand over his face and glanced around the hostel—where they could talk and where he could report to Thomas all that he knew, for Thomas was a man now and should not be spared.

So Thomas led him to a tavern for the English and selected a dark corner where he could sit and hear of home and none should see his face. Edmund sat across from him, sometimes passing both his hands over his face or pausing between sentences to open wide his mouth and smooth his cheeks and beard. It was a nervous habit that he had, and in a little while Thomas stopped looking at him and gazed off across the room.

"Things are not the same in England as when you were there," said Edmund. "Perhaps you've heard?"

"We've heard some things," said Thomas absently.

"The king's turned soft," Edmund said very quietly. "And treacherous men rebel against him. Some of the barons have made their castles strong against him and take the law into their hands so that there is no law where they rule, only lawlessness."

He glanced around and then leaned over farther on the table. "A man came into London from out by Hereford and said the baron with his men had come into his village and carried off the sheep and then set fire to the houses and the land around and took the villagers for ransom—any who had property. This man escaped. And after that . . ." Edmund's hand went rapidly over his face from forehead down to chin. "After that they went into the town and right into the churchyard where they carried off the chattels that the country folk had brought there for safekeeping. They went into the bishop's own cathedral and seized the sacred goods and drove the monks away and turned the church into a fort . . ."

Thomas looked at Edmund now, and Edmund nodded.

"Aye, they made of it a fort so that they might attack the castle of the king nearby. A garrison of fighting men into the choir, a catapult into the bell tower. Aye, and they dug up the graveyard to make earthworks! The man who told us said the townsmen cried aloud to see the bodies of their forefathers—some of them only lately buried, some half-rotten, all dug up from their graves and flung aside!"

"What has the king done?" Thomas asked.

"What can he do? When he goes out to put one of these barons down others rise up behind him. And when the bishops threaten them with excommunication and anathema they laugh. What does it mean to them? They are all cursed already, and foresworn and lost."

"What of my father and my mother?" Thomas asked. "Is it as you say in London also, lawless, and at the mercy of these lawless men?"

"In London we are many," Edmund said. "We are strong together and no one touches us. But food is scarce—grain, cheese, and butter very dear. Some go hungry. Even some wretched men who once were rich must ask for alms to feed their families. They come in numbers to St. Paul's. It is a job for me!" He pushed his fingers in his eyes, then looked at Thomas. "But your father is all right. He is a man with many friends and does not want. And we are in no danger in the city."

"How soon must I return?" Thomas asked suddenly. "The letter does not say."

Edmund drew away and looked at him, his hands for once upon the table. "Why, I don't know," he said.

"How long does she have yet to live?"

Now Edmund seized his face in both his hands and rubbed it hard. He did not like the question. "Why, *I* don't know," he said again. "I am no leech."

Thomas saw he must explain himself. "You think me very hard of heart," he said. "You think that even now I should be on my way instead of sitting here." He paused. "I will defend myself. My father gave me the last of his small treasure, skimping my sister's dowry, to send me here for education. My mother blessed me when I left, instructing me to turn aside for nothing, nothing, till I should master what there is to learn. Now it is April, and in a few more weeks the schools will close; I will have had two years of study under famous men. It's not enough, I will not be a master as my mother wished. But it will be two years . . .

"Now comes this message from my father, 'Son, your mother longs to look on you before she dies.' What does my mother say?"

Edmund did not know. He had not seen her, only Gilbert when he came to St. Paul's looking for some person who was traveling to Paris. "Why, I don't know," he said for the third time. It seemed to come as a surprise to him to know so little. "You must make your own choice. I will take your message back to London if that is how it is to be."

So Thomas chose, and sent word he would meet his father's steward Ebert—for he had strong instructions not to attempt the trip alone, no man did that these days—at a certain house in Sandwich late in June, as soon after Corpus Christi as he could manage.

Ebert was waiting at the waterside, wiry-thin and older, his pale straight hair no longer gold but gray. He embraced Thomas, letting his tears fall on the tall shoulder, as they stood upon the mud-washed cobbles of the landing place. He told the news of home: times were very hard but Gilbert Becket managed to provide and Thomas' mother wanted for nothing. But she would not last long, not long, for she was wasting badly and the time was gone when she could rise and be about the house. She lay abed and they must even prop the bedclothes up lest with their weight they crush her wasted bones. The doctors came and went and drank up all the wine, but she was beyond their art. Roheise came every day to see her mother and to cheer her—she was a fine cheerful matron now with her own firstborn on the way already plain to see. And they had rushed betrothal plans for Agnes, though she was so young, to please her mother, that all should be well settled. They waited only for the son's return.

Eagerly Thomas spoke of setting off at once, they could reach Canterbury by night. Having delayed in Paris these two months he could not bear to wait another day. Ebert was cautious, arguing that they must join themselves to some large party on the road. Brigands were everywhere. Men traveling alone were kidnaped, held for ransom, murdered.

Thomas knew only one thing, that he must go home. He overruled all Ebert's pleas and warnings and they took their horses and set off along the London road between the summer fields.

It was on the second day, when the road took them through a stretch of woods as they neared Rochester, that Ebert suddenly reached out and clutched at Thomas' arm and whispered that he had seen horsemen on the road, just round the bend. "I saw them through an opening in the trees. Come quickly!" And he turned and rode his slow unwilling horse, with frantic kicks and slaps, up the soft dirt of the embankment into the shelter of the underbrush and trees. Thomas followed, half-amused, half-fearful. But he halted and would go no farther when he felt they were well-screened. He wanted to stay close enough to watch the road.

Ebert slipped from his horse and put his hand upon its nose, hoping to silence it if it should whinny at the sight of other horses and, whispering still, he ordered Thomas to do likewise. Thomas smiled, dismounted, and took his horse's head. All these precautions made him feel a fool. And he laughed outright when he saw the men upon the road: three sober clerks on quiet palfreys ambling round the bend. He would have stepped into the open and hailed them to exchange the news, but Ebert clasped him and hissed in his ear: "No, no. You do not understand. This is how brigands go about these days. This is their way! No longer do they go by secret ways and lie in ambush—too many people have grown wary these last years. Now they ride openly in daylight on the well-worn roads, like these below. They wear false clothes . . ."

Thomas was doubtful, looking down on the unwary men sitting so slovenly. But Ebert's words continued to flow from him in an agony of earnestness. "Be quiet, oh I beg of you. You do not understand. This, this is their disguise, their very counterfeit by which to know them. They keep their daggers hidden beneath that downcast look and modest way . . ." He would have jabbered on but he had left his horse untended when he turned to plead with Thomas and it moved now, crackling the underbrush and snorting as the dust rose to its nostrils.

Down in the road the three men heard the noise. Three faces turned to stare into the woods, their mouths open in surprise and fear. Then in one motion they turned back, gathering their reins in shaking hands, flapping their legs against their horses' sides, crowding each other as they galloped off pursued by their own dust.

Thomas' laugh broke loud, so ludicrous they looked, so foolish he and Ebert seemed. But then he turned to make amends to Ebert, for it was clear now what had happened since he went away. No longer did man trust himself to man with the old confidence. Instead, in daylight, on the king's highway, they trembled when they sighted one another and hid away or fled in terror down the road. He saw, now, how it was with England. And he could have wept, remembering how fearlessly he used to ride alone in old King Henry's time.

Soberly the two led forth their horses from the wood and mounted and rode on for London.

Thomas knelt beside his mother's bed and heard her prayers for him. But he could not be sure she knew that he was there. The priest was often with her, an old man wise in necromancy, and he seemed to comfort her. She died on Lammas Day, quietly, without a word, while the soft air brought scent of newmown hay into the sun-filled solar. Her daughters came—Mary from Barking, Roheise from her new home near at hand—and Agnes, still a child, was there. They laid out their mother under Alfleda's guidance. Then she was buried and the girls returned, Agnes to Roheise's house, and Thomas and his father were left alone. "I will be going soon myself," his father said. But Thomas surmised that all men said this when their wives, whom they had loved, were dead.

Friends came to fill the hall and bring some comfort to the lonely men. They were impressed by Thomas, said he had turned out well, as, let it be remembered, they predicted. What would he do now?

"I have already spoken to my kinsman Osbert Huit-deniers," said Gilbert. And to Thomas: "Son, you should know your cousin takes a leading part in the affairs of London and it is expected he will be chosen to be justiciar at the Michaelmas folkmoot."

In these past years the burgesses of London had been granted a new freedom by King Henry: the right to choose their own justiciar who was the royal representative in town affairs and pled the Crown pleas in the city courts. He was a man of more importance, even, than the sheriff. Now, Gilbert said, the aldermen and rich men of the city were prepared to give this office to the wealthy merchant Osbert. If he were chosen he would need a clerk. And a man trained in Paris, and a trusted cousin, would be more than welcome.

After Michaelmas the great bell of St. Paul's rang out in summons to all citizens of standing to attend the folkmoot and be shown their sheriff, hear his commands, and to accept their new justiciar: Osbert Huit-deniers.

Osbert was a large man, portly and full of dignity. He wore a wide hat and a robe of crimson velvet girdled with gold and a large golden bawdrike round his neck and hanging down behind. He stood upon the church steps, facing the square, and raised his hands and spoke in a loud voice with great solemnity about the troubled times and his determination as a Londoner to keep the king's peace in the city.

The crowd was with him, but it was a ticklish business, for it was known to some that he held a knight's fee from the Earl of Gloucester, brother of the Empress Matilda. And at the very time Osbert was speaking to the folkmoot as the king's representative—September 29, 1139—the empress with her brother Gloucester landed in England to make war against the king.

But this news had not reached London. Osbert was installed, set up his court, and graciously included Gilbert

Becket's son among his clerks. And a new life began for Thomas.

The empress and her brother made their way to Bristol and from there launched many bloody raids against the cities of the west. All through the winter of 1139, the spring and summer of 1140, the civil war went on. By the September folkmoot of that year the knight's fee that he held of Gloucester became too great a handicap for Osbert, and his friend Gervase of Cornhill was selected as justiciar, replacing him. Still Osbert was a powerful man in London and he remained one of the inner group whose words were listened to in council. And Thomas, invaluable to him now not only for his ability to read and write but for his gifts of everyday diplomacy and swift decision, stayed with him.

The summer of 1141 was the decisive one for London. Stephen, to whom the city was still loyal, had been captured by the empress and put in chains. Then she had ridden south to Winchester to claim the royal treasure and the crown. There she arrived in royal dignity, flanked by her brother Robert, Earl of Gloucester and her uncle David, King of the Scots, leading an army of their combined men. And there she confronted Stephen's brother, Henry, Bishop of Winchester and papal legate, "lord of all England" as he sometimes styled himself, and said that she would have of him the crown.

The wily bishop made a bargain: she should leave all ecclesiastical affairs to him; he would arrange she be elected to the throne. And publicly, in the town marketplace, he showed her deference and instructed all to call her queen. She in return spoke haughtily to him and spread her insolence even to her brother and her uncle Scotland—though he be a king. And when these three great men came to her chair with bended knee she did not rise as would have been becoming. Nor did she listen when they bowed before her with petitions but often and again sent them away rebuffed with arrogant answers to their good advice and soft requests. The bishop hid his feelings in his beard and waited to see what end such a beginning would have.

Nevertheless, with Stephen in her prison and his forces scattered, there was none to stop her. Soon she brought the greater part of England under her dominion, receiving homage from the barons—and their hostages as surety for their oaths. In April, there in Winchester, she was elected queen.

As Osbert's clerk Thomas went with the London deputation to the ceremonies, watching with keen eyes and remembering all. The Londoners stood out alone against the empress, reiterating loyalty to Stephen, but they were ignored and overridden by the great magnates and shortly were dismissed. They had been ineffectual and overbold, perhaps, but they rode home with dignity, feeling proud.

The empress gave out word that she would receive the crown in London, at Westminster as the ancient custom dictated, on St. John's Day, midsummer. Wise men who understood the dangerous uncertainties of time argued against so long a wait—for the election did not make her queen; only the coronation could do that—but as in all other things she would not listen to advice. She laughed at the reports that Stephen's queen had raised an army from Boulogne, was strengthening it in Kent. The empress knew this weak and womanly queen of Stephen's who had come in person, on her knees, in tears, begging her husband's freedom. No, Stephen's wife was not the sort who could lead formidable armies.

The day before midsummer, then, the empress came to Westminster accompanied by the earl her brother and the king her uncle and many other lords but without her army. She set up silken tents among the gray old buildings of the palace and the church beside the Thames. It was a festive scene, the gardens at the fullness of their flowering, the water sparkling, and she herself arrayed in bright green silk and heavy gold embroidery.

There was one bit of business yet to complete before the coronation: the consent of the London citizens. Afterward all could be feasting and gay celebration. And for this business she commanded that her chair be set up on a purple dais in the huge empty Rufus Hall, named for her father's brother, William II. Then she sent messengers requiring that the burgesses of London wait upon her there. "Tell them to send their richest men," she said.

Thomas stood behind his kinsman's chair while Osbert and Gervase of Cornhill and the other city magistrates held their despairing conference.

"What is to be done?" asked Osbert heavily.

Everyone knew the answer to his question, it was as unavoidable as Doom: they must accept the empress as their queen. But there were arguments, factors to reconsider before they would admit defeat.

Thomas knew them all. He had rehearsed them several times for Osbert whose reluctant mind was slow to understand the facts. And they were these: London could raise an army of some thousands but not soon enough or strong enough to march against the empress alone. They could not hope the army raised by Stephen's queen would join them; it was still a nebulous grouping of French and Kentish men, unformed. Had they the stronghold of the Tower of London on their side they might resist the empress and withstand a siege. But Geoffrey de Mandeville, Earl of Essex, whom they hated and who hated them, was constable of the Tower. And although he had supported Stephen while he was victorious he had allowed himself, on the king's downfall, to be bought. London could not withstand a siege while in her very heart the enemy sat in his Tower.

Reviewing all these facts for Osbert, Thomas had seen for himself and thus advised—reluctantly; he would have liked to fight—"There is no hope. We must submit."

Now, at the council, Gervase the Justiciar made the decision for them all, speaking these same words: "There is no hope. Tomorrow, as the empress demands, we must go to Westminster and pay her humble duty."

It was a perfect summer day and in the unmarked oval of the sky the small soft clouds sat airily like cherubs, above the earth. The delegation of five somber men, their clerks, their standard bearers, rode at a walk. The people eyed them as they passed out of the city and along the strand, wondering what these magistrates would do. Many among the townsmen had gone secretly during the night to see the staller of his ward—his captain should it come to battle—and to arm himself. Thomas could feel what they were thinking, for his own desire to fight still rankled under the cool decision reason had forced upon them. After a little while he did not look around him but rode with head bent till they reached the palace at Westminster and dismounted in the court.

The empress received them in the Rufus Hall, immense and dark, a cavern of a hall. After the glare of sunlight Thomas could see nothing but the paving at his feet stretching away to blackness. A sergeant stamped his mace upon the floor and they were orderd to go forward. Only then, as he walked haltingly behind the magistrates, did he perceive the empress at the farther end, seated upon a dais with her retinue about her. He saw that she looked thin and somewhat worn. Her thick and tawny hair which she displayed without a wimple had lost its luster with the years. But she was regal and sat as straight as a young woman, or a man. And she surveyed them in kingly silence as they knelt before her throne.

At last she said, "You are the men that London sends to honor me? I bid you welcome." She seemed to swallow down the phrase. But her next words were strong and clear. "I will receive of you, you men of London, the sum of five hundred pounds in tallage to your queen."

Thomas saw the shock of this go through the men before him; he could read dismay in Osbert's heavy shoulders and Gervase's thin back. Five hundred pounds was more than they could raise. Even in good years, and with the freedom granted by King Henry, the sum that London offered the royal exchequer was less than three hundred pounds. And this year . . .

Gervase of Cornhill spoke for them. "Domina," he faltered, for this was the title she now held.

"Imperatrix," the empress corrected him.

"Imperatrix," Gervase began again, "our city has lost all of its accustomed wealth owing to strife within the kingdom. Famine has threatened our poorer citizens and now we find ourselves reduced to the extremity of want. Otherwise we would most gladly raise the sum. But as it is, may we make dutiful and humble mention of the charter granted to our city by your father our most gracious king . . ."

"You are very impudent," the empress broke in, "to mention privileges and charters to me when you have been foremost in support of those who are my enemies! You need say no more of charters or the extremity of want."

Gervase was silent. What could he say next, caught as he was between anxiety and outrage. And in the silence the Earl of Gloucester leaned beside his sister's chair and spoke into her ear. She did not answer and the earl straightened and addressed the delegation very civilly. "You citizens of London, styled as in the old days barons, as we know, have been most gracious in coming thus to add the strength of your great city to our support. And now that you have given honor to the empress as your queen, we ask that you pay tallage as you are able."

Thomas saw Gervase nodding in relief. A moment could be bought. "We beg your leave," he asked the empress, "to withdraw, so that we may hold council in our own hall and deliberate how we can raise the sum."

"Five hundred pounds," the empress said.

Again they stood in silence and again the earl bent down. "You have my leave to go," she said at last, staring above their heads.

They held their council in the hustings hall and all the

aldermen were present, questioning, discussing, until well after dark. But nothing new was said. Matilda would be queen; she would not keep her father's promises to London; five hundred pounds could not be raised—but must be. The alderman from Farringdon Without said that the men of his ward would choose to fight, and others nodded, but they were reminded that the Earl of Essex held the tower as it were a knife against their backs. So late they broke up, gloomy, and went home.

Thomas, back in Osbert's house beside the river, went up the loft stairs to the little room where he slept with the other clerks. Godwin, the merchant's secretary-clerk, was looking out the window at the soft-smelling summer night, the river running peacefully below. "What is that little light in Southwark?" he asked Thomas when he came to stand beside him. "There on the other bank?"

"It is a fire," Thomas said.

"And there's another. Farther down," said Godwin.

The lights leaped up and spread, till they could see the very flames jumping and throwing sparks into the night.

"And yet another—right down by the bridge!" Thomas gripped Godwin's arm.

The other clerks came crowding to the window. Now they could hear the tiny piping cries of men in fear or anger far away, and flames had spread to many points. It even seemed that they could smell the smoke.

"Someone is burning the crops and houses! Someone is harrying the land!"

Thomas turned and bolted down the narrow stairway to find Osbert. In the hall he saw Gervase push through the door followed by his men.

"Someone is burning . . ." Thomas said to him.

"Osbert Huit-deniers!" Gervase commanded at the same time, as he had commanded at the door. And Osbert came in running from his chamber, his heavy face dismayed.

Gervase gripped him by the arms to steady him. "King Stephen's army has reached Southwark!" he said in a shaken voice. "They are burning crops and houses. They are taking people with the sword."

"Why . . ." asked Osbert, not yet awake to what was happening.

"A messenger came to my house just now. He brought the word. Stephen's army has marched up from Rochester. And they are harrying our lands."

"Why do they spoil our lands?" asked Osbert still perplexed. "We have been true to Stephen."

"They heard we made submission to the empress." Gervase still gripped his arms. "They think we have gone over. Don't you understand?"

"Are there many men among them?" Osbert stared back at him.

"It is an army. Stephen's queen is with them. And they are captained by William of Ypres."

"William of Ypres." The fact shot into place in Osbert's mind and all was clear to him at last. "Why then it *is* an army . . ." and his face changed while he looked in Gervase's eyes and saw the hope beginning there . . . "Strong enough to hold the Tower do you think?"

"We must negotiate," said Gervase.

Thomas knew every turning of the negotiations, heard the word sent out to every alderman and staller of each ward to be prepared, lie low; saw every embassy depart to row across the river—for the city gates were shut, the bridge was guarded; helped to compose the letters in their proper terms when the justiciar spoke the gist of them aloud. Paris had not trained his hand for elegant copying, but that was not of such importance now as clear decisive thought coupled with delicacy of presentation. In these he proved his value.

Slowly the night went by. From time to time some of the aldermen, keeping to the shadows of the streets, had come to join them in their deliberations. When the dawn came, early summer dawn, the faces of the magistrates were gray; some slept, their chins upon their beards. They were not young men to withstand a night of waiting and of doubts, of fearful hopes, without a fainting of the spirits and the blood.

Thomas sat with the other clerks behind their table, resting with his arms stretched out before him but with eyes open and his mind awake. He heard the bells for Lauds in nearby churches; the sun was up. He heard the bells for Prime; fresh daylight filled the hall. The sleepers stirred. But still nobody spoke and still they waited.

At last the knock upon the door, the messenger returned. Thomas and the other clerks rose as he passed their table. They saw the letter he had taken from beneath his cloak; it bore the queen's own seal. Thomas knew even then, seeing the letter and the bearer's face, that they had won their point and that his own hand and his mind had helped to change the destinies of thousands.

The justiciar's chief clerk and secretary left Thomas' side and went to stand behind his master's chair. And Gervase, breaking the heavy seal and spreading the letter on the table, stared at it while the clerk murmured the contents in his ear. Then he rose and looked around the room—the tired men past middle age who with him ruled the city and with him spent this night and morning of decision—and his voice trembled as he spoke.

"Now do I thank you all," he said. "And God be our judge, I think we have done right."

The others, knowing what would come, stood up. The faces even of the oldest of them were alert, untroubled.

"William of Ypres, with Stephen's army, will occupy the city and surround the Tower. The men of London must drive off the empress." He stared a long time at them and they nodded.

"Then sound the tocsin now! Let every man take arms as he is trained, and come full speed to Ludgate. We will take Westminster today!"

Thomas saw Osbert coming toward him across the hall with arms outstretched and his broad face all wet, for he had given way to tears. Others ran from the room to spread the word abroad. And even as the merchant clasped him, murmuring senseless words in his excitement, then turned away to grasp the next man in his arms, Thomas heard the first bell, hesitant, begin to ring. He stood, head up, and listened as the other bells across the city took up the alarm—the voices of St. Trinity . . . St. Martin's . . . each in its own tongue . . . the sweet peal of St. Mary Colechurch where he had been born, he knew it well . . . Loud did they ring, each clanging bell. Then came the deeper tolling of St. Paul.

Laughing, he grabbed the long skirts of his scholar's gown and ran with leaping strides across the hall and down the stairs into the street below.

The empress was dining in her tent. She had brought with her excellent men from France to prepare her meals and this was to be a feast of some proportions, second only to her coronation feast to which she summoned all the great lords of her realm. The tent was very gay, with silken hangings on all sides and carpets softening the flagstones of the ancient Saxon court. Her brother Gloucester sat with her on one side and her uncle Scotland on the other. They were awaiting London's delegation with the tallage that they owed. But while they waited they would feast.

One of her sergeants came in hastily from the far end. He caused commotion for he came, careless of what lords or courtiers he passed, through the long tables set below to the high seat where the empress sat. There he went on one knee before her and exclaimed, even before she gave him leave to talk:

"Imperatrix, there is a noise from London like a hive of bees, and the bells ring!"

She sat nonplused at this incomprehensible outburst but the Earl of Gloucester understood. "Are these alarm bells?" he demanded. "Are these what make the sound of bees? Make yourself clear."

"It is the church bells, sire. They ring out all at once, a clamor. I would take it for a tocsin, sire. It is an alarm of some sort. So I would interpret it."

The earl rose. The King of Scotland had already risen. Only the empress sat uncomprehending.

"Come," the earl said to his uncle. "Let us hear these bees." And they took their leave with speedy ceremony and left the tent.

Out in the court they saw the guards standing atop the crumbling walls, staring toward London, and Gloucester called to one of them. He turned and jumped down and, like a man in battle, neglecting the obeisance of peacetime knowing it would be overlooked, spoke without preamble as man to man.

"There is a sound as of a giant crowd, a mob, sir," said the guard. "And I was just now watching a lone horseman, seemed to be galloping this way in haste."

"Robert," said the King of Scots aloud, for he too was a man of battle, unashamed to speak his thoughts at such a time, "if this is an uprising of all London we must perforce withdraw. We have no more than two hundred armed men with us and this castle offers no fair chance of keeping off a siege." And this was true, for the old palace and its walls, even King Edward's abbey, had been allowed to rot under King Stephen's rule.

"*If* it is a rising," Earl Robert answered, unconvinced. "How could they dare rise, those fat burgesses, under the nose of Geoffrey de Mandeville, and no hope of aid from anywhere?"

His answer came from the horseman who rode through the gate. He was brought forward by the guards, a slim, small man, a weaver, panting and somewhat frightened, usually a man of peace and quiet but now, for some small reason of his own, angry with London and thus loyal to its foes. He told the story clearly enough, that Stephen's queen was entering the town by London bridge and that armed men of London, uncounted thousands strong, had rallied at Ludgate and soon—even now—were marching from the city against Westminster. And around them gathered a howling mob.

"God's blood, how did this happen and so speedily," the earl said angrily, half to himself. "Stephen's queen in London and the town against us! William of Ypres is with her, you can be sure of that." He turned away. "Our armies spread from Bristol all the way to Oxford—and none here!"

He found the empress where he had left her, anger in her scowling face, and without ceremony told her bluntly they must fly. There was no choice. William of Ypres could easily contain de Mandeville in the Tower, and all of London marched against the empress' person.

The sergeant brought their swiftest horses; there had been no need to tell him what to do. They mounted and the lady empress with her two kinsmen, escorted by their closest guards, fled from the palace and along the road to Oxford. Behind her all the other lords who had attended her, waiting the coronation, gathered their retinues and fled. And in the tents the empress' clerks, the stewards of her household, butchers, cooks, butlers and larderers, ushers and servants of all kinds, even her priests, were left to gather up their own possessions hastily and take the Oxford road or else melt off into the countryside.

Even as the last of them fled straggling through the fields and forests to the west, a mob of London citizens, great beyond calculation, entered her abandoned lodgings and her sumptuous tents and plundered everywhere all that the foolish empress had left behind.

Stephen's queen was very gracious to Gervase and all the London aldermen. Gladly they raised a sum of money for her armies, and in return she gave them surety for some of her fine estates in Cambridgeshire. Likewise, with diplomacy, with promises and bribes, she won back to her husband's cause the Earl of Essex and his Tower.

The price she had to pay for Essex was somewhat higher than a few estates in Cambridgeshire, for he was powerful. Perhaps it did not seem so high a price to her, but for the citizens of London it was the price of honor. For among the titles she conferred on him were Sheriff and Justiciar of London. The barons, as they called themselves, of London had for a short time ruled themselves in dignity. Now Geoffrey de Mandeville ruled them, and from his tower he was paying off old scores. There, in his cells and dungeons, wretched poor men suffered the most ingenious tortures that the experienced earl could dream up or adapt from all the methods of inflicting pain that he had ever heard.

The year 1141 dragged on. In London a white icy fog lay on the river and the marsh. A gray fog, turning yellow where it mingled with the city's smoke, drifted and settled in the high-streets and the lanes, stood thick in crooked passages and underneath the eaves, and every sound was muffled at its source.

The city was subdued by more than fog and autumn cold. It was the eve of All Soul's Day but there was no revelry. Instead, long lines of hungry people stood at the bell tower by St. Paul's or grouped beneath the stairs of Bayard's Castle and the great halls of the wealthy, waiting for a dole of food. Hope burned very low this hallowed eve. And bitter as was the taste of fog, there was a greater bitterness within the heart.

Thomas was idle in the hall of Osbert Huit-deniers. The clerkship in the merchant's household was still nominally his but there was no work for him. Osbert sat idle too, and Gervase and the others. There was no work for them.

That morning, standing in the fog by Tower Gate, Thomas had watched with many others while a man was hanged. He did not know the man; who could have recognized him, stripped of his clothing, even of portions of his skin, eyeless, toothless, and emasculated? He was hanged not once but three times, for three times the halter was put around his neck and he was strung up till his life was almost gone. Twice they brought him down and let him lie till life returned and he began to scream once more. On the third time they waited till his body ceased to twitch and then they cut the rope and let him drop. And what remained of him was left to lie there, broken, naked, splotched with blood, and no one dared move forward to keep off the dogs.

When Thomas returned home and could speak of this, he asked Osbert what the man's crime had been and Osbert told him that he was a staller, one of the leaders of the rising against the Tower when they had driven off the empress.

"But so did we all do that!" said Thomas.

"Yes, yes," said Osbert somewhat impatiently. "So did we all in spirit perhaps. But of course we were not at the Tower at that time. Perhaps this staller showed himself too plainly or perhaps threatened the earl himself. But who can know? Besides which we have bought our pardon from the earl for all that we did then. Presumably this staller could not raise the sum."

At twenty-three Thomas was still capable of righteous shock. "I have not paid the earl!" he said.

"Oh yes," said Osbert, speaking of practicalities. "I paid for you—for my entire staff, of course. Why"—he looked in some surprise at Thomas' face—"surely you did not think that I would let the members of my household suffer, did you?" Thomas was silent. "That staller had no patron, I should judge," Osbert continued, "to raise the ransom for him."

"I see," said Thomas. But what he saw was only the white naked body dangling in the fog, the twitching blood-splotched limbs and blackened face . . .

"You must not be concerned with one man's death," said Osbert watching him.

"No," Thomas said. He was not so concerned. He had seen men die before, or suffer for their crimes in other ways. After all, the Cheapside Standard stood not very far from his own father's gate and often when he was a boy he had seen men put into pillory while their false weights or merchandise were burned before them. He had seen robbers blinded there, after their thefts were shown. Those men had suffered, surely, but their guilt was there before them, clear for all to see—just like the rotting fish hung round the neck of a cheating fishmonger. And he had seen men of rank beheaded there, a solemn sight. Twice he had seen it. But always justice had been done and always, it had seemed to him, the men went to their punishments and death content that it was so. He could see no justice in the death at Tower Gate.

Perhaps there was no justice among kings and earls. He, like all the Londoners, had welcomed the gentle queen and loved her as he had hated the haughty empress. How kind her manner when she had repaid their loans with promises—and then how slyly she had won over the Earl Geoffrey. And paid him with the lives of London citizens! So that was how it was, and he had had a taste of royal politics—perhaps enough to last his lifetime. He wanted no more part.

CHAPTER VIII

AFTER THE NEW YEAR, Thomas left Osbert Huitdeniers and went back to his father. There had been nothing for him to do at Osbert's; there was little for him in his father's hall. He kept his lonely father company and helped him to collect his dwindling rents—a cruel task these days—and sometimes went down to the hustings hall to hear the news, or to St. Paul's for talk with educated men.

The news concerned the war. The queen had gone on, after winning London, to win back the powerful and wily Henry, Bishop of Winchester, to his brother Stephen's cause. On hearing this the empress turned in wrath upon the bishop for his defection and besieged him in his castle. But while her armies tightened around him and he in turn poured fire down upon them from his walls, William of Ypres with Stephen's army crept up behind the empress' back. His forces ringed hers in the burning city; she was trapped and forced to wriggle through his lines and flee. Her flight turned to a rout, her armies scattered, and she alone escaped. Her loyal brother Gloucester, defending her retreat, was captured. Thus it was, as the year rounded toward its end, that an exchange of prisoners was made—King Stephen for the Earl of Gloucester—and once again the sides were balanced, with their forces and their castles, one against the other. And as before the country and the people suffered.

It was the year 1143, the year, men said, that Christ slept and with him all his saints. The empress held the west, the king the east, and earls and barons shifted from king to empress, from empress to king as they saw opportunity, and over all was anarchy.

In London men were safe once more, though times were grim. The Earl of Essex, caught changing sides too often, was summoned by the king and stripped of all his castles and the Tower as well and he retired to the fens of Cambridgeshire. There he lashed out from the fortress he had made, killing and torturing, and still unsatisfied. After his plundering of the countryside came famine, and after famine plague. And it was said there fell a rain of blood three days and a great swarming of black flies whereof men died.

All over England the land was dotted with these rough castle-forts put up in secret, without royal leave, and from them lawless knights went out to rob and burn. Men of free lance and outlaws followed after them. Sometimes, around these barons' strongholds, a man might walk for twenty miles and never see a house or plow or any living thing where once had been the little villages and manor farms with oxen in the fields and mill wheels slapping merrily beside the streams.

To east and west the shadow of a peace prevailed, but even here, men said, it was like ancient evil times when three men could not come on two but they put them to death. Only the Church and the peace-loving archbishop held fast to order and the protection of the poor.

When Thomas went to the cathedral of St. Paul's he found relief from his preoccupation with the affairs of kings and his dismay over the state of England. Here his old masters from the school spoke frequently of other things: of what he learned in Paris, of the affairs in Rome, of the new sorts of reading—in Church law or in the ancient history of Britain now being brought to light.

He met again the lord Rahere, the courtier and canon of St. Paul's, the churchbuilder. Rahere remembered him from when he was a student. It was he who spoke most frequently of ancient times and of the marvels done then and of the prophecies, for he had in his keeping a copy of a manuscript not long since written by a fellow-canon, an Augustinian like himself, from Wales but now of Oxford: *The Little Book of Merlin.*

He lent the book to Thomas, and Thomas, reading the prophecies that Merlin made, saw in them veiled descriptions and allusions to his own time. The things that Merlin told of brought to his mind the acts of queens and princes that he himself had witnessed: " 'Three eggs shall be laid in a nest,' " he read, " 'wherefrom shall issue forth a fox, a wolf, and a bear. The Fox shall wear an ass's head and in this guise shall she affright her brethren and make them flee. And when the fight between them hath begun she shall feign dead and move the Boar to pity her. Presently he shall go unto her and standing over her shall breathe upon her eyes.

But she, not forgetful of her ancient cunning, shall bite his left foot from his body, and snatch away from him his right ear and his tail, and slink away into her cavern. Thereafter she shall turn herself into the Boar and then abide the coming of her brethren. Them also shall she slay with sudden-snapping tooth, and she shall be crowned with the head of a lion . . .' "

No, not crowned, thought Thomas, for we denied her that. To him the Fox who wore the ass's head was surely the Empress Matilda as the prophet had foreseen her in those ancient times, though Rahere told him that it was not of today that Merlin spoke but of another day.

He and Rahere sat together, while they read, in the canons' library of St. Paul's.

"But it is like today," said Thomas. "For today we have these same portents that Merlin speaks of. Here," he said, putting his finger in the little folio, "he speaks of London: 'London shall mourn and the Thames river shall be turned to blood.' Or here—for that could be in other times; I know our history is long . . ." He turned the pages. "Here, the very story of Merlin Ambrosius himself. Born of no father. This is repeated in these days, for only yesterday I heard a story out of Kent of such a man—born of no father—who was swallowed up into the earth by fairy-men. His child was taken with him and a monster fairy-child left in its place."

Rahere said, "There is more of magic in that story than of prophecy. Such things occur but are no proof that our times are the times that Merlin spoke of."

"But here again," said Thomas eagerly. He had not such a firm belief in what he said, and both knew that the canon Geoffrey wrote with some little twinkling of wit when he translated this ancient tale of Wales into the Latin, but he enjoyed the argument. "Here again: 'Saturn the star shall fall upon the earth with a rain of heaven and shall slay mankind as it were with a crooked sickle.' " He looked up. "As happened in the fens when the rain fell like blood and men were slain. Or here: 'A worm whose breath is fire shall burn up the trees with the vapour he shall breathe forth.' We have had many fires recently. And following . . ." His finger was upon the page as he read on, " 'And out of him shall issue forth seven lions disfigured by the heads of goats . . .' " Again he looked at Rahere eagerly. "And that same story out of Kent I told you of—about the man who disappeared into the earth—told of a flock of seven she-goats that were seen to

the field (the manor was not large; the house itself but slightly bigger than the villeins huts, the land just half a sulung cleared from the scrub oak along the river bank) and took the rents when they were due: three shillings to the monks of Christchurch and six shillings to his cousin Elured who was a Canterbury moneyer; and tributes, also, as they were required, of wool and cheese and honey and all the other produce of the little farm—apples at Martinmas and eggs for Easter.

Elured never spoke to him. The boy would come into the forge when all the craftsmen were at work and hang inside the doorway while his cousin stood beside the oven, tense and sweating, with the red glow of the fire on his sinewy arms, yelling at the young serf Azo to work the bellows harder. The place was dark yet fiery, smelling of smoke and of hot metal, of leather aprons and of earthen floor and the faint scent like some far forest when the molten silver hit the hardwood molds. And it was crowded with busy men: the prentice boy ran with the molds, full of their silver ribbons, to the flogging block; the flogger beat each ribbon with his mallet, pounding it thin; the cutter snipped it into little discs. The master craftsman took the dies that had come down from London with the silver bricks that day and rammed the spike end of the lower die into the cross-cut log. Then Elured himself stepped up—he liked to do his own work when true mastery was called for—and took the coining hammer and, when the first disc was in place upon the lower die, the upper die set on it straight and true, brought down his hammer with a ringing blow. Then he stepped back and peered at this first coin and found it good: well-centered, clean. And only then did he turn to his cousin from the manor and the produce he had brought, grunt at him indicating he should take it to the house, and turn again to work.

At Christchurch the monks asked Robert who his father was and eyed him strangely and Robert said, he always said, that he was Alfrid's son. This he believed—he had it from his mother's lips—until the time came, when he was sixteen, for him to marry and he heard his mother talking to the strong girl he would wed, Wulviva, the miller's daughter of Certeham. They sat within the little scrubby hall and Robert came into the doorway, silently, half shadow and half boy. He had a way of quietly appearing thus out of a clump of bushes or in the dim house where there had been before nothing but bushes or a cloak that hung upon its peg beside the door. They did not see him.

"Tell your father he is Alfrid's heir, no matter what the villeins say," his mother said. "Sometimes a child may linger over long within the womb . . ."

"Oh yes," the girl said brightly. "I have seen our old cow do the same."

"You must not listen to this villein-talk of fairy men . . ."

The words flew like a sudden spark spit by the fire, straight into Robert's ear. They burned him. He had long known that he was not like other boys, that people eyed him, but he had never thought to doubt that he was Alfrid's son. Now, with a whispered word, he knew. He was no son of man but of the Other Folk. As silently as he had come he left the room.

He never spoke of this to anyone—except, years after, sometimes, to his little girl, not that she listened, she was too small for that, but just to hear the words. He married the strong girl from Certeham and when his mother died succeeded to the manor, although he didn't own it—he held it of his cousin Elured who held it of the monks—and with time he had children of his own: the little black-eyed girl named Hawisa and the boy Almon, who was born that year the goats walked in the sky, the year men suffered—as was written in the chronicles.

The boy was born—nothing unusual, except his mother bled too much. The midwife had to call in three old women past their change to say the Lord's Prayer over her nine times, which was the course prescribed in cases such as this. No one thought much about it—except the little sister Hawisa who saw the blood drip on the floor and heard her mother scream. Her father picked her up and took her out. And then he put her on his shoulder in the way she loved and wandered down, beyond the shade and the manure pile where the flies buzzed, beyond the well, beyond the gate. Walking more steadily he went—as he had often done before—across the bridge, along the cart road, into the woodland on the other side.

He knew the paths made by the forest animals and followed them, some haste now in his stride, holding the child with one hand and with the other keeping the branches from her face. He felt her little fists clenched in his hair and smelled her strong wet baby smell and loved her. Yet he went on, now almost running, slapping the leaves and branches, till he saw the open space among the trees. And there he stopped, and gathered himself in, and stood and gazed a long time at the sunshine—watching the shadows run across the meadow and then back again as the wind moved the trees, noting the zigzag flight of insects and the flick of turning leaf, cocking his head to listen, sniffing the warmth of grass and herb and sun-baked lichen on the stone.

And then he put the baby down and stepped into the meadow and stared across it at the fairy hills. They had been houses once—these little grass-grown mounds—with deep-dug, earth-packed floors and rounded roofs. Now their earthen roofs had fallen and the tufted grass and waving starflowers sprang from their slanting sides. They were not half as high as Robert as he approached them, moving steadily, intently, searching for something there. There was no sign of life around them, nor had been even when he first found them. Yet he came searching for it often, too often.

Suddenly he went down on all fours and burrowed, shifting the rotted wattle sticks, scraping the earth around the hole that once had been a door. The birds cried out a warning and Hawisa whimpered in the grass. Warning! The father vanished and the baby left alone!

It was too late for warning. What harm was due them had been done, long long before, when the young widow had danced here among the fairy men. This was the year for suffering. And Robert suffered, smothering beneath the fallen sod-roof, dirt in his face.

They found the baby in the morning, still in the fairy field, and found the father, also, where he had gone into the fairy hill. And they were frightened, fearing the power of the Other Folk, and word went round that in Hortone—not three miles from the seat of the archbishop himself—the arch-flamen had come again and swallowed up a man and left a baby for a human child.

This was the story Thomas heard. And though Rahere assured him that it was merely magic and not to be confused in any way with Merlin who was a prophet and possessed of a true spirit of God, Thomas could not help but see about him the fulfillment of some of those prophecies told to King Vortigern in ancient times by that strange youth to whom God gave a forward-seeing eye.

This was a time of violence and evil portents such as the times that Merlin spoke of, so Thomas thought, a time that his own life came to a seeming halt. This was the year that noble men as well as fairies fed on the lives of other men. This was the year Christ slept.

BOOK TWO

THOMAS OF LONDON

CHAPTER IX

DURING THOSE BLEAK and brutal years when Thomas lived at home and time was stagnant for him, there was one place in all of England where he longed to be: the household of Archbishop Theobald, primate of England. His court at Canterbury was the one stronghold of peace amid the anarchy, the seat where men of learning gathered and where power accrued. It was the place where young men schooled abroad, wise in the world's ways and yet devoted to the Church, were molded by the gentle Theobald and trained to be the future prelates of the land.

Thomas would have liked to think this was the place for him—this august household with its brilliant coterie of clerks, this small exclusive school, center of calm authority—but he had no connections, no introduction, no reputation that could recommend him. So he had little hope.

And then one windy summer evening that year, 1143, two old friends came again from France to visit Gilbert Becket's hall—the brothers Baldwin and Eustace of Boulogne. It was an occasion, these days, to have guests of rank like these. Baldwin was now Archdeacon of Boulogne, grown somewhat sharp and bossy on his way up in Church politics, and wore three rings upon his fingers and a robe trimmed with marten skins. Eustace remained his gentle self, vague and devoid of envy even when his brother took all honors for them both.

Thomas saw all of this now with an informed eye, newly taught by his experience. When he had been a little child and gone with them to see the skating, and later when their trips to London coincided with his own short visits home, these men had been to him simply two more figures of his father's world, men who smiled down on him and brought him gifts. Now he saw clearly Baldwin's round proud eye and calculating mouth, the high soft gestures of his hands and condescending attitude. Clearly he saw the bland smile on Eustace's empty face, the slack and happy look of one who long ago gave over all the taxing functions of the mind to someone else to cope with for him.

Had the world been less kind to Thomas as he grew up he might have written them in his now adult mind as "schemer," "fool." But he did not. Measuring them against the other men whom he had known he saw their faults. But these were only flaws upon the surface of their aspect; primarily these men were friends, who liked him, who meant well. And he liked them.

Baldwin, speaking to Gilbert, swept his hand high in the air, indicating Thomas. They sat at the table with their supper finished. "All very well, dear Gilbert, to have placed the boy with your distinguished kinsman as you say. But what has it got you? Where is he now?"

"Just now we men of London bow our heads and wait," Gilbert conceded. "There will come a time . . ."

"Let us grant that there will come a time," Baldwin broke in. "What then? Is he to go on as clerk serving some merchant, running the mercenary errands of some city government?"

Gilbert drew a breath to speak but Baldwin did not stop. "Oh yes, dear host, I know you take offense when I say thus of London, 'some city.' " He laughed, and Gilbert smiled because he was the host and Thomas smiled because he was his father's son. And then he said: "I would prefer if I, like you sir, could serve the Church."

Baldwin was gratified. "Eustace and I could ask no better life," he said.

"I have long thought about it," Thomas said. His father looked at him. "But as it is in England these days," he continued, "I have not found the opportunity."

"No opportunity? Why you are tonsured. You can read and write. Surely there must be someplace here nearby, safe here in London which you love so well."

"I'm sure," said Thomas. "But there is in England one place where men schooled in Paris, as I have been, most truly and most powerfully serve the Church. Where men of experience are needed."

"Yes?"

"And it has seemed to me that I should offer myself there."

"There? Where?"

"In Canterbury, sir. In the archbishop's household."

"Oh."

"But I have no introduction."

"Oh?"

"Someone of standing in the Church, someone of stature, the sort of man whose word would carry weight with the archbishop would have to put my name to him."

"A man whose words are heard by the archbishop?" Baldwin asked. "Or perhaps another bishop? The Bishop of Boulogne?" He pursed his lips.

"Yes, such a man," said Thomas.

Baldwin sat back and looked at him. In Eustace's mind a thought was forming; he looked at Thomas, then to his brother, then at Thomas, breathing as though he might soon speak, but he said nothing.

"If somehow I could have an introduction from such a man," said Thomas, "perhaps the archbishop would receive it favorably. My father's family and the archbishop's both come from Thierceville, as perhaps you know." He did not add that the archbishop's family were of knightly rank and Gilbert's common. "This might appeal to him, might carry weight. But only, of course, if he first knew that a man of reputation spoke for me."

"Aye, it might carry weight. Perhaps, perhaps," said Baldwin. "But who do you have in mind to introduce the name?" He pursed his lips and raised his brows and let the question hang.

Then Thomas' chin went up and he spoke boldly, formally: "I know this favor is within your power, Archdeacon Baldwin. You are indeed a man of reputation." Thomas said. He watched the other closely. "Echoes of your fame have often come to us, here in our little backwater." He grinned. Then, serious again, he added, "It is true I have been searching for just such a man as you to help me. And because you have known me so long, and known my father, I ask this favor now."

Baldwin leaned back again. He swept his arm around and rested it on Gilbert's shoulder next to him. "I have had many favors in this house," he said. He smiled. "Yes, I can do it, I think, very easily. I am not without some influence, as you say. Oh, nothing very much. A little power in my own diocese. But to speak frankly—without false modesty—my bishop listens when I speak. And owes me something, too, a little something."

He broke off, put his hands upon the table and rose up. "No thanks. No thanks," he said, and turned away to go and take the seat beside the fire. The others followed him. "It will be done," he said. "But not overnight, you understand that. These things take time. But I will do it. I have always liked you, Thomas. You know that."

It did take time, while the archdeacon put in his word for Thomas here and there as he found opportunity and sent a long and flattering letter off to Canterbury. But in time the thing was done, and Thomas received word that when the primate traveled to his manor house at Harrow in the fall, for Martinmas, he should present himself there for an interview.

"Now," said Gilbert, full of life once more. "The question is: Who is to accompany you? It would have been better if you had been invited more directly, if the archbishop had sent someone to accompany you. But as it is . . ."

His father's eagerness and his awareness of their lack of standing rubbed on Thomas till he would have spoken rudely, but for pity when he watched his father's face. Instead he only closed his mouth in a thin line. He did not need to be reminded how precarious was this introduction, how more than likely it would come to nothing, how foolish he would look arriving at the archbishop's brilliant court without escort, a nobody. His father's talk of it made matters worse. He rose and would have gone, as he went frequently these days, into the little parish church of his baptism, there to pray for strength and resignation. But his father spoke before he reached the door.

"Squire Ralph!" Gilbert blurted out. "Baillehache the marshal's man!"

Ralph Baillehache had frequented the merchant's house when it had been a gayer place. He had been, long ago, a promising young squire, an armiger. But with the passing years, due to this circumstance and that, he had remained an armiger and his duties ever more menial. Now, the promise gone that he would rise to knightly rank or make a name other than that of "hatchet-bearer," he performed still, alongside younger, fresher men, those tasks he once hoped were a path toward dignity. His hair was grizzled and his stocky figure thick with years, and he made much of his seniority among the marshal's men while they in turn curled up their lips at him.

Thomas knew none of this and Gilbert only by surmise; he had not seen Baillehache in several years. He only knew there was a man in the archbishop's service who owed him favors for past hospitality.

"I'll send him word at once," he said, "that when he comes

to Harrow with the archbishop I shall be much obliged if he will come and fetch you there." And thus it was arranged.

* * *

One bitter evening in November of that year, Archbishop Theobald rode on his gaited Spanish mule up the steep cobbled street of Harrow-on-the-Hill, smiling and raising his hand in blessing on the villagers who crowded by the way to see him pass. In his wake there ran a little hissing sound, the people whispering to one another how "I saw him pass," "He looked at me," "I touched his mount; I touched his gown," "I saw him pass." And gentle Theobald, cold to the bone in his fur robes, rode on.

His marshals had come several days before to hang the tapestries and lay the fire in the long drafty stone-and-timber hall that was the primate's manor house of Harrow. Now he arrived with all his retinue—clerks, stewards, huntsmen, men-at-arms, and servants of all kinds—and the great sloping courtyard of the house filled with men and mounts as darkness fell and the little crusts of ice froze solid in the mud. Pack horses were unladen in the dusk and led off steaming to the stable sheds and the wains unloaded and the chattels carried in: the curtains and mattress for the primate's bed, the linen sheets and the fur covers to be warmed beside the fire in the hall; the records and the writing tables of the clerks set on the benches hidden by the chancel screen; the altar cloths and monstrance, ciborium and chalice, and all the precious relics borne to the chapel by the sacristan.

All who had rank went stamping up the stairs into the hall. But outside tired men still worked. By the kitchen huts, where the hot fires drew idlers to watch, the slaughterers split the carcass of the deer the hunters carried in and kitchen-boys hacked off the heads of squawking fowl the villagers had brought as offerings. And bakers, already sweating though their breath blew steam, pushed the long ladles piled with loaves into the glowing ovens.

Among the lookers-on stood Ralph Baillehache. He had come earlier with the other warders, and his tasks were easy so he had already made his bed in a warm corner and drawn from the chandler his daily ration of two candle-ends and from the butler his half-measure of wine. Now he stood waiting for his bread. His rank did not permit him to take supper in the hall.

The moisture glistened on his rough wool tunic and in the

firelight his grizzled hair looked white. He shoved a little to make himself more room and others, feeling the push, looked round at him. "Well," he said pleasantly, his eyes still squinting into the heat, "I ride tomorrow into London."

There was no answer to his words. "Aye, I must fetch a young clerk back who is to serve the archbishop." Still there was silence and he carried on. "A brilliant lad. High-born, and schooled abroad. His father is an old dear friend of mine."

Someone behind him snorted in the dark, and to the faces in the firelight came the curve and glint of soft derisive smiles. But Baillehache, squinting at the ovens, paid no heed. "He always welcomes me," he said. "And of course it is my policy to grant a favor when it is asked . . ."

Thomas, as soon as he saw Baillehache, knew that his father's choice of guides was a mistake. The man came stamping into the hall midmorning, announcing he would stay for dinner but would not spend more time; his duties pressed. In fact, he had been able to obtain leave from the marshal for only one day—not because of his importance, but because the marshal did not like him well enough to grant him favors. He rose from dinner just as soon as he was full and urged his hosts to make their farewells brief. And so it was in haste that Thomas went off to procure a horse—his father had none now, and pack a few belongings—what would he need?—and put on his scholar's gown over his heavy cloak and he was ready.

Midafternoon, in the cold drizzle under the thick-drawn clouds, he stood beside his father in the empty court, his horse in readiness and Ralph already mounted waiting impatiently. The father and the son turned, faced each other, sought in their minds for words. "Godspeed," said Gilbert, showing a shadow of his old, bold smile. And Thomas' heart winced painfully within him when he saw how little of the old-time pride and energy were left. He nodded wordlessly, stooped to receive his father's farewell kiss. Then still without a word he turned and mounted and rode out.

All afternoon they rode, silent and hunched against the cold, out through the wet gray fields and little farms, the dripping forest paths and open glades of Middlesex, twelve miles, till they approached the slope of Harrow Hill. Ralph reined his horse. Above them climbed the narrow cobbled street and at its top, crowning the hill, the tower of the parish church. Evening had come and men and beasts were home now. Here and there among the village houses a lantern glowed or, as a door was opened, warmth of firelight fell upon the night.

Ralph spoke. "This, here," he said, "is Harrow-on-the-Hill."

This much was obvious. "Where is the archbishop's manor house?" Thomas asked.

"That. That is farther on. Beyond the church. A good distance. Not too far." Ralph's hesitation indicated there was more to come, so Thomas waited till, with a breath, a change of tone, Ralph went on. "You had better know," he said, "that the archbishop keeps the morning hours for discourse with his clerks and other learned men. That is the time when you should come to him. Not after dark. Not suppertime like this."

Thomas said nothing and Ralph shifted in his seat. "That being so, I know a lodging house where you could spend the night both safe and comfortable. That's in the village. Then in the morning you could ride on to the manor."

Thomas felt despair come on him. So Baillehache had no place within the court even to introduce a friend or offer him a bed.

As they had ridden through the darkening afternoon he had been conscious that, as his own hired horse was second rate, so was his escort. And with a winter chill about his heart he saw the bleakness of his chance. Tomorrow he must come before the great Archbishop Theobald in his wise, witty court, so lavish and so learned; this household where the bright young men came to be trained as deacons or as bishops; where when kings fought and the land fell into chaos, strength of government was stored; where business with the pope was carried on and all decisions for the English Church were made; this holy court of Canterbury.

As Baillehache nudged his horse to move ahead he could have cursed him for a failure and a broken prop. But then the truth came gently to his mind. It was not Ralph's weight in the balance here, but his. Had he come with a great procession heralding him, would that influence the archbishop? He thought not. Theobald was known for kindness and fair judgment.

Let me come to him like some unknown knight, he thought, with no fame of my own, no patron, riding a borrowed horse, led by a broken squire. Then let him judge me!

"Yes," he called out to Ralph. "It is a wise plan. I'll do as you say. Lead on."

The hostelry where Baillehache left him was a cottage with a loft, a mud and thatch affair with sty and dovecote close behind, much like any cotters home, although perhaps a little larger, with a carved wooden doorway and a bush, now dried up, hanging from a pole to show that ale was sold here. Inside, a smudgy fire filled the room with heavy warmth and smoke. The air was laden with the smells of animals and dung, of wet wool and of doubtful mutton cooking in a pot. The landlord came to scrutinize him before he let him in, a man quick in his step but very slow to smile. His wife likewise looked up with thin unsmiling face from where she stooped beside the cooking pot while from a corner three of her half-grown children stared through the smoke at the new visitor. Two men sat slumping wearily at a small trestle table.

Thomas, standing with his head bent in the doorway, saw it all. It was from homes like this he had received with thanks a bit of cold food handed out to him when he had been a student traveling to the schools. And though he might move in the high company of bishops, as he would do tomorrow, he was always in their debt. Stooping to enter, he smiled his merry smile at them as though he was delighted to be there. Their faces did not change but later, when they spoke among themselves it was with warmth as "the tall stranger with the blithe countenance." For he was gay, keyed up and talkative, that night, feeling the challenge of tomorrow.

After supper he entertained the company with marvels and weird tales that he had learned in reading and in traveling. Had they heard of Nicholas Pike, the merman, who was shaped like a man in all particulars but lived on the ocean bottom like a fish? Or of the knight of Barfleur who found a shipwrecked maiden on his coast and married her and by her had two children before it ever was found out—it was his mother who discovered it—she was a dragon? "The children and the knight and mother are living yet," he smiled, "although the dragon vanished."

They sat long at the table, Thomas and his hosts, after the two other travelers had gone up to the loft to sleep. And Thomas told them of the wondrous tales he had been reading about the kings of Britain and of the prophet Merlin, how Merlin proved the power of skill and cunning over strength when he moved the towering boulders of the Giants' Dance from Killare in Ireland onto the plain of Salisbury. "For at that place," he told them while they stared at him, "four hundred princes died by treachery and Merlin kept alive their memory by placing there this magic monument. 'The Dance,' they called it, 'of the Giants.' "

They stared in silence, gathering his words, till the host's son spoke up. "These giants," he said. "Do they dance yet?"

"Oh yes, by the town of Amesbury, there they stand today, so I have heard, in a great circle staring at the sun."

"Staring at the sun," the boy said. "Is it at night they dance then?"

Thomas laughed. "They stand there in a ring. As men *might* dance around a Maypole in the spring," he said. "But I have not read that they take a step, but only stand."

"Do they not tire, standing there?"

"They are great stones," Thomas explained. "They do not tire."

"Then they are not real giants? Only stones?"

"Aye," Thomas smiled upon him gently. "Only stones. The name is fanciful—the Giants' Dance. They are the great stones that the prophet Merlin brought here out of Ireland for King Aurelius."

He saw their disappointment and said quickly, "There is another king whom Merlin helped, the great King Arthur, conqueror of all Gaul." He paused to choose a tale of Arthur's prowess out of the many he had read when suddenly his host spoke, full of fire: "Arthur will come again!"

Thomas stopped, amazed, and saw they were all staring at him with their dark eyes full of mysteries.

"Arthur will come again," the man repeated, leaning across the table poised and intense, "out of the Isle of Avallon where he is resting." His eyes were fixed on Thomas'. "He will come again to rule in all his glory!"

There was silence for the man spoke his faith as passionately as any priest of God. This was the hope they lived by, man and wife and son and little children moving closer at the words. He saw now they were Britons, their lines going back through all the generations—son to father to father's father, back beyond Norman, Saxon, Dane—to that time when Britons ruled themselves. And Arthur was their hope that they would once again be masters of their land.

Thomas, a Norman, dedicated to the Christian faith, thought differently. Yet he was touched that they should honor him—he with his tonsure and the accent of the conqueror—with this, their deepest secret. He looked a long time into their faces, at the wild hope in his host's eyes.

"Aye, as you say," he said at last. "So be it."

Next morning Ralph came for Thomas soon after sunrise and he left the hostel with his host's smiles to follow him and all the children standing in the yard to see him go. He followed Ralph's directions up the hill, beyond the church and out of sight, and still they looked after him.

The wife came to the doorway where her husband stood.

"I dreamed of that young stranger in the night," she said.

"Dreamed?" said the host.

"Yes, very powerful and strange. I dreamed I saw him take his cloak and with it cover up the spire of our church." She turned and stared again with wonder up the hill.

"Yes, very strange," her husband said. "Perhaps it will bring luck. What was the garment? Like a bishop's robe? They say to dream of bishops' robes brings luck."

The woman shook her head. "I don't remember now," she said. "Only the young man and the tower I remember, very powerful."

Mornings, between the hour of Terce and dinnertime, Archbishop Theobald set aside for meditation and for discourse with learned men. The hours before this—after his celebration of the Mass—he usually devoted to the business correspondence of his see, closeting himself with his young clerks and secretaries. And in the afternoons, when he was on tour as now, he went about his lands blessing the common people and visiting the churches of his suffragans.

Therefore it was at Terce, as Ralph had said, that Thomas would do best to introduce himself, when the archbishop was in his hall but not yet taken up with men of dignity and rank. They heard the bell strike for the Hour as Thomas, following Ralph, rode down the slope and through the manor gates.

The court was crowded but no one took much notice of him and he was glad to tie his unprepossessing horse among the rows of them that stood beside the stables and head resolutely for the hall. Ralph left him there, below the steps, and Thomas was grateful to be done with him as well.

The hall was large, though only half as large as Pevensey, and with a softer tone. The canvas hangings on the walls were new, a snapping fire burned and on the floor was fresh clean straw. Thomas paused, as he was trained to do at Pevensey, forbearing to stride forward overboldly yet not hanging back as one of menial state. He stood straight, pushing back his hood. Then with a quick look he sought out and recognized the steward standing at his station near the door and bowed to him, not deeply but as a man invited would introduce himself. And when the steward, taking the size of this newcomer, returned the nod, Thomas moved forward easily.

"Welcome-may-I-know-your-business," the steward said, wary lest he give too warm a greeting to some stray young clerk seeking to break in on the archbishop.

"Thomas, son of Gilbert of Thierceville, bidden by the Archdeacon of Boulogne to present myself, and his respects, to the archbishop."

The steward looked again at Thomas' lean, impassive face and bowed. "If you will come with me," he said.

Thomas saw that the archbishop had come into the hall surrounded by his learned clerks, all talking among themselves, and chairs were being placed beside the fire. He took his seat as Thomas and his guide approached and looked at them with mild and questioning eyes.

"My lord Archbishop," the steward said. "May I present Thomas of Thierceville, sent by the Bishop of Boulogne."

The archbishop's face lit up to hear the name of his old home and he put out his hand as Thomas knelt before him.

"Thierceville!" he said. "You are of Thierceville, my son? Welcome."

"No, my lord," Thomas said flushing. "But my father's family has its roots in Thierceville, and from my childhood I have heard the name spoken with love . . . and come to know the fields and little running streams . . ." he stumbled on.

Some of the light had faded from the primate's countenance but he still smiled. "Yes, I know the little streams of Thierceville," he said. "And you pronounce the name as native-born. Well, where *do* you come from if not from Thierceville?"

"I am from London," Thomas said.

One of the clerks behind the archbishop turned and whispered in another's ear and snickered as he spoke. Thomas did not look up nor did the archbishop. Instead he motioned Thomas to come sit beside him while they talked.

"Now, if I heard aright," he said, his smile a little quizzical, "you come to me with recommendation—or bring a message from—the Bishop of Boulogne?"

If he had ever felt more agony of hot embarrassment Thomas could not remember it. He did not even try to smile. "From the Archdeacon of Boulogne," he said. "I am afraid I mumbled to your steward . . ."

"Ah, the Archdeacon Baldwin! Yes, I know him," the archbishop said. "Surely. I have had a letter from him recently. Indeed. Of course. He spoke well of a certain youth." Then, "Roger," he said without turning round, "will you please fetch the letter from Boulogne which came some days ago. I have brought it with me I am sure. It will be in the chest."

The clerk turned from his whispering, bowed quickly and went off.

"Then you must be that youth," the archbishop went on to Thomas, and again his look was quizzical, "whom the archdeacon praised so lavishly?"

Thomas, feeling relief come creeping back, said, "Archdeacon Baldwin has often been a guest in my father's house and I have known him since I was a little boy. If he spoke well of me it was because of old times' sake and friendship for my father."

"But more than that, I think," the archbishop said, remembering the letter. "You had some years in Paris at the schools?"

"Two years."

"In the study of dialectics I suppose?"

"Yes, my lord."

"With the brilliant Peter Abelard?" Archbishop Theobald looked into his lap and brushed at a little piece of fluff that clung to the fur trimming of his robe.

"No, my lord," Thomas said noncommittally. "Master Abelard had left, the year I came to Paris."

"A pity that you missed his teachings."

"Perhaps, my lord. Yet there are many men who could not stand the liquid fire of his argument and went astray, far from the teachings of the Church—through no fault of the great Abelard, perhaps."

"What do you think? You think his theories of rational inquiry heretical? What of the *Sic et Non?* Harmful to men of faith?" This was a central question of the Church; the long-worn argument had flared again since Abelard's death a year ago.

"I am not qualified to judge, my lord. I put my trust in those who are. Surely Abbot Bernard of Clairvaux knows the intent of God as well as any man. As he judges, so I believe."

"Aye, so do I," said Theobald. "You knew that, didn't you, when you chose your words?"

Thomas was nonplused. What had the archbishop expected him to say? Did he take him for a bumpkin? . . . Or was that perhaps the very thing he had been wondering?

"But I think you spoke the truth," the archbishop went on. "You would have said the same in any case. Now tell me honestly if I am right."

"Yes, my lord," said Thomas. "It is the truth." And he was

grateful that he could say this from the heart, without a reservation.

"Roger, have you found the letter?" the archbishop turned.

"Here it is, my lord," said Roger handing it to him. "It is from the *deacon* of Boulogne rather than from the bishop as we had supposed."

"Thank you, Roger," Theobald said crisply. "Thomas has told me." He glanced a moment at the letter. "So you would like to serve me as my clerk? Here we seek piety, sobriety, and righteousness. And you must give your best to all your work—that I demand—and study, too. England cries out for learned men . . ."

He broke off and looked searchingly at Thomas. "Well," he said finally, "Roger will see to all your needs."

Thomas sprang up, ready to fall before the archbishop in gratitude but Roger touched him on the arm. And the archbishop had already turned away. Others were waiting to speak to him.

Roger led Thomas across the hall and round the corner of the chancel screen. There he turned and looked him up and down. "I suppose you left your things with Ralph Baillehache, the marshal's man?" He smiled, but Thomas knew the words were meant to hurt. And he had hoped no one had noticed him with Ralph.

"No, I did not," he said.

"No? Where did you leave them then?"

"I brought nothing with me," Thomas said.

"No?" the voice was light. "Baillehache should have told you. You will need a bed here, and your books. You do have books?"

"Yes, I have books," and Thomas' voice was even and his face as calm as ever the Lord Richer could have asked. "I will go and find my friend Baillehache and ask him to ride to London for them. I have a hired horse that I must send back to its owner." He spoke the words "friend," "hired horse," clearly and evenly.

"By all means," Roger said. "One must not keep a hired horse too long. The cost mounts up."

"Aye, as you say," said Thomas. And he turned away and went out to the court to find Baillehache.

When he returned he had no choice but to join Roger once again. He found him laughing with another clerk in a far corner behind the screen, and heard him saying ". . . I shall call him the baillehache clerk for the name is apt—he came in like a hatchet, battering his way, without a proper invitation and unheralded . . ." He broke off as his eye caught Thomas where he stood beside the screen. He beckoned him. "Come and be introduced," he said.

Thomas advanced. The other clerk rose shyly, a small slender boy, younger than Thomas. Roger was more nearly Thomas' age, taller and more fleshy than the boy beside him although shorter by almost a head than Thomas. They made a threesome like a set of stairs as they stood facing each other warily.

"John Belmeis, of Canterbury," Roger said, naming his small companion. "And I am Roger of Pont l'Evêque." He bowed.

Thomas returned the bow unsmiling. "Thomas," he said. "Of London."

"Of London?" Roger asked. "I thought by your scholar's gown you were from Paris."

"London and Paris," Thomas said.

"London *and* Paris," Roger echoed. "Until now we had considered John here our most learned. John speaks all languages. He is our genius. He is our brightest star." John blushed and Roger went on, "But I can see you may replace him. London *and* Paris. Do you know Hebrew?"

"No . . ." Thomas said.

"Greek?"

"No."

"Latin?"

Thomas smiled grimly. "A little."

"A little," Roger said. "John is above us all in knowledge of these languages. Is it not so, John?"

John waved away the claim and stammered, "Oh not at all, not really. You, Roger, are far quicker than I am to learn . . ."

"Oh, I am quick," Roger broke in. "I am the man to run your errands and fetch your letters. If it is speed you want, I am your man." He had a long face with a well-fleshed curving nose and mobile mouth. His lips were soft and pointed at the center, always moving, and conveyed his feelings better than his eyes.

"And what is *your* gift?" he asked suddenly, turning his soft pointed smile on Thomas.

"My gift?" said Thomas. "Oh, I am handy with the hatchet."

Roger laughed and for the first time looked at him with warmth. "You have the gift of wit," he said. "Come"—he put a hand on Thomas' shoulder and the other around John's—"we will make a threesome." And in a voice like a conspirator, "The other clerks are old and sour, always looking for mistakes. Isn't it so, John?"

Thomas saw surprise and doubt in John's face, but Roger went on, still with his hands upon their shoulders, "We will make a threesome and stand against them all. Learning and lightning youth . . .

"Oh," a thought struck him and he dropped his arms. "Minerva, Mercury . . . and Mars. A classical triumvirate! The gods demand it, don't you see? Minerva, Mercury and Mars!"

He laughed the loudest at his joke but John laughed too and Thomas, looking at them, could not help but smile. The hour of Sext had not yet rung and he was one of them—a long step from this morning.

CHAPTER X

ARCHBISHOP THEOBALD REMAINED at Harrow well into Advent. Then with his court he made a leisurely return to Canterbury for the Christmas feast. Thomas went with him and for the first time came to know the great cathedral and the monastery buildings of Christchurch.

As they approached it from the hill of Harbledown the church looked like some dark and massive jewel. Its stones were carved, its wooden roof was painted red and blue and black, its turrets all were topped with gilded pinnacles and from the apex of its central tower a golden cherub rode against the sky.

The dark monastic buildings nestled by its side around the great quadrangle of the cloister with its wintry garden and its pillared walks; the dormitories for the monks and their refectory and library and chapter house. The palace stood somewhat apart and stretched a covered walk to join them as though to emphasize the primate's dual role as Archbishop of Canterbury and as Abbot of Christchurch.

Beyond this somber cluster lay the outbuildings and halls: the jumble of the kitchens with their sculleries and larders, bakehouse, brewhouse, buttery; the home for aged monks and the infirmarian's lodging by the long infirmary hall and little house for letting blood; the school for novices and prior's hall nearby; the baths; the guest halls for the rich and for the poor; the farm buildings and workmen's huts; the byre and sheepfold, sties and goatsheds, houses for the hens and ducks; the hives, the dovecotes and the tanks for fish; the small walled gardens and the open fields.

It was a great establishment, center of wealth and power, seat of God's highest representative in England, and all its business was conducted by such a complex of strong personalities that Thomas' bright perception was engaged, all the first weeks, simply in learning them and their relationships.

The strange triumvirate that he had joined with John Belmeis and Roger of Pont l'Evêque prolonged itself for many months, though never did the two antagonists become true friends. But it was advantageous to them all, especially to Thomas, as it gave him some distinction in the populous court.

All three young men were called upon from time to time, as were the other clerks, to write the archbishop's letters, witness agreements, observe his councils and, occasionally, give opinions. Thus hardly a piece of business was done—a prebend granted, a prior reprimanded, the right of sanctuary given to some parish churchyard—that one of the three had not direct and intimate knowledge of it. Details of correspondence with the king, the pope, with other men of power were, almost without exception, known and shared among the three. They soon became the best informed and the most balanced in their understanding of all the clerks in the archbishop's chancery.

Thomas and Roger were both quick of mind and apt in citing precedent. But Thomas was less prone than Roger to rely on personal bias in his judgments. John was more scholarly, devoted to his books, and found less pleasure in arbitration and diplomacy. He lived somewhat withdrawn. Thus he was unaware when Roger found pretext to slander Thomas, carrying tales to the archbishop of his moral laxity.

The charge was false but had the ring of credibility because it found its shape in Roger's own abnormal practices. For it was Roger's sin at this time of his life to prey upon the little boys who studied singing in the monastery school, luring them, using them, and then so frightening them to silence that they dared not speak—nay, so the monk who was their choirmaster said, they dared not open up their mouths at all and were a total loss to him for days. He did not say he knew the reason why, for he did not. Only the little boys—each frightened boy alone—knew why and did not speak.

At this time Thomas was by contrast as far from the temptations of the flesh as he had been at any time since he left Pevensey. His were the sins of pride, ambition, lack of charity in judgment, not of moral laxity. Prayer was a daily, almost hourly ritual at Christchurch and an antidote to craving. Denial had some purpose now that ambition had a goal. Therefore he was amazed when Master Hubert of the Chancery came to him suddenly as he sat studying a writ and told him without preamble that there was no longer any place for him within the primate's household. He could collect a small remuneration from the steward and it would please them all if he were gone by noon.

Thomas sat open-mouthed when Hubert turned as though from dirt and left. Then hatred and a passion for revenge rose burning in his throat. The accusation came from Roger he felt sure, it smelled of him. He jumped up, ready to seek him out. Then—caution. What would that bring? A cheap exchange of insults, pain and disgust to the archbishop, laughter from others, and a world lost for him. Better to let all thought of vengeance go, for now.

He left the little room where the clerks sat, all eying him, for they had heard the words and seen his face grow terrible. He crossed the hall and left the palace and the precincts, driven out by fury and the need to think. It was impossible to go directly to the archbishop crying for mercy, or for justice even. There was a wall about the gentle Theobald he had not learned to vault. One must be found to intercede for him.

Under the open skies outside the gate, with all his wrathful thoughts still flaring in his heart he sought to pray. " 'Oh Lord my God,' " he groaned, "in thee have I put my trust; save me from them that persecute me . . ." Rebellion rose up once again. "It is unjust, unjust . . ."

Now for the first time in his life he felt the need for scourge to whip his body and his mind into submission. He crept into the wintry reeds beside the wall and knelt, a curious figure, forcing his knees and body to a humble posture while with his will he struggled to subdue his heart: "Oh Lord correct me, but in judgment not in anger; neither chasten me in thy displeasure . . . but have mercy on me, Lord, for I am weak . . . my soul is troubled . . ."

But all the while the little thoughts went chasing through his mind: One must be found to intercede for me . . . a friend . . . redeemer . . . Archdeacon Walter has been kind to me . . . accessible . . . and the archbishop's brother, dearly beloved . . . "Oh save me for thy mercy's sake . . ." If I should go to him he would have mercy and deliver—he would speak for me . . .

He smiled a little, shamefaced, stepped from the rushes and brushed off his gown. He had not prayed successfully or found his way to God. But he had found the path to the archbishop and—in that way—success. He looked around. He had not been observed.

He found Archdeacon Walter in the palace garden seated behind a little table in an angle of the wall. He was alone and counting coins upon a checkered cloth, preoccupied and happy. He smiled at Thomas, for he had not heard the news, then cocked his head to scan the young man's troubled face.

Archdeacon Walter listened to his story, pursed his lips, and slowly shook his head. "Truly, it seems an error has been made," he said. And then as though a novel thought had struck him: "My son, I think that you have come to the right man, for I can speak to the archbishop as can no other man. I have his ear." He touched his own and smiled. "Wait here." He rose, keeping his fingers on the cloth so that the coins were not disturbed. "And watch the tally for me if you will. Easter is such a busy time for me—with all the tallage coming in. These are the plow-alms, already counted. Keep them separate. I will be back directly, for I am certain of success," he smiled as though the two conspired.

"Truly," he said in parting, "it was a lucky chance that brought you first to me. Of all men, I am the one my brother listens to."

Thus was the plea sped by the best channel, brother to brother, and the misunderstanding, as it was termed, smoothed over, all forgot.

This happened once again in those first months: again the accusation, again the story brought to the archdeacon, and again the reconciliation. And through it friendship grew between the easygoing Walter and the tall young clerk. And each time Thomas moved a few steps closer to the Canterbury throne.

* * *

Four years passed and Thomas found his place in the archbishop's chancery: the student and the clever diplomat. When Theobald, wishing to introduce to England the new study of law that flourished in Lombardy, brought from Mantua the noted teacher Vacarius, it was Thomas who profited. And when King Stephen, fearful of new ideas within his kingdom, banished Vacarius, it was of Thomas that the master spoke on taking leave of Theobald: "Send him to us in Lombardy when you can spare him for we have much to teach him and he is quick to learn."

But Theobald could not spare Thomas yet. The pope had called him to a synod to be held in Rheims. King Stephen, fearing what might be worked against him there, forbade the archbishop to leave. The king was now victorious in the land: Empress Matilda, losing heart, had left her English castles and what followers she had—so few since her dear brother Gloucester's death—and fled to Normandy to join her husband and her son. Stephen was undisputed king at last. Or was he? Surprising was the number of those who disputed him, the gentle Theobald not least.

"What is the duty of the primate in a situation such as this?" Theobald said dryly, gently testing some of the clerks who sat with him the day the news was brought that Stephen with a heavy guard had come to occupy his Canterbury castle for the Easter feast. "The pope has called me and the king forbids me go." He looked at all their faces. "Thomas?" he said.

"My lord," said Thomas, "we all know that while the king derives his power from God he must receive it through the hands of God, the Church. So is the call of Church that much superior to the demands of kings. And as for precedent: Archbishop Anselm long ago faced such a test of duty and defied King William. Does that suffice?"

"It does," said Theobald in his dry voice. The lessons had been learned. He sighed and for a moment sat in thought. Then he straightened, smiled, and said: "With that decided comes the question of the means." He looked around the room. All present knew that since the king had come the gates were guarded and the roads were watched.

John Belmeis leaned forward speaking eagerly: "My lord, I know a little hidden harbor north of Sandwich where we might find a boat." And the archbishop nodded calmly as though he planned a ride to Rochester.

"John and I could ride there after Compline tonight . . ." Thomas broke in.

"Softly," the archbishop held up his hand. "No haste. Tomorrow you and John may ride as though with messages to Rochester. I will provide you with letters that you may show the guard if they require it. Then you may double back. You know the roads, John? Send me a guide when all is ready. Roger and I will join you."

Roger, who had been made archdeacon only three months before, when Walter was elected Bishop of Rochester, spoke now as one of standing. He was no longer willing to play the eager clerk or young adventurer as John and Thomas seemed to be. "My lord, would it not be more fitting to your position if I should go to Dover and persuade the sheriff to look the other way while I procured a proper ship and guard to see us safely on our way? I know quite definitely that the sheriff can be bought . . ."

"It would be more fitting, Roger, yes," said Theobald. "But it is not the better plan, for there are hazards in it that I do not like. No, I prefer the humbler dangers of John's little boat—and the safety of small numbers. If I recall the flight of Anselm"—he shot a little twinkling glance at Thomas—"as I heard of it, it was both swift and silent. There is our precedent. And we shall follow it, I think."

Had the archbishop known what "little boat" his eager clerks in all their haste had settled for he might have bowed his neck before the king and stayed at home. But on the next dark night when he and Roger with two of his marshals, all disguised as monks, rode down the slippery stones and gravel of the landing place and watched the tiny bobbing light offshore come closer in to fetch him, it was too late. The fishing smack was old and scarce equipped for such a sail, and when he and his little retinue—there were just five of them, for John was left behind to cover up their tracks—grasped with reluctant hands the rough hands of the fishermen and scrambled in, the little vessel dragged its keel and sluggish water slapped along the gunwales.

It was too late to reconsider, too late even for comment or complaint. Wordless and with a little smile that none could see, Theobald wrapped his robe about him, grasped with both hands the little columbe with the Sacred Host he carried in his breast, and settled down to pray. And there he sat, all night and all next day. All night the blackness of the water rose and fell against the blackness of the sky. All day the boat rose sliding up each dark green crest and wallowed in each trough, slapping its lonely way across the Channel while the fishermen pulled at the oars and worked the flapping sail.

Thomas and Roger, with no word between them, worked till their arms ached bailing out the seas that splashed over the gunwales and leaked between their feet. So low they lay upon the water that they did not see the flat gray land of Flanders in the dust till they were almost on it. The fluttering sail came down, the sailors rested on their oars, and they came gliding on the final swell and grounded on the sand. The beach and looming dunes were all deserted at the end of day. Silently they left the boat and crept ashore wringing the water from their clothes.

When darkness fell the lighted windows of the fishing village led them to a resting place and there they dried themselves and ate and slept the night. Next day, before the sun was strong, they had procured five ambling horses and were pacing silently along the road toward Rheims. And it was then that Roger, at long last, gave voice to what he thought:

"It is a miracle, the hand of God, that we are not all dead!" His voice was angry and no one replied.

He rode in silence for a time before he spoke again, this time more calmly but still bitter: "Could it be possible for any man so to devise such danger for us all through sheer stupidity—not by design?"

Thomas looked sharply at him over his shoulder, but as no admonition came from the archbishop he did not speak and Roger went on softly: "How many times, when the water threatened to engulf us, the thought came to me how the king would laugh to see us now. He himself could not have planned it better . . ." He paused to test his ground and then, emboldened by the silence, still went on: "I could not help but think, then, of Our Lord, and what He said when plots were laid against him for his life. What were His words?" He looked aside at Thomas. " 'Verily I say to you that one among you shall betray me.' "

Thomas' senses sharpened and his muscles tensed as for a pass in jousting but he kept himself in check. This much had Richer l'Aigle taught him.

"Then might we each one look into our hearts and say . . ." Roger had brought his horse up and leaned forward so as to look directly into Thomas' eyes, " 'Lord, Master, is it I?' "

Theobald, rousing, caught his glance. He used the gentle word, "Forbear."

"I will forbear," said Roger quickly, settling back. "For your sake, Father, I will forbear to torment him. Conscience is torment enough . . ."

"I meant," said Theobald, cutting across his words, "forbear to jeopardize your own soul, Roger, with such unworthy thoughts."

The blood, released, rushed into Thomas' face. He would have laughed but caution stopped him. Only he checked his horse's pace and dropped back so that only Roger could observe him. And then he sent him such a gleeful smile, tinged with derision, that Roger never more forgave.

Pope Eugenius was at his dinner table in the monastery

outside Rheims. He ate as though the food meant nothing to him, sparingly, his face composed. All the misfortunes of his short and turbulent reign—his quarrels with the senators of Rome and his expulsion from the Holy City, the capture of Edessa by the infidels and the dissentions on the great crusade that he had launched to free it, the enmity of kings—had deepened his humility and brought out all the stoic qualities that had been nurtured in him in the cloister.

The guest who sat beside him was Abbot Bernard of Clairvaux, the voice of Christian conscience, who was so seldom lured from his small cell under the stairway of his austere house. The fare was simple and they ate in silence, in the Cistercian manner, while a monk read to them from his high corner. Other, more worldly Churchmen seemed to endure the meal with less composure, furtively signaling to each other to pass down the salt or with imperious glances summoning the stewards for more wine. Their clerks sat down below them with the monks, snatching such quantities as they dared. John of Salisbury was among them, head up and listening, a vessel of perception. He had left the schools of Paris and of Chartres and for the past year had been a secretary to the pope, a valuable man.

Suddenly a whispered word was brought to the pope's ear—and was sent rustling through the tables—that Theobald of Canterbury had defied the English king and fled the land and even now was entering into Rheims. Eugenius, so stoic in misfortune, showed suddenly his radiant side the others had not seen. Leaping up he broke the silence and cried out, "Come, let us welcome him!" The unaccustomed buzz of voices rose in the refectory and even Bernard left his meditation and rose smiling.

"Fetch me my miter. Fetch me my staff," the pope cried, almost running to his rooms. And when his man had helped him don his chasuble and his dalmatic, heavy with gold embroidery, and laid the pallium around his shoulders, he ran out again, holding his miter steady with one hand and asking, "Where shall we go to meet him? Where?" for he was not familiar with the monastery grounds.

When the archbishop came at last into the council room, bedraggled but undaunted, and would have stooped to kiss the papal ring, Eugenius swooped down to take him in his arms and with a rush of tears wetted his cheeks and mouth.

Thomas, too, was welcomed like a brother. John of Salisbury, whom he had not seen for ten years, came to him and embraced him—a rarity with him—and then stood back. "I see that you have grown to be a man," he smiled his quiet smile.

"John!" Thomas cried out. "John! I saw your hand in letters from His Holiness. I knew that you were destined for great things. And here you are!" He spoke delightedly but felt again a little awkward, over tall, as he had done so long ago.

About them milled the other clerks, asking for mutual friends, about their status and their health. This was an international group who knew each other from the schools or visits with their overlords or from great councils such as this. They asked each other news of England or the Frankish court, the Curia, about the schools of Paris or Chartres or this new study of the law in Lombardy. Their gossip and their jokes were light, but always softly spoken and they kept their eyes turned frequently to watch the pontiffs on the dais. When the pope rose they all fell silent. And as he passed between them out of the council room they stood aside with closed and pious faces till he had gone. Then they broke out in talk and laughter once again.

The council had on its agenda matters of Church decrees and jurisdiction, matters of politics, matters of faith. Eugenius presided from his throne with Abbot Bernard as his guest beside him, the cardinals behind. The papal secretary, Geoffrey of Auxerre, who read his proclamations stood at his shoulder and his recording clerks sat at their tables in the rear, half-hidden by their screen. Below him, each with his crosier beside him and his clerks all gathered round, the bishops stood and jostled for best place. Their chairs were empty for there had been arguments among them as to precedence.

This matter had caused uproar in the chamber earlier when the Bishop of Lyons had gone to take his place and, finding Tours before him, pulled him from the chair. Their clerks had struck each other and before the melee quieted, Sens had slipped into the seat in question. Treves as well had run to put himself above his host of Rheims, causing an outcry from the others. Therefore the council opened with all bishops standing and the first matter undertaken was this of their relative superiority.

Theobald, as all knew, had the place of honor nearest to the papal throne. But the matter carried far beyond the seating at the council; it was a fight for power. Thus Theobald brought up his complaint against the absent Archbishop of York who claimed that he was equal to Canterbury in the

English hierarchy. To this Eugenius gave ruling: "Canterbury, both by ancient usage and by our present declaration, is superior to York. And he alone may crown the English kings."

On the next day when all were seated, each according to his rank—if not content, resigned—the Church decrees to be agreed on by the council were announced. Geoffrey of Auxerre read them as they were written by the papal clerks, his voice resounding through the hall: "No clerk or deacon, priest or lay brother may wear a multicolored cloak." He paused, then added as the custom was: "Do you agree?"

The voices of the prelates mumbled in unison: "We do."

"No bishop, abbot, deacon, priest or monk may take unto himself a wife. Do you agree?"

"We do."

"A person who attacks or strikes a man in holy orders, be he high or low, that person must then seek his absolution from the pope. Do you agree?"

This last brought querulous discussion from the floor: "Suppose a choirmaster strike a stubborn pupil with the birch, or master of a household strike a tonsured servingman?"

"Suppose a doorkeeper in holding back a crowd of clerks all rushing through a door at once should happen inadvertently to strike one with his staff?"

"If one monk strike another, lightly, in irritation—must he then go to Rome?"

For the first time Eugenius himself spoke, lightly, drawing laughter from the crowd. "With these exceptions shall the decretal hold," he said. "For we all know that it is better to resolve such little questions in the school or cloister than to provide excuse for dissolute men to roam about the world under pretext of going to the pope."

"Do you agree?" the monk called solemnly.

The laughter lingered in the voices from the floor. "We do."

On the third day the serious matter of the English king was brought before the council. Eugenius himself spoke, listing Stephen's act against the Church, and Geoffrey called them out: "Instance one, this sovereign set his hand against our legate, who should be sacrosanct, and barred his passage into Ireland. Instance two, he forced on our unwilling prelates, and in contravention of our will, election of his nephew William to the Archbishopric of York. Third and most grievous instance, he forbade the English bishops to attend our Council."

Here the pope rose and took his staff in hand. "For these things and for others we propose . . ." he said, with the monk echoing in his sonorous voice.

"The excommunication from the comforts of the Church. . . ."

"The excommunication from the comforts of the Church," the monk intoned . . .

"Stephen of Blois, the King of England."

Thomas, standing in the shadow behind Theobald, felt a queer thrill of horror for the king. He knew that it was not for him to question any action of His Holiness—yet Stephen was his sovereign.

About him was a rustling in the chamber as the bishops rose, some with stern faces set but some, he saw, with doubt or even disagreement. Friends of the House of Blois looked to each other furtively to see which one would speak in their behalf. But they delayed too long. Even as they sought to phrase their pleas, candles were brought and lighted for the awful ceremony.

Thomas, with his eyes fixed on their flames and the pope's face flickering in the light between them, was surprised to find that Theobald had left his place and gone to kneel before the pope in supplication, begging for mercy for the king.

Eugenius was thunderstruck that such a plea should come from such a quarter. He stood in silence for a long time after the archbishop had finished until at last the softness of his heart engulfed his somber judgment. Tears on his face, he raised his arms as though to call attention of the angels as well as of the men assembled and in a trembling voice, "Behold," he said, "this man enacts the gospels in our time. He loves his enemies and prays for them that persecute him."

He dropped his arms and looked at Theobald. Then in a changed and gentle voice he said, "For your sake, brother, for your sake alone, will we have mercy." And to the prelates: "We will allow the king three months delay in which to give us satisfaction for the wrongs he does the Church."

On this high note the council ended, but the pope stayed on, giving his time to those who clamored for it: Ralph, Count of Vermandois, had followed him to Rheims as he had followed him about the past three years, seeking divorce so that he might have legally the mistress whom he now possessed in fact; John, Archdeacon of Cologne, stayed on to beg for absolution for his archbishop who was suspended from the Church for disobedience; and Abbot Bernard, burning with zeal, sought papal sanction in his attempt to censure Master Gilbert de la Porrée, as he had censured Master Peter Abelard and made him burn his books, for teachings inconsistent with accepted faith.

To these the pope and Curia gave ear. Divorce was granted to the Count of Vermandois and absolution to the Bishop of Cologne. The abbot's case against the learned Gilbert took more time, full of crosscurrents as it was, and ultimately failed because the cardinals were jealous of the power of Clairvaux.

At last Eugenius found time to speak to Theobald in private on a subject to be kept between the two of them: the matter of succession to the English throne.

"Stephen has proved himself an enemy," the pope said. "England, the Church, would be well rid of him."

"But he was recognized by Innocent himself," the archbishop replied. "And crowned by my own predecessor, William."

"Yes, yes, by that we must abide. Stephen is king. But Stephen's line has not first claim upon the throne?"

"No, Stephen's line, the House of Blois, is not direct. The Empress Matilda's line, as all the barons and the prelates of the Church swore before Henry's death, has the first claim."

"The House of Anjou?"

"Yes, the empress' son, young Henry."

"And Stephen, too, has sons. Tell me, what sort of men will these young princes make?"

"My lord, they are both young. Eustace, the eldest, is not yet fifteen. And therefore wild, not caring for affairs of state."

"And Henry Anjou, is he not also young?"

"Yes, young, but raised to be a king, so I have heard, ambitious and well schooled."

"Then would it not be better, Brother Canterbury"—Eugenius leaned forward, placing his hand upon the other's arm—"for England, for the Church, if this young man were on the throne—rather than Stephen's brood?"

"It would, my lord."

"Why then, we shall remember this, we two—and act upon it when occasion comes to act!"

The news of all that had occurred at Rheims came swiftly to the king in England and it shook the throne. More fighting man than diplomat, Stephen swept aside the cautions of his courtiers concerning excommunication and gave way to unconsidered wrath. By royal edict he condemned the archbishop to exile and seized all the Canterbury lands, giving them out to friends of his to farm. And only after that he thought to send his own commissioners to plead for him before the Curia.

Thus when the archbishop set foot again on English soil, and even while he still stood swaying with the motion of his boat upon the landing place at Sandwich, he was confronted by the king's justiciar, Richard de Luci. When he observed him there, the royal standard by him and his guard behind, Theobald knew before he spoke what he had come to say. Nevertheless he raised his hand in benediction saying, "God be with you, Richard. Welcome."

"Not so, my lord," de Luci said, his voice compassionate but his face stern. "The king bids you leave England. Your lands are confiscate and you are no more welcome here."

There was a silence while the archbishop looked with deceptive smiling eyes at the justiciar. And Richard, swayed by pity, dropped his formal role and stepping forward bent to speak into his ear. He would do well, he said, to step again into the very boat by which he came and quit the country while there was still time, and from his own purse gave him money that he might sustain himself abroad.

Theobald already knew where Pope Eugenius would stand. And he knew, therefore, that King Stephen once again had erred, playing from weakness as he so often did, discounting Theobald's strong influence on the Curia.

Therefore he only asked: "And my companions?"

"The king is not concerned with them," de Luci said. "They have their choice—to go with you or to remain."

Theobald turned to those who stood by him. "I will take Thomas with me now, the rest of you may follow as I have need of you." Thomas he chose because he was the strongest horseman and he had a mission for him to ride speedily ahead with letters of petition to the pope, "adding your own words, Thomas, as you think best, when you have gauged the temper of the cardinals."

De Luci, seeing Thomas' eager face, was touched. He too had loved adventure as a youth. So while the archbishop spoke to the others of his following, each one in turn, he took the younger man aside.

"Though I am loyal to the king," he said, "I am not bound to hinder you. The king is a true knight and gentle with his enemies. Therefore I may tell you that we have had news the pope has just these few days since left Paris and is on his way to Brescia. If you are fast, which I am told you are, it may be you can overtake him there." Then, cutting off all thanks, he added dryly that the prelates loyal to the king preceded him by several days. "They left the king in London when I did. And I have waited for you here some time."

"How long a journey is it," Thomas asked, "London to Brescia?"

"London to Rome takes seven weeks as I account it," de Luci answered. "But some say if you travel fast and kill your horses you can accomplish it in four."

"And Brescia is how far short of Rome?"

"By which account?"

"The latter," Thomas said earnestly.

"A week, perhaps—killing your horses," de Luci smiled, "if not yourself."

Now Thomas thanked him, smiling that eager, all-devouring smile that made so many friends. And the justiciar, acknowledging the debt, looked to the future with the thought he might have made a good investment.

Thomas left the archbishop at St. Omer and traveled through the villages and farms and the deep forest lands of Europe, starting each day at Lauds and stopping for Compline after the long-fading twilights of the early summer, procuring fresh horses as he could find them from the archbishop's friends along the way.

On reaching Brescia he was made welcome by the pope for Theobald's sake and there, for the first time, tried out his eloquence before the Curia, asking permission to place England under interdict unless the Canterbury properties were all restored and restitution made. His plea was granted. And in addition the pope promised that if this was not done by Michaelmas he would carry out his threat to excommunicate the king.

Theobald, at St. Omer, blessed Thomas for his speed and for the news he brought. Straightway he sent instructions for the interdict to all the English bishops: No more would Mass be said in any English church, would baptisms or marriage take place within the precincts, would the last rites be given to the dying or services be held to speed the dead to heaven. Thus would all England suffer till the king relent.

So spoke the pope from Italy, the archbishop from France. The bishops were in England and their allegiance torn. They found many ways to circumvent the order. Only in Canterbury was the interdict observed. And even here Prior Sylvester of St. Augustine's—long jealous of Christchurch—led a revolt among the monks and still presumed to celebrate the Mass.

The roads were busy now—London to Brescia to St. Omer—

with letters and petitions to the pope from England's bishops and from Theobald, with bribes and promises from Stephen. But as the summer ended and Michaelmas drew near the king thought longer thoughts about the papal threat. And Theobald, as well, grew weary. In mid-September he crossed quietly to England, taking Thomas with him. There, in the friendly castle Framlingham, he called his Church about him. One by one the English bishops came to beg his pardon and make peace. And as the time grew short the king relented and restored his lands.

On Michaelmas the sun was golden on the unkempt fields and on the gilded turrets of the cathedral church as Theobald rode into Canterbury to the sound of bells and cheering and the chanting of exultimus at Christchurch. Only at St. Augustine's, as Thomas noted who rode close behind, the bells were silent.

Prior Sylvester was to be flogged. He took his punishment with equanimity, but there were others whose rebellious spirits were not put down so easily. Elured Porre, the moneyer, who saw injustice in the very rising of the sun to shine on some (those who were in the fields at dawn) more warmly than on others (who were in the forge) cried out as though he felt the lash himself.

"There's justice for you, Walter. See and remember." He sat astride his low workbench examining a silver cup which had been brought to him for mending and lectured to his son.

Walter was eighteen now, a man. Thin, wiry, less than average height, he was more noticed for the hump between his shoulders than for his face that could have given more observant people than his neighbors pause and delight in the clear beauty of the human mind. Not that his face was comely: his eyes were hazel, small, deep set; his nose was large. But on it were the planes and lines already molded by a deep perception tempered with humor. He had that rarest combination, wit without malice.

He smiled a little wryly now. "You taught me as a baby, Father, never to look for justice . . ."

"Don't interrupt. I'm telling you things that you ought to know. You see here the archbishop's justice. What is it? Nothing. Injustice! Then there's the justice of the king. We tasted *that* while the archbishop was away. What of God's justice, you may say?"

Walter said nothing.

"Here is God's justice: some are punished, others go

untouched. Some are hardworking, others do no work. Some are born healthy, others are crippled. . . ." Elured stopped. Then in a changed and lowered voice he ended: "There is no justice. That is all I meant to say."

Thomas was a man of great importance to the archbishop these days. On their return from exile he had been rewarded with the livings from two of the Christchurch holdings: from the wealthy church at Otford and from the smaller parish, Certeham, as well. The incomes that these brought seemed luxury to him who had been used to the small stipend of the clerk, and to receive them he had been admitted into the lower orders of the Church. He was a lector now.

His duties in relation to his holdings took no time. He must see to it that the local priest was competent and that the rents and taxes came to him on time, no more. But since these were his first preferments he was conscientious; he rode out to see each one in turn.

It was a cold spring morning, early, when he went to Certeham and he had with him several friends. They took good horses and a pair of hounds, for hunting on the way, and Thomas carried on his wrist an excellent peregrine. He wore a riding cloak of rich dark wool, furred at the sleeves and neck and with an underjerkin also furred, for being thin he felt the cold more keenly than most men. Around his waist he had a leather girdle studded with colored stones and at his neck a silver clasp the archbishop had given him. But it was his bearing and the way he sat his horse and held the hawk, rather than the clothes he had put on, that made the villeins by the road stop and look up at him.

About two miles from Ridingate they turned off Stonestreet as they had been directed and took the track through the scrub forest down toward the Stour. Ahead they saw a wooden bridge and to their left a little way the peaked roof of a mill, but budding trees cut off their view of any houses near.

"Could that be Certeham?" Thomas looked around. But no one knew.

The trees grew thinner and now, through them, they could see a line of gray-thatched huts between cleared fields. A little manor house scarce larger than the huts stood in a court surrounded by a wattle fence with its gate open to the road. Thomas looked for a church but there was none. Could this be Certeham? It was not much and he was disappointed.

Some villeins worked the fields far off but he saw no one in the manor yard except two little children running to hide behind the fence at their approach.

"Children, where is this?" he called in English, reining his horse. There was no answer.

"Is this Certeham?" his voice was loud and tinged with irritation, for it was a foolish situation and his companions laughed.

No answer, so he rode his horse up close beside the fence and, looking down, saw two small heads, one tangled, very dark, that of a little girl, the other smooth and brown. The children did not move but like small frightened animals crouched quivering, their eyes fixed straight ahead.

"Children," he said more quietly, "from where I am I could pour boiling oil or other things upon your heads. . . ." The men behind him laughed. "So you had better answer me. Now tell me. What is the name of this place?"

The little girl looked up. Her eyes were round and snapping black. She stared at him until she saw that he might speak again, and then she drew a breath. "Hortone," she said in a small voice.

"What?"

"Hortone," she repeated, staring. Furtively she nudged her brother who had begun to cry.

"How far is Certeham?" Thomas persisted.

She raised her arm and pointed, still with her eyes fixed on his face. "Over there," she whispered.

"How far?"

"A little ways."

He dropped a penny to her but she did not move. He saw her brother scramble to take it from the ground and then look up. His head was tipped so far back on his little neck it made his mouth hang open, and his eyes were wide and wondering. Thomas saw the tears form in them and was sorry.

"Thank you. I shall be always in your debt," he said with formal grace. Then he swung back to his companions and went on.

The children waited till they heard the sound of hoofs and creaking leather die out along the road. Then Hawisa reached out and took the penny from her brother's hand.

"Why are you crying now?" she asked him, for he often cried.

He did not answer, simply looked at her with the tears swimming in his large gray eyes.

"Here"—she held out the penny—"you may hold it half the time."

Still Almon looked at her, his vision blurred.

"Doesn't that make you happy, Almon?" she asked anxiously.

For answer he said only: "Was that God?"

Hawisa shrugged impatiently. Almon, at this stage in his life—he was just five years old—seemed always to be watching out for God. "Oh, Almon," she said scornfully. "That was a man."

She did not remember that it was she who had put such ideas into the infant Almon's head some few years back and that she too had suffered from such trembling hopes and fears. The difference was that Hawisa had looked for fairies everywhere. She had talked about them to him many times, for from his second year, when Almon could just barely walk, she had been given care of him. And all the thoughts that formed in her bright mind—she knew not how—she handed on to him while he sat stolidly hunched in her lap or on the ground beside her under the fruit trees while she tossed pebbles from a sling to keep the birds away.

"God lives up above us, Almon. Father Lambert says so," she had told him with her fingers busy fitting the pebbles to the sling. Then: "Fairies live down below the earth in little huts.

"God wears bright-colored clothes with jewels and feathers like the pictures in the church. Fairies are ugly. They wear little pointed hats. I hate them."

The fairies were more real than God to Hawisa when she was little. But with Almon, hearing the words and forming hazy pictures in his mind, not really comprehending and never to remember how he had known these things, it was the other way around. God was more real.

Thomas rode on to Certeham and met the parish priest, a conscientious man who farmed his little plot of land and said the Mass and knew the secrets of the villagers and brought in all the money due to Christchurch regularly. His name was Lambert and he was a local man. No one had any fault to find with him and Thomas was well satisfied. Therefore he did not listen when the priest spoke to the woman who was sweeping out the church, calling her "wife." He chose to think this was a general term, as one might call an old man "uncle" whom he hardly knew.

He and his friends had supper at the manor house of Certeham with Haimo the Falconer and saw the little mews. Then in the fading twilight they rode home again. He was delighted with his little parish lying snug among its fields between the scrubby forest and the river running by. He would have gone there often, so he said, but Theobald had other plans for him.

CHAPTER XI

HE WHO MAKES his son a lawyer fashions a mighty weapon against his enemies and a machine to help his friends.' " Archbishop Theobald looked up from reading this and smiled at Thomas. "Do you recognize the words?"

"The thought is surely that of Master Vacarius; he often said the same," Thomas replied.

"A man like him," Theobald nodded. "A teacher of the Roman law at Auxerre."

Then he put the letter down and stared at Thomas, closely examining his face. "Thomas, I shall make of you that son, that strong machine," he said. "These days we all have need of such."

It was a somber time for Theobald and all the Church, for news had come to them this summer of 1149 that the great crusade against the infidel had failed. The noble armies, scattered and demoralized, were drifting back to Europe—all but the King of France who lingered in Jerusalem, avoiding all responsibilities.

"Therefore I have decided," continued Theobald, "that you shall go to Auxerre in a month, when the schools open. I shall see to it that you are well supplied."

Again he paused and studied Thomas' face before he said: "And now you have my leave to go."

Thomas rose and would have left the room but Theobald called him back. "Thomas," he smiled, but tears were in his eyes, "do not forget us in your new adventures."

"Father," Thomas knelt and took the old man's hands. "Father, I am yours and at your service always. No matter when. No matter where."

"Yes, I know that," the archbishop said gently. "And I will call you when I need you."

Thomas had been in Auxerre less than a month when John of Salisbury knocked upon his door. He had brought secret letters from the pope to Abbot Suger, the strong man of France who held the throne for Louis while the king was on crusade. The abbot was expected any moment in Auxerre. And while he waited for him John spent his time with his old friend from Paris.

At first they talked of old times and of mutual friends. But then they talked, as all Churchmen were talking now, about the failure of the great crusade and what this meant for France. John, indeed, was very close to this. The letters he had brought concerned it, and they were written in his own hand at the pope's dictation.

"And I can tell you this much," John said quietly, "in private, for your ears alone. His Holiness is much concerned the king and queen should stay together, man and wife. He is strong set against divorce. It would shake France."

"The Church leans hard on France," Thomas agreed.

"It does," said John. He shook his head as in dismay. "I must confess, it is beyond my understanding why God should let the French—who of all people in the world have deepest faith and do most honor to Him—why He should let them be destroyed by His most bitter enemies."

"You think the French might really be destroyed because they failed against the infidel?"

"I see it this way," John said. And he went back again over the history, how when Edessa fell nearly five years earlier Pope Eugenius, although beset by enemies himself, called first on France to save the Holy Land and how King Louis in his piety was first to take up arms, and Abbot Bernard left his cell, reluctantly, preached the crusade with all his fire and eloquence and won the Germans and their emperor . . . "The best of Christendom, the strongest, all went forth, bearing the cross . . ."

"Yes," Thomas interrupted. "But isn't this the point? Were they indeed a holy army? Or were they, as so many say, merely a horde of warring factions set against each other in their jealousies and with their hearts fixed on the hope of plunder rather than God's glory?"

"Perhaps," John nodded, "though I would except King Louis."

"Ah, yes. The king. But in his case may we not point to treachery among our allies—both in Byzantium and Palestine? I've heard the Prince of Antioch himself hindered rather than helped the cause of Christendom. And I don't even mention Antioch's personal treachery to his guest the king in his relations with the queen."

"Perhaps," John said again. "But Abbot Bernard blames no single man or group of men. He speaks of all humanity. He writes that these are evil times and that it almost seems to him the Lord has been provoked so by our sins that he is judging all of us before the time—the final Judgment—and with justice, but forgetful of His mercy."

Thomas' face had taken on a very somber look. "Yes, I heard that. 'Forgetful of His mercy!' Could it be that God would judge us so?"

"No, but Thomas," John said, "that is the abbot speaking. The pope takes no such pessimistic view. Surely the crusade failed; surely the king did wrong to linger so, a full year, in Jerusalem when all the whole world knew the impact of his failure and when his land stood leaderless . . ."

"Yes, that's my point," said Thomas. "Why did he do that?"

"Ah, why. Perhaps you may be right," John said. "Perhaps it was the queen and the trouble with the queen. He had to carry her by force from Antioch, you know, and he was never one for force, being so close to Godly counsel . . . But let me tell you how the pope views this. *He* does not throw his hands up, blaming God . . ."

"Neither does Bernard," Thomas said sharply.

John raised his hands and smiled apologies. "No," he said placatingly, "I know. Neither does Abbot Bernard. But His Holiness has set himself to save what may be saved and does not speak of such calamities." Again he checked his friend, still smiling, and continued:

"Let me tell you what the pope has done. You know the king and queen came separately to Tusculum where the pope stays, having been parted from each other in their ships by storms and pirates and all manner of trials. They came exhausted and dispirited. I saw them and I could not help but pity them. And the queen talked repeatedly of only one thing: of divorce.

"I tell you it was wonderful to watch the pope in this contingency. He was benevolent but firm with them. He listened to their grievances and then he told them, in the name of God and for the sake of France, what they must do. With his own hands he made a bed for them—spread it with his own brocades and furs—and told them they must sleep together, sharing the couch. They had not done this for some months, I understand."

"And they complied?"

"They did. Indeed, the king was eager—almost to tears."

"He needs a son," said Thomas. "Only one child—and that a girl—in almost thirteen years. There is a shaky reed on which to build succession to the throne!"

"But it was more than that," John said. "The king was like some green, infatuated boy. Thomas, I was amazed to see him so enamored, so enslaved, after so much has happened."

"And the queen?"

"Oh, the queen spoke again of consanguinity. They are distant cousins somehow related, as you know; that is the ground on which she seeks divorce. But, privately, I think that she is angry simply because the king took her from Antioch so ignominiously—as though he didn't trust her with the prince her uncle."

"With reason," Thomas interposed.

"Perhaps. But I can see it must have hurt her pride. She spoke of her position as a leader on crusade, chief of her own contingent and all that. . . ."

"Yes, I remember," Thomas said. "Dressed like a man. She went out on crusade an Amazon—and now returns a whore."

John laughed. "Well, she complied at any rate; they are together once again. And they will be here soon. They left Tusculum for Rome when I left to come here."

King Louis and Queen Eleanor stayed long enough in Rome to tour the apostolic shrines and kneel before each one. It was a tour the king enjoyed, if not the queen. And then they traveled through the passes of the Alps and entered France —just thirty months since they had left it in the cause of God.

At Auxerre they conferred with Abbot Suger, secretly, for as the regent he had private information that he wished to give the king before he entered Paris once again and took the throne. It was a shaky throne just now and he must mount it swiftly for a firm seat.

But all went well. The royal couple crossed the Seine to sounds of clamoring bells and shouting in the streets, and the flags flew to welcome them. The king, quite overcome, wept tears of joy; Queen Eleanor was less happy to be home.

It was November when they came. The winter drew on fast. All the dark months the queen kept to herself, indoors, remembering the heat and color of crusade, the high adventures and the gallant men of her own company. The bloom of southern suns which so became her lustrous coloring soon faded from her face and left it pale. She was, indeed, with child, and heavily so, taking no pride or pleasure from it. Daily the sound of plainsong drifted to her from the monasteries down below and nightly her patient husband filled her ears with everlasting counsel.

"I thought that I had wed a king," she once broke out, "but find that I am married to a monk!"

Louis bore all with patience, hoping that somehow things would right themselves or that a prince born of their union would cement it and bring joy to France.

But when the child was born it was a girl, a second princess, cruel joke of fate.

The year went by, another winter and another spring. With summer came a visitor, belated, to pay homage to the king. Geoffrey Plantagenet, Count of Anjou, should have renewed his fealty to France when Louis first returned, but he was a wayward nobleman and there were feuds between him and his overlord. Now he found it in his interest to come and bring his young son Henry with him, for he had made Henry duke of Normandy and needed royal confirmation of the investiture.

Thus they came as vassals to the Frankish court, ready to bend the knee and place their hands between the royal palms. But if one saw them—let us say a listless queen feeling herself a captive in her high room—as they came riding through the gates, their knights and squires following, their banners flashing and their bonnets sprigged with yellow broom, one might have thought they were two kings arriving at some castle of their own.

The Count of Anjou had the name "Geoffrey the Fair." He was a handsome, dashing, willful man and he would catch the eye of any lady as he rode by. But his young son was something more. Henry was eighteen and a belted knight, son of a count but also of an empress, Matilda. He was a duke, but more important he was pretender to the English throne. From infancy he had been raised to be a king. This showed in him.

Although his face was not so fair as Geoffrey's and his frame more powerful than tall, although his whole demeanor was more restless, pent with unused energies, than regally deliberate, and though his mind was quick and curious rather than grave, he had in him the essence of a king. He had been born so, trained so, and he saw it in his destiny.

He rode now like a centaur on his stallion with his thick legs melting to its sides, his broad back straight, his rough and callused hands gentle upon the reins. His face was open, courteous, and his gray eyes took in all that there was to see. One would not know, except by reputation, that those eyes were capable of bloodshot rage and this firm body could convulse with passion, rolling and kicking on the floor. Eleanor had heard. She smiled a little, looking down, and turned and called for mirrors and her new embroidered robe.

She was a woman whose great beauty lay not so much in rounded features or the warm coloring of the south as in her quick intelligence and passionate heart. Trained in the southern school to elegance and taste, to sing the songs of troubadours as well as to read Latin, and to ride a destrier as well as to preside with wit over a royal table, she led men by her charms as naturally as other women followed.

When she had married, as a girl of fifteen, she was already formed and educated. Now, after fourteen years as Duchess of Aquitaine and Queen of France, and after two years spent in all the fascinating cities of the East, some of the bloom was gone, some of the softness from the rounded cheek, but all the charm remained. And it was heightened by the glamour of sophistication.

Geoffrey knew her story very well, and something of her discontent. During his stay at court he ventured to speak to her alone. They sat together, side by side, in the warm garden on a marble bench and, after he had flattered her and she had laughed at him, he mentioned cautiously his son's position as the Duke of Normandy, heir to Anjou, heir to Maine, and claimant to the English throne. She did not speak but fixed her eyes on his until he dropped them to his hand that rested on the bench between them. Drawing it toward him, with the fingers spread as though he drew a map, he murmured softly: "England. The Channel." Here his finger drew a line. "Normandy," his hand was spread once more and lightly drawing southward. "Maine. Anjou." Then he looked again into her eyes and whispered as his hand continued: "Aquitaine." The hand had traversed all the bench—from north to south, if one could see it as a map—leaving scant room for France.

The queen said nothing but Count Geoffrey knew from her slight flush and quickly lidded eyes that the idea of new alliance had struck deep.

This was the month of August of 1151. In September Geoffrey and Henry took their leave of Paris with the king's Godspeed and rode for Angers, the count's capital. But softly and unseen another rode with them, invisible, unwanted, least expected by this strong ambitious pair of men. The third who rode with them was Death. He overtook them at the river Loire where Geoffrey suddenly was seized with chills and fever, lay for three days ill, and to his own amazement and his son's, on the third day gave up his life.

Henry, Duke of Normandy, pretender to the English throne, was now as well the Count of Anjou-Maine. And furthermore he was possessed of all his father's schemes for Aquitaine.

Queen Eleanor for her part laid her plans for freedom from her husband—using her doting husband's aid. Even as Henry, carrying his father's body, rode for Le Mans to bury it, the King and Queen of France left Paris for their last progress together through their southern lands. They spent their winter there and in the spring they said goodbye and Louis rode back lonely to his capital while Eleanor remained.

The pope had done all that he could for Louis. Suger was dead. Abbot Bernard, long set against the match, sent comfortable words to Paris from his cell: "Good riddance." Nothing was left but the formalities.

The date set for the synod was the twenty-first of March, 1152. The Archbishop of Sens presided. The church of the king's castle Beaugency, near Orléans, was the site. From here the king could return north to Paris while the duchess could withdraw southwest to Poitiers in her own domain. The charge, brought by the king as prearranged, was consanguinity: Louis and Eleanor were within the prohibited cousinship of fourth degree.

The king asked that the two small princesses might be declared legitimate and that they be awarded to the crown. This was agreed. The duchess asked that her domains, as she possessed them before marriage, be returned to her. She would, of course, remain a loyal vassal to the king. This also all agreed. And so they were divorced and the decree of separation read aloud to all the company.

The duchess and her little entourage withdrew from Beaugency. The court, the bishops, all the highest men of France came rallying round the king to say that all was for the best. The thing was done. And none among them could foresee what it would bring about.

In her high room of the old tower Maubergeonne, that lofty keep that rose above her castle city of Poitiers, the Duchess Eleanor sat with her sister Petronilla while her ladies dressed her. The liquid sun of May came through the pointed door that led onto the ramparts, and the sky about them, filled with little twittering birds, was blue. Already in the seven weeks that she had been at home the duchess' cheek had taken on a golden glow and the old castle had been brought to life. Her vassals came, great noblemen in their own rights, to do her homage. And the Churchmen of her large domain came also, with advice. But those who gave her court the color and the character reflecting hers were the young poets and romantic troubadours who brought their songs of love and the fair ladies of high birth who bloomed in this new atmosphere of chivalry.

"What will you wear to meet him?" Petronilla asked. The younger sister, smaller, darker, even more headstrong than the duchess, reveled in Eleanor's bold scheme. "What will you wear?"

Eleanor sat musing. "The green I think," she said indifferently.

"Will he notice? Is he the sort who cares?"

"I wonder. I think not. His father would have cared."

"Why do you fuss then?" Petronilla glanced with envy at the corner where the duchess' robes hung from their poles to lose their creases in the air. Like some bizarre and vari-colored army on the march they followed each one close upon the next: soft mossy wools with golden threads, silks from the Orient, brocades.

"Why fuss?" the duchess murmured, catching her sister's glance. "No, not because he cares or doesn't care. Because I care." She smiled and turned away.

Her waiting women brought a bowl of water so she could wash her hands, and then the perfumes for her limbs. She rose and let her robe fall and stood naked while they dressed her in her linen under skirt, her inner robe of saffron colored silk bound from the wrist to elbow with gold cords, her outer wide-sleeved robe of cypress green, her rings and bracelets and jeweled girdle for her waist. She wound this twice about her and smoothed down her robe so that it hung correctly, showing the curve of her small breasts and the long gently swelling line from waist to hip. Satisfied, she kicked the train behind her and sat down again and called for mirrors. Then with both hands she squeezed her hair back from her forehead and above her ears.

"Why do you do that?" Petronilla asked. "You look like a man."

The duchess did not smile. "Sometimes I think I am a man," she said.

She stared again into the mirror and took from her woman's hands the fine white square of lawn that was her wimple, holding it gingerly on outspread fingers over her head.

About her wimple Eleanor was most particular. She held it floating and then placed it very gently so that one corner hung down longer than the others, over the left sleeve, like a soft caress upon the stiff green of her robe. Then she quickly took a little tuck in each side, by her temples, while her woman placed a small gold coronet upon her brow.

The golden circlet gleamed. The wimple fell as flattering as candlelight beside her cheeks. She tilted back her chin and turned her head from side to side, her eyes fixed on her image, pleased when the wimple floated free to show the line of cheek and neck as firm and supple still as in her youth. She plucked two matching pendants from the tray and put them in her ears and with a practiced motion set her rings and bracelets straight. And then at last she turned and looked at Petronilla.

"Now you see me," she said soberly, spreading her arms wide, "like a man full armored. I am ready."

She had timed it well. It was not long before the duke came riding, as his messengers had promised, into the courtyard far below. The sound of hoofs, the horn, the yap of dogs and the deep voices of the men rose to her window but she did not stir. The seneschal had his instructions; he would greet her guests. When all was set and ready for her, when they were waiting, then would she go, descending the long winding stairway into the hall.

But what was this? Hardly a pause, and feet upon the stairs! The seneschal came in, red in the face, "My lady . . ." but he had not time. The women, snatching up discarded clothing, backed to the corner, to the chest, and stuffed things in while Petronilla stood beside the window giggling. Only the duchess, having risen, stood quite still.

The duke was here. He stopped inside the doorway long enough to look at Eleanor from golden circlet down to little pointed shoe, an avid look. She felt a blush come to her face, a long-forgotten flutter of the heart and sickly sweet confusion. A thought, hysterical, came to her mind that this rash boy intended to snatch her up.

But Henry, though he might have waited in the hall, was versed enough in etiquette. He bowed and called her cousin, said the proper words. Then he stepped forward, took her hand, and with formality embraced her, drawing her to him with his hard arm to bestow the kiss of greeting on her mouth. The Duchess Eleanor responded with grave formality.

And yet his body close to hers—how young!—felt like a kitchen fire.

Henry had little time to spare. His newly acquired lands needed his presence and the affairs of England grew more perilous. King Stephen was negotiating even now for sanction from the pope to have his son crowned king and undisputed heir to England. Also Henry knew the duchess could not long be left alone. Her trip from Beaugency to Poitiers showed the risk: twice was she ambushed by young nobles eager for her person and her lands—once by King Stephen's nephew, once by his own rash younger brother Geoffrey—and twice she had escaped. He did not think it wise to wait a third attempt.

Four days of preparation for the duchess, for it was imperative the wedding be attended by men of the Church who could forestall some later charge of consanguinity and by some powerful vassals who could raise an army should the need arise; four days for hawking through the countryside for Henry, seeing how the land lay, how the peasants looked, for he could not abide to sit and wait, and on the fifth day, in the morning, they were wed.

The dinner afterward was sumptuous and long. The poets and the troubadours of all Provence had gathered at the lovely duchess' court. All the long afternoon they spoke their exquisite verses until the light had faded and the candles cast their wavering glow on all the dreaming faces of the guests. Then the duke and duchess rose from their high chairs set side by side, bid all good night, and left. Softly, heads bent to watch their feet upon the shadowy stairs, the duchess lifting up her robe, the duke's rough hands hung limply at his sides, the bride and groom ascended to that lofty room where the wide bridal bed was laid. There, all alone, they stood and faced each other, looking each other in the eye, and understood each other well.

That morning Eleanor had spent two hours with four ladies donning her wedding robes. That night, lost in her husband's eyes, she spent three minutes casting them upon the floor. In doing so, for the first time in all her thirty years she fell in love. In Henry youth, excitement, ardor and ambition were all mingled in a hot emotion which, for the moment, took the guise of love.

Thus was the marriage consummated. And the union shook the world.

The court in France cried out in horrified recoil. King Louis' holy wise advisers, in agreeing to set free the queen, had carefully examined all contingencies but this. But who, they asked each other now, could have foreseen this bold stroke from the boyish Duke of Normandy? What of his oath of fealty so lately sworn? What of the duchess' duty as a vassal to seek the king's permission to remarry? And what of consanguinity?

Louis, dumfounded, asked no questions such as these. He only saw with chilling clarity that overnight his once-beloved wife lay with another man and that the map of Europe had changed face. The newly combined lands of Anjou-Aquitaine added to Normandy had given his young and ambitious vassal territories more than equal to his own. Honor demanded that he seek redress and dutifully he launched his armies against Normandy. But when the duke appeared like lightning from the west to give him battle, he fell sick with fever, turned and left the field. A truce was made between the two, the doubtful deed accepted as a fact, and history proceeded on its way.

* * *

Thomas had spent the winter in Auxerre, and in the spring, when men turn to the open roads and pilgrimage, he went to Italy. He had suffered from the cold that winter but the warmth that lured him south was not that of the sun that warms the body only; it was the rising sun of the new study of Church law that glowed among the red bricks of the ancient city of Bologna. Two years before a monk of this same city, Franciscus Gratianus, had published to the world his vast and systematic treatise on the rulings of the Church from the first dawn of Christian history. The news of it had thrown a ray of light into the darkest cloisters and the most obscure cathedral schools, drawing scholars and inquiring clerics to its source. Thomas was likewise drawn and with the archbishop's permission left Auxerre for Bologna.

He found the city was awash with foreign scholars. Within the walls the streets were crowded almost beyond endurance and the air was thick with dust. Men of all nations passed and repassed each other, sweat on their sour faces, elbows pushing.

Thomas withdrew and left his horse and mules outside the town and then through inquiry from the Confederation of the English Scholars found the place where his old Canterbury teacher, Master Vacarius, lived and taught. Through him he was admitted to the cloister where Brother Gratian himself discoursed on canon law as well as to the lecture halls of other masters like himself, not so revered as the great scholar-monk but able teachers of his profession.

This was a serious time for Thomas. There were no drinking bouts, few jokes and little singing in the streets as there had been in Paris. The students for the most part were men of his own age and position, Churchmen of rank and of a sober, cold ambition. For them an education at Bologna meant a furtherance of their careers. They had a year or two—and they were conscious of the fleeting time—to make themselves that newest breed of men, the legalists of the Church.

Only in summer did the work let up. Then Thomas left the city for the freedom of the roads. Once he went to Tusculum, for John was there and many other Englishmen as well, and there was business he could do for Theobald. But when the fall came he returned to study and the staid companionship of students like himself.

One day soon after Lady Day, in March 1152, a letter came from the archbishop full of affairs of state and with a grave commission for "his dear son Thomas." It was a welcome letter for the schools were closing soon, and out beyond the window and the crowded roofs cuckoos were calling and the hills were turning green.

The news that Theobald wrote was that King Stephen, anxious to have his young son Eustace succeed him on the throne, was seeking the pope's sanction to have him crowned while he, the father, was yet strong enough to see the ceremony through. "For this matter of succession is precarious indeed, as none knows better than the king. Was he himself not the first to break his oath to old King Henry that he would support the Empress Matilda on her father's death? Such oaths to uncrowned princelings have no meaning for him now . . ."

Especially, thought Thomas, now that Matilda's son has grown to be a man. Therefore, the letter said, King Stephen had required the archbishop to crown the prince, as was the ancient right of Canterbury. But Theobald had pled he could not act in this without the acquiescence of the pope—and he recalled to Thomas what he and Eugenius had agreed at Rheims: that they would favor Anjou for the English throne over King Stephen's House of Blois.

Now came the urgent portion of the news: Stephen had sent the Archbishop of York to Tusculum to plead his cause. The party even now was on the road. And York, as Thomas knew, was ever jealous of the rights of Canterbury and would himself crown Eustace if he could sway the Curia to Stephen's side. Thomas must ride to Tusculum without delay and use his eloquence in Canterbury's cause and that of Anjou.

The cocks were crowing and the donkeys braying the early dawn when Thomas left his rooms and made his way out of the city and, with a lightness of the heart like that of early youth, rode down the old familiar way beyond the city walls and then branched south and took the road to Rome.

He came to Tusculum in early April and for a week he argued before the Curia against the Archbishop of York who pled for Eustace's coronation. Wisely, he did not mention, other than to the pope in private audience, the cause of Anjou. He only cited precedent, and Stephen's history of quarrels with the Church, and the uncertain claims of the whole House of Blois and other matters of this sort. But like the good and faithful servant of the parable he took his master's interest to heart and added to it from the store of his enthusiasm and imagination. The cause of Anjou suddenly became for him the cause of God and the young duke the hapless victim of an Evil Power. Fired by this, he took each cardinal apart and joked with those who liked to laugh or discoursed seriously with those whose pride was in their learning, and on some others when he had sounded them, he spent wealth of Canterbury as he was authorized to do.

By these means, and through the predilection of the pope, the Curia was swayed to favor Canterbury over York. "The Church can never sanction Stephen's coronation of his son," they said, "since it appears he seized the kingdom for himself contrary to the oath he took before the Church."

With this achieved Thomas set off for home to take the word to Theobald. As he rode northward over the plains of Rome, the rocky hills of Tuscany, the mountain passes where the wildflowers rimmed the melting snow, he reassessed the shift of royal power in which he had a hand. What he had urged upon the cardinals were his own true beliefs. Stephen had sinned in breaking his oath to God, therefore he forfeited his right to dynasty. Matilda . . . he hesitated, looking back, remembering her as she sat high upon her throne while he knelt down below with Osbert Huit-deniers . . . Matilda, woman, full of the sin of pride, had forfeited her right to rule—even though she was the daughter of an honorable king and mother of a son as honorable . . .

This brought his thoughts to the young duke. Young Henry, grandson of the old, born of an awkward union, destined to be brought to England time and again in boyhood only to witness how his mother failed to hold her throne, only to return to Normandy each time in ignominy . . . Thus had the boy been tested under the eye of God. And now God through His Church—and he, Thomas of London, the instrument—was seeing justice done. The boy would be raised up; the Church would raise him. And the humility that he had learned while the usurper wore his crown would make him open to instruction from the Church.

With this thought Thomas smiled a little wryly to himself. Humility was a virtue he had trouble nurturing within himself. Yet, now that he looked at it in this way, it was of all the virtues most to be commended in a man of power.

The trip was easy, and his thoughts, running over the affairs of state that he had entered once again, were pleasant, self-congratulatory. He reached the Channel at Boulogne after six weeks upon the road and took up lodgings at a quayside inn to wait a boat. It was the twenty-fifth of May. And it was here, amid the smells of salt and fish, the cry of seagulls in the air, he heard the news—for it had traveled up from Poitiers even faster than had he—that Henry, Duke of Normandy, had married Eleanor of Aquitaine.

He heard it first as gossip and was angry in his disbelief. He heard it next as fact. It was as though a friend had snatched a proffered gift and laughed and thrown it in his face.

He was a fool to think that he could make and unmake kings! In one bold cynical stroke Henry had done more for himself than all the loving plans that he, the archbishop, even the pope had done. This is the world of kings; he should have known, should have remembered what he had learned with Osbert Huit-deniers. It was a world not meant for him. I will not work for kings again, he said.

CHAPTER XII

THOMAS THE ARCHDEACON was holding court on the north porch of the archbishop's palace in the Christchurch precincts, Canterbury. He heard the urgent whisper in his ear and felt the cold cheek of the messenger tremble against his own. The man had dashed into the courtyard reining his horse so tightly that it backed and sidled through the gate and splashed the water of the puddles onto the petitioners who waited there.

Thomas, sitting in his carved wood chair upon the high stone-pillared porch to hear the cases that were brought before him saw it all below. The western sun of the late afternoon just topped the walls enough to touch his hands and face with a last hint of warmth but in the court the crowd stood in the shadows of the cold October dusk. He saw the horse, the rider, the movement of the crowd as he came through. Then, as the intruder put his foot upon the stair, he saw his face and recognized him, knew his name—Arnold, a lay brother from St. Martin's Priory in Dover.

The man came slowly up the stairs because his legs would not support him faster, but his gaze ran on before as though to tell the news straight out from eye to eye. Full of his message, he was unaware his hands shook from the killing ride or that his lips puffed rhythmically, blowing the air against his beard. He came and fell upon his knees, his eyes still fixed on Thomas' searchingly.

"Archdeacon Thomas?" he asked hoarsely.

"Arnold, you know that I am he. What is your news?" He took his hands and drew him close, bending his head to listen. He heard the panting breath against his face and heard the whispered words: "The king is dead."

King Stephen dead! It seemed to Thomas that he had known this since he first heard the urgent clatter of the hoofs outside the gate and seen the wheeling horse.

"Dead," he repeated. "Where?"

"At Dover Castle."

"When?"

"About the time of Nones."

And it was not yet Vespers! He rose and gently pushed the messenger into his chair to rest.

Then to the crowd below he said in a loud voice: "This court is ended for the day." And to his clerk: "Take the petitions that have not been heard and I will give them ear tomorrow at the same time. And ask the cellerer to feed this man and give him lodging for the night."

The whispered words from mouth to ear, "the king is dead," were secret. There was no wind within the court to carry them away, nor were there eavesdroppers behind the chair to overhear. And yet as though the very pillars of the steps had caught them up and passed them, one to the other down the stairs until they reached the ground, the crowd below buzzed with the words: "The king! Did he say king? The king has died. Is dead."

Wulviva, standing in the crowd in matronly gray wool and dangling kerchief, felt the news as much as heard it. She was not one to notice cold; the racing of her blood was fast enough to warm even her ample limbs and large square hands—in fact the young boy Almon, standing beside her, was warming both of his in one of hers—but now a strange chill struck her and she moved her shoulders restlessly. She felt a sense of loss, though she had never seen the king or anyone who had. But there was something gone, as though a mountain long familiar in the distance had been leveled to reveal blank sky.

"Nineteen years," a voice said. "Ranno was born that year."

Wulviva, too, remembered. Nineteen years since Stephen had been crowned, since she had married Robert.

Robert was dead a long time now. Ten years. She crossed herself, remembering how he had disappeared and how she searched for him and made the villeins search and how they found him, underneath the fairy hill.

Wulviva ran her hand across her face as though a cobweb clung there and then looked down at Almon. It was a look she often gave him when she noticed him, as though she had been caught forgetting him and he might see it. Indeed, she did forget him often. Hawisa was closer, being a girl, doing a girl's work by her side, and taking care of Almon. Again that twinge of guilt came to her face.

She leaned down, taking Almon's hands in both her own. He was a tall boy for his age—ten years—but very thin and somehow faint and far away from her. His narrow head, his long jaw and his steady, somewhat vacant eyes under the fringe of fine brown hair gave her back nothing when she spoke to him.

"Almon, did you hear?" She spoke close to his face. "They say King Stephen's dead."

"Yes," Almon said politely. "Yes. I heard."

"And the archdeacon says that we must come tomorrow . . ."

"Yes," Almon said.

". . . with our petition." Here she sighed and straightened up. It was not her idea to come.

Then a thought struck her and she leaned to him again and smiled, a bright smile, showing all her teeth but little gaiety. "And Almon, perhaps, if we come tomorrow, Father Lambert will come with us."

"Yes!" Almon's face showed animation. "I will ask him."

Lambert, their parish priest at Certeham, was childless, although married, and he had taken Almon to his heart. It had been his idea that Almon should be trained in singing at the cathedral school, and since the new archdeacon was that same clerk, Thomas, who received the living from the church at Certeham and who had been so friendly on his visits there, Lambert felt that an appeal to him to help the boy might be received with grace. Wulviva had had little voice in all these plans; the boy had long been warped into the pastor's mold. But it was she—she twisted up her lips and sniffed as she reflected this—who stood among the puddles in the Canterbury court and had the long walk home ahead of her. Lambert was busy with some funeral or other!

Abruptly she turned the smile on Almon once again, and squeezed his hands. "We can go home now. And in the morning you can ask Father Lambert."

Thomas pushed the heavy door and walked into the hall. Inside the yellow light from the tall western windows fell in shafts against his eyes and stopped him short, although the urgency was great. He turned and walked as in a dream the length of the long room until he reached the chancel screen and rounded it. Within the chancellery some clerks were working late, straining their eyes in the near-darkness, but he strode by as though they were not there and went on until he came to the small door that led into the inner room where Theobald, as Thomas knew because he knew his habits well, was sitting in discussion with a chosen few.

He knocked and opened the little portal, pushing aside the heavy curtain that hung there. The inner room was small and there the night already hung, for Theobald had had a candle lit and its soft flame roused shadows in the room. The archbishop was resting on a wooden couch while Eudes, his confessor, read aloud a passage from the Scriptures. John Belmeis sat on the floor to listen and Philip, the Bishop of Bayeux, a favored guest, sat on a stool, his chin upon his hand.

They looked at Thomas, each of them in mild surprise to be thus interrupted, and he hesitated for he was not sure how much to say before the bishop.

"Father, I beg your pardon," he said after a moment. "I have brought news."

Theobald raised his eyebrows but did not fail to smile. "What is your news, Thomas? Come, what I can hear my friends can also hear. We are all friends."

"A messenger has just arrived . . . this moment spoke to

me . . ." He paused and then plunged on, "He brought you word from Dover where the king . . . The king is dead."

The old confessor gasped and John leaped from the floor. But Theobald said quietly, "God take his soul." And then: "We must make plans immediately to keep the peace until the duke arrives."

The bishop made a move as if to leave but Theobald put out his hand. "No, Philip, you must stay by me. You have a level head and we can use you. Thomas, my son, come closer here." He pointed to the couch beside him. "We have a long night's work.

"John," he said next, "go to the sacristan and tell him we will hold Mass for the dead tomorrow. No need to tell him who. And fetch my brother Rochester; he should be somewhere on the precincts now, I see it has grown dark. And find me John of Salisbury too, and send him here." John had come to Canterbury from the Curia the year before, after the death of Pope Eugenius, and shown a learning and a wisdom both so deep that he had soon become one of the inner circle around Theobald.

"And John," he said, as Belmeis made to leave, "make my excuses to those who wait for me. And tell the stewards to bring candles here, and someone in the chancellery to bring my writing desk and pens and all the necessary things." John bowed. "And do not stop for courtesies!"

"Now Thomas," Theobald continued when he had left, "what is our first move—for we must move fast? Is the news out about here do you think?"

"I do not think so," Thomas said. "The messenger came straight to me and whispered in my ear. But swiftly as word came to us it will have gone from Dover by all roads. The barons all had men at court . . ."

"And as we sit here planning to keep peace we know that others will be plotting how to seize more power for themselves. We know that, don't we? So we must work fast." Despite his words, Theobald sat quite still and gazed a long time at his folded hands.

"Well then," he said at last, still looking at his hands. "A message to the Duke of Normandy. Where is he now?"

"At Rouen, I believe," said Thomas.

"A message to King Stephen's brother, Winchester. I know that he will keep the peace with us. We work in amity together now, you know"—he glanced with a small smile at Philip—"all our past quarrels swallowed by our mutual aims.

"A message to His Holiness the Pope. A message to Gilbert Foliot at Hereford; his family has great power with the barons as he himself has in his bishopric as well as that of London. And one to London also. A message to the Archbishop of York . . ." He glanced at Thomas reassuringly. "Roger will help us; he does not forget old friends." He was aware, although it was his policy to stand above such things, of how things were between these two, of Thomas' swallowed jealousy when Roger was elected Archbishop of York and Roger's cutting comments when his rival had been given his old place as archdeacon.

"And one to Abbot Walter; one to Ely . . . Thomas, can you keep track of this?"

Thomas nodded, then said quickly breaking in: "May I suggest this, since the time is short: that I go now, at once, to tell the marshal to have horses ready and that I give word, now, secretly, to two of our most trusted couriers so that they may start at once for Normandy by different roads. Thurstan is trustworthy, though young, and Adam Beale of course. Later, when the letters are prepared, someone of higher rank can take a guard and bear your formal greetings with the written news by a third route. There may be those along the roads or at the Channel ports who seek to stop a Canterbury man . . . and storms at sea . . ."

Theobald sat nodding as he talked. "Yes, yes. Go now. Send them. Then return to me."

But Thomas spoke again, still somewhat breathlessly. "Father, may I suggest another move as well. If there are men who seek to seize the throne in this unguarded moment, their thoughts will turn, as mine do, to the treasure of the king. Perhaps it went with him to Dover. In such a case it will be in the hands of Walerun of Meulan before now. But if some part of it remains in Winchester it is the duty of the Earl of Leicester to protect it for the duke. Also, he has some power over his brother Walerun. Therefore, I think it of the first importance that one of us should ride to Winchester taking your greetings to the earl and the reminder of his oath of fealty. In Winchester I can inform, consult, the bishop also—in whose power we must put our trust. Someone should go who has authority to make your meaning clear."

Theobald looked at him quizzically. "Yes, you are right, my son. Your plan is sound, is quick, is like you. And I know who you would send—your tongue betrayed you. Well, may the blessings of Our Lord . . . the love of God . . . go with you. Take a detachment of my guard."

Thomas sprang up.

"Make your arrangements," the archbishop said, "and

then come back to me. I will have the letters written first for Bishop Henry and Earl Robert."

When he had gone the archbishop spoke to the two old friends beside him, men who were aging like himself. "Thus it is to have young blood," he said, "young brains. Quick to think and quick to act."

The bishop nodded absently. His thoughts were drawing him to Normandy where his own interests lay.

"Quick to think and quick to act," the archbishop repeated, almost to himself. "But is he trained for the long thought, would you say? There are other matters which are our duty to compose. The news must be got out, yes; the peace be kept. But what of the new king?

"We speak of youth. The duke is what? Twenty? Twenty-one? A boy! And he must take divided England in his hands and mold it once again into a nation of Godfearing men, united with the Church.

"He will lean heavily upon the men around him. Who knows what court he brings from Normandy . . ." He stopped and looked up, realizing for the first time that the bishop, having risen, was now standing foot to foot. "You, Philip, know this better than do I. God grant you may be one of them . . ."

"God grant . . ." the bishop murmured. "And now I must . . ."

"But some men also—men who know our English ways, love England—must be found. Richard de Luci is a loyal and an upright man; he has been long justiciar to Stephen; he would serve the new king just as well. And there are others like him. I would have a Churchman close to the king though . . .

"You must remind me, Philip, to put a hint of this into my letter to Bishop Henry."

"Yes, yes. No doubt," the bishop said so curtly that Theobald sprang up.

"Forgive me, brother, I have kept you and I see impatience in your eye. Forgive and go. I have my duties here and selfishly forgot you have your duties also. Go." The two embraced. "May God protect you in the name of Jesus Christ Our Lord."

The bishop left; the curtain swayed behind him and the candle jumped. The two old men remaining in the inner room exchanged a quiet look. Then suddenly their silence was invaded by the clangor of the Vespers bell.

Thomas took the horses at a walk along the road toward Rochester. With him went eight men of the archbishop's guard and two pack horses carrying their food and arms. The trip to Winchester, when he had ridden it before, had taken him two days and a third morning. That had been traveling in the style he learned from Richer l'Aigle: at a fast steady pace but changing horses often and resting overnight. Tonight he had decided not to stop at any inn or monastery on the route and not to change his horses, for he hoped to go as far as possible unrecognized.

When they had left Christchurch and Canterbury well behind and climbed the hill to Harbledown and entered, silently, the pitch-black precincts of the forest there, he spoke out softly to the men. They were close-packed behind him, for it was a fearful thing to be encircled by the trees at night.

"Now I will tell you all the reason for our ride," he said, his low voice carrying beneath the overhanging boughs. "Then, if we should separate, each one must make his way as best he can and bring the news to Winchester. The news is this: King Stephen died this afternoon at Dover."

There was a murmur from the men. They all had heard the talk that evening, after the messenger had come, but they were seasoned soldiers, wary. They had been deceived before—in some old battle or long march—by rumor's forked tongue. They were the last ones to believe all that they heard. Now they believed, for Thomas spoke as their commander.

"We are to take the news to Winchester, to Bishop Henry and the Earl of Leicester, and I plan to be there first. Others will be riding hard tonight. We will ride harder. And we will not stop."

They came out of the forest at Dunkirk and Thomas pricked his horse into a trot. The men came close behind. The jingling of the harness and the clack of many hoofs on the hard track carried in the night but there was none to hear. At Faversham, before they reached the monastery walls, they halted and dismounted. Thomas checked each horse himself and told the men to rest. They lay upon their backs and propped their legs up on the logs and tree trunks by the road as they had learned to do on many such long rides. They had not long before they mounted once again and, at a walk, went quietly around the monastery and the village huts and broke into a trot.

An hour's trot, a rest, an hour's trot again. Thus they went on until soon after midnight they passed Rochester, the sleeping houses and the castle keep shadows against the sky, and left all habitation once again. Then Thomas raised his arm, the signal for a halt. The men stopped, silent, and the breathing of the horses was the only noise. "Dismount, unsaddle, rub your horses down, and we will take an hour's rest and our first ration," Thomas said. "Each man a half a loaf and quarter measure mead."

While they were resting Thomas sat apart and thought about the mission he was on and all that led up to it. He had returned to Canterbury more than two years ago. It was the spring, he well remembered, lovely Kentish spring. The year, 1152. The duke had wed the French king's cast-off wife . . . and Thomas in the dark picked up a leaf and cast it down. He was remembering his resolution never to serve a king. That had come to naught! He had been caught and swept along in the world's great events. Troubled, he had revealed himself, one time, to Theobald. The archbishop had listened kindly, as a father, and had spoken like a father, frankly and not sparing: "My son," he said, "God gives us all our work to do and we must do it. As St. Paul tells us, the gifts that we possess differ as they are allotted to us, the gift of inspired utterance, for example, or the gift of administration. You, Thomas, have displayed a genius for the latter. But—we must be honest—you have shown little aptitude for matters purely of the spirit, not even—let us be honest—the disposition for it." Then, to comfort him, "God gives each man his talents and it is man's duty not to hide them but to increase them in His service."

With any other man Thomas might have urged that he be given time and opportunity. But Theobald, he knew, longed for the cloister which he had loved at Bec more poignantly than Thomas, very likely, could imagine, who had not known such blessed quiet since he was a boy at Merton. And Theobald carried the mundane burdens of his office cheerfully. A loving clerk could not refuse to serve him in his worldly just as willingly as in his spiritual work.

"Consider Abbot Bernard of Clairvaux," Theobald concluded. "A man so saturated with the love of God that in his cell he tastes the bliss of heaven. Yet he comes forth, when called, to mediate in the affairs of men. Think hard on this, my son. Can you refuse to do as much?"

There was no answer though in his heart Thomas rebelled to think it might be true—what the archbishop said about him. Yet that was how the matter was; there was no help for it but work.

Now he recalled the work that he had done for Theobald

and for the young Duke of Normandy when Henry had crossed into England over a year ago and given battle to King Stephen's son, the blood-thirsty young Eustace. It was he, Thomas, who at that time had helped the archbishop to reconcile himself to the king's brother, Bishop of Winchester. It was he, also, among others who had won so many barons to the Church's cause of peace and forced a truce on the young rivals and required Eustace to withdraw . . .

"The hour is past, sir." It was the sergeant who had come to rouse him.

They rode as they had done before, walk, trot, and rest, as far as Dartford where they crossed the river Darent by the ford and stopped and rubbed their horses down. Then they turned west from Watling Street and took the track that would lead them toward Winchester. The night seemed to intensify itself as though it would go on forever, but the rain held off, until, at last, they looked around and saw each other, nodding as they rode, and realized the night was gone. The light was coming up.

"Dismount and walk," called Thomas. Soon they would find a resting place and eat and take an hour's sleep. He was well satisfied. The sun was not yet up and they had ridden nearly half the way and still the horses showed no signs of weakening. With God's help they would arrive in Winchester before Compline that night.

He found a grassy place and stopped. The sergeant took his horse and he lay down. He would eat after the others had, when they were sleeping. He thought again of all that had been done to lead him to this march—halfway across the face of England—in the cause of Henry, Duke of Normandy.

Eustace had died that summer, strangled on a dish of eels. It was the hand of God and a sure sign to Thomas that his work was in the cause of right. He mused, then, on the role of death in this great game of kings he now was part of: how Stephen moved, retreated, held his place, and how those knights and bishops on his side—so few now—sallied forth, then stopped. How Henry, would-be king, had utilized his queen, and how the bishops moved to guard his interests and the barons each maneuvered for a better place. How castles stood or fell. And how the pawns—himself for one—were bandied here and there. He saw it all as on the checkered board: the sides arrayed against each other, plotting, intriguing, moving to take advantage.

And then came death. First Eustace, and now Stephen. What shape did death take in the game? It had no piece to represent it and it played outside the rules. Oh, if a pawn were taken, or a knight, one might say death had come for it and in a small way changed the pattern on the board. It is the death of kings alone, he thought, that alters the entire balance. And unlike the final checkmate in the game, death comes to kings regardless of the play.

Death came abruptly—but it did not come by chance. He knew his chess too well to credit that. Death was a knowing instrument, the instrument of God. And death had thrown the game—all England—into the hands of Henry.

Thomas had first seen Henry at that time, after the death of Eustace and the treaty with the king. He himself had been one—one of many—who had drawn that treaty up. And when it finally was ratified, in the great Rufus Hall at Westminster, just before Christmas of 1153, he had stood among the crowds of noble men to see the two kings meet—the present and the future—to make accord.

It was the second time that Thomas entered that great hall. How different it was from the degrading day when he and Osbert Huit-deniers knelt on the stones before the empress. This time the lofty room was crowded, swaying with noise and color. The brilliant costumes of the barons and embroidered vestments of the prelates swirled like bright oil on water before the muted tapestries. The golden coronets, the miters worked with pearls, the gaudy banners and the crosiers standing high all gleamed beneath the ancient timbers overhead. And this time two great thrones instead of one stood on the dais at the farther end, the king's guard in their little grove of polished spears by one, and by the other the duke's men wearing the golden lion of Anjou.

The call for silence and the trumpet's clear high note. The king appeared, and stepped onto the dais, turned, and when his aides had lifted and composed his mantle, bent and sat. His was a kingly posture, knees apart, jeweled hands relaxed upon the carved arms of his chair, head high beneath the heavy circlet of his crown. His handsome face was grave, his curling beard trimmed short, his dark eyes level and his whole being full of charm. A true knight, Thomas thought, and felt his heart go out, as did the hearts of others all around him, in a deep flow of reverence for his king.

The trumpet blew again. Henry Plantagenet came forth. A murmur rose at his appearance for it was different, something new. He wore his mantle short and his strong legs in gartered hose were muscled like a wrestler's and his thick trunk and short strong neck spoke not of princely grace so much as power, energy. His face recalled a lion rather than a king.

He took the step in stride and turned and sat. Then he surveyed the crowd. His gray eyes pierced them one by one as though he spoke to each by name, commanding their attention. Thomas, when the eyes glanced into his, felt a sharp thrill as though he heard a call to action and high feats. He felt the men around him merge, lifted above themselves, all drawn as by a magnet to that strong and stocky figure on the throne. Here was a king!

The charter had been read, that which the bishops had so carefully composed, consulting with each faction, over the past half year. By it King Stephen recognized the Duke of Normandy as his successor to the throne, promising to maintain him as his son and heir. Henry, for his part, promised to swear fealty to the king. The earls and barons of each side were to do homage to the leader of the other. The bishops undertook to punish any man who disobeyed these terms.

Now it was signed, and now the solemn kiss of peace exchanged. With this the ceremony ended; and with it ended civil war. In the great hall men sighed and smiled at one another, feeling the warmth of peace.

Thomas and his men rode all day long, their muscles aching, fighting sleep and Thomas thought no more of the affairs of kings. When darkness came they still had many miles to go and now it was a matter of endurance only, each man within himself, in darkness and in pain, until they reached the gates of Winchester. Here Thomas halted for the last time and the men dismounted heavily, in silence, and stood leaning on their horses as they tried to rub them down. Seeing them, Thomas wished that he could give them courage for the final mile. He would have liked to ride into the bishop's courtyard as he had seen Lord Richer ride, straight-backed and fresh as at the start, with all his men alert behind him.

He watched them for a moment and then spoke: "Good cheer," he said. "We have arrived. In a few minutes we will ride into the city and we will tell the watchman at the gate that we have come, since yesterday, from London. And from our looks they will believe us. Only we will know that we have ridden twice that distance in one night and day.

"Afterward, when I have told the news to those whose right it is to know it first, you can tell all the court—and all at home when we return—what you have done. And you can tell your children, too, and grandchildren. As for tonight, you will have comfortable quarters and you can sleep forever!

"Now let us mount and ride. I have but one more thing to say: that is to give my thanks, and the archbishop's thanks —and promise of reward—to every one of you."

Thomas found Bishop Henry in his hall conversing with his guests around the fire. The bishop greeted him with cold surprise when he strode in and hardly waiting for the courtesies asked if he could speak to him alone. But when they had retired and Thomas with scant preamble spoke the words: "Your brother, our Lord King, is dead," the bishop let the breath go out of him in a long sigh. He put his arms on Thomas' shoulders and leaned there, seeming to draw some comfort from the hard embrace.

Then with that lightning change that so distinguished him he dropped his arms abruptly and drew back. He fixed a piercing pinpoint gaze on Thomas and shot the questions at him: "When? At what place? Who knows of this? Why are you first to tell me of it? Was he attended? Did he die a Christian death?"

Thomas gave such answers as he knew and relayed the archbishop's message while the bishop stood pulling his beard and listening until at last the fierceness faded and he put his hand out once again, resting it on Thomas' shoulder. "You have done well, my son," he said. "From Canterbury in a single day! Yes, I will tend to everything. The treasure will be held for Henry; I will see to that. Go rest. Go sleep. And we will talk tomorrow."

All at once Thomas felt the weight of the great weariness he had denied himself. His eyelids drooped and Bishop Henry seemed to recede into a little bearded figure standing a long way off. Faintly he saw the face change, lengthen, and heard the voice as from a distance, full of sorrow: "So he is gone—so soon." He paused, and silence buzzed around them. "A gentle-hearted knight. A gentle knight," the voice was dying to a breath.

Then suddenly the dark bright gaze shot out at Thomas once again, snapping him back to life. "But never a great king. You will agree? He never understood the art of being king. Generous when a show of power would have served him better. An upstart . . . don't you think? . . . imperious in his quarrels with the Church."

Thomas, feeling the eyes upon him, fighting his own exhaustion, managed to remain impassive, noncommittal, as he took his leave.

Next morning after Terce, Thomas was directed to seek out the bishop in the garden of antiquities, where he kept his statues bought in Rome. He found him walking briskly up and down the paths, his clerks in anxious stride beside him committing all he said to memory.

"Well now, Thomas," the bishop greeted him. "I am writing letters, as you see. Tell me to whom our father Theobald sent his dispatches and what he said. Bless you," he added as an afterthought.

Thomas told the list, as much as he knew of it, adding that when he left the plan was simply to send word of the king's death as fast as possible with the instructions to hold fast until the duke arrived. "I cannot say what has been done since yesterday."

"No doubt he will do more," the bishop said dryly. "Our spiritual father Canterbury has more aptitude for action and affairs of state than a first glance would indicate, eh, Thomas?"

Thomas, recognizing jealousy, recalled that Winchester had switched his friendship often. If he now agreed to work with Canterbury as he had done this past year, it was for reasons of his own. Last night, when he had criticized the king for opposition to the Church, Thomas had been too weary to reflect. Now he remembered Winchester's own bitter quarrels with the pope after he had lost certain favors. Moreover, he has much to lose in Henry's coming—so he thought—It is a gamble for him. At least two of the castles that he built when he was siding with the empress have no royal license—two that I know of—nor have they been destroyed.

Then thinking, Here is a subtle and a changeful man, accustomed to the use of power, subject to jealousy—but not an evil man, I think, he smiled but did not speak.

"How many knights has he at his command?" the bishop asked. "Has he sent word to all his tenants to be ready to supply the men at arms they owe him?"

"I think he must have," Thomas said. "I myself spoke about this to the seneschal before I left. It would seem likely that it has been done." And he thought: He himself must have the service of at least a hundred knights; be sure they were the first thing that he thought of, after the treasure.

"And from what quarter does he most expect trouble may rise?" the bishop asked.

The thought crossed Thomas' mind that danger might lie close at hand, but he said only: "King Stephen's Flemings are still under arms and their commander, William of Ypres, remains in Kent, but I know no one who could buy him. No, I think the greater danger lies to west and north. Hugh Mortimer is strong on the Welsh March, Roger of Hereford is dangerous, but the archbishop sent an appeal to Bishop Gilbert who has influence with him; I mistrust William Peverel and Aumale in the north . . ."

"Yes, yes," the bishop said, "I see the picture much the same. Who was it, do you think, made the attempt on the duke's life before he sailed for Anjou?"

"I do not know, my lord. The archbishop believes it had no influence on his decision to leave England."

"No, no. He had sufficient reason without that." He paused and Thomas caught the gleam of speculation as the bishop eyed him. "That was a strange, disparate tandem—the young duke and my brother Stephen—to have pulled together many years without the traces being broken, was it not?"

Thomas kept his wary silence and the bishop changed abruptly, drawing his breath in sharply in exaggerated self-reproof. He raised his eyebrows, shaped his lips into an O, and took the end of his long beard and stuffed it in his mouth. His eyes looked mockingly at Thomas. Then he spit the beard out, puffed, and said: "That's right. Keep silence. Hold your tongue—clever archdeacon!" And he laughed.

Thomas laughed in answer and then said, "Only a fool speaks when he is in ignorance, my lord. I do not know the duke or any of his plans. I only hope to hold the throne for him—as is my duty to the Church."

"Aye, so do I, my son," the bishop said, his face composed again. "I only hope he will come soon."

CHAPTER XIII

HENRY, DUKE OF NORMANDY, strode in the driving rain along the quay in Barfleur. The Bishop of Bayeux, the Bishop of Lisieux, the knight Sir Richard Brito and the stripling Count of Anjou trailed miserably behind him. They had walked thus—either they or others of his retinue—their soggy garments flapping in the wind, more than a hundred times since they had come to meet the duke and follow him to England. But the storm would not let up—"nor all the duke's impatience change so much as one cold drop of rain or whitecap on the sea," the bishops murmured to each other while they dried their steaming clothes.

The word of Stephen's death had come to Henry in the fields where he was on campaign near Gisors, relayed to him from his court in Rouen where his wife, his mother and his infant son awaited him. That had been on Allhallows Eve, as the month ended, and he had ridden to Rouen that very day. Less than a fortnight later he had gathered an impressive escort—prelates and noblemen, Norman and Flemish both—and they with their retainers and their men at arms had met him on the coast at Martinmas.

Now all November had gone by in driving sleet and spray, impatience and discomfort; and now the cold December days took their short course through time, driven to early dusk by gusty winds. The warsloops and the fishing smacks lay knocking on the wharfs, their colored sails all furled, their decks awash. The duke stood once again above them on the quay, his mantle black with rain, his hood drawn low, the sodden fur along the edge of it dripping in little points before his eyes.

"God's wounds," he said, searching the slanting rain for signs of lightening. "Who would have thought the sky had so much water in it!" He turned abruptly to the master mariner beside him. "When will it clear, think you? What are the signs?"

The mariner, afraid to speak out what he thought, grunted a noncommittal answer but the duke's brother, young Count Geoffrey, wishing to get back to shelter, spoke out somewhat bitterly: "Why don't you ask the necromancer, sire? Then we could all rest from our watching till the appointed day."

Henry whirled and shot an angry look at him out of the little cavern of his hood. "Go on!" he shouted. "Go. And take your ease among the ladies, little girl! God's eyes! Am I to take control of England with young ladies at my side?"

Then turning to the mariner again he said: "If we have red skies tonight as we had yesterday—if only for an hour's clearing—we will sail. Tomorrow. I can wait no longer."

The mariner said nothing, for though he knew the weather he also knew the duke. But Philip, the Bishop of Bayeux, after an interval, said gently: "Are we to take you at your word, my son?"

"How else are you to take me?" Henry said. "Do you call

me false?" He turned and stared at him. "Yes. Take me at my word. We sail tomorrow."

The bishop, hunched within his robes, was not afraid. "The waves are very high, my lord. One of the local men has told me he has not seen such a gale in twenty years. Your life is doubly precious now—to England and to Normandy."

"Spit on my life!" the duke roared. "What do you take me for? Do you suggest that God would let me die while England waits for me?"

"Absit," the bishop said. "Far be it from me to say so. But think of your wife and son, my lord—he so tender for so rough a trip, and she with child again."

Henry was silent though his breath came heavily. And then the agonies of his frustration seized him. Suddenly he doubled up his body and began to stamp his feet upon the sodden boards. He crouched, his face contorted and his eyes grown fiery, and beat his fists upon his thighs. "God's breath, I cannot stand it!" he cried out in a high childish voice, stamping his feet and almost weeping in his rage. The others stepped away and watched.

"I will not stand it any more! I cannot stand it! God, to be burdened like an ass," he sobbed, "with babes and women —when a whole kingdom waits! Is there a man among you? Is there a man? Or have I only women for my escort to the throne?"

They all stood quiet, watching him while the rain fell, slackening a little, and the waves slapped against the boats. Only the rash young Geoffrey broke the frozen silence of their group. He moved impatiently and shook the rain out of his cloak.

Henry whirled on him. "Go on, get out!" he yelled. "Go back to Anjou. I do not want you with me!" And as the young man hesitated, Henry ran at him, gave him a shove and, as he turned and slipped, a kick. "I will remember this," he shouted. "Go to Anjou! Someday I will see you there," he threatened.

Henry stood panting, as his brother walked away. At last he took a breath and flung his hands out, almost as though he flung his rage away. He peered into the sky.

"See, it grows lighter as the day goes by," he said in quite an ordinary voice. "Tonight it will show red again. I know it. Am I right?"

"Yes, sire," the mariner agreed.

"Then we will sail tomorrow," Henry said. "Make ready."

It took the little fleet a day and night to cross the narrow channel. Soon after they left land the mariners, peering and listening from the castle deck, lost sight of all the other steering lights and sound of all the trumpets blowing from the other boats. From then on each small bark alone, rocking and tossing in the storm, showed forth its tiny bobbing star of light for none to see, and sent its puny blast of noise into the whistling wind with none to hear.

Below decks men of the king's escort lay, pale as the fishes of the sea around them, caring nothing if they lived or died, rising to vomit, sinking back again into the sloshing bilge. The Duchess Eleanor was mercifully unaware. Impervious to fear, made—so she thought—immortal by the child within her, she lay upon the canvas of her bed half-fainting, half-asleep. The baby boy beside her slept as well—though he had turned pale green—while the nurse groaned and retched all day and all the night.

Only the duke kept on his feet. And he was first to see the land. "England!" he cried out to the sailors as he clutched the railing of the castle deck and strained against the storm. "England ahead!"

* * *

Thomas, with Theobald and all the bishops of the land, waited at Westminster for Duke Henry's coming. Rumors had flown before him, then the trusted news: the duke and all his party had arrived along the coast, in various havens south of the New Forest. He had brought a large and impressive train and gathered more to him as he rode up to Winchester where he was welcomed and the treasure put into his hands. He had not rested long but even now was riding up to London.

"He is determined to hold Christmas court in London," Roger, the Archbishop of York, told Thomas. "Therefore he rides the weather to his coronation."

"Oh? Do you have this information at first hand?" It was a pleasure to keep Roger on the old basis of familiarity, and it was thus that they had checked each other when they were learning accuracy as clerks together in the old days.

"Knowing the duke, I know it must be so," said Roger.

Thomas prodded once again: "Ah, do you know him?"

"I have seen him," Roger said impatiently. "And thus I know him."

"Yes, I have seen him also. Still, I do not know his mind."

"Close up, I saw him," Roger snapped. "Closer than you." He moved away.

Thomas was pleased with this exchange although he knew it was unwise. If archdeacons made enemies—or cultivated old ones—it should not be with archbishops. But he knew Henry's plans as well as any—better than Roger—for he had been with Theobald when the duke's men rode up from Winchester. And it was harder than it once had been, now that he felt the worth of his position and his own worth in filling it, to stomach Roger's smiling condescensions.

Thomas was in London for the first time since his father's death, six years before, when he had come up hastily from Canterbury to see to the estate. There had been little left—more debts than assets—and with his newfound wealth he had managed only to save the house. This he had settled on his baby sister Agnes, now a fine tall woman, married but in need of help because her husband, young Fitztheobald, had not yet come into his father's lands. Roheise and her stanch merchant husband already had their house in town. Mary he had not seen; she was not given leave from Barking Abbey since the death was sudden and the burial without ceremony. For Gilbert Becket and his household—faithful Alfleda and old Ebert too—had died together of the pestilence that swept through London in that year.

Thus it had been a sad, almost a furtive visit, with brief calls on creditors and shamefaced kindness to the sister-stranger Agnes before he said a short, almost a brusque, goodbye, all feelings stifled, to the house that once had been the limits of his world.

This time his stay was different. London was gay. For Thomas it was gathering of friends in old familiar haunts. He stayed with the archbishop in the priory at Bermondsey and there met many clerks, now risen in the Church, whom he had known as students, and when he crossed the bridge into the town itself he visited with friends whom he had known in London's evil days. His sister Agnes and her husband made the old familiar Cheapside house as full of life as it had been when Thomas was a boy.

The life at Bermondsey, although it was the center of power in England till the king be crowned, was orderly as the archbishop's household always was and followed the familiar hours of prayer that gave Thomas ease of soul. His work was hard but he was master of it, and he sent all the details of the archdeaconate to be worked out by his subordinates at Canterbury. He was employed, most of the time, in planning the king's welcome and the ceremonies at Westminster, and he liked to ride down through the wintry orchards to the old abbey and the palace there. Once he met Miles Mauduit on the road and they sprang from their horses to embrace.

Oh, friends were plentiful and warm, and they meant life to Thomas—for he still suffered from a craving to be liked. The hospitality of London and the sport, the food, the wine were good. He was still young at thirty-five. His work excited him. His health was excellent. In all the world he wanted nothing more. If nothing ever changed, then would he be content.

Henry arrived at Westminster on the eighteenth of December. On the nineteenth, in the sanctuary of the old abbey church, he and his queen were crowned. And after that, because the ancient palace of his grandfather had been so let to rot during the civil war it was not fit to live in, he and his entourage rode slowly down the strand into the city and across the bridge to Bermondsey to make their royal residency there.

Along the way the people waited in little clumps and gatherings beside the wide suburban road from Westminster as far as Charing and from there in stifling crowds between the houses, under the city gates, along the narrow streets and on the bridge. And as the cortege passed along, the single horseman leading, then the banners of the knights, the barons on their chargers and the silvery bishops on their mules, and then, at last, the king, a shout rose in the air—one roar that ran along the mass of people all the way from Westminster to Bermondsey: "Waes Hael!" and "Vivat Rex."

Vivat Henricus Rex! Vivat Fitz Empress! Vivat the Duke of Normandy, grandson of old King Henry, great-grandson of the Conqueror!

Waes Hael to Henry, grandson of the beloved princess, Editha-Matilda! Waes Hael, bold young descendant of King Edmund Ironside!

"Vivat! Waes Hael!" Thus London spoke, in two tongues, with one voice.

King Henry held his Christmas court as he had planned, wearing his crown before his people for the first time, in the long hall at Bermondsey. In the six days before this that he had been king, the men who had been strangers to him learned the meaning of hard work. Henry was up at dawn and in the saddle riding out to see his lands, a hawk upon his wrist in case the opportunity for sport should come. And while he rode, his eyes and ears alerted for every novel thing, he shot out questions at the men accompanying him:

"Whose are those ships across the river by the wharfs? Ah? What is the law regarding strangers here?" Then, with a change of thought: "How many men can Mortimer raise along the Marches do you think?" And as they crossed a marshy inlet: "How does that eel trap work—that one the fisherman is baiting. Come, bring it to me. How does one say 'come forward' in the English tongue?" His mind was restless as his body and his curiosity was of the touch, the taste, the smell as well as of the intellect.

Returning to his chapel in the priory for Prime he did not rest but went on questioning, his whisper and his restless fidgeting sounding in every pause of plainsong and of prayer. He sat to break his fast, to drink his beer, but soon was up again—consulting with the archbishop who liked him for his well-trained mind and literate discourse, or with the Bishop Nigel about the royal revenues, or with King Stephen's chief justiciar, Richard de Luci, whom he wished to probe to see if he might still be utilized.

Thomas was often in his presence but not recognized, for he was one of many. Only once the king took note of him with an appraising glance. That was one morning when the bishops would have kept him over long at dinner and Henry, wishing to extricate himself, broke in abruptly, getting to his feet and saying to the company at large: "Who keeps a decent gyrfalcon in London?" As there was startled silence, he continued, "You must admit it is a rather sorry lot of birds you keep for my amusement here at Bermondsey." The little line that always sat between his brows deepened as he looked around.

Thomas, in his place far down the table, at the very foot, had risen when the king rose. Now he spoke in a clear carrying voice: "The mews at Bayard's Castle are among the best in England, sire. There are some fine hawks there."

It was then that Henry looked at him and saw a fine, tall, glowing man, pale face, and ready smile. This was his impression. And, I like his voice, he thought.

"Thank you . . ." Henry bent his ear to catch a whisper from his aide, "Archdeacon . . ." but he had not caught the name. "Thank you." Then he turned and told his squire to bring his horse, and with his favorites following him he walked away. And that was all.

But later the name, Thomas, was brought to his ear:

"Thomas, my most beloved son and prop, is a young man I would commend to your attention," Archbishop Theobald told him when they discussed the court, hoping to keep the power of the Church close to this raw young sovereign.

"Thomas of London," Richard de Luci said when he was asked whom he might choose to serve with him if he himself were to remain justiciar, "is an energetic and an honest man, well versed in law."

"Ah, Thomas the Archdeacon," the Bishop of Winchester replied to the king's questioning. "Yes, yes, a charming man. Brilliant I have been told—but careful to conceal that dubious asset with his charm, I think."

And the two men on whom he most relied, Philip, the Bishop of Bayeux, and Arnulf, Bishop of Lisieux, had been well briefed by Theobald. On both their lists the name of Thomas had a place.

Theobald spoke to Thomas in his private room before they went into the hall for the high ceremony of the wearing of the crown on Christmas Day: "Thomas, you have served me well eleven years. Now it may be that you can serve me better—and the Church—if you will serve the king."

Thomas was hesitant. "I do not know the ways of royal courts," he said.

"Do you doubt you could learn?" Theobald smiled at him.

"Father, in honesty, I doubt my own desire to learn."

"But I desire it, my son. Will that suffice?"

"Father," Thomas was surprised to feel the tears lump in his throat. "If it must be . . . If you desire it . . . But I shall be sorry, very sorry, to leave you."

A little grimace flickered on the kind old face but Theobald was silent. He felt his heart cry out, but no words came. He raised his hand in blessing and then turned and signaled to his crossbearer to lead the way into the hall.

The hall of Bermondsey was narrow and it was crowded to the stifling point by all the court that gathered there before the throne of their new king. Thomas, in a far corner, saw the king advance and saw the men who walked with him. These were the men whom he had so far chosen to be close about him in the royal household and to rule the land.

Close behind him someone whispered, "He has chosen men of competence . . ."

"Yes, but it seems he is afraid to put his confidence in any one of them," another answered. "See, he has balanced the office of justiciar between two men."

"How so?"

"Why, there's the Earl of Leicester whom he has publicly announced will be justiciar, and—look there—there's de Luci also."

The king had stepped upon the dais, turned, and now was seated on his chair, his rough hands clasping the carved ivory of its arms. The marshal called for order and the assembly rose, closed ranks, and faced the king.

Again the whispering in Thomas' corner of the hall. "I see he's chosen Bishop Nigel . . ." "He is to keep the treasure and the royal revenues." "Well, he has long been loyal to the Angevins . . ."

And again: "I don't see Mauduit." "He's too old." "Then who is to be chamberlain?" There was a stifled laugh but Thomas could not hear the answer. His heart trembled when he thought that he himself might soon be called upon to walk beside the king while courtiers discussed his competence and snickered in their sleeves.

The business of the court was settled with dispatch. The king pronounced two edicts for the land: first for the disbanding and expulsion of all foreign mercenaries from the land and the destruction of unlicensed castles. The king spoke in his rough young voice. For many these were the first words he had said. "As was agreed at Winchester," he said in a clear strong Latin, "my lands shall be delivered from the tyranny of unlawful barons and from the instruments of their tyranny. Thus are these measures taken."

Second he announced he would reclaim all royal castles and crown lands that had been bartered off by Stephen in his desperation to buy funds and followers. For, "It is our intention to have one authority, the crown, as guarantor of peace and justice in our land," the king concluded.

Then he rose, and while men tried to reach his ear with flattery or with requests for favors, he strode quickly through the hall, smiling, clasping a hand here, patting a shoulder there, but never long detained, until he stood upon the porch without. There his quick eye caught Thomas in the crowd. "Is that the man?" he muttered to de Luci who stood next to him. De Luci looked and nodded.

"Here," the king raised his hand and beckoned Thomas. "I have a hawk for you . . . if you will join us in the hunt." He smiled, showing his strong young teeth beneath the tawny beard.

Thomas said quickly, "Sire . . . delighted . . ." as, feeling the eyes of envy on him, he pushed through the crowd.

The sky had suddenly grown lighter and the air tingled, for indeed he was delighted—and his own fierce joy surprised him—to be hawking with the king.

CHAPTER XIV

THE JANUARY WIND CAME unrestrained, laden with salt and sea-smell, from the narrow estuary where the river Test joined the Southampton Waters. It blew up from the Channel and across the sparsely wooded flat until it reached the castle on its little rise. Then it flared upward where it hit the palisade of spikes along the motte, rattled the timber keep, and then swept on beyond to toss the upper branches of the forest trees.

The king and his small party, scarcely thirty men, huntsmen and soldiers and a few courtiers, sat on their horses at the drawbridge gate. The sea wind, coming from behind, flattened the horses' tails against their rumps and pushed the riders' hooded cloaks hard up against their backs so that they all streamed forward in the wind—like the king's angry words that flew before him as he spit them out. Beside him Bishop Henry sat clench-faced, his long beard flying on ahead as though to point the way.

"What does this make, Sir Bishop—the fifth? the sixth?—of your unlicensed castles that remain despite my ruling? How many of these devil's nests do you intend to keep to breed rebellion in my realm?" The king turned toward the bishop as he spoke; the wind caught at the words and tore them from the corner of his mouth. But Bishop Henry understood their meaning well enough.

"It is not manned, my lord," he said.

King Henry shot an angry look at him. Turning, he cupped his hands around his mouth and hollered to the men behind: "Ho, trumpet!"

A huntsman blew. The brassy note was caught and carried, over the ditch, the motte and wall, over the bailey with its jumbled outbuildings, into the dark squat keep. A man stepped from the gatehouse, saw the royal banners, turned, and they could see him beckoning and running back into the house. Slowly the drawbridge lowered on its chains. The man with his companions ran across it as it settled, made it fast, then came, uncertain, to the horsemen and knelt down before the king.

Henry led his men over the rumbling boards and into the cramped and dirty bailey, looking about him with distaste. Then to the bishop, who still rode beside him, he said, "Call your seneschal."

The bailiff was already on the steps. He recognized the bishop, knew that the younger man must be the king. He started and exclaimed and then came running forward with a look of deep dismay, almost of horror, on his bearded face. He knelt before the king, sprang to hold his bridle, saying repeatedly the whole time, "Welcome, my lord, my king. Welcome, my sovereign," while his face, the brows drawn almost perpendicular, the eyes triangular in their alarm, belied the greeting. "Welcome, my lord," he said for the tenth time.

Henry laughed harshly. "Oh, welcome. Welcome. Welcome indeed!" he said as he dismounted. Then to the bishop: "Show me your hospitality, my lord. We will stay here tonight."

Together they went, straight-backed, up the steps and into the dim hall.

Thomas watched all of this and caught more of the words, the intonations, than most of his companions in the entourage. His hearing, like his understanding, was more quick than most men's, and his appreciation, too, was keen. He sat his horse, now, laughing at the bailiff's face, for he laughed easily these days. He had not felt such pure exhilaration all his life as he had felt this past month in the king's service.

Soon after Christmas the new king had started his first progress through his realm—how different from Archbishop Theobald's long-planned, well-ordered journeys from one holding to another. From London he had gone to Windsor, thence to Wallingford, thence down to Winchester. Sometimes he gave the word to start at dawn and then, while all the crowded courtyards and the roads outside were crammed with saddle horses, laden mules, carts of provisions and great wains of royal baggage; while men and women pushed and haggled, loaded, unloaded, mounted, dismounted, ran to the kitchens or the stables for forgotten things, ran out at the alarm to take their places once again, the king turned his attention to some other business and they did not start till noon.

Sometimes they did indeed start out at dawn, while sleepy grooms tugged at unfinished harnessings as the procession rolled along and laggards, still with their belts unfastened and their hose undone, ran to find their horses in the dark. They stayed in quarters unprepared for them, ate in the open, waited, squabbling for their shares of bread or candle ends, while their young restless king rode off on some side trip to hunt in every forest that they passed.

They had come into Winchester the day before: the king, his earls, his bishops and his knights; his chaplain and his master of the writing office and his clerks; his chamberlains, his stewards, butlers, ewerers; his constable, his marshals, huntsmen, guards; his porters and the man who kept his bed; his extra horses, hunting dogs and hawks; his coterie of strumpets and his dancing bear—nearly two hundred of the court in all, and half again as many animals.

They had been welcomed in the castle and the town—though Thomas could perceive the leaden hearts behind the gracious smiles. It is the welcome that the wheat field gives the locust, so he thought. It also smiles and nods at the approach of hordes.

The purpose of the king's procession was to see his lands and to be seen, to receive homage from such lords as had not come to London, to reap his royal harvest of the goods his crown lands owed him, and to destroy those castles that had been built for civil war.

The Bishop of Winchester had played a double game, hoping to have the favor of the king while clinging to the power he had built against the king. But Henry was familiar with duplicity; he had been taught it at his mother's knee. And there were men enough to tell him of old plots, new-made alliances, or hidden forts.

Thus he had graciously invited Bishop Henry to ride out with him along the Test and to the New Forest which lay beyond. The invitation had been made in public, in the hall, and Thomas, like many others, heard and understood. The bishop also understood and smiled and nodded— Nodding and smiling in the wheatfield of his beard, thought Thomas. He had been captured by the bishop's personality and now he felt with him the silent power making its approach.

Thomas was chosen to accompany this somewhat awkward party. The king had marked him for his laughter and his merry voice as well as for his knowledge of the hawks. And thus he rode, observing, free of responsibility, into the unkempt bailey as the light began to fail that afternoon.

The hall was dark, barren, smelling of moldy straw and of the garbage and ordure that lay beneath it. There were few benches and Thomas, with many others, had to heap the straw to sit upon while the villeins who did service in the place brought them stale bread and sour wine for supper. The bishop, with great grace, sat with the king at the one table and amused him, entertained him with fine conversation through the meal.

Afterward Henry went aloft to sleep, taking with him only his chamberlain and two men of the guard, leaving the bishop sitting at the table, lonely with his thoughts. He had gambled and he had lost. He could thank God the king was lenient, feeling his power secure. He could choose exile and the king would let him go. At last he looked up, searched the hall, and with his eye caught Thomas whom he beckoned.

"Archdeacon Thomas," he began when Thomas sat beside him on the bench, "my plans are somewhat changed, as you may guess." Thomas said nothing.

"Yes," he continued, "I shall take up monastic life once more . . ." He shot a glance at Thomas, smiled, and went on, "You may not think it suits me, but it does. I shall return to Cluny for a time. I spent my childhood there, you know. To read, to study, follow the Hours, tend the bees—these are pleasant occupations . . .

"Have you brought pens and parchment with you? You have been so long a conscientious clerk," he pursed his mouth in half-apology, half-speculation. "I am afraid there would be none kept here."

"No, my lord, I have none," Thomas said. "But I know one who has, I think. There is a young clerk with us whom I have seen frequently scribbling in a corner."

Thomas had noted this young clerk, taken his size, as he was constantly observing all men of the court, their characters and their relations to each other and to the king. William Fitzstephen was his name and he was new to royal service as was Thomas, but somewhat younger and of even less position. He was but one young clerk among the many in the chancellery and was included in the party only because he longed to come and for his passionate love of horses and of the hunt.

Thomas, looking round the hall, soon picked him out and caught his eye and called, "Fitzstephen!"

When the three sat close together Bishop Henry said: "Master Fitzstephen, may I call upon your generous offices to write a letter for me to my chancellor? I would apprise him of my plans to go abroad." He watched with some amusement all the various thoughts that flashed as clear as glass across Fitzstephen's face. "So that arrangements can be made for my . . . unruffled, shall we say, departure. I do dislike unnecessary haste—don't you agree?"

Young William grinned—unwisely, for he found himself alone in this and staring broad-mouthed into the bishop's steely face. "So, if you will kindly take your pens and little parchment there I see; and have you an inkhorn handy? Yes, I see that you are very provident. And if you will kindly write as I dictate . . ." The bishop gave his orders in precise, pure Latin while Fitzstephen wrote.

Thomas, observing all, thought: This is what it is to be a great lord of the Church, well-armed against adversity. He had forgotten much of his reaction, long ago, to the first secular lord he knew and how he had longed, then, to be like him, above all weariness. But what he felt now followed the same line: it was an admiration for, and a desire to emulate, true courage.

Next day the king took only a few huntsmen and those courtiers who were addicted to the hunt and rode on, into the deeps of the New Forest beyond the bishop's fort. The bishop had been left behind to oversee the burning of the keep and palisade and to give orders to his bailiff to destroy the motte, fill in the ditch, and leave no trace that ever castle stood upon that spot. Then he was free to find his way out of the king's domain—to exile.

The hunting party left at dawn. In midmorning they stopped and lit a fire and the huntsmen carved a doe that they had shot and hung a haunch above the flames to roast. The king and followers grew close in silence and in easy converse under the barren branches and walled in by fog. This was a royal forest; to the king it was his hall and throne, the heartland of his realm. The doe was his, a royal doe—raised and pursued and slaughtered to provide his food. The men were his, sworn to him, trusted. For once the king relaxed, stretched on a bed of winter leaves, and slept.

By noon the hunt was on again, through oak and beech grove where the wild pigs scurried at the approach of man, through the thin growth of marshy land, through open meadow, into the deep forest where the deer turned for last desperate hiding.

The men were scattered. Thomas, all alone, pulled in his horse and listened for the horn. The wood was very dim and still. The panting of his horse was loud. Around him fog crept up between the trunks, stood hesitant beneath the arches of the boughs, lay drifting eerily upon the ground that he had traversed and must traverse once again. It closed him in as though some presence waited there to speak to him, and Thomas, listening, paralyzed, was thankful to hear human voices up ahead.

His horse moved forward and he saw, standing as in a bed of steam, King Henry and one other with the horses' reins looped on his arm—the king quite still, his face turned up, the huntsman fidgeting.

He heard the king say: "Is this a holy wood?"

"No, sire," the man said doubtfully. He was a native of Rouen.

"A sacred wood, then?"

"No, sire, not to my knowledge . . ."

The king looked at him, scowling. "Do you not know my uncle was killed here?"

"No, sire," the man said miserably. "Uncle, sire?"

"The king, you fool. My grandfather's brother. Do you not know he gave his life here . . . here in this forest? Are you so ignorant, or merely stupid?" The king broke off. "Oh, God's wounds, what's the use," he said more quietly.

Thomas heard it all, knew the king's anger, far from over, was still smoldering. He must decide now whether to withdraw. It would be prudent, yet he hesitated.

He knew the ancient story well, the bloody story of those dark, mysterious times before his birth. Alfleda told it often: how King William, called the Red—although he was a dark-faced and dark-bearded man, Alfleda whispered—had foretold his death and manner of his passing in the sacred year—or so Alfleda called it, for it was a mystical year, 1100. How he had disappeared into the forest with a friend—his acolyte, Alfleda used the Christian term—and there beneath a mighty oak . . . beneath, before, spread out upon? Alfleda did not know—his throat was pierced by an arrow and he died. And how the blood dripped from the corpse the whole way from the New Forest to Winchester with, so Alfleda said, the awestruck people following the cart—for they had waited for him; they knew he would die.

Thomas felt the hair prick on his scalp as it had done in the old solar long ago.

The king had stopped abruptly and turned from the huntsman as not worth his words. He stood for once as still as baited breath and with a solemn listening look upon his face. Thomas dismounted and moved forward quietly, taking the risk because he could not help himself.

The king looked at him, watching his approach, bringing his thoughts together. Then he said as in discovery, "Ah, it is Thomas the Archdeacon. Ah, it is you." And, formally, "You may approach."

Turning to the huntsman he said, "Take the horses off a little way and let them feed."

He was silent while the hunter took the horses crashing through the underbrush, silent while the silence of the woods closed in. At last he said with slow deliberation: "You are a learned man I understand, Archdeacon Thomas. Then let me have your most informed opinion. Is it the duty of a king to die?"

"Absit," said Thomas automatically. "It is far from me to say so, lord.

Henry smiled a little at this answer but pursued. "Yet many say so. And many kings have died. King William Rufus died in this very forest for some reason. What was that?"

"He was a pagan, lord," said Thomas softly.

"Pagan?" the king said sharply. "What does that word imply?"

Thomas felt his danger but he answered doggedly: "He was an enemy of the Christian Church."

"The Church! The Church is sometimes grasping—as you may not know who have not ruled," the king said with a rather heavy scorn. "But Rufus was a noble king, a good king to his people, and he died for them."

Thomas was silent and his face showed doubt.

The king looked at him as a man looks, with some pity and some humor, on the child who first knows disillusion. "You have never heard this said before?"

"I have, sire, as a boy," Thomas admitted.

"And you did not believe it, even as a boy?" Henry said gently. Then, with a changed, harsh voice demanded: "What, was it murder then? By treachery? Was it an accident?" He hit the last word with a bitter sarcasm.

The stillness of the forest seemed to give the lie to this. The fog, alive and moving up behind the trunks, the overhanging branches where an owl might roost, the dried fronds of the braken listening, each with a separate ear. Thomas had often been aware, when he was in the forest depth, of other voices saying other things. Prayer had been his weapon of defense before. Now it was the consciousness that he was talking to the king and that it was the Church who placed him by the king.

So he said strongly, "I believe it was an accident, my lord."

Henry laughed, still looking at him with appraising eyes. "Do you! Yet you look very troubled when you say so!

"Tell me"—now his voice was serious—"from the heart. Do

you believe sometimes a king may die, must die, so that his people and his lands may live and prosper?"

"No, sire," Thomas said firmly. The king was but a boy and full of troubles. Suddenly he felt this and his heart warmed to him. He forgot fear and caution. "No, sire. These are heretical beliefs."

"Do you call me heretic?" the king snapped. But the question, meant to be frightening, had but little bite.

"No, my lord," Thomas said gently. He was wondering, now, how he might help the king, no longer how he might escape his wrath.

Henry looked away from him, then down. For a long time he stood, picking a rough nail on his hand, silent and thinking. Finally he said, as though he formed each thought with gouge and hammer as a mason carves a column from the block:

"King Rufus so believed. The time came in his reign. It was foretold long long before. The time came for the king to die. And he was king. And there was none to die for him. He had not made provisions; he was the only king. Thus, when the time came, he died by the arrow in the sacred wood. It was a noble death. It was a sacrifice . . ."

He looked up. "This is a belief. Is it heretical?"

"It is, my lord."

"How so?"

"Because it is the Devil's teaching, not the teaching of the Church."

Henry looked very queerly at him and his voice was soft as fog: "Do you not know that I am of the Devil's family—as was King Rufus?"

Then he changed. "All right," he said abruptly. "Tell me the Christian truth."

"The Christian truth," said Thomas, "is the truth of God—that He, our only Lord, a greater king than William or than any man, made that same sacrifice upon the tree for all time and for all mankind. No man, no king, can make that sacrifice again. To say so would be blasphemy."

Henry's laugh was like a bark. "Oh, but I blaspheme often! It is my greatest fault!" He laughed again. "Don't look so startled. You will get to know me and my ways."

Turning, he shouted: "Huntsman. Bring the horses."

Then again: "You are a very solemn archdeacon, Thomas! The bishop said that you would charm me . . . Well, perhaps you will . . . How do you serve me now? I promised the archbishop I would use you somehow."

"In the office of your chamberlain, my lord."

"Yes, in the chamber. Well, you will be my chancellor from now on. I have found no one yet, and Leicester nags me. Yes, you must be my chancellor and keep my thoughts from blasphemy and all my writs correct and keep my seal inviolate, and all my secrets . . ."

Then he turned serious. Subtly, with an adjustment of the head and neck, a regal stance, the tiniest thrust of chin, he changed and imperceptibly grew into the very image of a king. "Chancellor Thomas," he said softly, "swear to serve me."

Thomas knelt and placed his hands—as he had never done before, for he was not a landed man—between the open palms outstretched before him.

"Swear to serve me . . ."

"Lord, I swear."

"Until you die."

"I swear."

The huntsman, gaping, came upon them thus. The king turned, drew his hands away, and like a small boy shoved at Thomas saying with a little laugh, "Come on. Rise, rise!" Then he threw his arm about his shoulder, hugged him, and still laughing went to take his horse.

Thomas, smiling, took the reins of his own horse and waited for the king to mount. But while the huntsman stood by with the stirrup in his hand, the king stopped, hesitated. Then he turned.

"Thomas," he called, his hand upon the pommel.

"Yes, sire," for there was a pause.

"Thomas. Never trust me."

"No, sire?"

"No. I will use you." And the voice was deadly serious.

Thomas said nothing. And he saw the king smile sadly, a strange wise smile upon so young a face—before he swung into the saddle.

BOOK THREE

THE CHANCELLOR

CHAPTER XV

THE HALL WAS WIDE and clean and smelled of the drying field flowers caught in the rushes on the floor. The windows, open to the city sounds, let in the pure late-morning sunlight of a summer day to wash the pictures painted on the walls and gently fall upon the rushes, golden-green. About the hall a scattering of servingmen worked quietly, setting out the trestles and the boards for dinner, floating the linen cloths out over them. These servants were all dressed alike in short green tunics and long hose, their hair was neatly trimmed, for they were of the household of the king's chancellor and they were conscious of it—better than others of their station. Thomas the Chancellor selected for his own only the best.

Conrad the Steward stood beside the door that led out to the pantries and the kitchen courtyard, checking off each plate and cup and bowl as it was brought before him into the dining hall: the set of gilded platters from Cologne; the bone and silver tankard, "Inge's horn," named for the King of Norway who had given it; the chancellor's own plate of silver etched with the scene of Lazarus the Beggar, a gift of gratitude from Walter, Abbot of Battle; the ancient cup of mottled glass from Rome, and many more. The pages carrying them paused by the steward and then crossed the hall and set them out along the upper tables, silver and gold and horn and polished wood and here and there a little cup of ivory tusk, until a treasure fit for a king was ranged along the cloths.

Now, at the steward's signal, the heavy iron-studded doors that led out to the porch were opened wide—the day was fair and warm—and men began to gather and come in. It was the hour for dinner in the chancellor's hall and men of every rank were welcome to sit with the chancellor and share his food.

Thomas had been chancellor for two years, and in two years he had become the first in all the land, after the king.

He lived, indeed, as though he were a king, and better than the king. Men commented on this.

Reginald Fitz Urse, baron of King Henry's court, was among the first to enter from the porch. He walked a little stiffly from an old wound in his thigh, for he had been in many battles, and his light brown eyes, set in a bed of leathery pouches, seemed to be weary of observing ugly things. He walked beside a shorter man, his arm upon his shoulder as he looked about and commented upon the elegance they saw around them. The two had lately come from Wales where they had been in battle beside King Henry, chasing the rebel Owain through his wild mountains, and like all men when they first come from the hard regimen, the dangers and the smells of war, they were resentful of easy living in peaceful places. The king himself had taken the long way home, making a progress through his northern lands of England so that his vassals there might view his power.

Fitz Urse's resentment was fixed on Thomas, for Thomas had not gone with Henry into Wales.

"Christ, he lives well," Fitz Urse said, thumping the other's shoulder with his heavy hand. "Better than you or I, eh?" His lips smiled but his eyes looked wearily about.

They found a table just below the dais and Fitz Urse, leaning, resting his knuckles on the cloth, looked along it at the bowls and cups, shaking his head, before he drew his legs up over the bench and sat. "Each time I see him he improves himself," he said.

The other picked up a polished bowl and turned it over in his hands. "At whose expense, I wonder," he asked, searching the tracery for a name.

Thomas had indeed grown rich at the expense of others. As chancellor he had custody of the Great Seal of England and every royal grant or charter, every document that bore the seal, passed through his hands, and every fee collected for its use was paid to him. But more than that he had the income from not only his own lands which he still held as Archdeacon of Canterbury, but from the lands of vacant bishoprics and abbacies which came under his care in the king's name. And when a bishop or an abbot died King Henry did not rush procedures to elect a man to fill his place; an empty bishop's throne or abbot's stall meant income for the king's government.

"It has been profitable for him sitting here with foreigners while we fought through the muck and mire with the king," Fitz Urse said sourly.

"He can fight well enough, though, when he wants to. Grant him that."

"Aye, as you say. Aye, well enough," Fitz Urse conceded. It was a fact that he could not deny. He had himself fought under Thomas in the campaigns of Maine and Anjou the year before when Henry—true to his angry threat—attacked his younger brother Geoffrey's strongholds of Chinon and Mirabeau and conquered and deposed him.

Thomas had shown himself a skillful and a ruthless soldier in the field and Henry, pleased with his new friend, put many knights at his command, Fitz Urse among them. But on their return to England, when the news came of Owain's uprising in Wales, Henry bade Thomas stay in London to entertain the King of Norway in his name—so much had Thomas grown in the young king's esteem. He was now his lieutenant on the battlefield and his ambassador at home; his confidential minister in court and the dispenser of his royal favor; his best and trusted friend; his favorite. So much in two years generated jealousy.

"Well enough when the king's eye is on him," Fitz Urse continued. "I would not trust him when the king's back is turned."

The hall was filling up as men of rank found places for themselves close to the dais and others farther down till, by the door, where wooden bowls were placed on barren tables, poor men of London, beggars and those hard hit by fate, came bowing in and settled silently. Only the high table on the dais remained unoccupied.

Robert of Melun, Thomas' old teacher in the schools of Paris and now a member of his court, brushed past them as he went toward the table for important clerks. He caught Fitz Urse's last words and stopped.

"You do not trust the chancellor, my lord?" he asked in his thin voice. It was a challenge he was used to tossing out, for he encountered bitter talk against his pupil-patron frequently and found amusement in defeating them in argument.

"I trust him, oh I trust him," Fitz Urse said, twisting around. "I trust him as I would trust my hound—a good hound," he added hastily. "The best. You could not match him in the field. But I must have command of him." He turned to his companion, speaking confidentially. "He'll tear a man to pieces if I'm not there to stop him." He turned again and fixed his weary eyes on Robert, smiling a little with his lips. "A good dog."

Before the learned doctor could make answer—and he had

one, subtle but to the point, ready on his lips—the door in the great screen behind the dais opened and the chancellor came through it with his special guests. His hand was on the elbow of the Justiciar de Luci as he spoke in confidence to him, but his eyes turned to look along the tables of the hall, seeing what men were there and if they were well placed, according to their rank. He caught the eye of Master Robert, standing behind the barons, and he beckoned him. "Come sit with us." Then he saw Fitz Urse staring at him and he smiled especially at him and raised his hand, a soldier's greeting.

Fitz Urse half-rose and put his hand up in an answering greeting then sank back, the quick smile vanished from his face, and mumbled half-ashamed, "The way he enters you would take him for the king."

The steward came in from the kitchens, bearing in his own hands the roast for the high table. Behind him came the servingmen, holding the platters and the skewered meats high up above their heads, and set on every table haunches of venison and roasts of beef, mutton in pastry, pheasants and geese and ducks done up in many ways, and piles of tiny partridge with their little legs like twigs in a dry forest sticking out, and fish both from the river and from the chancellor's pond, and stacks of fine white loaves and apples stewed in honey and many other things. As every dish was brought, the steward called it out by name. And after them the pages came with wines both red and white.

The Bishop of London rose from his place by Thomas and held his hands aloft (where none could help but see they were already shaking with senility) and asked God's blessing on this food and on those who would partake of it and then sat down and Thomas with great solicitude helped him to a bit of pap cooked for him specially and then took for himself a breast of pheasant.

"Aye, like a king," Fitz Urse repeated, leaning across the table to spear a piece of the beef.

"Much better than a king," his friend corrected. "Haven't you eaten at Westminster when the king is there? The wine is often sour and the fish is spoiled."

"The king is occupied with other things," said Fitz Urse, staring somberly at the high table where bishops, abbots, men of the king's curia and of the chancellor's court were gathered and the young upstart Walter Map, just come from Paris, was making them all laugh with his droll wit. "It looks as if all England dines with the chancellor," he growled.

"Except the queen," his friend corrected.

He smiled and Fitz Urse smiled. The whole court knew the queen felt greatly slighted when the king had given Thomas the commission to entertain the King of Norway in his absence, even though King Inge's visit was a matter for Churchmen to handle. Indeed, the Norseman had come at the urging of his bishops—though there were matters of trade between himself and England he wished to see to for himself—for Norway was a newly Christian country and until four years before all of the prelates there had been sent out from England. Now they were subjects of King Inge and they could not control him as they wished. His was a bloody past: when he was a boy, Inge with his two brothers Sigurd and Eystein had ruled jointly after the murder of their father. When they had grown to manhood, Inge and Eystein had together murdered Sigurd. This year, Inge, quite on his own, had murdered Eystein. He saw no harm in it for all his prelates' talk; he had no use for them in any case.

But Thomas, even though a Churchman, he had liked. They had sat late together in this hall, Inge with his great horned helmet and his uncouth ways telling dark tales of ancient battles and intrigues against the gods and drinking the strange English ale he liked from his own royal cup. This was the cup that he had given Thomas—token of friendship for all Englishmen—when he departed. He had not seen the queen but once, at Westminster where she gave lavish entertainment for him and where he had been ill at ease, drunk too much wine, and did not go again.

"Aye, she was angry when the king took his leave," smiled Fitz Urse. "I'd say the king will have a hard time of it with her when he returns."

"The king has found a way to manage her," the other murmured. He wiped the grease off his mouth with the heel of his hand and smiled. "He times his visits so as to keep her busy—producing an heir each twelvemonth. The French king couldn't do it, but he can. You saw there is another on the way?"

Fitz Urse, his mouth full, nodded.

"It was a sad thing when the young Prince Geoffrey died."

"No matter, there is another," Fitz Urse said brutally.

The dinner was well started and here and there among the crowded tables men rose to stretch themselves and belch before they settled down to eat again. Musicians of the chancellor's court, a little band of six, came through the doorway from the kitchen courtyard and began their small procession around the hall. They wore the flowers of late summer in wreaths around their heads and walked with lilting steps, the finger-cymbalist leading the way.

Fitz Urse, still chewing, listened a minute. Then he said, "I heard a song when we were in Chinon. Something about 'I wish the Queen of England lay with me.' Students were singing it."

"Aye, they sing it in the taverns," his companion said. "I heard it. It has a solemn tune though . . . 'If I owned everything . . .' Something like that. I can't sing it against that tune they're playing." He paused and tried again. " 'If I owned everything, from the sea to the Rhine I'd throw it all away—if the Queen of England lay in my embrace . . .' "

"That's the one," Fitz Urse said. " 'If all the world were mine.' It is a womanish song. These students are not really men." He paused to drink. "The king heard it," he said. "He laughed."

"He can laugh well enough. He owns everything and the queen too—in his embrace, as they say."

"And anyone else he takes a fancy to," Fitz Urse said into his cup. Then suddenly his dark face brightened and he turned from his food to speak. "Nay, did you hear how he sloughed off the Lady Beatrice?"

"Sloughed her off?"

"Got rid of her. She had grown tiring. It happened just the last time he rode up to Stafford, after we got back from Anjou. As usual the lady sent him gifts and promises, suggesting he should come into her house again. But he had other plans. . . ." Fitz Urse leaned closer, bent his head and put his elbow on the table so that his hand could shield his mouth. "You know the chancellor"—he tipped his head toward the high table—"celibate, afraid of women and all that. He was with the king. And so the king arranged the lady should come to a certain room. When she was there and waiting for him and the king knew of it—they brought him word—then he said, 'Thomas . . .' They were still in the hall together. I was there. Then he said, 'Thomas, you shall have my room tonight.' "

"What happened?"

"Well, we gave her ample time with him—the two together in the room—and you know the Lady Beatrice. And in the morning we went up, and gave no warning, and broke in the door. The king was first."

"What did you find?" They were both grinning in anticipation.

"The chancellor was on his knees beside the bed, hunched over, either asleep or praying, I don't know. He had his clothes on. And over in the corner sat the lady, very sour. God, how the king laughed when he saw her face! The chancellor never touched her."

They laughed so hard that Fitz Urse, rearing back, slapped on the table and the board resounded. Then, with a guilty thought, he glanced at the high table, stopped himself and coughed, for Thomas' eyes were on him. The other too stopped laughing and wiped his hand across his beard and frowned as though he pondered something very deep, and Fitz Urse raised his wine cup, shielding his face, and from behind it murmured, "They say he can hear through the thickness of the Tower walls."

He sneaked another glance at Thomas but the chancellor's eyes were elsewhere and he was laughing now. Young Walter Map was entertaining the high table with a story of a certain monk—one of the Cistercian order, who, as all know, wear no underclothing on their nether parts lest they be heated and thus tempted into adultery—who, said monk, on a windy day tripped on the cobbles of the street and fell headlong within the full sight of the king who at that moment passed by on his horse. The wind caught at the garments of the wretched brother and blew them around his neck, exposing all his naked private parts. The king rode on, pretending not to see. But one who rode in the king's company, a monk himself, but of a rival order, saw it and could not help himself from crying out, "God's curse on a religion that bares the rump!"

The bishops and abbots—there were no Cistercians there, Map had been quick to see—laughed as loud as any of the barons or the courtiers, and Thomas too threw back his head and laughed. Thus was the hall alive with all the sounds of eating, talk, merriment and music when suddenly a horse and rider clattered up the porch steps and into the hall.

Those by the door were first to recognize him and fall still. A hush fell, table after table, back through the hall, till only one last tag end of a laugh was heard in a far corner. An instant only of full quiet, then the wave of noise came rushing back, the scrape of benches and the thundering of feet upon the oaken floor, the clattering of plates and cups, the voices: "Who is it?" "It is the king." "No, tell me." I say the king, you fool!"

Henry urged his sidling horse up past the lower tables where the poor men stood, mouths open. But here a foolish servingman—perhaps he was half blind—came carrying a platter right before him and the horse reared up and threw the froth out of its mouth and backed into a table with a great scattering of men and food and barking dogs. Henry looked back and grinned to see the chaos he had made. Then he jumped lightly from the saddle, tossing the reins to any who would catch them, and came laughing up between the tables to the dais and leaped with dirty boots upon the cloth and then jumped down by Thomas. He caught him by the shoulders and embraced him, turned and embraced the bishop, waved to the others all along the table, and sat down.

"What have you here to eat? My stomach rumbles." He looked at Thomas' plate. "A breast of pheasant in a savory sauce!" He held it up, all dripping, and then pushed it in his mouth. "God's eyes, you eat well, Thomas," he said while he chewed. Then he reached out and heaped the plate with meat and fowl and pulled it toward him so that it lay between the two of them.

And while the whole hall watched them, bishops and barons and poor men by the door, some with envy, some with open hearts, King Henry and his chancellor reached with their hands into the food and bent their heads together and ate from the same plate together, side by side.

That afternoon Thomas and the king went hunting in the Forest of Essex and sighted a wild boar and gave it chase for several miles to no avail and came back through the streets of London in the evening, dirty and worn but in high spirits. The citizens stood staring at them as they went laughing by, jousting with bare fists like two raw boys, heading each other off. Henry was the better horseman but Thomas longer in the arm, and neither would give way. Thus they went shouting and brawling by and men gaped after them and said that never since David and Jonathan had two such friends been seen.

But in the morning there was work to do. The Palace of Westminster had been rebuilt and furnished, under Thomas' stewardship, to house the king and queen in a fit manner and to become once more the royal court in London. This work had been one of the first commissions that the king had given his new chancellor. And Thomas, determined to do well, had hired the best architects and masons and seen to it that all was done between the times of Easter and Whitsuntide—to the amazement of London citizens who daily heard the noise of winches, rumbling carts, hammers and chisels, and of shouting men come floating down to them as though the tower of Babel were being built anew.

It was here the king held court whenever, in his incessant travels, he abode in London. And it was here, in his own private chamber, that he conferred with Thomas and with the other officers close to his person—those who ruled the land.

This morning he and Thomas worked alone together as they often did, Thomas sitting on the step below the king's high, curtained bed and Henry moving restlessly around the room. Thomas was the man on whom the king most heavily relied and there were many reasons for this. Thomas, unlike the landed barons of the king's Grand Council, derived his power solely from the king. The fact that he had come into the court through the archbishop's backing and was still of certain consequence within the Church no longer troubled Henry. In the great controversy over Battle Abbey the spring before, Thomas as advocate before the king in judgment, and in the face of his old father Archbishop Theobald, had delivered the final telling argument in favor of royal charters when they conflicted with episcopal authority.

Thenceforth the king felt that he had in his new chancellor a stanch, unwavering champion of royal rights. In this perhaps he underestimated the effects of Thomas' legal training and failed to understand that with this man the weight of law might fall on one side whereas his heart was on the other. But be that as it may, the king had trust in Thomas.

Further, he discovered him to be above his other councilors in many things. His mind was quick, his memory long; his temper hot in battle and cool in diplomacy; his actions quick, his judgments sound. And in the hours when he put the weight of his crown aside, he found in Thomas a good companion in the hunt and at the gaming board, an excellent host well versed in food and wines, a witty conversationalist in light discourse and stimulating teacher.

In one thing only were the two apart. Henry loved all women—or called it love. As king he could command *their* love, and this sufficed him. It was a pleasure to him just to see a woman bend to lift her cloak or send a laughing look into his face or sit before him combing out her hair. His rough hands loved the softness of their skins. If he was tired from long riding their flesh was cool as water next to his. If he was cold on winter nights their little supple bodies warmed him.

Thomas looked at women with distant eyes, nor would he touch them or make light discourse lest the temptation of his old desires lure him from his vows.

Just now their thoughts were far from sport. They were

upon the king's high constable, the captain of his armies, Henry of Essex, who was accused of cowardice on the campaign in Wales.

"What shall we do with him?" asked Henry. "God's eyes, Tom, my own life was in danger and he flung the standard down! I was surrounded and they tell me he would have cut and run!"

"What does he answer to the charge?" asked Thomas mildly. Sometimes, in conversations such as this, he was acutely conscious of Henry's youth and of the fifteen years that lay between them.

"He says he didn't do it." Henry tossed away the straw he had been plaiting. "Montford says he did."

"And *did* he leave the standard? Did you see it?"

"Are you cross-questioning me?" Henry wheeled to shoot a look at him. "Are you the judge here?"

"No, my lord," Thomas said smoothly. "You asked me what should be done with Essex. And my advice is of a very meager value if I am not to know what happened. Where *was* the standard? It should have been by you."

"No, no. The fact that it was not with me is understandable. That part is not in question. You do not know the way you have to fight those Welshmen. . . . You should have been there, Tom." Suddenly the king's mood changed. He came and sat by Thomas on the step and bending brushed away the straw beside his foot and with his finger drew a rough map of Wales upon the floor where chaff and dust lay thick.

"We landed here," he said. "Most of my men, the main force, came up along the coast from Chester here. I knew I'd never get to Owain that way; wildmen like that won't risk a battle in the field. They fight a new way; it is a different sort of war. You have to follow them, back into their mountains, cut them off and wear them down. God's breath!" He sat up laughing. "They nearly cut me off!"

He looked at Thomas. "You should have been there! I took along a company of archers, good men, very good men, from Shropshire. We traveled very light, way back into the hills. My God, what hills! It's like a hog's back there: up one side and through the bristles and down the other. Black as a sow's belly underneath the trees!"

"Did you take Essex with you?"

"Essex, of course. And Montfort and a few others. We cut back up in here," he moved his callused finger along the floor. "Kept moving, never saw a soul. Then on a barren knoll, along about in here, I said to Essex, 'Keep the standard here,' and took a few men down into the valley where the woods were thick."

"You should have sent a scout," said Thomas.

"I felt the need of action," Henry said briefly. "We got down in there, thick as the Devil's beard, and looked around and never saw a thing till somebody sent an ax at me. Then we heard our trumpets blow; Essex and the others had seen the Welshmen filtering through the trees behind us. By God they're like a pack of devils. Shadows. I never saw a one. Somebody gave a whoop and arrows came down in around us. Not much. The trees were thick. I never saw a soul!"

"Did Essex get down to you?"

"No. He lost us. We went on around and came back up the other side."

"Where was the standard?"

"It was there, Essex and Montfort both holding on to it."

"What did they say then?"

"Say? Why Tom, we were cut off, entrapped! Not just the few of us in the defile, the whole damn lot of us. We were surrounded. Say! Why we said, 'Damn the bastards, run for it!' We didn't stop to *say*. We ran. We flew."

The king was so delighted with his adventure that Thomas was caught up in it. His eyes shone as he echoed Henry's earlier words: "I should have been there!"

"You should! You should!" said Henry, smiling. Then his face changed and he frowned, scuffing the reeds back over Wales with his soft boot. "So, what shall we do with Essex?"

"Montfort has accused him? And he's denied it?" Thomas thought a moment. "Let it rest a little while. Essex has been a valuable man."

"Wait and see, eh?" Henry asked.

"Yes, wait and see. And keep an eye on him. We shall have opportunities to see what he is made of."

"Have them, or make them," Henry grinned. "All right, I'll do it your way. But I will keep you by me." He paused and stared, a curious look, at Thomas. "I wouldn't want to have you for my enemy, my friend."

"That I shall never be, my lord," said Thomas.

"No, God forbid," said Henry, still with that curious look. "For I shall need you one day, it may be, as I need no one else." Then he jumped up and moved about the room once more. "Where's Nigel?" he said abruptly. "We are wasting time."

Nigel, Bishop of Ely, was the king's treasurer. It was he who presided over the checkered board where the accounts were reckoned—all the fees and taxes, scutages and escheats that came into the king's treasury and all the payments that went out for the king's household and his holdings and his mercenary men at arms. It was the bishop's clerks, not Thomas', who kept the records of these matters and of the coinage of the realm.

Thomas went to the door and called a clerk and soon the bishop came into the chamber, a parched and upright man with the bright burning eyes of genius. His summer robe, soft boots and jeweled belt were those of an officer of the court; there was about him nothing of the Church except his tonsure.

He entered and approached the king with dignity and welcomed him to London once again. Henry returned the greeting somewhat formally, for Bishop Nigel had his trust and his respect but little more. And as for Nigel, Henry was to him a kinglet still, a novice; he had been treasurer to the kings of England since before this one was born.

Henry shook some coins out of his purse into his palm and held them out to Nigel. "These are the coins of my realm," he said, showing his scorn. "Some I collected in Northampton. What do you think of them?"

The bishop barely glanced into the open hand. "Aye, these are your inheritance, my lord, from years of anarchy."

"Well, my inheritance, as you say," Henry repeated. He took a coin, since Nigel had not done so, and made as if to weigh it in his fingers. "This one's not more than fifteen grams, if that." He tossed it as if it were some dirty thing to Thomas, saying, "What think you, Tom?"

"Not fifteen grams," said Thomas, weighing it in his palm.

"And what is the prescribed weight for an English penny?" Henry asked them in a rising voice. It was impossible to tell if he was asking them for information or merely driving home a point; there were so many things the King of England knew about his English lands, so many things he didn't.

"Under your grandfather, my lord," said Nigel in his very quiet voice, "the weight was fixed at twenty-two grams and one half. Under King Stephen there was some debasement and you will find—as you so graciously have shown us—many short-weight as well as squalid coins of various sorts."

Henry grunted. Then he held up another penny and said angrily, "Look at the effigy on this! Is this a king?" His brows shot up, his eyes were smoldering. "Is this the way my people see their king?" He held the penny out for them to see but his hand shook; they could not make it out. "Just look at that! The crown's half off, not even sitting on the head. Look at the face, all holes and slashes. God's blood, this is my ancestor! What do they make him out to be—an ape? A juggler?" He paused so long that Thomas made as if to speak but Henry cut him off. "So this is the work of my engravers and my moneyers who think because King Stephen let them cheat and slop their work that I will do the same! 'Oh aye,' they think, 'let men mock the king and scorn his money so long as I grow rich; let foreigners refuse to take it as a standard of exchange, it matters not to me!' God's blood, I'll have them hanged for this. I'll gut them with their own engraving tools!"

Both treasurer and chancellor were silent, Nigel with his eyes upon the rushes, Thomas with his upon the king.

"Well, what is to be done?" asked Henry, somewhat calmer. "How shall we punish them?"

"I would suggest, my lord, the fault is with the money rather than with the moneyers," said Nigel in his whispery voice. "And it is here, I would suggest, you seek a remedy."

"What does he mean?" asked Henry bluntly, turning to Thomas.

"I think my lord the Bishop would suggest that you recall the money."

"How, recall it? All of it?"

"So I would suggest," said Nigel. "It has been done before and it is time that it be done again."

"That's it. God's eyes, we'll do it," Henry cried. "Recall the money. Every penny that's been adulterated or chopped down or shows the king to be a monkey. . . . Every defective coin of any sort in all my realm shall be recalled. Any man holding such a coin shall take it to the moneyer. And every moneyer shall be responsible for minting full round decent coins. And every man who does not do it shall have his eyes out and I know not what else. . . . He shall feel my wrath. See to it."

The king had spoken and his word was carried out by Thomas and Bishop Nigel and the Justiciar de Luci. At Michaelmas when, as was required every year, the sheriffs and the custodians of the king's lands brought in their revenues to Westminster, the counting-clerks examined every coin when they recorded it and if it was defective they withheld and sent it to the minters to be melted down.

And further the sheriffs were instructed to command all persons in their counties who held defective coins to take them to the moneyer nearest them and all moneyers were ordered to accept such coins and melt them down, assay their metal on the touchstone and from it mint new pennies, returning weight for weight what had been brought to them.

If anyone should fail in this he risked the king's displeasure.

* * *

In Canterbury angry fires raged in all the forges of the moneyers and craftsmen sweated at them while outside, along the Highstreet and in White Horse Lane and Pillory Lane, reluctant men stood waiting to have their pennies melted down and given back to them—not coin for coin but weight for weight, a very sad exchange. Nor were the moneyers happy. The royal minters, Mainer the Rich and Solomon and Luke and Lambin Frese, worked in grim silence; they were accustomed to make a heavy profit on their coinage and now had to spend their time and energy for nothing—and pay their craftsmen out of their own pockets. They shot out angry looks at all newcomers but they bit their tongues in prudent silence and said nothing.

Elured Porre, however, could be heard all down the street. Of all the Canterbury moneyers, he was the one who always gave full value, who never minted any but a full round coin, who never practiced usury. He was the only one who had no hidden wealth to cushion him. And he was loud in his complaints that he must work for nothing in order to undo the faulty work of other moneyers.

"Look at that, I pray you!" he shouted at the unhappy man before. "Do me the honor, look at that!" He held a chopped and mutilated coin up in his fingers. "Have you been calling this a penny? Or perhaps has it been cut in half? A ha'penny, may be, or a fourthing? You need not answer; I see your blushes clear enough!" He flung the coin into the crucible and took another while Simon Crudde, the burgess who had brought them, stood by looking glum. Walter, sitting by the doorway, watched his father with a tiny smile.

Elured took another worn and grimy coin and rubbed it on the touchstone where it left a dull gray streak. "No pride. No pride at all," he muttered. "Probably London." He turned it over and peered at it; the moneyer's name was crudely stamped and was so badly worn he could not make it out. "Probably London," he repeated. "I never trusted any of those London minters . . . high-stomached . . . double-tongued. They'd make a penny out of solid copper if they could, and spit on it and call it silver And then they look you in the eye and tell you they are better men than you!" He peered at Simon with a pale blue eye

"What are you standing here for, taking up room?" he

suddenly burst out. "Walter has the weight and tally of all you brought. You'll have your pennies. Don't you trust me?" He glared so fiercely that Burgess Crudde, a peaceable and pious man, found not a word to say but simply backed away and left. He did not even stoop to touch the lump on Walter's back as he went out the door, though he had meant to.

Walter watched him go and smiled, his lips closed and the creases in his thin cheeks deepening. He knew the gesture well. He knew all kinds of men: those who touched him crudely, making no remark; those who touched him and explained themselves or even thanked him; and those who wanted to—but caught his eye before their hands went out.

Walter was twenty-seven now and full-grown, five feet tall. His head seemed large on his sharp crooked shoulders and the early beauty of his face was gone, sunk back, far back behind his eyes, leaving it lean, large-nosed, thin-lipped. Sometimes, unhardened people, looking at it, felt a pang.

But recently, since spring, something had softened Walter's face, for this late in his life—he knew it to be ludicrous—he fell prey to the passion of desire, both of the flesh and of the soul. He was in love. And when he thought about it, or when he saw the girl he loved, all his defenses dropped away; his face grew fuller and even beautiful, as it had been before.

The girl that Walter loved was Hawisa, the black-eyed daughter of Wulviva of Hortone, whom some called changeling. Walter had known her well enough over the years: a queer little round-faced child of five when he came into manhood at fifteen; a wild unruly girl of twelve and thirteen, given to strange moods and fits of silent madness, now as a maiden of seventeen, so softly rounded and so unpredictable.

This last spring Walter had gone often to Hortone because there was another crisis in the family there. Almon, the only son, had failed in his responsibilities. At fifteen he should have been the one to give the orders to the reeve, to oversee the sowing and the reaping, to keep account of what was owed to Elured and the monks. But often when his mother came to look for him from working in the fields herself (she had no pride) she came into the house all sweating, kerchief askew, glancing about her wild-eyed, only to find him gone.

Hawisa, silently carding wool in a dark corner, could not or would not tell her mother where her brother went. But that did not matter; Wulviva knew. How many times had she not begged him, ordered him, seized him by the hair and shaken him; how many times had he not promised never again to leave his duties and go off to Certeham, to the priest Lambert and the church? And yet he did it, over and over again.

Almon truly meant to be a dutiful son. There was no evil in him. But when his mother spoke of "owing," he could think only of what he owed to God. He was possessed by God—a quiet, very happy boy. And for him God dwelt in the little church in Certeham. He was not sorry that he had not been accepted in the choir school at Christchurch—though Lambert was. Almon found all that he was looking for without the monks. And more and more he spent his days, and even nights, away from home, with God in Certeham.

This spring, at last, Wulviva had given up the struggle against God and Lambert for possession of her son. She came again to Canterbury with her shoulders sagging (Wulviva was nearing forty) and her eyes bewildered to ask a man's help on the farm.

To satisfy her Walter had gone out to Hortone but he found the reeve was competent as always and that the manor and all the villeins on it prospered. There was no need for Almon, or for him. Nevertheless he made the trip again and yet again, till Elured remarked on it and he could give no reason even to himself. He simply went, spoke to Wulviva and to the reeve, and went away again. And yet, somehow, no matter how he occupied himself or where, around the manor grounds, there he found Hawisa: Hawisa sitting in a corner carding wool, Hawisa in the herb yard working in silence and oblivious to sun and scent, Hawisa standing by the apple tree, her hand upon its trunk, looking at nothing.

Who was this dark-eyed sullen girl to draw a man, all unaware, three miles from Canterbury every day? What could she offer, she who had not long ago taken a flight from life into the realm of madness only to be clucked and scolded back against her will, like some young crazy chicken, into the home yard once again? How could she comfort loneliness who did not even raise her eyes to him?

Yet there he stood, the hunchback, in the house or in the yard, day after day, surprised at finding her and ready, on seeing her, to leave as though released from something till the following day.

One time he came upon her when the bees were swarming. He heard their whine as he came down the lane and then he heard another music, blending, rising, dipping lower: it was Hawisa's voice and she was speaking to them, singing the charm to keep them at the hives.

"Fly here my little cattle,
In blessed peace.
In God's protection
Come home safe and sound. . . ."

He smiled as he came through the gate because this was the old spell that his mother used to use and here was Hawisa, so like a child and sounding like a child. He saw her, then, where she stood by the dusty cypress hedge and weedy garden of the bee yard in the sun, her round young arms outstretched. He stopped and watched her, listening.

"Sit down, sit down bee,
St. Mary commanded thee
Thou shalt not leave;
Thou shalt not fly to the wood. . . ."

Walter's smile had gone and he stood, crooked, ungainly, by the gate, amused no longer but—the thought struck him with a thrill of fear—enchanted.

The angry whining of the bees increased and Hawisa's small voice was almost lost, yet Walter heard it:

"Thou shalt not escape from me,
Nor go away from me,
Sit very still."

The bees had risen and were taking off into the sky, a furry comet, circling. "Sit very still," said Hawisa again. They spiraled upward, humming their single note with such intensity one could not tell if it was rage or joy, and wheeled in a great arc, away and free. Walter it was who stood there, very still.

Hawisa snatched a stick up and threw it after them, a childish gesture, and her voice was peevish as she repeated futilely, "Sit very still, I said. Await God's will!"

The smile on Walter's face made anguished creases down his cheeks. He thought that he might laugh. Instead a sort of groaning came from his chest. O Christ my Savior, it is love, he thought. I love her.

Thereafter Walter did not come to Hortone for many weeks. His heart ached and he stayed away. At last he came, though; he was a man—no matter what his shape, no matter how he ridiculed himself. He came but did not enter in the house. Instead he crossed the yard as though on urgent business and tossed the merest glance into the doorway as he passed, a glance devoid of interest, one might say, the merest wheeling of the eye to one side and then back again. And after that he closed his eyes and tightened up his fists as though he cursed himself and blundered on so fast he nearly ran into the cypresses around the bee yard. He dodged around them as though he did not dare to stop and went on to the little millrace that ran into the Stour and there he squatted on the grass and stared into the water, breathing hard.

Wulviva had set out a little fish trap here where the stream ran shallow over a sandy bed. The trap was empty and the water tugged at it and caught the slippery ribbons of the river weeds, yellow and green and black, and trailed them in long streamers toward the mill. Walter stared with fixed eyes, but he did not see the trap, the water and the pebbles under it.

He heard a step behind him. It was Hawisa. He knew this and he felt his body tremble and he cursed himself. He did not look around.

She stood behind him for a moment and then said, "Why Walter, you are here!" A foolish exclamation, for she had followed him. And then, "It's me; it's Hawisa," as though he did not know.

He did not answer and in a moment she crouched down beside him and looked where he looked, into the water running swiftly at their feet. "What are you looking at?"

To feel her, sturdy yet soft, beside him took all the strength from Walter and he lay back on the grass and put his arm across his face as though to shade his eyes.

"What are you doing?" she repeated.

It was an effort for him to get out the words: "Looking for fish."

Hawisa laughed. "Up there?" She glanced into the sky.

He rolled his wrist back and looked up at her but did not smile. And then at last—a boulder rolling from his chest, a weight of anguish from his throat—he said the words, as though he spoke of death: "I love you, Hawisa."

He closed his eyes and lay there, taut and quivering. And Hawisa sat quivering too. They were so silent, listening to themselves, that the smooth waters of the stream sounded like winter torrents and the soft droning bees like thunder at their backs.

At last Hawisa looked at him and saw his jerking eyelids and drawn cheeks and all the other marks of pain and then leaned over him with shining eyes and said in her child's voice, "I love you, Wat." She touched him very softly with her fingertips and Walter's face broke, and his arms went up and pulled her down to him.

They lay together on the grass, her lips upon his lips. And then they were no longer on the grass, no longer by the millrace in the summer sun, but off together in some secret region of their own, spiraling upward, singing a single piercing note, away and free.

Where did they take each other for that moment out of time? They did not know. And when they asked each other, wondering, when they lay once more upon the grass, their only answer was, "I love you."

* * *

Eleanor the Queen of England sat in her wardrobe chamber in the Palace of Westminster with her mirror propped before her but she did not see herself. King Henry stood behind her and it was his face she watched, reflected in the hazy surface of the metal speculum. They had been talking of affairs of state which in this instance were affairs of family.

"You of all people should understand what this alliance means," said Henry. "As long as we do nothing, just so long the castle of Gisors shall stand affront to us, breathing down on Normandy, a constant threat. I need that stronghold. I need all the Vexin lands. For my own, as they were my father's."

"But I mistrust the French," said Eleanor. "The monks who minister to Louis see with a double eye. I am uneasy." She peered into the mirror, up at her husband, and her face was somewhat pitiful. for it had lost its freshness.

"You? Uneasy?" Henry's tone was teasing, like a caress. He smiled and touched her hair and ears and noticed in the mirror how her lips swelled and her eyelids drooped. Gently he cupped her neck and then he ran his hands down hard over her breasts and squeezed them. She leaned back against him, ready to have him any time he wanted her, but Henry turned away.

"There is no need either to trust or mistrust the French in this," he said. "It is as much of interest to Louis to have his infant daughter betrothed to England as it is for us." His thoughts were clarifying and he began his customary pacing of the room. "Already he has shored his borders to the east by the betrothals of his first two daughters . . . yours." Henry shot a look at Eleanor. "He will be eager to 'entrap' us—that is how he'll see it—in an alliance to safeguard him on the

Norman side. When we have made him think of it, then it is he who will come begging for the betrothal. We shall comply—and ask the Vexin for the dowry."

Eleanor had seen her own face in the mirror when he caressed her and then turned away. Now with a gesture of self-scorn she rose and moved about the room, as he did, prowling, using the very act of walking to fight down desire. She did not hear his arguments, and when she spoke her one thought was to hurt. "You do not know him as I know him," she said, "as a woman knows the man she lies with."

"I know him better," Henry retorted. "As one king knows another."

"And how would you go about this miracle of persuasion?"

"It is no miracle. The Frankish princess is no more than three months old. And our little prince is what? Not yet three years. Louis will think of it as merely a protection, a means to keep us quiet, a long betrothal." He paused. "And on their marriage I shall have the Vexin."

"Either you do not understand men's pride, my lord, or else you underrate the prize you took from Louis. The Franks have not forgotten Poitou and Aquitaine—if you have."

Henry smiled mirthlessly in her direction but she had turned away. "Don't fear, I understand pride well enough," he said. Still pacing, he stared at her back. She was no longer slim as she had been; four children born to her in middle life had thickened her. And he was silent for several seconds before he added in a level voice, "It was indeed a prize, a noble prize, a prize most undeserved. There's no one in God's world who's more aware of that than I—unless perchance 'tis you."

He waited for some outburst but she did not answer. She was not ready yet for open quarrel with her king. Indeed, when she next turned to him she laughed.

"Well, well, my lord. We are to hoodwink Louis once again, is that what you propose? Aye, good, we are the ones to do it. How shall we go about preparing him? He is a simpleton but even simpletons must be prepared."

Henry was gratified that she had come around and dropped his cutting tone. "I shall send an embassy suggesting the alliance. I shall make the idea come into his head that since fate brought him only daughters he had better use them to good advantage. I will make him see that his advantage lies in making a marriage with a prince of England so that someday, perhaps, his grandson may wear a double crown."

"There's sense in that," said Eleanor. "And do you also

look into the future in that way and see our grandchild ruling France and England both?"

"My eyes are on the Vexin," Henry said bluntly. "I see no further."

The queen winced. It had been obvious to her a long time that Henry looked at lands alone and at the ruling of them —seldom at his wife and children other than as pawns with whom to gain these lands. She did not say so now, but in her heart she chalked another mark against him. She only said: "And who will lead this subtle embassy?"

"Thomas can do it. He has already fleshed out some of my ideas."

"I see." Her voice had winter in it. "Why do you come to me then?"

"For your experience," said Henry. "You know the Frankish court." And feeling the chill about her, he came forward once again to touch her, but she pulled away.

"Aye, I know the Frankish court," said Eleanor. "And does the chancellor know it? Why is it always and always the chancellor? The chancellor must entertain the King of Norway and the chancellor must go to France. He sets himself up so that he lives better than his king. And you allow it. You conspire with him to set you in the shadow!"

"Thomas is valuable to me, you know that," Henry said, and then he paused and looked at her, a long compelling look. And when he spoke again his voice was grave. "He is a man whom I have need of, whom I may need above all others some fateful day. Come, give me your understanding." He took her hands and held them and she let them lie in his. "You of all people know the need and duty of a king—to rule his people and to lead them, and to take their sins upon him and to die for them if that is called for—or to stand ready with a servant to play the king for him. Thomas is my chosen servant, have you not seen that? I thought these things more understood in Aquitaine than England."

"We have been far apart," she whispered. "I did not know."

"You know," he said, still in his low grave voice. "We need not speak again."

"He is a Churchman. Does he understand?"

"He understands and does not understand. The thing is far away and may not come at all. He knows that I have chosen him above all others. That is enough."

Suddenly he smiled and pulled her to him and kissed her quickly, a married kiss.

"And with your wisdom and your knowledge of the Frankish court you'll help me with this embassy?"

She nodded.

"Come then," said Henry. "What is the best way, would you advise, to get the better of the French?"

"The best way, yes the best way," Eleanor smiled, and once again the youthful sparkle came into her eyes. "The best way is to dazzle them. How dull they are! Give them pomp and splendor. Show them your wealth—your gold, your jewels, your wine—and it will stupefy them. Aye, let them taste your English beer; that will surprise them! Parade the wealth of England in their crooked streets—all of the marvels that come into London from far places. Make their mouths hang open. Then you can stuff whatever thoughts you have into their foolish brains!"

CHAPTER XVI

"MAKE THEIR MOUTH hang open," the king had said to Thomas.

Henry himself had gone before and met with Louis quietly to broach the subject to the betrothal of their infants. But he left it to his chancellor so to impress the Frankish barons with the wealth and grandeur of the English court that they would acquiesce.

"You play the king for me in this," Henry had said, smiling, his hand on Thomas' sleeve. And Thomas eagerly accepted the new commission. It suited him; he loved magnificence.

He sat now in his silken traveling tent outside the little settlement of La Villette-Saint-Ladre, suburb of Paris where the forests ended and the city farms began, reviewing every detail of his entourage before his final sally across the Pont-au-Change into the Île. So far his embassy, starting from Rouen on a bright June morning of 1158, had done what he intended it to do. The gaudy mile-long train, passing through villages along the way, had left the peasants standing in their fields and doorways with their mouths agape.

Now, within sight of Paris, on the broad open ground where the great Lendit fair was held, Thomas called his final halt and for the last time had his tent set up. It stood, a high-peaked billowing canopy, green as an emerald, in the center of the camp. Around it on the meadow spread the tents of all his knights and squires, his chancery clerks, the shelters for the yeomen and the guards and menials, and the pickets for the horses, runs for the hounds, cadges for the hawks, and all the chancellor's wagons, wains and carts of costly goods well guarded against the rabble French. Never had the fair grounds been so gay, so full of men in costly dress and conscious of their finery. As night came on a hundred fires were lit. Across the Seine Parisians climbed the battlements and looked in wonder out into the darkness where the Englishmen were lighting up the sky.

When the sun rose it found the glorious chancellor and all his retinue upon their knees for Lauds. Then they were up and doing, breaking their fast on travel rations while they struck the tents and loaded up the carts and groomed their horses and themselves. Paris was up too, in anticipation: King Louis and his Spanish queen, his court, his prelates, and all the wealthy merchants of the Île, making their preparations for a decorous reception of this fabulous embassy. More eager were the shopkeepers, the cooks and vintners, even the poor scholars out of curiosity.

The light was rosy and the mist of a warm summer day was rising from the fields. The woodlarks sang as though to entertain the company. And then a silver trumpet blew. The chancellor's entourage rolled out.

Far in the lead the guards and trumpeters went forward to clear the way. They wore the scarlet livery of the king and carried staffs with silver tips or yard-long silver trumpets. Behind them and between their ranks the wagons rolled: eight four-wheeled wagons, carved and painted, drawn by five dappled horses each and carrying the chancellor's personal gear; the high-wheeled wain that bore his chapel, marked with a gilded cross; the wain that held the mattresses and hangings for his bedchamber; the kitchen wain with pots and buckets dangling underneath. Then came the carts with casks of beer for the amazement of French palates, the carts of food, the hoop-topped wagons covered with hides in which the bags and coffers of the chancellor's wealth lay hidden. Beside these walked armed guards with bristling mastiffs snarling on their leads.

Twelve sumpter horses followed, each with its load of table plate or books or parchment rolls, each with its groom in scarlet livery and each with a little liveried long-tailed monkey riding on its back. The Frenchmen laughed to see these. Here was diversion!

After the sumpter horses came the huntsmen, very proud: the stag-hunters and wolf-hunters and cat-hunters each in his own regalia and each with his own pair of greyhounds or brachetti or with a heavy-bodied liam hound, and after them the hawkers with their falcons and gyrfalcons hooded on their wrists.

Now the procession walked in rhythm for behind them came the marching lines of flax-haired English yeomen—twenty-five companies in all, of ten men each, singing in turn the songs of their own native villages. Oh, here the mouths hung open as the sturdy English lads went swinging by singing such tunes as Frenchmen never heard before. But the parade had hardly yet begun. Now came the bright young squires bearing the painted shields of the knights who were to follow, then the pack train servants with their mules, then Thomas' household servants, swaggering in their new green tunics and soft leather shoes.

There was a space, a silence, a settling of the dust, and then the mounted cortege came on, two by two: the knights in parti-colored surcoats riding their sleek-skinned destriers and then the clerks, perhaps more somber in their dress but no less rich, pacing on little palfreys or soft-gaited mules. They did not look to right or left but each aware of his own elegance rode easily, a little smile upon his lips. Only the clerk Fitzstephen, now a deacon in the chancellor's court, let his eyes dart here and there upon the long procession and the watching French.

Oh yes, indeed, their mouths hung open now! Here came the chancellor himself at last, riding among the dignitaries of his court. Their robes were gaudy-bright and shone with jewels, their spurs were silvered and their horses draped with strips of colored silk. Thomas rode tall among them, sitting the springing step of his high-mettled destrier as though he sat upon a throne. The horse itself was cause for wonder, a black and shining stallion standing full eighteen hands, but the chancellor more wondrous still. He rode bare-headed and his hair, still dark, was cut short like a clerk's, showing his ear lobes. His face, austere and pale, shone with a light of pride. His dark eyes flashed. The silver-thread embroidery on his cloak was of such simple elegance that no one of the populace could guess its worth. His gloves were gilded, crusted with jewels, and his spurs were gold. Around his neck on a broad jewel-studded chain he wore the Great Seal of the King of England. He did not seem to be aware of all the gaping crowds, but as he passed across the bridge he heard a man say to his neighbor: "If this be but the chancellor, God grant me sight of the king!" And he was happy.

"You play the king for me in this," Henry had said. And Thomas, hearing the surface of the words alone, had done his best to fill the role. "He understands and does not understand," Henry had said to Eleanor. And Thomas, the politician now above all things—as he had been a student once, a clerk, an archdeacon—understood only the politics of this commission: his embassy must awe the French. In this he was successful, as in all things it was his habit to succeed, and did not question the king's words. He sent rich gifts, of cloaks and plate and vestments, horses and hounds and hawks, to every man of standing among the French. He gave a feast of such proportions that the eels along cost more than one hundred shillings; the barons fell to him. He paid the debts of English scholars in the schools; the merchants fell. He opened up the casks of beer for all to come and try as freely as they liked; the populace fell. Nor was it only pomp and wealth that he displayed. Mild Louis was not one to fall for these; Louis had seen the Emperor of Byzantium, the King of Sicily, with all their gold and silken garments, gems and fruits and strange wild beasts, and he was not impressed. He liked simplicity and gentle discourse, pondering aloud on all the ways that men seek God or hide from Him. And so with Louis, Thomas slipped into the old simplicity that he had known with Theobald, and made his mark.

The stage was set, and in September Henry returned to Paris with a small company. He spoke with all the modesty of a true vassal to his overlord, King Louis, and he visited the shrines and gave largesse to lepers and the poor. Into his gentle care was given, then, as was the custom, the betrothed—the infant Princess Marguerite, just six months old—to be raised in the domain of her future husband, the baby prince, young Henry.

The French were not such fools—they told themselves—as Henry and his Eleanor might think. They made some stipulations: the princess was to live in Normandy rather than England; the castles of her dowry, the Vexin, were to be held in custody by three Knights Templar until her marriage; Louis himself would ride with Henry when he took her, seeing her safe to Newburgh where she would live and grow to marry and, perhaps, to be a queen.

The two kings had parted friends. Nearly a year passed

thus with peace between them and Henry would have kept it so, for to be free of quarrels on this front allowed him the more strength to deal with his own restless barons. But then came an opportunity Henry could not resist, an opportunity to gain more lands.

The Mediterranean county of Toulouse had long been claimed by Aquitaine (the duchess' father had been born there; her grandmother had owned it) and Henry always kept an eye on it to see when he might press his claim. Indeed, as he had used his first son to secure the Vexin, he had used his second, Richard, to make alliance with the Count of Barcelona, enemy of Toulouse. Now, as he held his Lammas court in Rouen in the late summer of 1159, the news was brought him of a fresh quarrel between the Count of Toulouse and the Count of Barcelona, Raymond of Berenger, his neighbor to the south.

"It is inopportune," Henry complained.

"And yet imperative," said Thomas.

"And yet imperative," Henry agreed. "We cannot let it slip."

They spoke no more before the company but afterward, when they came in from riding, they paced together in the covered walk beside the garden, out of the sun. The shade was deep here, and in the courtyard a little fountain splashed, but it was hot and close. The gnats swarmed round the sweat upon their faces.

"It will be good to be out in the field again," said Thomas.

"Are you war-hungry?" Henry asked him, almost lazily. "You have had very little of it then."

"No, only restless," Thomas said easily. His footing with the king grew ever more casual as they spent more time together. He did not drop his guard but gradually, over the years, his tone had changed.

"This campaign will need a good-sized army," Henry continued. "I foresee it will be long." He turned to Thomas suddenly. "How many knights can you supply me, Tom, now that you've grown so wealthy? Fifty? A hundred?" His tone was goading but Thomas smiled. "I haven't reckoned them," he said. Then he continued, almost carelessly, "You should use mercenaries for so long a campaign as you foresee."

They walked in silence to the worn steps where the door led to the passage and then they turned and walked back down the colonnade.

"I shall use mercenaries of course," said Henry. "And how shall I pay for them?"

"There is the scutage tax," said Thomas. "It's my belief you have not used that to its full advantage."

"I've used it," Henry contradicted him. "I hear the outcry yet. You think my barons will pay it this time without pressure?"

"I think that they will welcome it," said Thomas. "De Scalers spoke to me only yesterday of the hardship of bringing knights to Normandy for more than forty days. Others have mentioned it."

"De Scalers complains of me, does he?"

"No, not complains. But he would find it easier to pay the scutage of two marks on every shield than bring the knights themselves. Then there is the scutage from the Church. Surely you would rather have Church money than Church knights."

"No, I don't want the riffraff Canterbury calls *his* knights. God's breath!" The king broke out in laughter. "Don't you remember what he sent me for the campaign in Anjou? No, I'll take the scutage." Again there was a silence while they walked, the young king scuffling thoughtfully along the worn stone corridor, his head bent and his fingers pulling on his lip. "It's not enough," he said at last. "I've used the scutage tax before," his voice was almost hurt, "although you say I haven't. . . ."

"To its full advantage," Thomas corrected.

"Let me finish!" the king snapped. "I say I've used it and it's not enough. I've used it and I've used the borough tax. I've used the Jew's tax. What more is there? I do not want to borrow from the Jews. . . . What of the Church?"

"The Church cannot lend money," Thomas reminded him. "That's usury."

"God's wounds, Tom. What do you take me for? A child? 'That's usury!' " He imitated Thomas in a prissy voice. " 'O, God forbid. Absit, absit. That's usury!' " he mocked.

"Look ye, Thomas," he stopped and faced the chancellor and spoke more soberly, "the Church is rolling in its wealth. I need the money and they have it. And they owe *something* to their king. What do you think?"

"Since the need is pressing," Thomas said thoughtfully, "perhaps the bishops would be willing to send a gift. Some of the abbots could be approached. . . ."

"Approached? In what way? On my knees?"

"Approached by me, my lord."

"Approached. Approached," cried Henry. "Thomas, you stink of Church; you crawl to them and you disgust me. Yes, by God's eyes, I will approach them! I will approach them with a message you can send from me. Here is my message." He stopped and glared at Thomas. "Send them this: 'I, Henry, King of the English, send you greetings. I will accept from you for my campaign in Toulouse a gift of' —so many pounds—you work it out—so many pounds from this one, so many pounds from that. You work it out. You know what each can give. And do not stint."

"As you will," said Thomas soberly.

"You work it out," repeated Henry, happy with his idea. "You know the Church. That's your domain." He smiled to see his chancellor's somber face. "And while we are about it, what can *you* give? How many knights did you say? Two hundred? Three hundred?"

"I am not in your good grace this afternoon, I can see that," said Thomas.

"Five hundred?" Henry was grinning.

"You have hit very close to home," said Thomas.

"Six hundred! Six hundred, then it is," cried Henry.

"No, not six hundred," Thomas said. The king was speechless. "And I am sorry," Thomas went on in measured tones, "to find you underestimate my worth and my desire to please you. I shall not furnish you six hundred knights, nor five, nor four." He looked a moment longer, down into Henry's frowning face before he smiled. "But seven hundred."

Henry was startled. "Seven?" Then he reached out and punched the chancellor on the arm and cried, "Tom, you have topped me! You've topped me once again! You sneaking devil, seven hundred knights! And foot soldiers to match." He laughed and shook his head.

"And foot soldiers as well," Thomas agreed.

"And gifts from every tenant that I have among the Churchmen."

"Yes."

"Yes," the king echoed. "Yes, we shall have our army. And we shall have Toulouse. Cities shall fall to us, Thomas, in such a fashion as you have never seen. And one day I shall ride from Scotland down to Aragon, the outer limits of the empire, and never leave my own domain."

No other man could match the army Thomas raised. Full seven hundred knights were sworn to him, as he had promised, and four thousand foot soldiers as well. It was a mighty force.

Because of this King Henry sent him to join the Count of Barcelona. Better, the king had said, that it appear this war was Barcelona (with his English allies) against Toulouse than that the Duke of Normandy dared to defy his overlord the King of France by marching in directly to snatch a wealthy county from beneath his nose. King Louis' ties with Toulouse, his loyal vassal, were far closer than with his restive vassal the Duke of Normandy; his sister was the Countess of Toulouse. Henry held back a little while Barcelona went ahead.

Thus was Thomas in the van, both of his own force and of the army of Barcelona, when they came on Cahors. The stronghold stood encircled by the river Lot, high on its rocky ledge, barring his path as he came southward toward the city of Toulouse. It was a golden autumn evening. The grain stood high and yellow in the fields outside the town, the fruit, the purple plums and orange apricots, were ripening on the trees, the grapes were hard green clusters under the broad leaves of the vines. No men or beasts stood in the fields, no smoke came from the cottage chimneys and no dogs barked. Everyone had fled before him into the city, taking their chattels and abandoning their homes.

Thomas topped the final rise before the valley, halted, and like a hawk hung poised in his progression under the wide pale sky. And like a hawk's his keen eyes picked out everything about the scene: the undulating farmlands in the late sun, the shadows stretching long blue fingers beside the poplar trees, the gleaming river and high-towered town, all silent and untouched.

Behind him lay a path of devastation, a broad swath of blackened fields, burned crops and plundered villages marking the route that he had taken through this sunny land.

He sat his sweating horse in silence, one hand on the heavy reins, the other on the saddlebow before him steadying his helmet which rested there. His face was darkened by the sun, his neck was leathery. His hair was plastered down with sweat for he had worn his helmet earlier, when they rode through the smoking ruins of a town. His linen undercoat, once white, was stained with soot and his soft leather buskins grimed. Only the polished handle of his sword gleamed in the slanting light. On this hot day when they had ridden far and done no fighting he did not wear his mail. Two sergeants carried it, stretched on its pole between them, and his squire bore his shield.

The Count of Barcelona stopped beside him and their captains halted, just within earshot, ready to be called. Their armies spread out fanlike over the countryside behind them, the mounted troops in clusters with their lances throwing spidery shadows on the stubble fields, the infantry sprawled on the grass or in the shade of trees wherever they had halted, already sleeping as they hit the ground. Far in the distance the supply train crawled along the road: the mules and wagons loaded with the tents, provisions and the loot of the campaign.

The count surveyed the empty fields and town as Thomas had. Then he said with a small dark smile, "A merry welcome."

"Aye," Thomas nodded. "It is no matter. They cannot long withstand our siege."

"You think a siege is necessary?" the count raised a brow. "I think, sir, they cannot long withstand a bold attack from such a force as ours. Why, should I take the bridge and you the postern gate we'd pinch them in a minute."

"You are my master in such things, my lord," said Thomas graciously. He could afford such courtesies since both knew he commanded seven knights to Barcelona's one. "It will be well, then, to talk to someone who knows the city and its garrison."

"I have no such person in my company," the count said. There was impatience in his tone. He was a man whose habit was to strike and afterward to think.

"Giles!" Thomas turned and called his captain, as though he had not heard the count. "Send out a party to bring us someone who knows the town."

"If it seems wise to you, my lord," Thomas said deferentially, "shall we set camp there by the river for tonight? And rest our men? And on the morrow fight?"

"As you would have it, sir," the count said with great courtesy. He was not easily offended by a man with seven hundred knights.

The camp was sprawled along the river bank, the morning fires dying in the sun, the ashes white, the damp low-lying ground already hardened under many feet. Mass had been said, and the field rations, salted beef and bread, had been doled out—though many men ate better on the plunder of the day before. Thus spiritually comforted, well fed, and conscious of their strength the army waited for the sun to climb. Surprisingly, perhaps, there was but little noise in all the camp, no laughter.

Thomas sat on a little folding stool before his tent, hunched over with his knees apart, his elbows on his knees, and squinted down the river toward the bridge. He spoke but little though four men sat with him: the Count of Barcelona and his constable, the Bishop of Le Mans, and King Henry's constable, Henry of Essex, who had been sent to join them from the king's forces. At the mere sight of Essex when he had ridden into camp that night, Thomas had caught the message from the king: "Devise an opportunity to test him out," as though the words were said aloud. Thus he smiled when he greeted him; and Essex took it for a smile of warmth.

The captain, Giles, approached, begged pardon, and announced he had the prisoner Thomas had sent him for, a man who knew the town.

He was a short and stocky man, a craftsman by the look of him for he had on a leather apron over his cotton shirt. His hands were bound behind him and he staggered when the soldiers pushed him forward and then slowly, almost lazily, sank down upon his knees. His eyes were closed, his lips were swollen, and the blood ran down his chin. From time to time his tongue came out to soothe his battered mouth, and when the blood collected he leaned forward and spit it on the ground.

Thomas was irritated. "Did you have to be so rough?" he asked.

The soldiers stood back, wooden, and said nothing. "He gave us a bad fight, sire," Giles explained.

Thomas looked at the man. "Well, what is your name?" he asked.

The man made no reply and Giles spoke for him: "He says his name is Ponce, sire, and that he is a coffin-maker for his trade."

The soldiers smiled and would have made remark on this, but Thomas glanced at them and they were silent.

"Well, Ponce," he said, "now that you've had your fight, tell us about your city. How many men do you have in your garrison? Who guards the bridge?" The man said nothing and Thomas continued calmly, "You are a man of spirit; you have shown us that. Now we expect that you will talk to us. Who is the garrison commander? How many men has he?"

The man of Cahors never raised his eyes. He bent his head a little farther and let the blood drip from his mouth.

"Answer me!" Thomas said sharply.

Giles took a quick step forward, grabbed the coffin-maker by the hair and jerked his head up while he rammed a knee into his back. Here for the first time Ponce's eyes flew open, wildly, and he made a sound.

"Answer me."

Giles pulled the head back till the neck was stretched and Ponce's jaw gaped open and his eyes rolled, searching the sky. He made a noise as if to speak. His throat constricted and his tongue came out.

"Ease up a little," Thomas commanded, his tone hard. "You choke him so he cannot speak."

Giles loosed him and the prisoner fell forward with his face upon the ground. His shoulders heaved. A long black stream of blood and vomit gushed from his mouth.

Thomas stood up in anger. "What sort of fools do you have in your company?" he barked at Giles. "They've beaten him until he is no use. Take him away." He looked down at the prisoner, then up at Giles again. "I want the men who did this punished."

"Yes, sire," said Giles, unmoved. Then: "What shall we do with him?" He nodded toward the coffin-maker from Cahors who lay curled up before them on his knees, beating his cheek against the ground.

"Hang him up before the bridge where all can see. And let him be a warning." Thomas turned and walked away from the unpleasant sight. The others followed him.

"Perhaps it would be wiser," the Bishop of Le Mans said, "if we sent an emissary to the bridge demanding parley. Then we shall know just where we stand."

"We will do that, my lord. Of course," said Thomas. "Wisely spoken." His courtesy increased proportionately with his irritation. It had been his idea to enter parley with some prior information but he had only wasted time. He looked to Barcelona for his confirmation and the count looked at him. But while their heads were turned, thus, and before they spoke, they heard a trumpet blaring from the city walls and then the grinding of the city gate as it was lifted on its chains. They turned and stared with startled faces toward the bridge.

"What's this? Do they come out for parley?" the bishop asked.

There was commotion down along the river bank. They strained and stared, but from their low position they could see nothing of the bridge except the tips of lances and the banners flying—a long procession riding out.

"No. Not for parley," Thomas said.

"My horse!" the Count of Barcelona shouted as he turned to run up toward the higher ground.

Essex the Constable grabbed Thomas' arm. "To higher ground," he said. His voice was hoarse but on his broad and bearded face there was an eager smile. "They mean to fight!"

Thomas grinned back at him. "They're fools!" he said, as

he and Essex cut around the tents and bounded up the hillside after the count.

"Foolhardy!" Thomas repeated as they ran. "Why? What is their meaning? How do they dare to sally out against a force like ours?"

They reached the crest. "There! There's their reason!" Essex shouted, pointing ahead. And Thomas looked, and saw drawn up along the farther ridge a line of armored knights with foot soldiers. They flew the banner of Toulouse.

"Sound trumpets," Thomas said. "I must find Barcelona."

He found him in the midst of turmoil, standing immobile while his armorers bent down before him to tie his leggings. He was already in his hauberk and the close-fitting coif made his dark narrow face seem narrower still as he looked right and left—first at the hilltop where the horsement of Toulouse were gathered, then at the riverside and bridge below—scanning the areas of battle.

"My lord," said Thomas, panting, "if you will let my army take the hilltop and yours the valley, we will have Cahors before this night."

"As you will have it, Chancellor," the count said calmly. "I will engage Cahors and you engage the army from Toulouse. And the first one triumphant shall join the other."

His horse was brought up and his armorers stood back. He put his hands on Thomas' shoulders and the two embraced and then he turned away and stepping into his sergeant's cradled hands he swung into the saddle. "God protect you," he called down to Thomas.

"And God be with you," Thomas answered, smiling up.

The count was gone and Thomas turned to search the hillside for his standard and his horse. Soldiers were running by him, shouting, their mouths wide and their eyes absorbed, desperate to find their companies. Thomas saw his standard riding high and made his way to it. Essex was waiting there, already mounted and Thomas' captains had gathered round it. His horse was saddled and his squire was ready with his shield, his sergeants with his mail.

"We take the hilltop," Thomas shouted up to Essex, and the constable looked down and grinned, his white teeth gleaming in his beard beneath the heavy nosepiece of his helm.

Then while he slipped into his hauberk, feeling the weight of metal on his shoulders and the constriction of the coif about his head, he spoke to his commanders: "I want the lines drawn up along the ridge. Roger to take the right wing by that line of poplars. The left wing over beyond the gully."

He pointed down the slope. "Bertrand, you rally there. Essex and I will take the center." He helped his sergeant to slip his sword belt out through the side-slit of his hauberk and buckled on his sword. "Tell the trumpeters to sound the call," he said, "and send precursors with my orders. Foot soldiers to the fore, the mounted troops behind. I'll keep the archers in the center, on the highest ground." He nodded at the hillcrest and then turned and took his horse's reins and heaved himself into the saddle without aid.

He looked around him from this added height, a first clear view. Behind him Barcelona had already drawn his army off, down toward the city. Across from him the Toulouse forces waited his advance. A single horseman had come forward from their ranks and rode along them, a tiny prancing figure. His own contingents were taking order now; looking right and left he saw his flanking forces coming to position. Then he stared out across the draw again, sizing his enemy. "How many do you make them out to be?" he said to Essex.

"Three hundred at the most," the constable answered.

"Will they stand? Or will we have to chase them, do you think, when they have seen our number?"

But Essex did not answer. He was staring at the Toulouse horseman still riding back and forth. "May I have leave," he asked, "to take that knight who flaunts himself before us? Who is it? Can you make him out?"

"I cannot see," said Thomas. "But you may have him." This was a sacrifice. He looked away—to judge how near to readiness his forces were, but also so that Essex might not see his face. He would have liked to take that horseman for himself. Thomas had never been in single combat against a worthy enemy. But stronger than desire was the king's voice in his ears: "Devise an opportunity. . . ."

He looked again at Essex. The constable had taken up his shield and slipped his arm through it. His lance was resting in his gloved right hand. His massive shoulders settled and his head moved forward in its pointed helm. He is already in the fray, thought Thomas.

The precursors came racing back; all was in readiness. "Lift high the standard," he commanded. He drew his sword and pointed it aloft. The line grew silent, all heads turned to him.

"Set your hopes only in the Son of God," he called, "and fall upon the enemy and they are yours!" He brought his sword down with a sweep, pointing it out across the battlefield. "King's men!" he shouted, and "King's men!" came echoing down the line. The trumpets sounded and with a roar the foot soldiers ran forward, pell-mell down the slope.

The constable's horse leaped in its place, feeling its rider stiffen. But Thomas put his hand out and grabbed Essex's arm. "Not yet," he said.

The foot soldiers had drawn the enemy infantry to meet them. They mixed, now, in the little valley, the spearmen pausing to throw their javelins and then hang back, the swordsmen and the men with axes charging in to lay about them in a yelling tangled mob. Already from the farther side a few lone figures broke away to scramble up the golden hillside in retreat.

Thomas turned and spoke to Giles. "Keep the bowmen on the hill," he said. "We may not need them." Giles turned to go and Thomas leaned and took his helmet from his armorer and then his shield and lance. His horse was sidling impatiently.

"All right," he said to Essex. "Now!"

The constable's horse broke like an arrow from beside him and all along the line the knights released their tight rein and their destriers plunged forward. Thomas could feel the earth quake as they rode, himself among them. They thundered down the slope and through the heaving knots of fighting foot soldiers, across the shallow draw and up toward where the knights of Toulouse waited them.

Thomas saw it all with utmost clarity: his horse's ears, the ground before him, Essex to his right. He saw the forces of his own right wing draw out ahead of them, close in around the enemy, and saw the wavering in the Toulouse line. "They cannot stand," he thought despairingly. "There'll be no battle."

He let his horse out and rode close to Essex. "They will break!" he yelled. And even as he spoke he heard the frantic trumpet call and saw the brave line of the Toulouse horsemen turn in confusion, knight crowding neighbor knight for room to flee.

Essex was cursing as he galloped, searching the backs of the retreating army for his challenger, but it was hopeless. They could no longer even see the enemy; the men of their right wing had broken in ahead of them and it was they who had the honor of pursuit.

Thomas followed till the scattered enemy and their pursuers were swallowed in the distant woods. Then he called halt and rallied those he could of his remaining force and turned and headed for Cahors.

Cahors had fallen to the Count of Barcelona and there

rose from it the smoke of many fires and the screams of those pursued within its walls. All afternoon and late into the night the sack continued. Thomas restrained his own men, out of courtesy to Barcelona, making them camp outside the city walls, and himself waited the count's invitation to enter in. Thus it was after dark when he rode down the market road and past the body of Ponce the coffin-maker, hanging in chains and still alive, and crossed the bridge.

Essex and the Bishop of Le Mans rode with him and he noticed how the bishop winced to hear the bellowing of the soldiers and the screams of those they came upon, the running feet, the thud of ax on iron-studded door, the shrieks of women and the drunken laugh. He made no comment and they rode on through the battered city gate and up the street behind the captain who had been sent to guide them.

In the poor section of the city the fires blazed in wood and thatch and it was scorching in the street and glaring bright. But in the merchant's quarter where the stone houses stood, the cobbled squares and alleyways were dark, lighted only by the sparks that flew above them, and by a windy torch that here and there bobbed in an empty window. Here soldiers crowded in black doorways or staggered shadowy along the walls, their arms piled full of linens, plate, or fur-lined cloaks. The flicker of a torch shone through a splintered door as they passed by and lit upon the bodies of the householder, his wife and children where they lay, draining their blood into the running gutter.

Around an angle by a little cluttered square they came upon a group of their own foot soldiers who had sneaked off into the city without leave. Thomas recognized them by their surcoats and he stopped. They were already drunk as pigs, their mouths wet and their faces urgent as they crowded round a woman in their midst. She was half naked and she clasped her hands across her breasts as she turned in their circle, pleading for mercy in little yelping shrieks while they snatched at her, tore her clothing, and made pig noises in their throats.

Thomas rode in among them and they turned and growled at him, then recognized him and fell back and hid among the shadows, waiting for him to go. "Disperse!" he bellowed at them. "Back to your camp, you dogs!" They did not answer and he heard the woman whimper in their clutch. He rode at them and found himself in empty shadow, turned and rode back across the square, peering in doorways and up crooked stairs. The others watched him and the captain said, with just a touch of scorn, "My lord, the Count of Barcelona waits."

They went on silently until the Bishop of Le Mans, made bold by Thomas' action, spoke. "I wonder," he said, keeping his voice as mild as he could manage, "if it is necessary to sack such a town as this." He knew Cahors and loved it.

"It is a matter of war," said Thomas curtly. "For men of war to say." After a little while he spoke more gently, soothing the bishop, "These men are mercenaries," he explained, "and they expect it. They count it in their pay. You may not find it pleasant, Richard. I do not relish it myself. But it is necessary."

King Henry's army had come on the city of Toulouse in August. Another month and Thomas and the Count of Barcelona joined him. Bound by such massive force the city had but little hope. Then came surprise: King Louis sent word to his vassal, Duke of Normandy, that he himself was in the city and charged him with his sacred oath not to attack his overlord.

It was a blow, a master stroke. Who would have thought the dovelike Louis would have flown to make his nest within the red-walled city of Toulouse and thus defy his vassal to attack it? King Henry raged a day, flinging the furniture around his tent and cursing all who came within his sight, and then he called his captains and announced he would withdraw.

It was a disappointment to the king but even greater to his chancellor whose lot had been frustration all through the long campaign. But Thomas did not dare to speak against the temper of the king, although his thoughts were clear.

"I leave tomorrow," Henry said sullenly, as though in answer to those thoughts.

Thomas said nothing.

"I shall withdraw to Poitou." He glanced up at his chancellor's dark face and suddenly burst out again: "You do not understand these things!"

"I do, my lord," said Thomas to placate him.

"How can a clerk know the affairs of kings? I cannot, cannot take the town while my liege lord is in it. My oath to him cannot be broken. My honor rests on that!"

Thomas knew very well that honor did not carry so much weight in this as caution: the Duke of Normandy and King of England dared not risk a personal assault upon his overlord; too many vassals of his own, restive themselves in Aquitaine and Anjou and in the far-off reaches of Northumbria, waited just such a precedent for action of their own. King Henry was outplayed.

"I understand, my lord," Thomas repeated tonelessly, although his face betrayed he understood perhaps too much.

"You do not understand!" cried Henry. "I see it in your stubborn face. And you will never understand. You are a butcher's son parading as a knight. The whole world laughs to see you! Yet you rise up before me and council me to go against my honor! I will not do it!" His voice dropped and he continued with cold cruelty. "I may not. But since you have no honor to defend, my chancellor, you stay. Aye, you can keep your splendid armies. You can defend what we have taken against the French—aye, show them that King Henry's second best is better than their best. Eh, Tom?" His smile was a mere show of teeth. "Show them for me."

Thomas said nothing, though the blood burned in his face. And in his heart the hot vindictive spark that always lay there flamed into hatred for an instant before caution smothered it.

King Henry took his forces and withdrew; the Count of Barcelona led his army off to garrison Cahors. Thomas deployed his knights and companies in a wide circle around Toulouse, but he did not attack. Instead he took a troop of his best men and rode about the countryside seeking out skirmishes with local forces, besieging castles, plundering towns and villages. And still the spark burned in his heart and would not let him rest. He rode away from burning towns with half a hundred prisoners and his men jubilant; he listened to the abject words of castle seneschals surrendering their strongholds and their goods; he sat with Essex on a forest road, sweat on their faces and their horses done, and laughed to see the enemy flee through the trees. And still he could not rest.

There was a bold young knight, and famous, Engelram de Trie, who had come with King Louis to Toulouse, and he was restless too. He swore a heavy oath that he would meet the chancellor and spit him on his lance as he would spit a chicken or a suckling pig. And he went out at night by secret ways and threaded through the sleeping soldiers, leading his horse with cloths around its feet, and though he slew a score of knights, in fair fight, in as many days, he did not come on Thomas.

Thus it went on until the winter months set in, ending the time for war. Thomas sent word back to his captains to lift the siege, rally their forces all together, and move out.

And he himself came riding, stained and weary, back along the forest roads and into camp.

It was a moist November day when dying leaves fell slowly from their trees and squirrels and little vermin scurried among them storing their hidden nests and winter birds came winging from the north that Thomas watched the last of all the long processions of his armies draining out along the roads from Toulouse, moving north. He sat with Essex and his sergeants as the final overloaded wagon trundled by them, and when the last recurring shrieks of its ungreased axles died away, they heard again the sound of church bells in the city and the cheering of the people on the walls.

Thomas looked back and shrugged, then looked again. A knight was riding toward them, armored and helmeted, bearing a shield and upright lance. They heard a shout and saw him cut across a low brown field, then disappear behind a grove of trees.

"It is a challenger!" said Thomas.

"But too late," the constable said mildly. "He only means to crow in safety, now we depart."

"No, not too late," said Thomas. "Bring me my hauberk and my shield." He jumped down from his horse and armed himself and mounted once again, feeling the flame leap in his breast and hatred for the church bells and the cheering from the town. He did not take defeat with easy heart.

"Wait here," he said, and put his horse into a trot across the desolate and littered field where they had camped.

He heard the sound of Essex's horse behind him and his rough voice, "I will be your squire," but his attention was fixed on the grove of trees—whether to risk a ride through it or wait the challenger in the clear.

He may now come, he thought, and boldly put his horse into a lope downhill into the gully. The path went winding through the trees, bare trunks, bare ground, denuded by the soldiers in their search for firewood, and overhead a network of bare twigs and brittle leaves. The horse moved forward, walking now, picking its way down the smooth slope and up again, and Thomas looked from side to side, searching the columns of gray light between the trees. A crow rose suddenly ahead of him, flapping its wings and cawing, and Thomas felt a sweat start out of him.

"There! To the right!" cried Essex as they came into the clear. Thomas wheeled and saw the stranger, sitting a heavy dappled horse, shield raised and lance upright, not thirty yards away.

The knight had seen them and he jerked his lance into the air. "Ho, knight," he called. "Who goes there? Give me good reason why you ride toward Toulouse."

Thomas settled in the saddle and felt the muscles of his horse quiver beneath him, a powerful machine—as he was—for destruction. Now he was happy. All the crows of hell could flap their wings at him and he would feel no fear. "I ride where I have mind to," he replied. "Who bars my way?"

"I bar your way. Because you are a Norman dog!"

"Sir, you shall die for that," said Thomas. "What is your name that I may know whom I have killed?" His voice was steady and while he spoke he took the measure of his challenger: a brawny man and young, wearing the squared-off helmet of the French and on his shield a blue device, a branching stipe and star.

"You know me!" jeered the challenger. "Shall I list off the names of all your fellow knights whom I have slain?"

So this was Engelram de Trie! Thomas felt a surge of exultation that God had given him this opportunity. "Holy Mother, I thank thee," he breathed.

Essex behind him in the shadow of the trees bellowed against his silence: "Beware, Sir Engelram. You face the chancellor of the King of England!"

Thomas smiled grimly to see the horseman start. He has been looking long for me, he thought. He saw the lance come down and level at him.

De Trie rose in his stirrups. "Now we have met," he called, "I mean to kill you, Chancellor!"

"Now we have met, look well on me," said Thomas, "for I am the last thing you shall ever see before you die."

"*You* die!"

He heard the Frenchman's shout and saw his horse bolt forward as his own horse surged beneath him and he raised his lance and leveled it above his shoulder, ready for the thrust.

He heard and felt no more until they met. The shock of lance on shield tore through his body as his horse plunged on. The wrench upon his shoulder told him that his own lance had struck square. He felt no wound and wheeled to see the Frenchman struggling to regain his seat and stop his horse and turn him. Then they came at each other once again.

Five times they passed thus till their breath came rasping and their shoulders quivered when they raised their arms. But they were unaware of pain or weariness; only their thrusts were not so true or powerful. On the sixth charge de Trie's blue shield came up too late and Thomas' lance struck at an angle, with such a shock it splintered and broke off. He pulled his horse back on its haunches and wheeled, keeping the other close. The Frenchman's lance had grazed his shoulder and Thomas threw his own shaft down and grabbed it. They grappled while their horses plunged and turned. Thomas was the better horseman, though he was older and he was tiring. He had advantage of de Trie in height and length of arm and he rose in his stirrups to stand over him. Their knees were locked against each other and their faces close. Thomas saw de Trie's lips stretched back over his clenched teeth and felt the frantic strength of his young shoulders as he tugged on the lance. He saw that he was fighting like an animal, by instinct, and his own mind cleared. With a quick feint and thrust he let go of the lance and seized the Frenchman's helmet by the nosepiece and backed away, pulling, yanking, jerking with all his strength, and dragged him from his horse. Then he leaped down while yet de Trie lay stretched upon the grass, the wind knocked from him and his helmet rolling free. He drew his sword and had it at the other's throat before he could rise up.

"Pause, Chancellor!" The voice came from a horseman standing not twenty feet away. Thomas stood still, his eyes fixed on de Trie and his sword steady in his hand. He was aware of not one horseman only but a company, in arms, beside him, but still he did not look around.

"Have mercy," the voice said, "and let this knight go free, as you are sworn to serve a merciful God."

Thomas' breath burned in his throat, his shoulders heaved as though he sobbed, his legs were quivering, but he held his pose. Slowly he felt the rage of battle drain from him. At last he spoke, though he did not look up. "I hear you," he said, panting, "and I will have mercy if this knight will yield."

"Have you heard, Engelram?" The voice was gentle but had deep authority. "Do now as you are told, and yield. We will have no more blood."

De Trie lay pinioned and he rolled his eyes to where the horsemen stood, then back to Thomas and the sword. His broad scarred face contorted with the words he had to speak. "I yield," he said.

Thomas stood back, sword still in hand, and watched him rise. "I claim your horse as trophy, Engelram de Trie."

De Trie stood with his head bowed, eyes upon the ground. It was his first defeat. "Aye, he is yours," he said.

Now it was time for Thomas to turn, face the horsemen, and find out if they were honorable men or if they meant to take him prisoner. He wondered whether Essex stood by him still and, if he did, what chance he had to make escape and ride to their own forces, what he would tell King Henry of the combat, and what the king would say. He turned.

Above him sat three knights on three tall destriers with a full company of bowmen drawn up behind them. His eyes went to the central figure and he saw, beneath the crowned helmet, the long and concave face of Louis, King of France. He went down on one knee.

"Strange meeting, Thomas," the king said. His eyes were mild. "You have shown wisdom in your mercy," he added gravely.

"My lord, I am within your power, thus I am content," said Thomas.

King Louis' smile was without mirth. "You may go free," he said, "and back to Henry." He made a little gesture. "Tell him you owe a debt to me, and he on your behalf."

Thomas rose and would have gone to him to kiss his stirrup, a formal gesture of his indebtedness, but Louis waved him off. And then, as Thomas backed away, he called out after him, "Thomas, try to remember—keep it in your heart—that you serve God."

Thomas walked to where the gray horse cropped the grass, took it and led it to his own and mounted. Essex was waiting for him, sitting rocklike in the shadow of the trees. They did not speak as silently they turned together, feeling the bowmen's eyes upon their backs, and rode with slow deliberation into the grove.

When they came out into the field beyond they broke into a gallop, still not speaking, and rode until they knew that they were free. Then at last Thomas stopped and took his helmet off and wiped his face. He glanced at Essex.

"You should have made off when you saw the company approach," he said. "You could not know the outcome."

Henry stared at him, half incredulous. "Leave you to face them by yourself?" he asked, a dark flush mounting in his face.

Thomas turned his head away and tugged at the laces of his coif to loosen it. "You could accomplish nothing by remaining," he said carelessly. "You were unarmed and we were two to twenty."

The constable grabbed Thomas' arm and jerked him round. His bearded face was very close and hot with wounded pride.

"Aye, I could leave you, Chancellor. I could have left you twenty times when danger threatened in the last months. Do you believe it of me? That I could run away from danger? Is that what you think?"

His eyes were black with anger and Thomas met his stare with a deep-searching answering look. "I do not think so, Henry," he said quietly. "I know you well; you are a man of honor."

The constable relaxed and they moved on, keeping their horses to an easy lope, their lonely hoofbeats echoing on the beaten track, so as to reach their column before dark. After a long time Essex spoke again, his rough voice jolting to the rhythm of his horse. "You will have much to tell the king," he said.

Thomas laughed shortly. "Aye, I will tell him all he needs to know."

CHAPTER XVII

THOMAS JOINED HENRY in Falaise where he was holding Christmas court and found himself so warmly welcomed by the king, so drawn into the revels of midwinter and made much of, that his pride was soothed. They stayed in Normandy throughout the coming year, a year of many happenings, 1160.

Pope Adrian died; two rival popes were then elected his successor, and there was war between them. Henry, like Louis—it was agreed between them in friendly concourse—backed Pope Alexander. Louis acted for the love of right; Henry for the promise of a favor when it should be asked. The kings retired, each to his own strong city, friendly still.

Then in July the news was brought to Henry from his listeners in the French court that the French queen was with child again. Henry sent for Eleanor to come from England and bring their eldest daughter, Princess Matilda, four years old, to have in readiness should Louis' fortunes change and God send him a son. She brought the young Prince Henry also, so that as heir to Normandy he might renew his pledge of fealty to Louis as his overlord; it would not do to let the

French forget him in their rejoicing over a new heir. The three arrived in good time, early in autumn, but their concern was premature; malicious fate brought Louis one more daughter and the good Queen Constance, worn with the effort, conscious of failure, closed her eyes and died.

Then came another of those lightning moves, so unexpected in the monklike Louis and so unsettling to the Angevins. Before the month was out he took another wife, potential mother of strong sons, a daughter of the powerful Houses of Champagne and Blois, those ancient enemies of Anjou.

But Henry would not be outplayed again. Foresight had brought him what he needed for his next move and, as Thomas pointed out, one must not put his hand upon the plow and then look back. While Louis was preoccupied with his own nuptials, Henry arranged a nuptial ceremony of another sort: in Newburgh, Normandy, before two legates from Pope Alexander (paying off his debt) he hurried through the marriage of Prince Henry, five years old, and Princess Marguerite, just three, and took the Vexin castles of her dower from the Templar's custody. Then he said to Thomas, "Take the future King and Queen of England into your famous household for their nourishing," and turned to face the wrath of Louis and his lords.

But soon again the winter put a term to war and he withdrew with all his court and captains to Le Mans, his ancient capital, snug in his power and contented—for the moment—with his gains. And Thomas, his right hand, too busy for reflection, thought himself contented too. Then came a messenger to Le Mans from Canterbury seeking the chancellor: Archbishop Theobald, ill for so many months, lay dying.

This cold news was brought to Thomas one dark, frostbound January day, 1161, as he sat close beside the fire of his private room dictating correspondence to his clerks. It sent a sudden chill of desolation to his heart, as icy as the fingers of the cold that reached through all the layers of his clothing to his skin.

His father, Theobald, was dying and he called for him. He had sent word before, when he was ill, last summer. Thomas had been busy then; the king could not release him to go home. And in the autumn. No, King Henry was not yet persuaded that he should go. And now.

The firelight flickered on the folded parchments in his secretary's hands: letters from Canterbury, and he knew their contents.

"From the archbishop?" He looked up at his secretary, Ernulf, as he stood before him, high bare forehead shining in the light.

"From the archbishop, and from Master John," said Ernulf, the shadows moving by his moving lips.

From John of Salisbury. Thomas had written John in secret: "Our lord the King has kept me here, but should our father write commanding me, perhaps then I may come."

"Let me read that one first," he said. Then he looked about the little room, the moving firelight on the dark folds of the hangings, the tonsured bent heads of his scribes who paused, their eyes averted, over their manuscripts. "And I should like to be alone."

The stools knocked gently on the floor and parchments whispered as they rubbed together. The hems of long robes crackled on the rushes as they swept over them, and sandals scraped. The door was gently closed, the scribes were gone, the swinging curtains quiet once again in firelight and in shade.

Ernulf remained, and Thomas took the letter from his hand. "From John of Salisbury," he read the familiar script, "To Thomas, Chancellor of the English: In reply to your command, dear friend, I had drafted my lord's letters to our lord the King and to yourself . . ."

"*Had* drafted." Was not this the one?

"Had drafted . . . in such austere terms that the necessity of your immediate return might be impressed upon you and the king. But the unexpected arrival of the king's request that you remain has forced me to temper my language and we concede to the necessities of state. . . ."

Thomas' eyes skimmed on: "We hear that the king and all his court are utterly dependent on your counsel . . . that you and the king are of one heart and mind. . . . But our father asks, then, whether there may be some collusion between you in this matter. . . ."

No, this was not the answer he had hoped for.

He gave the letter back to Ernulf and took the other, from Theobald himself. The archbishop came strongly to his mind and he recalled the quiet voice from long ago: "Do not forget us in your new adventures," and his impassioned answer—he was young—"No, Father, I am in your service always." What was it Theobald said to that? He said that he would always trust him . . . something like that. He had great faith. He meant: "I know that when I need you, you will come."

So long ago. He opened up the parchment and saw it shake,

the shadows jumping in the folds. He read the salutation: "Theobald, Archbishop of Canterbury, to his archdeacon." Cold greeting from his father. But the message, worse: "You have often been recalled and you ought to have returned in answer to a single summons of your father, now old and ill." Was this his conscience speaking? Was this Theobald? "Indeed, it is to be feared that God may punish your tardiness if you shut your ears to the call of obedience forgetting the benefits you have received and despising your father whom you should have carried on your shoulders in his sickness. You were wholly inexcusable and in great peril of our curse had not our lord the King excused your absence on the pretext of his necessity. . . ."

Thomas remembered the light words of the king: "How can I spare you now, my friend?" My friend. "The wrath of Louis and his court and all those angry men of Champagne and of Blois come down upon me. I cannot spare you now!"

Thus spoke the king: "My friend. I cannot spare you." And thus the king had written to Canterbury.

And now Theobald, "to his archdeacon" (he had not written thus before): "Because we set the welfare of the state above our private gains we do not murmur that the king's will has gone against our own. Indeed, we fear that you might be in peril if you returned under his displeasure, for you might be unable to recover his favor through any influence we may have. For the days that are left us are brief, and the favor of the dead is generally of little value. . . ."

The words blurred and Thomas felt the tears well in his eyes. He knew that Ernulf watched them glisten in the firelight but he did not wipe them off.

"Will you go back, my lord?" Ernulf spoke quietly.

Thomas made no sound but shook his head. He did not know. And still he could not read the words.

"Shall I read on for you?"

Thomas gave the letter up and leaned his forehead on his hand to listen.

"Nonetheless," read Ernulf in his pure Latin, "we place our hopes in the love which by the grace of the Holy Spirit we know to be strong in your heart. But beware lest in any way you abuse this indulgence of mine; for you may be sure that the justice of God is not deceived by the error of any man. And we have decided to make a trial of your devotion. . . ." Ernulf hesitated and took a breath, for his eye had run on before. "Your devotion and your diligence," he read, "by noting how you further our petition to the king concerning the business of the church at Exeter. . . ."

Thomas rose abruptly, letting the cloak fall from his shoulders and the lap robe from his knees. The candles jumped and flickered with his movement and Ernulf looked up with the shadows dancing on his long smooth face. "Will you hear more?" he stammered.

"What more?" Thomas' voice croaked and he cleared his throat. "What more?" he asked.

"Only this more," said Ernulf, flustered to see the chancellor towering before him with the shining streaks of tears upon his face. "Only: 'Let us know your will and the will of our lord the King,' and that is all."

Thomas said no more but left the room and went to find the king.

King Henry was in the guardroom of his castle, and he had with him a learned doctor just returned from studying in Salerno, for there was sickness among his men that winter, coughing and strange night howling, lethargy, convulsions, sometimes death, and neither the monks of nearby La Coutoure nor his own court physicians could prevail against it. He looked with blank eyes up at Thomas when he came in winded from climbing the narrow streets, chilled by the wind that blew between the stony walls, breathless with urgency.

"My lord," said Thomas, "I have had word from Canterbury and I must go."

But Henry did not hear his words. "What think you," he asked the doctor. "Is it the plague?"

"It is a plague," the doctor said, "but not of the evil kind. I see no swellings in the groin."

A soldier sat up in the straw beside them with his eyes staring and his mouth stretched wide. Then he bent forward over his knees and coughed, and coughed again, while the men watched him fearfully. At last he straightened up his body and drew in his breath, making a hollow moan, the sound an owl makes in the dead of night. The doctor crossed himself, and so did Thomas. But Henry only watched with narrow eyes. "Is it the Devil's work?" he asked the doctor.

"It is a sickness not of the Devil but of man," the doctor said. "It is a sickness only time will cure—a conflux of those heavenly bodies that pertain. And certain potions I will mix."

"Then go and mix them," Henry said.

The doctor bowed a graceful bow and left.

"My lord," said Thomas once again, scarce breathing in the tainted air, "I must go now to England."

But Henry hardly looked at him. "Not now, not now," he said, as he had said so many times before, and turned and prowled along the row of helpless men stretched out upon the straw, staring at each one, sometimes questioning, touching them even. Thomas walked behind him, tall and silent, heavy in the heart.

Again and yet again as the days passed Thomas brought the subject to the king: "My lord, Archbishop Theobald lies very ill and calls for me." "Yes, yes, I know." "Then have I leave to go?" "Yes, later, when my affairs allow it; yes, of course." "I have been called to come at once." "Why, why at once? He has been ill since summer and still lingers. He will mend. Now, for the present, I have need of you." "I have a duty to him. . . ." "You have your duty to my son, the future king, whose person I have given you to nourish. Speak no more of 'now.' "

Or in the course of business: "There is the matter of the vacant bishoprics. It has been brought to my attention once again the Church at Exeter is now without a bishop as well as those of Worcester and Chester-Coventry. The archbishop awaits your will as to appointments there. . . ." "Yes, yes, a matter; not a pressing matter. Bishoprics are always falling vacant." "Sire, there is talk that you have put at my disposal all the revenues of these three vacant bishoprics; I would return to Canterbury to quell this idle talk and to convey your will. . . ." The answer was a frank and friendly laugh: "Have I not done so?" "Not so, not so; I hold them for the crown." "And what comes to the crown from vacant bishoprics is yours, my Chancellor. Now speak no more."

Or, in a cry of desperation after a night of fearful waking in the stony bed: "Sire, you have called me friend. I ask your favor. Our father Theobald commands. . . ."

"Commands?" The red fires leaped and smoldered in the gray eyes. "Commands?" And the retreating back.

I am a courtier, thought Thomas bitterly, and thus it is to be a courtier, dangling upon the will of him who rules. I am a courtier among the wild beasts of the court, a man no longer. And yet he found no way to cut the cords that bound him to the king.

And in between his arguments, his pleadings and his prayers, he laughed—oh, shame to wake and think of it, deep in the frozen night—he laughed and joked together with the king, did business, hunted, hawked with him, and was his friend.

* * *

In April Archbishop Theobald, the gentle monk of Bec, scholar and king-maker, spiritual father of the English, died in an agony of pain and in the knowledge that of all the bright young men whom he had nourished in his house and sent on to high offices, not one was fit to take his place.

It took him many days to die. Outside in silver sunshine little blossoms sprouted on the twigs in Canterbury gardens as they always did, but in the palace, in the darkened inner room, death sat and waited, listening for the end.

The room was crowded. The carved bed was set up in the center, head to the central pillar, and the archbishop lay on it, propped high on pillows and so thin and wasted as to raise no shape at all under the brocade coverlet. Around him moved his doctors and his intimates. John was with him, faithful secretary, hiding his feelings, self-contained; and the archbishop's brother, Walter of Rochester, worn to a sorry lump with weeping day and night. His widowed sister Margaret had come to Thierceville to be with him and cook for him the clear soups that he had loved in boyhood but which he could not eat. Hubert his chancellor was there, and Eudes his old confessor. In the last days two doctors came to join the infirmarian Gilfridus of Christchurch who since the summer had fought the illness without hope. And nursing him, cooling his scorching skin with spring water, clearing away the sheets stained by his hemorrhaging, stewing fresh costmary leaves to cleanse the air, were two lay brothers, his personal attendants, who had seen to his little wants of daily life through the past years.

In the adjoining anteroom an altar was set up and priests said Mass before it almost continuously through the day and night while bishops, abbots, canons, clerks and laymen of high station came and knelt and heard the service, peered through the doorway to the inner room and went away.

For three days Theobald lay in and out of coma, waking to pain and struggling with it, sinking again defeated. Armed with humility and calm, those traits by which the world had known him many years, he opened up his lips only to pray and never once cried out or made complaint. Toward morning of the last long night when he was roused from coma it was to stare into the ceiling, to bare his teeth, but now he had no strength left even to turn his head or raise his hand.

He seemed to hear the intonations of the service in the next room and to be comforted, but soon he sank again into oblivion.

When the pale April sun had risen high enough to gild the turrets on the cathedral spires and the small thrushes were fussing loudly at their nest building, he opened up his eyes for the last time and seemed to look about the room. His chest was rising, falling, in an agony, sucking the breath in, squeezing it out as though a bellows labored deep within him. The doctor turned from leaning over him and whispered to the chancellor, "He has not long to live." And at these words death rose from his dark corner and came likewise to the bedside to lean down.

A long time since, the hair mat had been brought, and ashes in a little box. Now Gilfridus went to it and took the mat and stretched it on the floor and threw the ashes over it. The two lay brothers pulled back the coverlet and took the frail emaciated body in their arms, light as a little bird, and stripped the robe from it, leaving it only in its stained and wrinkled tunicle, and placed it in the bed of ashes on the floor.

No sound came from the archbishop, and Margaret, thinking him dead, cried out. The murmurs of the service in the next room lulled for an instant while the priests hesitated. Then once again the sound of the forced breathing rattled in the room.

The old confessor, Eudes, knelt by his friend and placed his hand upon the laboring chest, searching his face with loving eyes. "Now you are dying, Theobald. Have ought to say?"

A tremor like the shadow of a nod traveled across the sunken face. The words came, barely discernible, formed in a wheezing outrush of the breath, "Into Thy hands, O, Lord. . . ." The rattle of the indrawn breath was lost beneath the swish and murmur in the room as all those present fell to their knees in prayer and Eudes with shaking hands began the final sacrament. Again the grating exhalation and the half-formed words, ". . . do I commit my spirit."

Eudes crouched round-backed above the body where now the soul was struggling to get free, and death crouched with him, waiting, while the old man dipped his trembling fingers in the oil and touched the eyes, the ears, the nose, the mouth, the hands which he had crossed upon the breast, and then crawled out along the wasted body to touch the feet, whispering the words of exhortation over and over.

"And may the Lord forgive thee all thy sins." His voice was paper-thin and crackled in the room.

Margaret and Walter sobbed aloud; the voices of the priests before the altar rose and fell; outside the birds chirped in the ivy, fluttering their wings. And now the room grew lighter, emptier, for two had gone from it: death and the archbishop.

Gilfridus stepped up softly to the place where death had been and leaning over peered into the hollows of the dead man's eyes. He saw the pupils fixed and dilated. He turned to Hubert, whispered, and the chancellor rose from his knees and said in a firm voice so all could hear: "Verily, the archbishop is dead."

Now the sonorous voices swelled, joined by the prayers of those within the room, deep earnest words to God. And in a moment came the tolling of the mourning bells from the cathedral church, somber and heavy on the air, sounding the final note of death, and Bishop Walter slid from the bedside where he had leaned in prayer and lay flat out upon the floor, weeping into the rushes.

Death hovered over Canterbury all that year. Although he lingered long over Archbishop Theobald, he struck with sudden fingers at a young cowherd who fell in a ditch and drowned, at Anne of Ridingate while she was giving birth to her fifth bastard son, at infants stillborn and at gnarled old men, and many others. Quickest of all he struck at Sylvester, Abbot of St. Augustine's, who at one moment sat at lunch and in the next fell forward on the table and was gone.

From sudden death, Good Lord, deliver us.

Who was to mourn the abbot, Sylvester, having no father or no mother living, having no sister, brother, wife or children, having been contentious in his life, full of vexations?

Elured Porre and all his family mourned him. For with the abbot's death King Henry, through the person of his chancellor, took the monastery's minting privileges unto himself and then, finding no need for it, declared the mint closed.

Elured, who was sixty now, listened while the notice was read out to him and felt the strength go from him. His life was over now. Even his scarred and callused hands, so long of use to him, so long his pride, went limp.

How strange the household was, with Elured no longer at the center of it making demands and twitting them for fools; how quiet with the forge no longer busy all day long, with only Walter starting up the furnace now and again to make some trinket or repair somebody's clasp or bowl; how empty with ever fewer debtors coming to borrow money, knowing that the money was dwindling fast.

It was a household to be shunned. Hawisa, on her marriage four years back, had come to live in it and in the course of time she had brought forth a little son, whom they named Viel, to liven it. But with the birth, Hawisa had turned strange once more. Sometimes she did not know the baby; he became his father's child. Sometimes she sat silently all day long, a living silence that reached out and touched the others in the room so that the neighbors avoided coming here.

When Almon came from Certeham to see them he had a good effect on her. She told her brother that a demon sometimes came into the room at night to threaten her, and gave him a strange confidential look as though he were the one to understand. But Almon told her that the demon did not come and would not come, that she was safe. His smile and quiet eyes brought comfort no one else could bring.

When Elured, too, sat silent with the closing of the mint, Walter was left to keep the household going on his own. He could not do it. He went to Hortone to ask his mother-in-law, Wulviva, for her help.

Oh how Wulviva welcomed being asked! She came, the old life pumping back in her, and took her daughter Hawisa in hand, washed her dank hair and set her to spinning as she had done long ago. She bossed the servants and made old Azo scurry to clean up the forge and keep it all in order. Then she turned to Elured.

"You must appeal," she said. "It is not lawful for the chancellor to close the mint. You must bring suit against the order, Elured."

"Don't be a fool," the old man said. But his eyes lighted up.

"You must get legal counsel while there is money left to pay for it," Wulviva ordered.

"Oh, aye, a woman speaks!" said Elured. And Walter, in the doorway, smiled his thin smile to hear the old familiar nastiness rise in his father's voice.

"You hold the minting privilege from ancient times, isn't that true, Elured?" Wulviva prodded.

He looked at her with scorn. "It is beyond your understanding," he said. "I've minted coins since I was ten years old. My grandfather minted them before me and his father before that and back and back beyond your understanding." His hands were working in his lap.

"A court would need to know how long, precisely," Walter put in.

"Abbot Sylvester was the forty-fifth," said Elured. "Forty-fifth abbot of St. Augustine's who held the minting privilege, one following the other, in a direct line! They had it first of old King Athelstan." He rose and stood as though he were a king himself. "And in our family we have been the moneyers for them almost as long!"

"Call in a lawyer!" Wulviva cried. "Call in a lawyer and make inquiry before the judges of the court. You have a case!"

King Henry and his chancellor had many problems on their minds and one more suit of inquiry about a minting privilege was simply one more case upon the docket to be brought up some time, when more pressing matters could be set aside. No one accompanied the small petition that came from Canterbury; therefore there was no mute and nagging face hanging about the anteroom. Nor had it any man of rank to sponsor it and therefore no oblique reminders dropped into conversations in the hall, no letters to be read and answered, no bargains offered: this favor in return for that. Somewhere, among Ernulf's rolls of parchment, it lay and rotted.

The king and Thomas seemed as close as ever. There was no mention made between them of Archbishop Theobald. News of his death was brought to them and for a day they kept apart but after that whatever change there was in their relationship was not remarked among the people of the court. Thomas was seen more frequently to pray and sometimes was seen weeping when he prayed and this, some people thought, was new. But others said it always had been so. Hamon of Cricklade argued thus, and told a story of what he had seen:

Hamon had come to Le Mans from his home in Wiltshire to see the chancellor, hoping through him to reach the king with a petition. He did not come to town till evening, so he told, and put off bothering the chancellor until day should break. At dawn, as he was going through the streets, he saw a figure in a cloak kneeling at a church door, praying. The dew was very heavy and Hamon sneezed, at which the kneeling figure started, rose to his feet and walked away. Impressed by this devotion, Hamon remarked the gown and stature of the man. Then he went to the palace where the chancellor had his rooms, and entering them he saw the very man, even now putting off the cloak Hamon had noted!

Perhaps these night prayers were a contribution to Thomas' illness—for he did lie ill that winter, with fever and strange dreams and a wasting of the lean flesh on his bones. But with the warmth of spring his health returned.

The king, since Theobald's death, had not been given much to prayer—no more than was his wont, which was attendance daily at his chapel to hear Mass, obedient to custom if somewhat restless. But then, he had great problems on his mind that did not fly away simply because a priest said *Asperges me*. They plagued him through the service:

He and his Church in England had not been getting on well. . . . Both Theobald and now his suffragans annoyed him with complaints about the vacant bishoprics and pestered him for the return of Church lands which had been taken by the crown in Stephen's reign. . . . And on the other hand they claimed immunity from royal justice for all his subjects who could by any stretch call themselves clerks—mere scum, a lot of them, with nothing but a tonsured head to tell them from the ordinary thieves and robbers of his realm. . . . He sensed a restlessness among his barons, also, since he had been so long from England. . . . They did not threaten his own hold, of course, but who knows what they plotted as to succession? . . . He had presented the infant Henry to them for their recognition soon after he himself was crowned. But six years had passed since then. Perhaps the time had come for a reminder. . . . One cannot make an oath too often, the nature of an oath being to fade with time. . . .

This is how his thoughts ran while Mass was being said.

Early in spring he went to Falaise, that ancient seat of all the Dukes of Normandy, to hold his Easter court. Richard de Luci went as his close adviser; Thomas could not travel. And there, some final plans took shape within his head and worked themselves out to the last detail until he could not wait to put them into action. He called for Thomas to come from Le Mans as quickly as he could and bring the little prince, his ward.

Falaise was beautiful in March. Above the river valley and the little sloping town the massive castle stood upon a crag of rock, and trailed a scarf of cloud-wash like a wimple in the wind. Thomas, with his little friend the princeling at his side and followed by the members of his court, his clerks and guards and baggage train, wound up the narrow horse trail from the valley road. He found his heart was lighter than it had been for a long time and that the strength had come back to his limbs. He thought with pleasure of the excitement of being in the court again and he was gratified by his warm welcome. Henry, on the first notice of his arrival, had left his room and come down to the hall, and when they met it was like schoolboys who had been parted by the holidays.

Henry had a favorite room at Falaise, high in a tower that flanked the central keep, for it looked down upon the walls and stony slopes and tiled roofs of the town. Here it was his great-grandfather had been born, William the Bastard known as the Conqueror, son of that dark duke, Robert the Devil, and Arletta, daughter of a tanner of the town. He liked to think of these two, of the blood that flowed in them, and how it joined the blood of Anjou to produce himself.

"I am a man of many different bloods," he said to Thomas, turning from the window and walking back to the small table where the two sat to eat together on the afternoon that Thomas had arrived. They had taken the little prince up with them but no one else, and now the prince had been sent down again to join his mother for he was a lively, somewhat headstrong boy and had been fretful and become a nuisance after the tiring journey.

Thomas looked up at Henry where he stood, the light behind him, and noted once again the burly shoulders, the square head and ruffled hair, the short strong neck. One glance could tell you, even in outline, that this figure was the seat of power in the land. He smiled and nodded.

"Did I ever tell you of my great-grandmother?" Henry sat down briefly at the table, opposite Thomas. "Not this one here, this tanner's daughter of Falaise. My father's grandmother. On the other side?"

"No," Thomas said, still smiling. It was good to be here with the king again.

"She was a witch, they say." He rose again and wandered to the window and then back. "She could never be persuaded to go into church until one day she was at last compelled." He laughed. "She disappeared, they say, in a great cloud of sulphur, during the Mass."

Thomas laughed with him, somewhat carelessly and caught off guard. "Such idle tales are told . . ."

Henry's frown stopped him. "Who speaks of idle tales?" he snapped. "When I speak of my ancestors, I speak not idly!"

"Yes, yes, of course, my lord," said Thomas softly, rising and walking to the window. Sometimes he sat before the king; at other times he found it wiser to stand up. But this he did not do so one could notice it; he kept a certain dignity.

"You would do well," said Henry staring at him, "to take more seriously what I say. I told you long ago that I am of the Devil's brood. It comes to me from both sides. Do you remember what they called my great-grandfather?"

"The Conqueror," said Thomas easily.

"No, no. It is his father that I speak of." He stopped and glared at Thomas' back a moment. "Do not be so easy in your manner with me, Thomas."

Thomas turned and faced him.

"What did they call him, that ancient Duke of Normandy?" Henry persisted.

"Robert the Devil," Thomas said softly.

"Aye, they called him that. The Devil. What do you make of that?"

"Nothing, my lord."

"Nothing? Then you are a dullard and an ignorant man! You should know that such men, with such title, are worshiped, worshiped by many. Their blood is precious to the people." He stared at Thomas and saw his face go troubled; this was one sure way, always, to make his chancellor uneasy. He smiled, a curious, cruel smile. "You drink the blood of Christ our Lord, do you not, Thomas? At the Eucharist? Is it not precious to you?"

Thomas said nothing.

"Was it not spilled upon the ground for you and all mankind? Did they not pierce his side and let the blood flow? Was it not so?" he asked. "I want your answer."

"Yes."

"Was he not king? Was he not Christ the King?"

Thomas said nothing, sensing the crooked argument, and Henry stared at him before he went on in a quieter way: "This blood is precious to mankind, we all know that, this blood of kings. For what is the blood of kings but the blood of all the people? Sometimes it must flow for them." He paused, his voice grown very quiet. "The blood of kings is needful to the people," he almost whispered. "Or, if the king desire and command it, that of another in his place, a second king."

"Sire, this is blasphemy. I do not understand . . ."

"You understand," said Henry scornfully. He looked at Thomas almost with hatred. "You were supposed to teach me, weren't you, Archdeacon? It was for that that Theobald put you beside me? Now it would seem I am the teacher. And you are slow to learn."

Suddenly he turned away and shouted, laughing through his words, "You upstart prelates, thinking to teach a king!"

He doubled back and came to Thomas and put his hands upon his arms. His voice, his face, his manner changed.

"Thomas," he said earnestly, "you are my teacher. You have taught me well. We have done many things together in these past six years, and my lands prosper. I chose you to be closest of all to me. Let us not break our friendship." Tears came to his eyes; he bent his head and rested it upon his chancellor's breast and his hands tightened for a moment, an almost desperate grip.

"My lord," said Thomas, greatly moved, "you honor me. Yes, through your gracious kindness, we are true friends and shall be."

Henry stood a moment, silent. Then with a final pressure of his hands he turned away. He stood a moment with his head down, watching his feet as they kicked at the rushes. Then he sighed and said, "I see we must not try to talk of these things any more."

Thomas was with the king all day and every day. Henry was eager to disclose his plans to his advisers and to put them into execution. Foremost was this: the time was ripe, nay overripe, to call the English barons and the bishops all together to renew their recognition of Prince Henry as the heir of England. His son should not face what he himself had faced when as a boy he sought his rightful place as king.

"Thomas," he said, "I charge you with this mission. You shall take the prince at once to England and call a Great Council—let it be at Whitsuntide, at Winchester—of all my lords both temporal and spiritual. Have them give their oaths of fealty to him as future king. You shall procure for him . . ." all these details had Henry worked out in his eager mind, all calculated to forestall some future question as to his son's succession ". . . you shall procure for him a golden circlet, like a little crown, and all regalia that is proper for such occasions. And first yourself, as chancellor, shall kneel to him and then the barons and the bishops in proper order. Richard de Luci will come with you and act with you in this. I shall not come myself, for this occasion shall be his, as future king."

Henry had spoken. As in the past, it was for Thomas to carry out his words.

On the departure day, Thomas, in his sumptuous riding cloak, came to the hall to say his farewells to the king. He knelt in formal salutation and bade the little prince kneel after him. Henry raised them and kissed his son and sent him to his mother, and the queen went with him to the great covered wain in which he was to ride. De Luci, having made his obeisance, stood by the door till Thomas should come with him and give the signal for the entourage to move.

Then Henry, as on some sudden impulse, stretched out his hand to him. "Wait there," he said. And taking Thomas by the arm drew him aside, into a window niche. They stood alone.

Thomas looked down into the strong, still boyish face. The light came slanting on it, on the weather-roughened surface of the cheeks, the craggy furrow between the brows, the penetrating eyes. He saw the look, like triumph, on it and the half smile in the indentations by the lips as he began to speak. He knew with sinking certainty the words the king would say, and inwardly he gathered in his forces to resist.

Persistently the rumors had come to him while he was in Le Mans: the king had fixed on a successor to Archbishop Theobald—himself, Thomas the Archdeacon. Henry of Pisa, papal legate, had even made the trip to Thomas' sickroom and spoken openly, thinking to benefit the Church. But Thomas had been troubled for he knew quite well, better than any, what the king had in his mind. He wanted his own man, his chancellor, under his thumb, as primate of the Church. Knowing King Henry, knowing the Church, knowing himself a little he knew it was unwise. He could not play this dual role.

But when the king had spoken not a word about it but seemed intent upon the homage to his son and nothing more, Thomas, perhaps with a faint flicker of disappointment but with an overriding feeling of relief, believed the king would fix on someone else. In this mood he was prepared to leave, when suddenly the king drew him aside. And now he knew the very words Henry would speak before he spoke them.

"Thomas," said Henry, "you do not know yet all that is in my mind concerning this trip to England. It is my will—and I have sent this word to Canterbury—that preparations shall be made for the election of the next archbishop. You are to be that man, Thomas. Primate of England."

Thomas could not bear to look at the triumphant face with its expectant smile. Uneasily he smiled himself, glanced down, and tried to hit upon light words to turn the matter off. He raised the wide sleeve of his cloak and showed the rich embroidery, the jeweled band around his wrist, and forced a laugh. "My lord, do these look like the trappings of a holy shepherd of the flock of Canterbury?" he asked. "Pray you, think twice. Go somewhere else for this."

Surprise and disappointment washed over Henry's face.

The smile was fading as he said, "Don't treat me like a boy. It is my will."

His will, thought Thomas. How well he knew the will of this young man, the king, who to fulfill this "will" would utilize his wife, his children, his empress mother when she would let him, and would now utilize him, Thomas to control the Church. How well I know him, and he knows me not at all.

"My lord," he said again, "I know of many men. I know of three poor priests alone whose elevation to the primacy I would desire above my own."

"I also know of many men," said Henry sharply. "And I have chosen you."

"You do me honor," Thomas said. Then with a last appeal he looked with gravity down into Henry's face and said, "My lord, we have been friends for many years, a friendship happy and unconstrained, for which I thank you. But now, my lord, I fear . . . I fear for our true friendship under such a change, for there are many who would come between us. I fear the future if you persist in such a course."

Thomas saw the warning flames leap up in the king's eyes. They did not frighten him. Instead he felt a wave of weariness, almost of boredom; he had so many times been called upon to calm those little fires. And in a moment of cold detachment, with an absolute lucidity, he saw the future and himself in it, a product of his past. He saw the vision of the Church as Theobald had seen it and saw himself as a young and, it seemed to him, pure-hearted man when he had been a party to that vision. The schemes and plans that he had been a party to with Henry, and all the work that he had done with him, seemed not so clear. The ground was shifting for him and he cried out, out of friendship: "No, my lord!"

Henry was grimly silent and looked long into his eyes, reading there what he could. Then with a start he forced himself to laugh. "Thomas, my friend," he smiled, "be not so fearful! We shall be together in the future as in the past. You shall be my chancellor, as you have been, and my archbishop also. Do not speak of the end of friendship but of a new beginning!"

He smiled, yes, but he turned his eyes away. And Thomas, too, withdrew into himself. The chill of dark mistrust had crept between them.

BOOK FOUR

THE ARCHBISHOP

CHAPTER XVIII

WHATSOEVER THING THE KING WILLED, that thing—in King Henry's mind—was good, was just, was an accomplished fact. Thus he brushed from his thought, his chancellor's words, his doubts. He said to his justiciar, Richard de Luci, before they parted at the door, while all the entourage was waiting: "Richard, if I were lying dead upon my bier, would you endeavor that my first-born, Henry, should be raised to king?" And on receiving the reply, "I would, my lord, with all my strength," said then: "I wish you, Richard, to take no less care for the promotion of the chancellor to the see of Canterbury," and he looked in triumph up at Thomas' face.

Richard de Luci did as he was told. He rode with Thomas and the little prince to Winchester, then left them and went down to Canterbury, taking with him three men of power and good repute on whom he could rely: the bishop Hilary, of Chichester, who having once encountered the king's displeasure was very eager to be active in his cause; the bishop Walter, of Rochester, brother of Theobald and Thomas' old-time friend; and his own brother Walter, Abbot of Battle.

These four, with their impressive trains of clerks and servants and with a large contingent of the king's guards, presented to the monks of Christchurch a show of royal and ecclesiastical strength not lightly contravened. The prior heard their will (he had already heard it from the king) and gathered all his monks together in the chapter house. There, behind the locked and bolted door, seated forlornly on the stone bench that ran round the room, the brothers looked each other in the eye, then looked away. If some were bold enough to whisper that a worldly man, a man who ate meat and drank wine the way the chancellor did, was not perhaps God's choice for shepherd of the flock, and the sub-prior Odo said that he had not forgot the levy on the Church for the Toulouse campaign nor yet the bloody deeds done there, they spoke as men whose cause is not worth speaking for, a cause already lost. When they emerged it was to say, with smiles for the justiciar, that in their chapter, gathered all together and in private, they had elected with unanimous voice Archdeacon Thomas to be their abbot ex-officio and their archbishop.

De Luci thanked them courteously, congratulated them, and then reminded them to send their representatives to Westminster forthwith in order that they might attend the council with the suffragans that their election might be formalized. Then he turned back for London, never resting, so as to prepare each suffragan bishop in the king's cause.

All England—that is to say, all those who mattered—had done homage to the prince in Winchester. Now all rode down to London for the election, still in a mood to give obedience to the king. Thomas rode with them but he did not go into the Hall at Westminster when they did; he waited in an outer room.

Some of the men who gathered had their doubts as to the wisdom of King Henry's choice, but of these doubters only two or three had courage also. And of them all, Gilbert Foliot, Bishop of Hereford, alone rose up and spoke aloud. And Gilbert was a man of such renowned austerities, such learning, such high connections, and such self-esteem, he knew not what it meant to be discreet.

The meeting opened with a prayer to God who seeth all men's hearts, and this was followed by the reading of a letter from the king—who seeth also, with an ever-watchful eye. The king commended to their attention, in their election of a new archbishop, Thomas, the archdeacon and chancellor.

Strange that it took these bishops, abbots, monks and notables so many hours to say yea to that. And yet it did. Even after Gilbert Foliot was silenced—and this took some hard words and some threats of punishment—an inconspicuous abbot was heard to mumble that to some folk it would seem more fitting to have a man accustomed to the cloister in the seat of Canterbury as had been the practice ever since St. Augustine.

"What! Do you think, sir Abbot," cried Bishop Hilary, "that no man be acceptable to God who does not live as you live? Far from it!" And the men around him laughed.

Then Foliot tried once more, that final tactic of the obstinate minority faced with defeat: he tried delay. Should they not, he asked, postpone decision until the king himself should be among them so that they all might join their voice to his?

"What, are there any who still want for knowing who the king is?" cried Bishop Hilary again. "King Henry vested power in his son but several days ago! The young king . . ." (thus they called Prince Henry since they bent their knees to him). "The young king is among us to give royal sanction to our election. I do not think"—he whirled his eyes around—"I do not think King Henry would play double with us in this affair!"

To this sally even Gilbert Foliot could make no answer. He kept silent while men looked at him and speculated how much jealousy had played a part in his objections—for Foliot might well have thought himself a better choice for archbishop than Thomas—and how much righteous consternation for the Church, for indeed Bishop Gilbert was a righteous man.

The senior suffragan among them, quiet until now but in control, rose from his high seat on the dais to dominate them all. This was Henry, Bishop of Winchester, returned but lately from his exile behind the walls of Cluny. His beard was whiter and his face pale from long hours with his books, but if one looked into his eyes one saw the world was with him still. He spoke so gently that some murmured to their neighbors that he seemed a changed man after seven years away. But it was only that, as always, he made accommodation in his speech to suit the mood of the occasion and thus play upon his listeners.

"We have all come here, friends and brothers gathered together, for the end that each of us should speak out that which seems good to him. Now all have spoken, before God." He looked about him with such mildness one might have called him saint if he had seen him now for the first time. "All have been heard. May I allow myself to make my own opinion known?" He did not pause for answer. "It is this: that I know of no one so well fitted to be archbishop as Thomas. And I urge, most humbly, that he be elected."

At this the cardinal and papal legate, Henry of Pisa, who had crossed into England for this purpose, rose beside the bishop, gravely nodding his assent. The legate's nod was thunder from the pope. The vote was taken and the ayes rang out. No voice dissented. Thomas was called in.

From all this, from the day he left King Henry, Thomas had kept himself aloof. Now he appeared in the great Rufus Hall—where he had knelt before the Empress Matilda, where he had seen the king for the first time—and heard himself acclaimed archbishop by all the men of power in the realm.

What man could hear his name called thus, unanimously chosen by God's representatives on earth to be their spiritual father, and accept the honor with less than overflowing heart? What man whose life had been spent fighting upward could keep reservations when he reached the top? Not such a man as Thomas. He stood among them weeping openly, humble and proud. And if he heard the scornful whispered words of Gilbert Foliot that the king had worked a miracle indeed—the transformation of a soldier into an archbishop before their very eyes—he put them from his mind with resolute forgiveness and was unaware that they had found a place deep in his heart beside that little hidden spark now lying dormant in the season of success.

The young king had given royal sanction to the election. Now Bishop Henry asked him in the king's name to free the archbishop from all financial obligations that he had contracted as chancellor. And this the kinglet granted also in his piping voice.

All was accomplished and the meeting ended as it had begun with the intoning of a solemn prayer to God who seeth all men's hearts.

* * *

Thomas lay full length, face down, on the stones before his altar in the sanctuary of Christchurch. Nearby, at the high altar, knelt his consecrator, Bishop Henry, and the two assistant bishops, deep in prayer. It was the morning of the Sunday after Whitsunday, June 3, 1162, and the warm sunlight filtered through the distant windows and touched the chalk-white damask of their miters and the green of their pontificals as in a forest glade, picked out the multicolored threads in the embroidered altar cloth, and warmed the yellowing marble where they knelt.

Behind their backs the shadowed caverns of the choir stalls were crowded with the dignitaries of the Church and with the black-cowled figures of the Christchurch monks; far off, in the arched corridor of the nave, the multitudes stood shoulder brushing shoulder. And over all, engulfing them, the voices of the monks soared clear and winging as the flight of birds, deep as the winter seas, as they intoned the plainsong of the Litany of the Saints.

This was the solemn moment in the Mass when Thomas

would be consecrated bishop. He had been elected archbishop, indeed, but it was from the rank of deacon that he had been catapulted upward by the king, and after the election it was necessary—two small points—that he be ordained priest and consecrated bishop. And so the great procession had taken to the road once more—bishops and clerks and monks, the cardinal, the young king, Richard de Luci and many other notables—escorting Thomas from Westminster down to Rochester. Here Bishop Walter in his own cathedral, proud as a father, ordained him priest.

All had been politics till now, the play of worldly pressures and persuasions. Thomas knew all the royal armory of threats and what de Luci had been armed with: the granting of favors—given to one man at another's cost; the confiscation of lands and properties; exile or the charge of treason with the penalties of multilation or of death. But as he rode on with the entourage, moving again from Rochester to Canterbury for his consecration, a priest now, sanctioned to say Holy Mass and bring the body of Our Lord down to the altar, he felt another power open up to him, a power greater than the king's.

He had been gathering to him, in these few days since his election, some of the men whom he would want around him in his household as archbishop. One he had called, whom now he bade ride close beside him, was his old teacher from his days at Merton, Robert, new prior there.

"Robert," he said to him, beckoning so that the prior should bring his little palfrey close to his own tall mount. Then he bent down and spoke in a low tone. "A vision came to me last night. I was approached by one, an old and saintly man, who called my name, and when I knelt before him—for there was that about him that made me kneel—he put into my hands ten talents, bidding me use them well.

"Robert, I think I know the meaning of this vision. I must increase all that the Lord has given me. I must do better than all who have gone before. Already I have made determination to give twice the alms that Theobald gave. And Robert, I call on you, if I should fail in any of my duties, or if men complain of what I do or do not do, to tell me of my faults so that I may correct myself."

Robert nodded, smiling, but he did not speak. Was that a hint of humor in his eyes, indulgence for a man who was as yet a child? or was it understanding and compassion? Thomas could not make out, and yet felt comforted.

This was on Friday, the first of June, 1162. On Saturday, while others made preparation for the consecration and for the feasting afterward, Thomas kept to himself and fasted through the day. That evening he went alone into the inner room, that room which would be his as archbishop, that little room where he had often sat with Theobald, where Theobald had died, and pricked his heart with many thoughts, as a man pricks his flesh with flagellation, all through the summer night. He rose for Compline, after dark, when the monks went into the choir for their final service of the day, although he did not leave the room. He rose again at midnight, when they did, for Matins, and again for Lauds as the sun gilded the horizon. At Prime they called him and he dressed himself, for the first time, in the white linen alb—too short for him he could not help but notice—and tied the amice round his neck, the cincture round his waist. He put the stole around his shoulders and, as he was instructed, crossed it on his breast. He set the small black cap upon his head and stood erect to let his chamberlain and helpers settle the heavy cope about him. And then, like this, accoutered for the first time in the garments of a priest, he prayed.

There had been some in-fighting among the bishops for the honored role of consecrator on this occasion. Roger of Pont l'Evêque, the Archbishop of York, claimed it on point of precedence. But he was put down, after some bitter arguments, because he was too proud: he had continually set himself as Canterbury's equal in the land. Walter of Rochester lay claim to it as the provincial chaplain, but Walter had but little power of person, his voice was very thin and weak, and he was easily brushed past.

The Bishop of Bangor Fawr said he was senior to them all—indeed he was a very ancient man—and claimed it for this reason. But he was in error. Henry of Winchester was senior in point of consecration. Besides this, Henry had provided for himself a letter from the London clergy giving him leave to act as the provincial dean in their own bishop's place—the Bishop of London having become an imbecile with age.

Thus it was settled, not without some very hard words passed among the bishops and some tussling among their clerks, and the victorious Bishop of Winchester took himself off to fast and meditate, the bishops of York and Rochester to niggle a little but to content themselves at last with secondary roles—assistants in the consecration—and Bangor Fawr to shake his shiny head and mumble through his gums at the presumption of all youth.

Truly the Lord is great, to mold from such poor pitiful clay as this a creature to stand at the apex of the hierarchy of His Church, next to the door of heaven, a creature little lower than the angels and above all the other men, a bishop. If a man wants a miracle, let him look here. Let him see Thomas, worldling, power hungry, and vindictive in his heart, stretched out before the altar. Let him listen as God speaks to him.

The prelude to the consecration had been concluded. Bishop Henry, seated on his faldstool on the steps of the high altar, had given the oath to Thomas who sat below him on the sanctuary floor with Bishop Roger and Bishop Walter seated beside him. He had made promise to obey the pope, promote his rights and his authority, to visit him and render his accounts to him. Seventeen times had Bishop Henry asked him questions of canon law and seventeen times had Thomas risen from his stool, taken his cap in hand and answered "I will" or "I do believe" as it was called for, and sat down again. The ceremony of High Mass had been begun, and after the *Asperges* and the sprinkling of holy water, Thomas had been escorted to his altar where he laid aside the cope and donned the sacerdotal garments of the tunicle, dalmatic and the chasuble. In unison with Henry at the high altar he had intoned the Introit and the Kyrie and Gloria. A second time he was escorted back to Henry and had been told the powers and the duties of a bishop. Then he had knelt and heard the multitude all murmuring together like forest leaves in a soft wind their prayers to God that He bestow his grace on Thomas.

Now he lay prostrate.

The marble on his cheek was cool; the sunlight, where it came slanting toward his eyes, was soft and full of golden motes; the plainsong of the Litany poured over him and washed his soul and made him light, as though he floated in the arms of God. He thought with love of Bishop Henry who like a father, like a strong comrade, led him through this ceremony, guiding his spirit . . . a man to lean on, venerable, eyes full of understanding . . . leader and helper, stronger even than Essex in the field whom he had come to lean on.

He felt again the pressure of Roger's hand upon his arm, guiding him surely . . . Roger whom he had hated . . . he saw again the scorn-filled youthful face at Harrow . . . and whom he now forgave . . . forgave . . . the animosity dissolving.

I do not condescend to Walter any more, he thought. Where God has given a good heart, there I give honor and respect . . . not counting certain weaknesses of mind . . . Love one another.

A flood of loving-kindness, an unaccustomed flood, brought tears. They slid out from the corners of his eyes and dropped upon the marble as he thought, "As I have loved you, love one another." Love all the world . . . love all men in it . . . love . . .

And it was here that God spoke, interrupting him: *"What is this evil thing the king wants of you?"*

The voice was large, so large it filled the air around him and the ground beneath him, shaking the stones; so large it seemed to burst his heart as it came thundering forth; yet at the same time it was gentle in his ear, soft with a deep concern for him, Thomas the little child; full of compassion.

It said no more than that: *"What is this evil?"*

And Thomas answered, with no pretense, no thought, an answer from a depth within himself he had not known, words that surprised him when he heard: "He wants me to deny you, Lord."

Here his heart broke; he wept in earnest as he lay upon the floor.

Walter and Roger came to him and lifted him to his knees. "Now bow your head," said Roger whispering. He was surprised that Thomas should forget the ceremony just at the essence of it. "Stretch out your neck."

Thomas knelt and bowed his head and felt the open Gospel placed on his neck and shoulders, felt how it trembled as Walter held it there . . . annoying. Oh to be left alone with God, a moment longer, just a moment. He felt their hands upon his crown, first Bishop Henry's, warm, "Receive the Holy Ghost," then Roger's, then the trembling of the Gospel as Walter let it go, the trembling of Walter's fingers on his head. "Receive the Holy Ghost."

His eyes were closed. He opened them to see their feet around him and the swinging hems of their pontificals. He saw the tip of Henry's beard as he bent down, and then the crucible of oil in his left hand. He felt the finger, dipped in the oil, slide up and down across his tonsure, making the cross. He felt the entire hand, the palm, anointing all his crown, and heard the voice reciting, strong and sure, the prayer that constancy of faith and purity of love, sincerity of peace, should be his and abound in him—him, Thomas.

Strange that the words should stab so; he had not thought himself so much worse in these things than other men.

The bishop took his hands and steadied them and with the oil he crossed their palms three times. "Whatsoever thou shalt bless, let it be blessed; and whatsoever thou shalt sanctify, let it be sanctified," he said. Firmly he folded Thomas' hands, the right one on the left, and placed them in a linen scarf and took the ends and tied it round his neck while Walter lifted up the Gospel to make room and Roger whispered to him, "Steady yourself!"

He longed to wipe his face for it was wet with tears and his nose clogged. He longed to be alone with God, but somewhere in the ceremony God had withdrawn Himself.

He was a bishop now, he knew this, and would receive all the insignia of his office, but he cared little. He suffered them to stand the crosier up before him, wedging it in between his middle and his index fingers, and to admonish him to temper justice with his meekness but never to neglect strict discipline for love of ease. He suffered them to put the ring upon his finger and to remind him that it symbolized fidelity. He suffered Walter to remove the Gospel from his neck and thrust it underneath his nose where he could read a verse from it and take it to his heart, a guide. His eye fell on the passage: "Let him which is on the housetop not come down to take anything out of his house." But he could make nothing of it, and he shook his head.

They raised him then, bestowed the kiss of peace on him, and took him back to his own altar and cleaned his tonsure with crumbs of bread and washed his hands.

He wiped his face and put his hair back into place and took a deep breath, sighing. "Come, courage," he said to himself, and felt some strength come back into his heart. He saw that Henry watched him from the high altar and he nodded and together they continued with the ceremony of the Mass. Before the offertory he crossed once again to the high altar and gave to Henry, as was the custom, two lighted torches, two loaves of bread, and two small barrels of wine. Then side by side, in unison, the two of them—as Henry had done many years, as Thomas, tall beside him, did now for the first time—blessed the bread and wine and then received the Body and the Blood of Christ.

Mass was concluded. Thomas received his miter and heard it called his helmet of protection and salvation, terrible to the enemies of truth. He took his gloves, the symbol of paternal blessing. Then wearing these, dressed in his glowing green pontificals, his crosier in his hand, his ring upon his finger, he was enthroned before the altar in all his majesty. And rising up from here, while Henry in his strong old voice intoned the hymn of praise, *Te Deum,* Thomas walked slowly, very tall, magnificent, down past the choir stalls and past the bishops in their seats and went among the multitude, blessing the people.

So it was over, and Thomas, drained, sat in the midst of all the prelates at the high table, feasting, with the young king prattling beside him, and was amazed that any could take easily what had occurred.

From then on Thomas himself was somewhat changed. He wore the costly robes that he had always worn as chancellor and drew about him men of learning and good discourse rather than the ascetics of the monastic world. He furnished the archbishop's palace as he had furnished the chancellor's hall in London and he served as always food and wine of the best quality. But he was conscious now of something to be nourished in his soul and while he watched out for his guests at dinner, sending down pittances of special delicacies from the high table to this one or that, he himself ate but sparingly and often drank instead of wine a broth of fennel, pungent to the taste. He banished jugglers and light musicians from his hall and where before it had been merely open to men of every rank, now he took care to see that never less than twenty-six beggars were invited in. He doubled the amount of alms that Theobald had given out and spent his days most soberly.

He rose at sunrise when the sky outside his window paled and went into the church for Lauds and then returned to his own room to make confession of his sins to Prior Robert and to repent of them. And afterward he called in others of his clerks and had the Scripture read to him and then discussed the meaning of each verse. When he dismissed them he sat alone within the inner room—and no one knew his thoughts—until the time for Terce when he went once again to the cathedral to hear Mass. On feast days only did he say Mass himself, and then he said it very quickly, though with devotion. Men noticed this, for many eyes were on him now, marking what he would do as archbishop.

At dinner he had twenty men of learning on his right, as many monks and canons regular on his left. Barons and knights were welcome in his hall but they sat farther down, where they could talk and laugh among themselves and not disturb the reading of the Latin text for those who sat with him. And after dinner till midafternoon he rode about his diocese or visited the sick in the infirmary or else he took his seat in court and heard the cases that were brought to him. And men remarked he took no presents but judged every suit according to its merits only. After the Hour of Nones he rested, for he was unaccustomed to the broken sleep of monks, but when his chamberlain brought candles in he called his clerks once more for discourse and correspondence until Compline, the final service, sung while the stars wheeled overhead.

Thus went the days of Thomas' learning—learning at forty-four the discipline of the Church, the discipline of his own soul, the duties of an archbishop. It was a task most difficult for him, and sometimes tedious. He did not take to it with ease, although he set his heart and will to master it. And God did not reward him with His presence.

He watched the monks with penetrating eyes and marked some few of them who seemed to ride the rhythm of the day, supported by the hours of prayer, the hours of meditation and the hours of work the way a soaring seagull is supported by the air. They did not fall, though with their piercing eyes saw many things below, but were invisibly borne up.

He spoke of this to Robert in confession, for it was envy that he felt for men like these, not love, and with a wry smile of self-knowledge said that he coveted their faith. "I would myself rise up as on the wings of eagles, and faint not." And Robert winced to hear him, for his heart was open to this strong and eager man and it was wounded by the picture, clear in his inner eye, of a fierce, grounded eagle beating his wings against the earth and floundering.

"Perhaps," he said, "you carry too much weight upon your wings."

"What weight?" asked Thomas.

"Only the weight of self," said Robert. "Only of self, the heaviest that a man can bear."

So Thomas set about to lose himself. He had been archbishop three months and he had mastered the administration of his see, mastered the daily routine of his office, but not himself. He added to his discipline three things: he sent his chamberlain to buy a hair shirt for him and he wore it always, under his clothing, pricking against his skin; he chose among his younger clerks a flagellator who would scourge his flesh each morning when he rose; he bade his almoner bring in thirteen paupers to him every night so that he might bend down before them in humility and wash their feet and give them alms in secret. All these things were done in secret, for he abhorred the thought of any praise that they might bring. He was in earnest.

So now he rose in the dead dark of night for Matins and after that, when the monks slept again, the brief sleep before Lauds, in that dread hour when godless men are apt to start awake and stare into the emptiness of all eternity before them and smell its breath like stagnant air seeped from a tomb, and pray to God to let them sleep again, that hour Thomas chose to make his secret way across the court and down the pathway under the shadow of the cellerer's wall to the small postern door into the almonry, the house where alms were given out, where the poor traveler could always find a resting place.

There the almoner gathered in his own small room, a room no bigger than a vault, lit by one rush light on the wall, thirteen paupers every night to wait for the archbishop to come and kneel before them and wash their feet. The almoner, as Thomas bade him, swore all to silence and to secrecy. But who could keep a secret such as this?

"Now he has taken to washing the feet of the poor!" said Elured snorting as he swung his cloak from his shoulders and hooked it on the peg inside the smithy door. "There's a charlatan for you!"

"Who's that?" asked Walter, turning from the furnace where he stooped.

"The chancellor. Every night he calls them in and they must sit there while he washes them in the dead of night, dead cold too, all for a penny!"

"He is the archbishop now," Walter reminded him.

"He is the chancellor all the same," said Elured coming to the fire to peer over Walter's shoulder. "He has not changed his spots. I've seen him in his embroidered robes!" He spit into the hot coals and stood watching them. After a little while he said, "I'd like to see him kneel before me! I'd let him have it."

Walter smiled into the fire. "Where do you hear such things?"

"All over town," said Elured. He was accustomed to the changed tone Walter took with him, no longer frightened of his father's words nor on his guard. The moneyer's household and the people in it had changed since the closing of the mint, the failure of their suit to re-establish it. Wulviva, after her whirlwind efforts and a few weeks of impatient waiting had gone back to Hortone, for the farm was all important now; all of them lived upon its rents and produce. Walter sometimes made a few pence from the trinkets that he made or mending dented cups or broken clasps, and he went out to Hortone to lend a hand. He was, at last, the man who counted in the house. Hawisa, too, had new responsibilities and for this time was steadier; the house was hers to care for and a new baby also, as well as little Viel. Only Elured, after his period of apathy, did not return to work. He spent his days out in the town, hanging around the other mints and making comment, gossiping in the taverns.

"They call in thirteen paupers every night. Everyone's doing it."

"Don't talk nonsense, Father."

"You're the one who's talking nonsense. That's because you never know whats going on. I tell you, Walter, they're plain desperate for paupers at the cathedral. Why, if you went around the town as I do and heard what men are saying, you'd learn how the clerks come begging: 'Come to the cathedral. Come before Lauds.' Bold dead of night they choose! 'The archbishop himself will wash your feet. Aye, and you get a silver penny too.'" He shrugged. "Some go. Some are repeaters; they go regular. Blind Odo down at Newingate, he's a regular."

"He is a pauper, too," Walter reminded him. "He begs a living."

"Others go. Lambin says he might—only he can't see after dark; his eyes are going out on him. Tom Slupe says he might."

"Might," Walter grunted.

"Oh, plenty go!" the old man insisted. "Somebody has to; they have to get their thirteen men there every night. Of course they get their transients but they need Canterbury men. They need them bad."

Three nights later Walter and Hawisa were wakened by something moving in the dark. They started, warm in their narrow bed together with the baby nestled in the curve of her mother's back, and lay breathless, listening, with their necks stiff and the prick of fear along their scalps. Then they heard Elured muttering across the room. They saw the glow from the banked fire pink on the naked flesh of the old man as he rose from the jumbled pile of bedding and reached for his kirtle.

"What are you doing, Father?" Hawisa asked.

The old man, shivering, did not answer as he slipped into his clothes.

"Where are you going?"

"To the cathedral," Elured grunted.

Walter groaned within himself and Hawisa, in wonder, said, "At this hour?"

The old man went on groping in the dark, pulling the bedclothes back and forth impatiently. "Just before cock-crow, that's when he does it. Before Lauds."

Walter crawled out over his wife to stand beside his father. "You can't go like this, without arrangement," he protested. "The gate is locked. They will not let you in."

Elured straightened, having found his buskins and thrust his feet in them. "It's all arranged. The almoner's lay brother will let me in. Where's that cloak?"

"You won't be welcome," Walter warned.

"Welcome!' the old man snorted. "Welcome or not, I'm going. Find me the cloak."

"Your cloak is on your bed. Father, don't go."

"Don't be a fool, not that cloak. Get me the cloak that Wilbert used to wear. He always looked a pauper in it. There." He found it, hunched it round his shoulders, and was gone.

Rumor was no more accurate in this case than in any other. In Canterbury at that time there was no lack of paupers. One of the legacies of civil war and chaos twenty years before was a sad crop of homeless children who had survived by wandering and begging through the land. They were grown men now, close to the end of life, for life was short for those who had no food, no places of their own, and no protection. There were the sick as well, and those survivors of the king's justice—blinded, mutilated and disfigured. The roads were crawling with them and by night the porches of the rich gave shelter to a crowd, and every monastery almonry and guest hall for the poor was full. There was no lack.

This much alone was true: word had leaked out of the archbishop's nightly humiliation and men talked of it with relish. The chancellor was not over much esteemed in Canterbury—no more among the townsmen than among the monks.

If Thomas knew of this he did not care, for he was on another path. This night he rose again as usual for Matins, as the hour of midnight rolled away. Of recent weeks he had begun to wear the habit of a monk over his hair shirt when he went into the choir. The brothers had been offended to see him in his chancellor's robes there and one had warned him—as he had been charged to in a dream—that the saints frowned to see an abbot at his devotions in such secular finery. And in this habit, with the cowl pulled foward to shield his face, he walked, a gaunt black figure in the shadow of the wall, alone across the courtyard to the almoner's door.

He pushed it open and saw there before him in the shadowy vaulted room the same array of wasted filthy remnants of humanity that he saw every night. He had not learned yet to distinguish one man from another behind the tangled hair and matted rags, beneath the stench of illness, of human excreta and crusted dirt, beyond the universal face of avarice and self-hate. There sat before him, abject and shivering, a world's diversity of men, each a creation and unique among his brothers, but he saw them not. He only saw with one glance in the flickering light, that the first man he knelt before looked at him with large limpid eyes as from a skull, the center of his face a mass of shiny scar tissue punctured by small, black nostrils and his mouth an open crescent from which the stench of hunger came in gusts. And after that he dropped his eyes down to the naked feet which he must wash.

Down on his knees he worked his way along the line. The almoner and his lay brother moved beside him with the basin and the towels. Some of the feet were splayed and thick with calluses. Some were so crusted over with years of dirt that when he had washed them every pore and crease stood out as though they had been etched in ink. And some were swollen into shapeless lumps although their shins were bone and nothing more, and these men groaned to feel his hands upon them and but for weakness would have drawn away.

Only at Elured Porre did Thomas pause in his methodical washing, drying, bending to kiss the feet, and crawling on. For Elured had refused to take his buskins off.

Thomas stared as though entranced at these two buskins planted before him on the dark stone floor, at the long dun-colored pointed toes, at the soft creases in the leather around the ankles, at a triangular blemish in the skin of one, for they were not of the first quality. It took him all this time to bring his mind back from the psalter which he had been saying over to himself, as he did nightly, while he washed and kissed the feet.

He did not hear the almoner's muttered explanation and apology. He slowly raised his head until the cowl fell back upon his shoulders and looked up into the blue, defiant, somewhat frightened eyes of an old, stringy, and yet well-fed burgher of the town. "Friend," he said, with some slight asperity, "I cannot wash your feet if you don't take your shoes off."

"I did not come for that," said Elured, blustering. He sent a guilty glance in the direction of the almoner. The whole scene had upset him. No one was there whom he had ever seen before, not even old Blind Odo who had claimed he came there every night. Just scum and riffraff whom he had never bothered with if he had ever noticed. He disengaged himself from them and stood against the wall instead of sitting down and would not take his buskins off when the lay brother told him to. He would have left except for pride. And now it was his turn.

"What for, then?" Thomas asked.

"I came so you could kneel before me, since it pleases you," said Elured. He had to clear his throat to get the words out for he was truly frightened now.

Thomas rose to stand confronting him, a full head taller and his black eyes piercing. "You think this pleases me?" he asked.

Elured looked to one side and another with his back pressed up against the wall. "You do it, don't you?" he said with the flicker of a smile before he shot a gleaming glance up into Thomas' face.

The whole thing was absurd and Thomas gave a little cough of laughter, taken by surprise. He would have turned away then, from this cheap intruder, but in turning his eye fell on the row of abject men along the wall and he remembered that he came here for the practice of humility. He took a breath and turned again to Elured. "Well, friend," he said, "I do it for my soul's good, not for pleasure."

Elured was made bold by this softer tone. "Aye, your soul is very dear to you, Chancellor. What of my soul? I cannot keep it in my body if I starve. Did you give thought to that?" To Elured the central glaring fact of the entire world was that he had lost his mint, and he expected this oblique allusion to it would strike the chancellor full of guilt. He watched for signs of this. But Thomas only turned a questioning look and asked the almoner softly, "Is it a madman?"

The almoner was shaking. "Father, forgive me. The man said that he was a pauper, recently struck down by some great tragedy. It was Hubert let him in." He gestured toward the lay brother, willing to pass the blame along. "I take responsibility of course," he whispered. And then to Hubert, "Take him away again," in a much louder voice.

But Thomas waved him off, conscious once more that

he was archbishop and shepherd of all their souls. "My son," he said to Elured, "if God has seen fit to chastise you, you must bear yourself with meekness . . ." He broke off because the man before him, grimacing either with laughter or with rage, burst out: "It was not God who punished me, but you!"

"But I?" repeated Thomas frowning down at him.

"You did it! Taking the mint from me!"

"What mint?"

"My mint! That you took from me, Chancellor!" Elured felt trapped against the wall, this tall and fierce-eyed man before him, towering over him. Panic was in his heart. But he had come to ease himself of the great blow that had befallen him and to cry out against injustice. Already he felt better. He squeezed against the wall, but he continued. "You sat beside the king and said to him: 'Let us take this man's living from him, leave him to starve.' "

"I do not sit beside the king," Thomas said stonily.

But Elured was not listening. He put a finger out and touched the habit on Thomas' chest, a pleading gesture, though his eyes were calculating. His voice dropped. "Give me my mint back, Chancellor," he wheedled, while Thomas stared at him, incredulous. "Oh do not let me starve," said Elured.

"It does not seem to me that you are starving," Thomas said. "And if you hunger, you are welcome in my hall. Are you a Canterbury man?"

"Oh Chancellor, do not let me starve," cried Elured again, "and all the little children bellowing for their food!"

Thomas looked at the bright and crafty eyes, so much at variance with the pitiful words, and laughed outright. "My friend, I do not know your game," he said, "or what it is that you would play with me. But I am chancellor no longer. You will get nothing from me that way." He stepped back. "Here is the penny that you came for." He took it from his pouch and put it into Elured's callused hand. "It is for that you came?"

He did not wait an answer, for there was stirring in the room as many heads turned toward him and his purse; the torchlight glittered in their eyes. He saw them and revulsion rose in him. He choked it down and went along the line once more, his eyes downcast, his shoulders stooped, and put a penny in each outstretched hand and murmured, with each coin, the ritual phrase, "May God the Father, Son, and Holy Ghost, bless you . . ." until he reached the end and straightened and went out the door. He felt the cold dawn wind upon his face with great relief.

Elured went out another way, clutching the penny in his fist and laughing to himself to think how he had stood up to the archbishop. Oh what a story he would tell!

Thomas spoke the truth when he said he was no longer chancellor. Only the week before he had returned the Great Seal of the King of England into royal hands, journeying to Winchester to give it to de Luci and the young king that they might send it back to Henry with Thomas' loving protestations of affection and his regret that now he was archbishop he had found himself unequal even to that one task, much more so to the task of both great offices with which the king had honored him; he must resign the chancellorship into more capable and worthy hands.

He did not linger to hear Richard's words or more than catch a glimpse of what was in his eyes—surprise, remonstrance, warning—but spent an hour only with the little prince, his ward, promising to have him soon again within his household, and departed humbly, without farewells, for Canterbury.

King Henry raised his eyebrows at de Luci's words. He did not take the seal which the justiciar had brought to Rouen with his own hands and laid upon the table while he spoke. Instead he let it lie there while he listened and then rose and walked about the room.

"So he has found the job too much for him" he said in a dry voice. "Did he say more?"

"No, my lord. He spoke most humbly, hoping to keep your love."

"Aye, so you said." The king was silent while he examined a portion of the wall and scratched it with his finger to see what would rub off. "I hear strange things of him," he said. "I hear he wears the habit of a monk and lives on bread and water. I hear he weeps a good deal; someone told me that." He turned abruptly on the justiciar. "What shall I think of all this, Richard?"

"I do believe his life has changed somewhat," de Luci said. "I did not see him in the habit of a monk. I think, my lord, such stories grow."

"Yes? How did you find him, then. Just as of old?"

"Subdued, my lord. Perhaps his duties weigh on him. Although your son the young king laughed and sported with him as of old."

Henry crossed his arms upon his breast and stared down at the table with blind eyes. "Does the young king forget his father in the company of archbishops?" he asked.

"Not so, my lord. The prince has been in Winchester attending royal duties."

"Aye, I know. And Thomas keeps to Canterbury?"

"Most of the time, my lord."

Henry looked up then with a piercing gaze. "I hear he has made claim to Tonbridge Castle for the see of Canterbury—on some forgotten pretext that King Stephen took it from the Church. Does he do this? He has not asked my leave. I hear he criticizes me."

"Sire, I believe he thinks now only of his spiritual duties. It would surprise me if he went against you in any way."

The king's smile twisted down the corners of his mouth and for the first time he reached out and touched the royal seal. "You bring me this, de Luci, and you are not surprised? Sit down." He pushed the seal aside as though it were some ordinary thing and sat across from the justiciar. "You were with us, Richard, when I arranged that Thomas should be my archbishop. Was it then your impression that he would no longer be my chancellor? You need not answer. It was very clear among us all." Suddenly he slapped the table with his hand and shouted, "Why does he cross me, then? What is his purpose? He knows my mind!"

He stopped himself, a new thing for the king to do, and put both hands up to his face, and said between them, with closed eyes, "He warned me, Richard. He said that there were many who would come between us, who would malign him and work upon my trust. He feared to lose my friendship."

He took his hands away and looked at the justiciar with a steady gaze. "He shall not lose it. No one shall come between us. Nothing. Until I hear from his own mouth what he intends."

CHAPTER XIX

It was three months before the king saw Thomas again, for he remained in Rouen for his Christmas court and came to England—after four years' absence from the kingdom that he ruled—only in January of 1163.

His little fleet put in at Southampton with Henry's royal smack, its painted sails arched in the wind, riding the winter waves ahead of all. The king stood, as he always did, upon the castle deck, the fog as wet as rain upon his face, and felt the calmer swell beneath him of the sheltered waters as they came into port and heard the wet snap of the sails as they were lowered. On shore he saw a multitude of people, blurred by the fog, and faintly heard—because the wind blew from him—their piping cry, no bigger than a bird's chirp in a winter blast, of "vivat rex." He heard it and he smiled.

At last the thump and grating of the boat against the dock and he jumped down, his strong legs bending, staggering a little as the earth rocked like the pitching of a ship, and looked around to see a little figure dart from the sheltering cloak of a tall Churchman and run toward him crying, "Father, Father, I am king!" He laughed to hear this, very proud, and while he held his son against him looked up again into the multitude. The Churchman—yes, that man was Thomas, somber in the black cloak of a canon of Christchurch. But he was smiling the old smile as he came forward.

The two rode up together from Southampton and at first the warmth between them held. They laughed together as of old, made plans for hawking when the weather turned—at least the king did. Thomas said nothing, but he had not lost the courtier's art of saying nothing gracefully, and Henry did not notice.

The long procession, like a festival, wound up the river road under the luminescent drift of sea-mist and the cry of seagulls overhead. But when, late in the afternoon, they came into the royal forest of Bere Ashley and the dark of sheltering winter trees was added to the dark of fog, the horses of the knights ahead of them receded and changed shape, lost color, and became blurred moving forms behind the blur of fog. Thomas and Henry rode as though alone. Thomas pulled the hood of his black cloak close up around his face. The king rode bareheaded.

"Thomas, some men have come to me with strange reports," the king said into the drifting fog.

Thomas, with the hood about his ears, said nothing and he did not look around. Perhaps he had not heard. Perhaps he heard some other words, spoken eight years ago upon a January day like this and in a forest much like this, into the waiting silence of a drifting mist and half-seen barren branches overhead. He heard again the words stir in his inner ear, words he had long forgotten: "Never trust me."

Now the king, riding close beside him, spoke again. "The Earl of Clare came to me, Thomas. He was very wroth. You know of this?" He kept his eyes upon the tunnel of the trees as they rode under them but when again there was no answer he turned his head and raised his voice until it barked. "What is the truth of this?"

Thomas turned his dark hood slowly to the king. "You speak of Tonbridge Castle, sire? I have informed the Earl of Clare he must do homage to me for the holding of it."

"How can that be, Tom? What are you talking of? Tonbridge has been in that family since the Conqueror's time! How should he do you homage for it? Have you gone mad?"

"Tonbridge was held by Canterbury before that, my lord," said Thomas undisturbed. "If property was wrested from the Church, I care not when, it is my duty to reclaim it, is it not?"

The king looked in amazement at his old-time friend. " 'Your duty is it not?' " he echoed. "No. It is not! The earl owes fealty to me, the king, for Tonbridge. It was my ancestor gave it to him. What are you plotting here? Would you take all my lands away?" Still he had not really lost his temper, for he would not believe it in his heart. "Come, Tom, reveal yourself to me. Are you so much changed since I saw you last?"

"Not changed toward you, my lord," said Thomas, though he looked away again so that his face was sheltered in the overhanging hood.

"I think you have!" said Henry, staring at him. "Yes. God's breath. I think you have!"

Thomas was forced to turn again and look his sovereign in the eye. "Not so, my lord," he said, his black eyes steady in the shadow of his hood. "I am as you have always known me."

Henry stared grimly back at him, the fog between them, and their horses gently moving up and down as they went forward. "Why have you crossed me then?"

"My lord," said Thomas, "let us look back through all the years to what it was we both set out to do when you came into England to be king and Theobald presented me to you. Then there was chaos in the land; the Church was ravished and the people at the mercy of wild beasts. Through you the royal power was established once again. The savage barons were put down. Men learned to fear the law once more. Your throne became a rock on which the nation rose, well-founded, prosperous, feared by its enemies. My lord, your power and the fear of your stern justice has spread throughout the world. You are a king above all other kings. Have I not helped you in this? Have I not given all my heart and mind to this?"

"Yes, Tom, but now you slide away from me," the king said almost plaintively. "Why, when we reach this power, do you seem to challenge me?"

When the king said "we" he meant himself; this was quite clear to Thomas. It was clear also that his somber flattery had slid beneath the king's defenses; Henry was pleased. So he continued: "When Stephen died the Church held power for you till you could come and seize it for yourself. Gladly we held it in your name and gladly we placed it in your hands when you arrived." He slid the subtle "we" into his discourse without emphasis. "For it is right, and God's will that the king rule absolute, by the grace of God. And when we placed the crown upon your head we swore our fealty to you as earthly subjects, tenants of your lands. . . ." He broke off, for he found himself feeling the pull again of Henry's magnetism and on impulse dropped his stately tone and spoke straight from the heart.

"My lord, do you remember how we studied John of Salisbury's essay on the ideal state and how we argued over it and, it then seemed to me, agreed? There on those summer nights in Rouen when we sat late at supper and the sweat rolled off us while we argued? That time you took the tun of wine and poured it over me, saying I grew too hot?" He smiled and Henry smiled abruptly, too, remembering.

"Do you remember how John said—and we agreed—that in the ideal state the king's the head, but that it is the clergy of the Church who are the soul?"

"Aye Tom," the king said, stopping. "But that was the ideal state we were discussing—and the clergy were an ideal clergy. Do you remember that as well?" He grinned.

"It is the structure only that we are discussing," Thomas said.

"You cannot build a structure with rotten timbers, Tom."

"The Church builds with what materials she has. Men are not saints."

"Amen to that," said Henry grinning once again. But Thomas looked away and when he spoke again his tone was formal as before.

"Let me resume my thesis. When Theobald set crown upon your head you then became the king of all the land. Is that not right?"

"So far," said Henry cautiously.

"When Theobald anointed you, you then became God's priest and servant of the Church."

"Well . . . yes."

"As king you undertook by oath an obligation to your subjects to rule them well; as God's own priest you undertook to carry out His will."

"Aye, in a manner."

"Who is to direct your own soul, then, in this great undertaking?"

"Well, Tom, I keep a whole swarm of you Churchmen all around me! I had you as my chancellor and chaplain, didn't I? I have my confessor . . ."

"Gilbert Foliot." Thomas said the name with some distaste.

"He is a very austere man, you will agree. Who better to chastise me?" Henry smiled.

Thomas was irritated and his voice grew louder as he said, "The Archbishop of Canterbury is your spiritual father, head of that clergy whom we have agreed are the soul . . ."

"Well, hell, Tom," Henry broke in, "this is neither here nor there. I never said you had no power to direct my soul. Didn't I make you archbishop? The point in question is not my soul but my authority, my lands. When you claim Tonbridge is that out of fatherly interest in my soul?"

"Yes, in a manner," Thomas said stubbornly. "Tonbridge was taken from the Church. The Church has been despoiled. Those who despoil the Church shall suffer for it—not only here, but hereafter. As shepherd of their souls I must protect them from their own misdeeds. Therefore, if I correct you in this matter, my lord, it is for the good of your own soul."

Henry was silent for a long time, biting his lips and tasting the wet-leaf taste of fog upon them, thinking. And when at last he spoke his tone was soft and angry. "I have heard what you have to say. Now let me give you some advice: go not so often into dark churches in the night, for there, I think, strange thoughts come in your head. It is not good for you. And you begin to bore me, Tom. As for the matter of Tonbridge, we shall bring that up in Council. For now, I shall drop back awhile and ride beside the queen."

At Whitsun, while King Henry wore his crown at Westminster before a gathering of all the powerful men of England and there was celebrating, feasting and May-dancing, Thomas responded to the call of Pope Alexander and went to Tours with many of his suffragans there to attend the Papal Council and to sit upon the pope's right hand and be made much of.

When he returned he felt strong in his power and was conscious of the backing of the pope in all he did. He sent reminder to the Earl of Clare to do him homage for Tonbridge; he placed a claim for Canterbury on the castles of Saltwood and Rochester as both had been bestowed—according to his records—on his predecessors at one time; and he presented to a clerk of his the living of the church at Eynesford, since it lay within his see. And when the Lord of Eynesford without ceremony tossed the young clerk out, he excommunicated him. The lord went to the king.

Thomas received King Henry's message, faithfully reported word by word—so many "God's eyes," so many "God's wounds," so many slammings of his fist upon the board—with a set stony face. It was an ancient principle, the king reminded him, that any tenant of the crown should not be excommunicated without his sovereign's leave; the archbishop was herewith ordered to withdraw his excommunication without delay. "Inform the royal messengers," he answered, "that such spiritual matters as excommunication and absolution are not the business of the king."

Henry's wrath burned slow and steady in him like the coals beneath the firecover after curfew time; the coals were hidden but the cover scorching to the unwary hand. He held his councils and he made his progress through the land and carried out the business of his realm, and all summer long he noted everything that went against the power and the order of his royal will. These things he kept within him, nourishing the fire.

With autumn he went to Woodstock where he had his favorite hunting lodge and where the game ran plentiful and fat, protected by his foresters. Here he summoned his two chief justiciars, de Luci and the brilliant hunchback Earl of Leicester, and others of his legal and judicial staff. All day he hunted and in the evenings when he came into the hall, face scratched and dirty, hands rubbed raw, legs swollen from twelve hours of the chase, he then conferred with them. He had the fires lit because these men of intellect were sensitive to cold. And while one of his chamber men knelt at his feet and chafed the muscles of his legs, he questioned them and listening with respect, the light from the log fire leaping, glittering on his face and glowing on the hewn pine walls and canvas hangings, well into the night.

His mind dwelt on the clergy, on those "souls of the ideal state" whom Thomas boasted of, on their encroachment of his power, and on Thomas' willful opposition to him as their leader. He knew them, all of them, from Thomas right straight down, and felt them to be just as riddled with ambitions, faults, and double-dealings as any other men. His stern face twisted in the firelight. De Luci thought it was the pain from his stiff, swollen muscles being kneaded, but Henry did not feel his legs at all. It was the memory of upstart clerks who flouted royal justice and laughed at the king that made him wince.

Since his return to England he had been told of many cases of tonsured men who broke the king's law and yet escaped king's justice because the Church claimed jurisdiction over them. This was no new condition. Archbishop Theobald had wrested from the royal courts a most foul murderer and breaker of the king's peace when he, Henry, had first come to power and—how crafty are these archbishops—before he had that power firmly in his hands. Did they think that he would forget this? Thomas had always sidestepped, slippery, around the subject when he brought it up. (Henry saw many double-sides to Thomas, now, that he had not seen before.) And yet it was a crime against the Church: a bishop murdered by his archdeacon. Poison in the eucharistic cup! The case was clear; the man was guilty. Even Stephen, struggling to keep the remnants of his power, would not let them gloss it over. The guilty man was taken from the Church and held for trial in the king's courts until, at that very moment, Stephen died. And then it was the Church—how crafty—when he himself was young and new, claimed they alone had right to try a man of their own order. They seized him back. And now he wandered free as an innocent man, a living challenge to royal power, laughing at justice.

"Where is Archdeacon Osbert now?" he asked abruptly.

De Luci knew exactly whom he meant. "I think he is in

France, my lord. He was on pilgrimage for some long time."

"Unpunished," Henry murmured.

"It is a form of banishment," Richard corrected quietly.

Henry did not move his head; only his eyes turned searchingly to Richard. "The Church has not the power to banish. Am I correct? That is the privilege of the king's courts, is it not?"

Roger Fitzedwards, one of the king's itinerant justices whom Henry had called in, spoke up. "My lord, the Church courts, as you know, cannot pass sentences of blood nor impose fines nor yet imprison, nor, as you say, are they empowered to banish culprits from the king's lands. However, as I have learned from many of the bishops who have sat in shire courts with me, the Church is sensible to the need for strong correction in many cases. Thus we may read "monastery" for imprisonment, "forfeiture of property to the Church" for fines, and "pilgrimage" for banishment, all in good faith." He smiled. He did not know until a moment afterward that he had touched the firecover and was badly burned.

"So we may read," said Henry in a voice as still as ice, "that 'all in good faith' the Church usurps our royal privilege and garners in our fines. And while we read, we smile." He looked at Roger and the firelight glinted in his eyes. Then of a sudden he reached out his hand, spilling the chamberlain from his feet as he half rose, and grasped the startled justice by the beard and yelled into his face, "Take your smile elsewhere!" and then let him go.

"Richard," said Henry, when all was quiet again, "how many murders, would you say, have been committed in my realm by clerks since I have sat upon the throne?"

De Luci glanced for confirmation at the Earl of Leicester. "One hundred would you say?" "A hundred more or less," they nodded, looking to one another.

"One hundred," Henry nodded in his turn. "One hundred murderers—how punished?"

No one was eager to speak up lest he should be found smiling while he spoke. De Luci therefore answered: "The heaviest spiritual penalty is degradation, the loss of orders."

"Aye," Henry nodded. "What would this mean to a clerk already in the lowest orders? May he not murder with impunity?" He did not wait for answer.

"Last month, was it? Just these few weeks ago, when we were in Worcestershire, you heard the sheriff bring complaint that he was not allowed to seize or try that rural deacon who raped the girl and then compounded felony by murder of her father? Surely a crime against the peace and order of our realm? Do I speak reasonably?" They nodded. "And yet we cannot touch him. No, the Church claims jurisdiction. The man is tonsured. What did the Church deem proper punishment for such a crime—two crimes? A loss of order? He is no longer deacon? And there the matter rests."

"There was some penance in that case as well, I think," de Luci said.

"And penance." Henry kept his voice most reasonable. "For such a crime—two crimes—what is the punishment meted out by our shire courts? No need to answer. For such a crime—for either crime, against a free man, as the victim was—the punishment is death.

"Now let us take the case of that Bedford canon, Philip of Brois." His voice grew harder for this was the case on which he meant to stand.

Philip of Brois, a man of good birth and a canon, as the king had said, of Bedford, was charged with the murder of a knight at Dunstable. Being a Churchman he was tried before the bishop's court in Lincoln and for lack of evidence was found not guilty, purged himself, and was acquitted. The dead man's family said that they were satisfied, but many others murmured at the case and, therefore, the sheriff of Bedford charged him for a second time and brought him up for trial before the king's itinerant justices when they next sat in Bedfordshire. Philip was not a humble man and thought he knew his rights; he would not plead before a secular court and used insulting words to the king's justices and left.

Of course the matter came quite speedily to Henry and he demanded that the Church turn over this unruly clerk to be tried once again for murder, since the case was anything but clear, and also for contempt of the king's court. The royal order sped from Philip's Church superiors at Bedford up to the Bishop of Lincoln and then on up to the Archbishop, Thomas. Thomas demurred: a man should not be tried twice for the same offense, he said. Philip had been tried once for murder and had purged himself. The Church was satisfied. As for the second charge: the Church did find him guilty on that count and would suspend his benefice for two years and—if the sheriff and the king insisted on it—they would have him flogged. Would this satisfy the king's most admirable thirst for justice?

It would not. "As things stand now that murderer, because he is a canon, is beyond my reach," Henry continued, staring at the fire. "Richard, can it be that ever a king before me was thus belittled in his own kingdom? How has this come about?"

"My lord, your ancestor the Conqueror made separate courts for Church and Crown when he came into England as you know. Churchmen construe this to mean that they have the right to try their own, no matter what the crime."

"Tell me something new," the king said gruffly. "You talk as if I did not know my ancestors or my laws. My grandfather had no such trouble as I have. When Henry Beauclerc sat upon the throne the king's law was supreme. Don't tell me that it was my mother's doing—or even Stephen's fault. He fought against the graspings of the Church while he had strength. No, it is the greed for power that has grown up around me among my prelates; it feeds on this new learning of the canon law. Churchmen have got a taste of law now and it has made them drunk. They do not even see the danger to themselves in laughing at the king!" He looked with wide eyes up at Richard. "The time has come to teach them. And I will do so."

The king held Council at Westminster on the first day of October in 1163. He had come up to London for the feast of Michaelmas and kept around him all his earls and barons and the other mighty folk who helped him rule. His prelates came as they were summoned: Thomas the Archbishop, with bishops, abbots, canons, clerks, riding with pomp and pageantry to the king's court.

Henry spoke calmly to them, very quietly, from his high throne upon the dais in the Rufus Hall and everyone leaned forward silent; warily, to listen, for they smelled a storm.

"I have been pondering how you bishops," he said, gazing out at them, "are willing to dispose yourselves toward royal rights and our rule here in England. I have been thinking, searching my mind, as to what kind of fault it is that you have found in me that I am deemed less worthy than those other kings, my ancestors who have been here before me." He looked at them a long time, though not at Thomas, and the bishops turned their eyes away.

"There have been no other learned men before you who have been disposed," he said, "as it would seem you are, to go against the rights of kings. I speak of criminous clerks and how you shelter them. There are among you tonsured men who murder, rape and rob and do all sorts of violence. These men are worse than laymen for they push themselves into the honors and the ordinations of the Church and turn her dignity and liberties into a mockery. They are the followers of evil rather than consecrated men.

"Yet you, you bishops"—here he raised a finger, pointing it at them—"maintain that it is written in your canon that such dishonorable things should be protected, in that you think that no one but yourselves alone are able to understand the laws of king and Church. But you had better know that we have other wise men with us, wiser than you." They murmured and he raised his voice to top them. "So wise in either law that they can see at one glance, and root out, your own misunderstandings of the law and utterly refute them. These men have testified to me the true interpretation of the law and it is this." He jabbed his finger at them, shouting. "The law is that all evil-doers, even such as are ordained, shall be delivered into rightful punishment by kingly power. That is the law! And I demand of you, you bishops, that you deliver all such criminal clerks into our hand for punishment!"

He stopped and there was silence in the hall while all the bishops looked to their archbishop, and the king likewise, finally, looked at Thomas—not with a query but with hard uncompromising eyes. "And I shall have your answer now," he said.

Thomas rose. "My lord," he said in his clear carrying voice, "your words are new and harsh upon our ears. May we have leave to go and speak among ourselves before we make an answer?"

"Aye, go." The king looked at him with disdain. "Go and confer." He waved his hand, dismissing them. "I am a patient man and can outwait you." They moved, all in a body around Thomas, down the hall and Henry watched them, frowning, and then raised his voice to call out after them: "And I shall want clear answers from you on your return!"

The bishops milled about the anteroom while servants ran to bring up stools and Hilary of Chichester began to talk even before they all were seated or Thomas put the question to them. "The king has reached the limit of his patience," Hilary said. "I know him well. It would be mad to go against him. No, his temper will not hold. What, do you think that he would brook an argument over a matter of the law when he has told us with his own mouth what the law is?" He swung his eyes to Thomas who stood dark and silent, waiting for his chair, then back again and in a lower voice, to Roger who was standing next to him, "Besides, the king has much on his side. It would seem to me that he is right in this—if

I am not mistaken?" He looked up at Roger's veiled eyes and the soft lips moving soundlessly, but Roger was not ready yet to be drawn out.

"Brothers," said Thomas, and all fell quiet, "let us look into our hearts and see our faults and with humility confess ourselves to God." They knelt, and having murmured through their prayers they rose again and found their stools and sat, each one where he could look at Thomas and appraise what he might say.

"Let us examine," he said, sitting with his knees apart, his hands upon his knees, a warrior's pose, "let us examine and discover what is our duty to the Church and, as shepherds of the Church, what is our duty to God's folk who are the clergy of the Church. The king would have us turn them over to the wild beasts of the court, judges of common criminals, to suffer at the hands of laymen such punishments as God's folk were not meant to suffer. The earliest fathers of the Church, surrounded as they were by pagan power and beset by worldly enemies, made clear to us in their decretals that ungodly men should never touch the lives or limbs of those for whom Christ died. Can we do less, to whom Our Lord has granted power and has given the duty to protect our sheep?" He looked into their doubtful faces and continued, "Would it not be blasphemous profanity to seize and bind behind the back the hands of priests, those very hands which consecrate the Body of Our Lord? Could we be party to such a sacrilege? Brothers, I say this cannot be."

The bishops all were silent, wary, except Roger who wore his irritation like a hair shirt, constantly tormented by the knowledge that the Archbishop of Canterbury—Baillehache the gawky clerk—was higher in the land than he, the Archbishop of York. He spoke with lazy insolence, casting aside all forms: "Thomas, the king is speaking not in generalities, as you would have it. He made no mention of godly men. His words were 'followers of evil' if I remember." He looked around for confirmation, pursing his lips out. " 'Evil-doers who push themselves into the Church.' You heard him. And you know as well as I do what has got him in this state; it is your foolish handling of the case of Philip of Brois—no priest, a canon and a criminal. If you had only handled that with tact we would not have this confrontation and the king's wrath to contend with. . . ."

"Philip of Brois was tried and punished," Thomas snapped.

"Not to the satisfaction of the king, most surely," Roger drawled. "Nor many others either."

"Would you have a man tried twice for the same crime?"

Bishop Hilary, made bold by Roger, assayed an answer, full of assurance at the first but limping at the last, under the piercing gaze of the archbishop. "What!" he cried out in his accustomed style. "What, if a man be tried and then degraded by the Church, then may he not be punished by the king, and that be only single punishment . . . tried once, then punished once . . . as I would count it . . . not tried twice . . ." his voice trailed off.

"Surely, my lord of Chichester," said Thomas coldly, "to a Churchman like yourself, degradation, loss of orders, must be felt as the heaviest of all punishments? What could such a man dread more than fall from grace?"

"Of course, of course," said Hilary hastily. "Put that way."

Thomas looked at him a moment longer, cold and unmoving, while the other squirmed, and then resumed his argument.

"We have it in the Scripture," Thomas said, turning to the others: "God does not punish twice, nor man should either." He saw that they were puzzled and he smiled within himself. Even Gilbert Foliot, he saw, had failed to put his finger on the source. " 'What do you imagine against the Lord? He will make an utter end to punishment; affliction shall not rise up a second time.' I speak the words of the Prophet Nahum as he understood the Lord. 'I have afflicted thee; I will afflict thee no more.' "

"My lord Archbishop," said Bishop Foliot, "this is a learned answer, but it is not an answer that will serve to calm the king. He speaks of worldly justice and worldly punishments that worldly men will fear."

"My learned brother," Thomas answered in the same tone, "can lay justice be as terrible as God's? I give you once again the Scripture, as the Lord spoke to Job: 'Hast thou an arm like God? Or canst thou thunder with a voice like Him?' What justice can be terrible as God's? The justice of the king? The justice of the shire courts?" He smiled a still, small smile. "I must remind you, it was I who helped the king to form those courts. Their purpose is to try lay folk. They have no jurisdiction over priests.

"No, brothers," he continued, looking out at all of them laying claim to each one with his eyes, "the king is seeking not for justice but for power, for the power that is justly God's. The right of it is that the Holy Church, who is the mother of both kings and priests, has two kings, two laws, two jurisdictions and two controlling powers. The first king is the King of Heaven, Christ Our Lord, whose body is the

Church, and there can be no limits to the powers and punishments of that King whose power is infinite."

He had them nodding. "Why do we speak, then, of thrusting Churchmen from the shelter and the justice of this infinite power into the lesser power of the king?"

He dared to let the question hang a long time in the air, for although Henry had quite obviously touched upon their fears, he knew that he had touched them in their vital spot: the power of the Church.

"What shall we say, then, to the king when we return?" asked Bishop Walter in an almost soundless voice.

"Our lord the king has our devotion and our loyalty and we will heed his will in all things—if it stands not athwart that which is right. But if it sets itself against the power of God, the laws and dignity of the Church, then may we neither wish nor dare give our consent to it. This shall we tell the king in all humility."

He gave the signal to the doorkeeper that they were ready to return.

Henry heard this speech through but he did not look at Thomas. His eyes went to the faces of the bishops, one by one, to see if they stood firm behind the archbishop, and anger flared within him when he saw they did. He rounded, then, on Thomas, interrupting him: "I ask you flat out for clear answer," he said, biting his words. "Do you, Archbishop Thomas, swear to uphold the laws and customs of my land—or not?"

"Indeed my lord," said Thomas levelly, "all praiseworthy customs here in your lands we will uphold, saving our consecration and the rights of God."

"I did not ask you 'saving your consecration' or your orders. God's eyes. I ask a straight out question and you slide away. Now, once again shall you give answer. And you shall not say anything of saving your order, but you shall agree outright, expressly, to my laws and constitutions. Answer!"

"My lord," said Thomas, "it is well known to all men present, an ancient custom, that a bishop's oath is always given saving his consecration. I cannot break this ancient custom of your land."

"So! Is this so!" said Henry, rising up. His wrath was terrible to see. The veins along his temples and in his neck stood out; his chest heaved and his eyes were red as blood. "Body of God! You slip and slide away from me, you bishops. All of you!" He glared first at the gray, unhealthy face of Gilbert Foliot, at Roger's hooded eyes and crafty mouth, at Walter in whom fright was battling with loyalty until the tears stood in his eyes. Only Hilary of Chichester was nodding furtively to indicate he sided with the king, and sight of him enraged him more. "So! Yes I see! You huddle all together, all of you, under one shield against me! But let me warn you, you shall have no victory to boast of! From this day on if any one among you shall presume to flout the power of my realm you shall pay dearly for it. Wait and see!"

Next day he sent a formal letter to his archbishop demanding the return of certain lands that he had granted him as chancellor: the honors of Eye and Berkhampstead. He notified him also that he was sending into exile his secretary John of Salisbury on whose treasonous theories he presumed to base foolhardy notions against royal rights. And last, he withdrew from his household and protection his little ward, the young king, lest he corrupt him. Then he left London, but he did not rest in his pursuit of Thomas for he had sworn to bring him low.

He set his mind to work upon the bishops one by one and, knowing human frailties, he worked them well, Roger of York through jealousy and Gilbert Foliot through righteous pride, convincing them that they must form a party among themselves to save the Church from downfall under one self-willed man. Hilary was persuaded to their cause through fear, and Robert of Melun, Thomas' old-time teacher and his one-time friend, through vanity.

Thomas watched them drop away from him and turned for his support to that key pillar of the Church, the pope. He found instead a slender reed. Pope Alexander, exiled from Rome, confronted by a rival pope, could not afford to go against so rich and strong a king as Henry, no matter what the cause. He sent mild words to Thomas: compromise, placate the king in this. And papal envoys, joined by the English bishops—Robert of Melun first of all, whom Henry had named Bishop of Hereford—came smiling softly, adding their own embellishments to papal thoughts: "Placate the king; he asks for nothing more than that you show him honor and keep the peace; he swears he will do nothing prejudicial to the Church."

And Thomas, listening and for once unsure, agreed. "I will meet him when and where he likes," he said, "and make amends."

They met, then, just the two of them, alone, outside the

town of Northhampton—for Henry said no town was big enough to hold them both—but evil winds were dominant and from the start all hope of easy concord was foredoomed. They met on horseback, or would have met except their stallions screamed on seeing one another, reared and lashed out with their hoofs, and would approach each other only to fight. The watchers from afar—for each had brought a mighty train and there were many there to watch—stood squinting with their arms upraised to shade their eyes and strained to hear what words would carry to them on the wind. The winter sun came from its screen of clouds and struck a burst of light behind the small black wheeling figures of the horsemen with their cloaks flung out like wings, and when it did the stallions' heavy legs turned thin as broomstraws, radiating light. The watchers squinted, strained, and shivered in the wind.

The sun shot straight in Thomas' eyes, he could not see the king. He only heard him cursing as he fought to hold his horse and he himself, with his whole body taut, intent, sawed at his horse's bit and jabbed his bloody spurs into its sides. He felt its muscles bunch and plunge beneath him as he kept it wheeling, tight upon itself, and with despair remembered he had come here to make peace and to submit himself to the king's will. What omen was this that the very horseflesh that they rode should meet like enemies?

He heard King Henry's angry voice commanding, "Go and get another horse. One you can manage!" And in obedience he turned and rode back to his waiting followers and took a docile gelding and rode out again.

The king came out to meet him on his own fresh horse, his brow like thunder though he had a smile stretched on his face. He did not speak until their horses stood neck beside neck and the two riders face to face and then he hissed at him: "You came to make submission to me, so I was promised. Yet you must first stand up against me like a fighting cock before the eyes of all! Have you learned only how to scorn your king through all the years he showed you friendship? Have you no gratitude?"

"My lord," said Thomas.

"I showed you condescension that I never showed another man. I have heaped favors on you. You were nothing when you came to me and it is I who raised you up!"

"My lord."

"Do you think anyone will raise you up, as I did, when I have cast you down? On no, you lean too hard upon the ladder by which you mounted!"

"My lord," said Thomas once again. But suddenly, his patience and his caution at an end, he added stubbornly, "I lean upon the Lord. For cursed is the man who puts his hope in man."

"God's eyes! Am I to have your mealy talk again?" the king broke in. "I did not send for you to preach to me. Who do you fancy that you are to speak thus to your king. You are the common son of one of my villeins, common born!"

"Aye, true," said Thomas, flaring. "I am not sprung from royal ancestors. Neither was Peter, prince of Apostles, who holds the keys to heaven!"

The king broke out in shrill derisive laughter. "God's eyes, you aim high!" He stared at Thomas with a kind of loathing, even as he laughed. And then his face grew still, as still as stone, his eyes like agates, only the tawny fringes of his beard moved in the wind. His voice sank to a whisper, knife-like, and he said, "Let me remind you that St. Peter died for his Lord."

Thomas too had turned to stone, a dark, carved gargoyle of a man. He understood the reference and the threat but he was not afraid. The furrows worn into his cheeks, the craggy nose and deep-set sockets of his eyes were hard as granite as he said, "And I, I also, I shall die, for my Lord, when the time shall come."

They sat, two horsemen with the winter sun upon them, silent, immobile on their stretch of grass. The watchers wondered at their stillness and the wind blew over them, and still they sat, locked in this hard cold glare of recognition in each other's eyes.

The king broke first. It was as though he had seen nothing and heard nothing of this last exchange. "I summoned you to make submission to me here," he said. "I had your promise you would make amends and swear to me you would uphold the customs of my land." And then his face changed once again, twisted as though in anguish as he blurted, "God, Tom, that it should come to this! That I need ask from you a promise to do me honor when I had thought you held that honor dear as I do myself!"

"I do, my lord," said Thomas, though he was not so moved.

"Then Tom, swear for me that you will uphold my honor and the customs of my lands."

"It was for that I came prepared, my lord. I swear it: all the rightful customs of the land I will uphold."

"Without reserve, Tom? In good faith?"

"Without reserve."

"Ah well! Ah good! And bravely said!" The king's smile

was a sudden slash across his face. "I have your word. You shall repeat this for me in full Council, with your suffragans."

"In council?" There had been no talk of council. "In what council, sire?"

Still looking at him, Henry pulled the reins so that his horse tossed up its head and backed away. "Since you defied me in the public eye, Tom, surely you see you must submit in public? Honor demands it!" Grinning, he swung his horse around and raised his gloved hand in dismissal. "I have your promise," he called as he rode away.

Thomas watched him: strong back, firm in the saddle, cantering lightly across the winter grass. "No, never trust me," he heard the voice again.

* * *

The smell of smoke hung over Clarendon all through this council, for it was to Clarendon, his hunting lodge near Salisbury, that Henry summoned Thomas to commit himself in public, and although he laid his fires well, the fuel was not quite ready yet for burning.

Thomas was lodged, with all his bishops, crowded in, in the new guest hall just completed: barren, raw, and smelling of the pitch that clung in golden droplets to the pine planks of the walls. It was the smell of the barbarian north from which these timbers came and there was nothing that was comforting, familiar, to an English bishop in his hour of unease.

The time was January of 1164, and on the first day of the council Thomas rode, his suffragans behind him, the short distance from the guest house to the lodges because the road and court were churned in mud. The great hall of the lodge itself was ancient and its weathered timbers blended with the gray-brown hillside off beyond. The woodsmoke pouring from its roof vent added gray on gray to the low winter sky and patches of thin snow lay in the shade of rain-soaked outbuildings and on the boles of trees.

Thomas saw that he must face full Council, "all the men of England," for every shelter here was crowded and there were tents set up in the wide park, and rows of well-fed horses, chestnut and bay and black, were hitched to every rack.

He rode on past and through the palisaded court up to the timbered porch and there dismounted on the lowest step. He was prepared to keep his pledge; he had rehearsed it.

"All the rightful" . . . could he say praiseworthy? no, he had promised simply to uphold the customs . . . "All ancient customs of this land will I uphold, without reserve, and in good faith." He would say nothing of the reservations due him as a representative of God. In this he bowed. It was defeat. But he must do it; there was no escape. The pope himself had urged him to it. It was in no way prejudicial to the Church the pope had said. And yet he knew it was. God give me strength thus to deny His rights, he thought, and anguish rose in him. Then suddenly: I wonder if I am the man for this? But that escape he could not take. He was the man. And he must play this through.

He walked into the chamber and saw the earls and barons, king and court, arrayed against him there. He held his head up. It will be brief, he thought.

The hunchbacked Earl of Leicester was presiding and after some preamble he came to the crux: "My lord Archbishop, you have come to swear, with all your fellow bishops, that you will uphold the ancient customs of this land. Our gracious lord the King, therefore, has caused us to reduce to writing, so that we all may understand of what we speak, these customs of his grandfather into a code of articles . . ."

Thomas' head jerked back as though he had been slapped. The broad oath to respect the customs of the land he was prepared to take; to swear to uphold a set of written laws he had not seen was something else. His eyes turned from the earl to find the king amid his courtiers, but Leicester, quick in speech as he was quick in thought, continued ". . . so that no one may, in after time, presume to charge the king with introducing novelties into these laws. My lord Archbishop, do you swear?"

Thomas had found King Henry, seated in his chair and leaning back, his chin upon his hand, as though he meant to draw himself into the smoky darkness of the room. It seemed to Thomas that he squatted like a waiting frog, half-hidden by his courtiers. Only his eyes betrayed him, gleaming a steely blue out of the gloom. He turned again to Leicester with his own eyes shooting fire. "I do not swear, my lords, to what I have not seen," he said.

Henry leaped up. "You know the customs just as well as I!" he shouted.

"I know not what is written there!" said Thomas, pointing at Leicester and the parchments in his hand.

"My lord Archbishop," Leicester said quickly, "these are the established laws, the constitutions of our land," he tapped the parchments. "Nothing more."

"Then I would have them read to us, my lord of Leicester, before I swear—and ask my suffragans to swear—the Church's rights away!"

He was surprised to hear the voice of Gilbert Foliot behind him whispering, "Hold fast!" and new determination rose in him. The bishops, weak though they were and sore disposed against him, would suffer trickery such as this no more than he.

"Then read them, read them," Henry cried to Leicester. "Let him hear them. He shall swear in any case!"

The list was long for there were sixteen articles in all, with many facets to each article, and each upheld the king. As Leicester read each one aloud the barons cheered, the bishops all kept silence. Only Thomas spoke, after each article, making a comment on each legal and each spiritual flaw. Henry had sunk back in his seat again, his mouth closed and his fist upon it, watching and listening to all.

"Clerics accused of offenses against the royal laws shall be tried by the royal courts," read Leicester. "And the king's officers shall have the right to watch the trials of clerics in the bishops' courts and if the accused are found guilty or confess to secular crimes, the Church shall no wise shelter them . . ."

"So now we see," said Thomas bitterly, "how Christ shall be tried once again by Pilate!"

Leicester paid no heed. He read on to the end, with interruptions such as this, as though he had not heard. "The revenues of vacant sees and abbeys are to be turned over to the king; likewise the king shall have his say to whom elections of these dignities shall go."

"No, no, my lords," cried Thomas. "I cannot, not without the sanction of the pope and of the Universal Church, forego the basic tenet of canonical election! Shall I, as father of our island Church, place her in schism from the rest of Christendom? It cannot be. I shall not!"

There was a roar within the chamber and King Henry's voice topped all as he leaped up again in fury. "You are foresworn and damned!" he shouted. "You pledged your word to do me honor! Now before all you throw your insults in my teeth. But I will bend your neck, you villeins' spawn! You ingrate! Pimp and protector of thieves and murderers! I will have justice in my land despite you!"

The barons stamped and milled about, infected by this fury, and the bishops all drew back. Only the Earl of Leicester and de Luci kept their heads, came to the king with quiet words, for they feared bloodshed if his rage went on unstemmed. But the king shouted out in answer to them while the sweat stood on his face: "Not counsel! This is not time for counsel! I will have recourse not to counsel but the sword—and they shall feel the edge of it, yes all of them, if I am not obeyed!"

"Withdraw, my lords!" the Earl of Leicester said in his quicksilver voice directly to the bishops from behind the king. "Withdraw, and we shall call you once again."

The bishops turned and Thomas felt them flee away behind his back. He saw two of the king's knights come at him, their cloaks flung off, their swords raised, and their faces red with anger. Fitz Urse was one of them. He shouted as he ran at Thomas, "You heard the king! Beware! This arm is his and it is ready!" And he whipped his sword back with a flourish, making it sing as it cut through the air.

Thomas felt Foliot behind him as he backed away, keeping his eyes on Fitz Urse's as he would on a wild beast's. He felt no fear and he heard Foliot's voice close in his ear, as calm as he himself: "We must withdraw until we stand on solid ground; but there is no retreating, now that we know the king's full purpose. Come with me." And they retreated through the door as from a lion's cage while other knights came rushing at them, one with a battle-ax upraised who swerved aside at the last moment with a shout, "Submit or else you die!"

Outside they saw the other bishops in a panic, some gathered in the corners of the courtyard and some running up the road. Their horses had been led away and they were forced to follow through the mud on foot. The Bishop of Salisbury saw them as they left the porch, ran back and said, all breathless and near tears, "What now, my lords, may God protect us! What is to happen now?"

"We must gather in the guest hall and stand firm," said Thomas.

They found some of the bishops there already and they had taken heart, as though this raw barn of a building were a cathedral church. Those who had peeled away from Thomas under the royal blandishments and those who had stood firm were now together of one mind against the king. Robert of Melun came to Thomas and bowed down and kissed the ring upon his finger; he said nothing, but his intent was clear.

They had no time for counsel when the Bishop of Salisbury ran in like a rabbit with the ferrets after it. He flung himself at Thomas crying, "Relent, my lord Archbishop.

Father, relent, for they are after me. They have selected me, with Winchester, as their especial victims!"

"What special victims?" Thomas took him by the arms.

"The barons say we are obnoxious to the king! Have been before times and are now again and he will have our eyes out . . . God knows what else . . . the Earl of Leicester said. Barons are ready to carry out his threats. I saw them! Father, have mercy and submit to him. Oh God, he has selected us . . . give thought to us . . . have mercy . . ."

He babbled on and Thomas looked from him to Winchester who stood inside the door and saw by his white face that it was true, but Winchester only nodded and forbore to plead.

Bishop Foliot stepped up to Salisbury and spoke impassioned words, his hand raised as in benediction: "Brother, have no fear. A warrior of the Church stands ever ready to face death and torture for the cause of right. Take heart and follow Christ—upon the very cross if need be—smiling at sacrifice!" He smiled his own dour smile but Salisbury only clung to Thomas, limp with fear.

Newcomers stood within the door: the Earl of Leicester and the king's uncle, the Earl of Cornwall, and behind them two Knights Templar in their white wool habits with the red cross of crusaders on their breasts. They called for Thomas that they might speak with him alone. "My lord Archbishop," Leicester said when he had joined them on the open porch, "things stand very bad for you. The king is not to be controlled. I fear that some unheard of violence may be done . . ."

Quick as he spoke, his face full of its quick intelligence turned up to Thomas—Thomas spoke quicker: "It is nothing new, unheard-of, that a priest should die for God. A multitude of saints have taught us that!"

"And that unfortunate bishop, he is to be your saint, and suffer horribly in life and limb?" asked Leicester with a darted look in through the door at Salisbury who had swooned against his brother bishops.

"My lord Archbishop," said the Earl of Cornwall, "though you may feel there is some right on your side, consider, please, your duty to the king. You make of him the laughing-stock of all the world if you deny him honor in his own Grand Council and leave his nation destitute of law. No matter what the rights here, what the differences—that all may be smoothed over by and by—it is our duty to uphold our king whom we have sworn upon our knees, in solemn ceremony, more than once, to honor and obey."

And the Knights Templar, seeing a wavering in Thomas' face, fell down before him at his feet, embraced his knees, and swore the king required nothing more than to avoid appearance of defeat before the Council; all would be peace again, his bishops safe, and he would hear no more of "customs" if he but give the verbal promise he had sworn to give; they pledged upon their souls' damnation this was true.

The power of these strong men's words and their impassioned wills, their high positions, and the power of pity, worked on Thomas. What was to be gained by more refusals? What, after all, would a few words said under such duress cost him or cost the Church? The pope said, "Placate the king." And afterward, if when the pope saw for himself these Constitutions written down as they were here at Clarendon, he took his stand against them—as he must—new action could be taken. But for now . . .

He nodded and the Templars sank away. He turned and walked back to the bishops where they stood, their eyes on him, and said, "It is the Lord's will, brothers, that I should foreswear myself and for the present yield."

They stood dumfounded at his words. "You speak of perjury!" said Foliot at last, his mouth tight with disdain.

And Thomas said, "If I incur the guilt of perjury, then must I hope for pardon through my penitence hereafter. There is no other way."

He led them back again, the earls and Templars going on before, and there before the hostile eyes of all the barons and the king he made his pledge: "My lord, I do consent to your demands and give my word I will observe the customs of the realm in all good faith." He hoped, then, all was over and that he would have leave to go, but Henry sprang up.

In full voice he shouted, "You have all heard here how the archbishop has made submission. Now let him fix his seal to this and prove his good intent!" and he snatched up the parchment where the laws were written down. His face was full of triumph for he thought he had won. But Thomas, seeing shock upon the Earl of Leicester's face and even Cornwall frown, seeing the Templars start up in dismay, knew he was not alone.

"No, never," he said firmly, "by Almighty God. As long as breath is in my body, I will not put the seal of Canterbury to this blasphemy." He looked long at the king, and Henry, staring back, read his determination.

So I have pushed him to the wall, he thought. Well, you

shall stand there, Thomas, with my sword against your breast, till I have done with you.

Aloud he said, his voice full of disgust, "You have my leave to go."

CHAPTER XX

THOMAS WAS SOMBER as they rode away from Clarendon. He had done nothing right there and he knew it, vacillating, perjuring himself, and then at the end when all was over taking from the hand of Richard de Luci, like some foolish and unwary child, the parchments—so that they now might claim he had accepted the Constitutions even though he would not put his seal to them.

The other bishops left him to ride alone, as though he were diseased, and when at Winchester they parted they had few words for him. Never in their memory had the Church suffered such defeat—when all might well have been avoided by careful leadership. Some found the king at fault and Thomas an accomplice to this fault by his submission; some found the archbishop at fault for rousing the king's wrath in the first instance. None knew what would come next, and all were troubled.

Thomas rode on with his own train of clerks, keeping a bitter silence, failing to call a halt for prayers, for food, to rest the horses or the men. After a long while Prior Robert ventured to ride close and speak to him. "Be of good courage and play the man," he urged him gently, "and the Lord will do that which seems good to him."

Thomas shrugged off his words. "I am an interloper in the Church," he said. His face worked while they rode a little farther in deep silence, then he went on: "If I, a worldly man, a courtier, a runner after honors and the world's acclaim, had not been thrust into this office by the king, then these calamities would not have fallen on the innocent. It is through me the Church and all her little ones are brought to this."

"These things are not for you to say," said Robert. "Wait on the Lord and pluck your courage up. And He will strengthen you."

"No. I am not worthy to be a priest of God. I shall not say Mass again. I am foresworn and perjured and a harbinger of evil and hard times."

"Wait on the Lord," repeated Robert once again, turning those open shining eyes on him, but Thomas did not turn to look, even when Robert for the third time begged him, "Wait on the Lord, I say."

"I shall withdraw myself," repeated Thomas stubbornly, "and I shall not say Mass."

But when they were in Canterbury once again some worldly matters made imperative demands. Thomas took up the reins again. He sent word to the pope of the king's Constitutions and of his own submission and of his penitence and his suspension of himself from saying Mass. And—knowing the pope's position, exiled, confronted by an anti-pope, dependent on the friendship of the king—he wrote as well to John of Salisbury to marshal every friend in Europe that he had and use what means he could to sway the Curia, for it was only prudent to be prepared against King Henry. Long years with Henry had taught him this. And such prudent habits are hard to break simply by willing your soul to trust in God.

His envoys reached the pope, who was at Sens, were well received, told all they had to tell into his sympathetic ear, and were again in Canterbury within a fortnight. The pope was most indulgent to his archbishop: he must not tax himself too much with self-incrimination; he must resume his office at the altar; he should seek out some skillful spiritual guide and make confession to him of those things that weighed upon his conscience and be absolved. One must not take oneself too seriously, he seemed to say.

"He had not seen the Constitutions," was Thomas' comment. And he wrote again to John.

John's answer came, a practical and realistic answer. Some things were hopeful in it:

"Everything that passed at Clarendon is well known here—better than in England. The Count of Flanders is most anxious to help you . . ." He has no love for Henry, Thomas thought. "And I have seen the King of France and he has promised he will write the pope on your behalf. And you should know, the feeling toward our king among the French is one of fear and hatred. . . ."

This much hopeful, but the rest: "The pope himself I have avoided seeing until now, though I have written the two cardinals, of Pisa and of Pavia, to explain the injury that will be done the papal court if these new Constitutions are upheld. I am not sanguine, though. Many things make against us, few in our favor, and I fear the pope himself is cool . . .

"You write that if I cannot succeed otherwise I may promise two hundred marks. The other side will give down three or four hundred sooner than be defeated, and I will answer for the cardinals that they will prefer the larger sum in hand from the king to the smaller promise from you. It is true that we are contending for the liberties of the Church, but your motive, it will be said, is not the Church's welfare but your own ambition . . .

"They may propose—I have already heard a whisper of it—that the pope cross into England in his own person and take your place at Canterbury for a while . . ."

Thomas stopped reading as a thrill of fear shot through him. Thus would his ending come—not two years from his consecration—in public ignominy. I must go to the pope myself, he thought.

Article four of those accursed Constitutions (Thomas knew them all by heart now) forbade the clergy to leave the country or carry their appeals to Rome without the king's consent. This one article alone, if not the others, must the pope reject, so sharply did it strike at his own power and prestige. I must be sure Pope Alexander knows of this and that the world knows that he knows, he thought. But am I bound by this same Constitution not to go? Since I took this cursed paper in my hand, must I obey its laws until the pope has ruled against it? He asked his close advisers this; they recommended caution. He must not go without the king's consent.

Henry was once again at Woodstock. And once again, although the roads were fetlock deep in mud and though the steady rain soaked through the layers of his furs, Thomas made the journey—four black and weary days and nights—to Woodstock Palace to seek audience with the king. Abruptly, like some beggar, he was halted at the gate.

"The king sees no one."

The rain fell in a silver curtain from the eaves. The guard stood shadowy behind it and his voice was muffled in the sound of splashing water where the gutters overflowed.

"Tell him the Archbishop of Canterbury waits."

"No one." The disembodied voice was insolent. "Not the archbishop nor yet the pope."

Thomas shook the water from his face. "Go tell your master the king's marshal that his wit is unappreciated here. The archbishop seeks audience."

"The order's from the king himself. He knows who waits."

"Get me de Luci the Justiciar."

"The king . . ."

"Get me de Luci!" The thunder of the voice, the lightning flash, jolted the insolence from the marshal's man. Without another word he pulled the cloak about his head and left the shelter of the gate to run between the puddles of the court to the great hall.

Thomas dismounted, left his soaking horse to twitch its ears against the downpour, and went into the guardroom, there to stand shivering in that airless hole until at last de Luci came.

"Richard, I have come four days' journey up from Canterbury to see the king."

"He will not see you, Thomas."

"Richard . . ." The black eyes bored into the other's, seeking to reach the man behind the royal justice. Where was friendship? "Richard, help me to see the king. If he knows I am here and on what errand he will receive me." He was aware that all the guards were listening but it had come to that, the end of dignity. "Tell him for friendship's sake and that it is a matter of importance."

Richard knew full well, as the king knew, what the errand was. Had they not spies? Did they not know of Thomas' plottings and of his journey step by step? Could they not guess with almost certainty his next maneuver? His face remained impassive. "He will not see you, Thomas, not for friendship nor for any pretext. But let us, we two, part as friends." And he stepped forward and kissed the wet cheek that was offered silently. Richard the Loyal.

The journey back was worse. His mind was tired out from scurrying this way and that in search of exit from the trap King Henry had him in, his body sick and shivering with fatigue. But when he reached the Medway outside Rochester he paused before the bridge and of a sudden swung his horse into the river road and headed south. His hand had done it on the rein, his foot on the horse's flank—neither his conscious will nor mind. But after that he traveled faster and at Snodland, where he stopped his little train for food and shelter at the village church, he sent them back to Canterbury, all but one serving man, and went on at an ever quicker pace.

At Maidstone they took fresh horses. It was noon then. But by the time they entered Romney Marsh the day was darkening and all the world lay flat and featureless under a lowering sky. Night closed them in. The servant whispered that he feared the marsh sprites lest they deceive their senses and ensnare their souls, but Thomas took his reins from him and bade him wrap his cloak about his head so that he might not see them and led on. He held both reins in one hand and with the other grasped his cross, and when the marsh lights danced obliquely from his sight—first over here, then there—or when strange spirits sprang up in his path, now looming in the darkness like an armored challenger, now like a maiden, now like a mocking dwarf, he turned a resolute and frowning face upon them till they disappeared.

The steeple of the little church at Snave stood like a beacon on the plain and when they reached it they dismounted and gave thanks before the altar of St. Augustine. Four miles to go.

At Ivychurch they paused again. The servant said, "My lord, where are you leading me?" And Thomas said, "To France."

The boatmen at the port of Romney, roused, could see no reason to put out at night. The tide was wrong. Why should a merchant and his man, they asked each other in the corners of their huts, feel such an urgency of haste? Why should a merchant dress thus in a canon's robes?

"A merchant's business for the Church," said Thomas, cursing his weary mind for carelessness.

"The Church moves very leisurely, in God's good time," they said. "The Church can wait for dawn."

"At dawn, then, from the churchyard of St. Nicholas," said Thomas, but he shivered at the price they asked because the size of it, the crafty looks that went before the asking of it, showed that they knew he was in flight.

He spent the night in the church porch, a hiding place where he could enter without key and shut the door behind, a sheltering place filled with the sounds of water lapping at the walls and of the creak and thump of little boats tied to the mooring rings. He did not sleep. Before the dawn he rose up from the stones on which he lay and went and knelt before the locked door to the nave and leaned his head against it while he prayed. Now it was time to go.

He roused the servant and they went into the air and found the boatmen ready with their oars. They did not look at him as one by one they climbed into the little smack and held it for him till he was settled and then cast off. Without a word they bent and dipped their oars together, stirring the blackness of the water while the sky turned gray above them and the land grew dim behind. Thus went an hour by of silence and of rhythmic work, of smell of briny water, while the dawn grew bright. And then they looked at him.

They rested on their oars and looked, sweat on seamed faces and suspicion in the eyes. "I said we should have none of it," said one.

"He is indeed a tall man, very tall. I noted it before."

"Why does a merchant go about in canon's dress?"

"I said I was a Churchman," Thomas snapped. "On merchant-business for the Church."

They stared at him. At last the eldest spoke, rubbing his hand across his grizzled chin so that the sound of bristles scraping could be heard above the silence of the sea. "Are you not he, that archbishop who quarrels with the king?"

"Not I," said Thomas.

But he heard a cock crow then. Out here, mid-ocean, far from land, the crowing of a cock! He closed his eyes. "Yes, I am he," he said. "In God's name, take me on to France."

The boat swung silent and the oars dripped motionless between the dark green of the swelling waters and the light green of the sky.

He heard them, then, on to the other, "Turn back." "Heave there, Saundi." "Bring her around."

"The price you named," said Thomas. "That can be doubled."

They did not answer as they pulled upon their oars.

"Have you no fear of God," he asked them, "to treat thus with God's representative on earth?"

Then softly, with persuasion, "I am your spiritual father, you know that, and as you are God's children you are mine; as I do care for you, so must you care for me . . ."

And yet again: "The Church commands you! Know you the power of the Church? Know you the hell of excommunication? Under the threat of this anathema, I tell you, turn for France!"

The oars dipped on in unison. The boatmen bent to them. They did not answer.

Now Thomas rose up from his seat and towered over them. "Have you no fear of God," he thundered, "and the wrath of God?"

At last the old man spoke. He did not look at Thomas but his words were clear. "We fear God, but we fear King Henry more." And after that no more was said as they pulled on for shore.

Thomas sat brooding, near exhaustion, till the boat touched bottom and with a burst of strength he jumped out, wetting his skirts up to the knees, and waded the few steps to the land. His servant, mute, ran after him and Thomas sent him to claim their horses at the stabling place. Then they rode, one behind the other, in the flat, cold morning light across the Marsh again. They had not eaten since the morning of the day before and Thomas had not slept for many nights. Now fever took him and sometimes he shook so in the saddle that he had to grasp it with both hands and bow himself over his horse's neck. The servant, nodding on his palfrey, dropped far behind. They made a strange procession under the windy sky, the tall bent man in black, the lagging servant, with the marsh grass blowing all about them as they plodded on.

At Ashford they crossed the bridge to take the winding road along the Stour. Thomas sat upright through the little town for he was conscious of the way the people stared at him, though none came forward to ask his blessing. Were they aware of who he was and yet hung back?

The numbing hours followed, each like the last. Sometimes he let his body slump, his mind go blank. Sometimes he dreamed. A cup was placed before him full of wine. It was a silver cup and set about with jewels: great lumps of jasper, topaz, tourmaline embedded in the tracery, the metal glowing softly in the firelight. A warm voice spoke to him, friendship, approval, even admiration in it. He did not recognize it and the words were blurred. But oh the warmth of it, the glow of pleasure to be here, the velvety color of the wine inside the silver cup. He drank.

Suddenly his body bolted upright in the saddle, stomach constricted, horror and revulsion in his throat. A spider sat within the cup. Its long and hairy legs were folded under it but it was still alive. It touched his lips when he tipped up the cup to drink. His eyes flew open and he looked about him: the day was almost over, colorless; the wind blew in the treetops up above the valley road; a little splatter of quick rain flew in his face. He looked down but the cup was gone, his hands were empty. Only the spider sat within his mind's eye, folded upon itself and yet alive, twitching, repulsive. His stomach lurched and he leaned out and vomited a spurt of burning juice into the road.

The dream stayed with him. Where was that place of warmth? Whose was that voice? Why had he felt so happy and contented there and who had put the spider in the cup? The voice was not King Henry's and the place not any hall that he had ever known. And yet . . . he knew it was the king. He had beguiled him. He had said, "Drink." Thomas shuddered and tried to sweep the dream out of his mind but he could not, and thus he knew that it was not a dream; it was a vision.

He tried to pray. But once again his mind deserted him, darkness encompassed it, he slept. Night came to meet them as they entered Godmersham: a clutch of villeins' houses and a church crouched by the forest wall. His horse stopped by a gate and Thomas jerked awake, his mind quite clear and speaking clearly, "Could you not watch one hour?"

A man stood by the gate, his pale round face a glimmer in the dark. He had been hoeing till the darkness closed him in; he used the hoe as though it were a staff as he came up the road. He was the village priest. He looked suspiciously at Thomas because he did not know him and he mistrusted strangers. Other strangers had come by that day: men of the king's guard, knights and their retainers.

"This is the Canterbury road?" asked Thomas. The place was strange to him. His head felt hollow, aching with fever, and his eyeballs like rough agates in their sockets. "This *is* the road?"

"It is."

"And this place?"

"Yes."

"And this place?" Why was the man so stupid?

"Yes."

"What is the name of this place?"

"This is Godmersham."

"Godmersham," repeated Thomas. He did not recognize the name. "How long a ride to Canterbury?"

"An easy ride," the priest said. He himself had never ridden it and not for promise of the highest seat in heaven would he have ridden it at night. He said "an easy ride" because he did not want this stranger staying here. "If you ride on without delay you may well catch the others."

"What others?"

"Those others who ride to Canterbury like yourself."

"What others?" The man's stupidity—perhaps his own?—was like a swamp in which he sank.

"The king's men," the priest said. "They did not stop here," he said significantly. "They must be close to Canterbury now, on the king's business . . . But you may overtake them yet," he tacked on quickly.

"What business?"

"How should I know what business?" The face grew fainter in the darkness as though it moved away.

"I myself have business with the king," said Thomas loudly.

There was a silence. Thomas could sense the indecision in that fat round head, the fear the man had of authority pitted against the stupid hope that silence meant safety. "My business with the king is urgent as the king's life itself," he added. It was only half a lie. "What business did these others claim to have? Be careful, lest you betray your king."

"Oh not so dire as that, my lord," the voice came quivering through the night. "They rode to meet the others, up from Saltwood, because the king has confiscated the archbishop's goods."

I knew it would be so, thought Thomas. There was no surprise.

"Tomorrow they will strip the palace. They say that there are coffers full of gold there, and silver plate, and cloaks worth a hundred shillings" . . . the priest's voice echoing the soldiers' greed . . . "all for the taking—for the king of course—because the archbishop has broken the king's laws and fled out of the land and all his goods are forfeited . . ."

The servant's horse came plodding up and stopped. The servant, rolling in the saddle, lifted his head a little, whispered, "I cannot go on," and let it drop. He was not heard.

"They say this is the king's will?" Thomas asked.

"I do not speak against the king," the voice was anxious and the moon face reappeared, "Nor yet the archbishop. God knows the right of it."

"God knows," said Thomas.

"St. Anselm fled from the king, you know . . . so I've been told," the priest said, fearful of saying anything too much and yet afraid to stop. "But Anselm was a saint and this one, so they say, a soldier. Still, he was chosen by the king, and that's enough. And yet he flees away." He could not stop. "A strange affair!"

The servant slid down from his horse. "I can't go on," he said. "Father, I can't go on."

"Nor can I, Thomas thought. And yet he must. They would not confiscate his property if he were standing at the door. He dug his heels into the tired horse and it picked up its head and started on. The servant and the village priest looked after him but he was soon beyond their vision.

A patch of low scrub forest and a patch of field, an oak tree standing shadowy within a glade, a night bird's cry—the terrifying mysteries of night lay all about him, and the wind moved in the hair upon his scalp. The fever came again and shook him and he hung his head. He dozed and, at a noise, he sprang awake. He dozed again. Again he dreamed. "This is my house," a voice said. "And my eye is on it and my ear intending night and day." "But it is *my* house!" Thomas exclaimed. It was his hall, the tables set, and laughter. He saw the starling in its cage and his sister Mary just beyond, dressed like a cymbal player. "But it is my hall!" He ran up laughing to the door. How gay it was! That was what made him laugh—the laughter, and Walter Map beside him, laughing. Someone shut the door. He beat upon it. How his heart beat! That was not laughter jumping in his heart but agony. It almost suffocated him. He woke and he was weeping. "But that was my house," echoed in his ears. Where was he now? He heard the Stour beside him purling in its shallow bed; above the moon was glinting on the edges of the clouds. He was alone.

A church rose up before him, gray in the darkness, ringed by the deep black shadows of a hedge. It blocked his way. His horse had stopped and he sat dumbly staring at the church, the gray hulk like a wall across his path, the white stones in the churchyard. Why did it block his way? Despair engulfed him. He put his face down, weeping bitterly, onto his horse's neck. He put his arms around it and with no effort felt himself roll from the saddle and fall heavily upon the ground. He lay there. It is the end, he thought.

He woke to find himself upon a pallet, soft as moss. Above him rafters wavered in a candle's light. There was a smell of incense and the feeling of a quiet presence in the room. Someone sat by him. "Where am I?" he asked.

"Why, you are in the church." The voice was of a young man but very mild and soft. There was an overtone of faint surprise.

"What church?"

"Why, Certeham."

Thomas closed his eyes. He thought he could remember Certeham. But darkness surged and jumped behind his lids, then suddenly a burst of light. His eyes flew open and he raised his head. "Is that daylight?" he demanded.

"No. It is night."

He sank back whispering, "No matter, It is over anyway." Despair crushed down on him. He felt its weight.

The young man watched him, then he leaned over. "You have been weeping," he confided, "while you slept."

"Aye," Thomas murmured with his eyes closed. "Likely."

There was a pause so long that Thomas raised his eyes and looked up at the young man's face—a pasty, concave, somewhat vacant face, but with such peaceful, childlike eyes it took on beauty. Just now it wore a puzzled, questioning look and Thomas felt compelled to add, "I have good cause." His voice failed and he closed his eyes again.

After a while the young man spoke again. "I think that you are hungry." He smiled a tentative embarrassed smile. When Thomas did not answer, he added in that shy and fluting voice, "We have both bread and wine." He meant the bread and wine that the priest Lambert kept for the Consecration of the Host. He went off in the darkness to take it from its hidden place and came back noiselessly, his bare feet treading with familiarity each ridge and furrow of the stones, so long had Almon known this church.

He knelt and put his hand in back of Thomas' head and with the other held the cup. "Now you must drink," he said.

The word "drink" echoed eerily in Thomas' mind. He shuddered and drew back and stared with terror at the young man hovering over him. The cup hung close above his face, blurred by its nearness and coming closer, ever closer to his mouth—the very entrance to his soul. He felt the strength go out of him and lay back helpless, weak with dread, and whispered, pleading, like a little child: "Is there a spider in it?"

Almon sat back and peered into the cup and swished it round. He shook his head and smiled. "It is good wine," he said. "There is no harm in it." And once again he pressed the cup against the folded lips and once more waited with that shy expectant smile, while the words echoed, high and soft, "No harm in it . . ."

Was it a demon speaking in that fluting voice? Was this indeed a church? Where was he, where was he? Thomas lay rigid with his lips clamped tight, fear and suspicion knotted in him, while he thought, Beware, beware, for evil stalks the world! He arched his back and with the last strength in him set his will against the cup, against the hand that held it and that empty and receptive face.

They held this pose together a long time—the strong man arched in panic and the weaker holding him—but never did the mild eyes waver in their curious gaze nor the cup tremble. Patience was there and time was his. In time, with patience, the most stubborn man must drink.

Unequal contest and unfair! There was no hope for Thomas. Deep in his inner being, and for the first time in his life, he weakened, softened, and forgot his pride. His stubborn will relaxed and yielded. And with an effort such as he had never made before he gave himself into the young man's hands, surrendered, and let go his life into another's keeping. Slowly, with his eyes fixed childlike on the face above, he put his hand upon the hand that held the cup and drank.

The wine was warming to his throat and tasted sweet. He drank it sip by sip as it was offered and when Almon sopped the bread into the dregs of it and fed him he ate eagerly. Afterward he lay back sighing and the world came clear to him; he saw the young man and the church for what they were and that he lay behind the altar in the narrow space before the apse. This must be the young man's bed.

"You were very hungry," Almon said.

"Aye," Thomas nodded.

"I think you were in trouble."

"Aye."

"Then you were wise to come and leave your troubles here," Almon said owlishly. "I often do. I live here."

The young man was simple. Thomas sat up and hung his arms across his knees and stared into the dark. "I cannot 'leave my troubles here,' " he said.

"Men often do," said Almon earnestly.

"Not troubles such as mine."

"Are they so terrible?" he whispered.

"Terrible enough." The youth was stupid but he owed him much. "Men plot against me and I have been deeply wronged."

"Is that so terrible? Oh, yes, I see it must be." Almon blushed.

Thomas looked strangely at him. "Has no one ever wronged you, then?"

Almon was startled. "I? I don't think so." He thought a moment. "Not that I know of," he said doubtfully.

"You are a fortunate young man."

"Yes," Almon said. "Who was it wronged you?"

Thomas looked down into his hands. "The king," he said.

"The king! Then it must be a great majestic wrong! So much to forgive!"

"Forgive?"

"It is God's will," said Almon solemnly.

"I know God's will," said Thomas sharply. "I can forgive the past. What of the future? He threatens now to seize my properties, my books, my horses, all the treasures I have laid up for the poor." His voice was bitter with new strength.

"Why, that would be a wrong indeed!" cried Almon, who had no property at all of any kind for any man to seize.

There was a look of deep concern, almost horror, on his face. "He must not be allowed!"

"One does not say 'allow' when kings are spoken of," said Thomas. Then, with a second glance at that distraught pale face, he asked, "Why do you care so much? You do not know me or even who I am." He caught a look of passing doubt. "Or is it I you care for?" he asked in a deeper voice. "I see," he added. "Yes, I see your meaning. You do not start and tremble that I should lose my properties. You do not even know whose properties they are. It is his soul in danger that you care for, not my properties." He dropped his head upon his hands. "I had forgotten who and what I am." He was not speaking now to Almon but to himself. "A child reminded me. So does God work!"

He turned again to Almon and took his hand. "What would you say," he whispered, "if I should tell you that it is I who am responsible for the king's soul?"

"Then you must stop him!" Almon's eyes were wide.

"Aye, I must stop him. Has the dawn come up?"

"No." Almon rose and peered around the altar toward the windows of the nave. All was in blackness. "Bu I hear the wind that comes before the dawn."

"Then I must go now."

Almon watched him as he struggled up and clutched the altar. "Have you the strength?" he asked.

"I have the strength," said Thomas. "Show me the way."

They left the little bed, the candlelight, with Almon going first, Thomas behind. His body ached, he limped, he held his hands out like a blind man to touch the garments of the youth who guided him. This way they reached the door and went into the night, and found the horse, and Thomas mounted and rode on toward home.

CHAPTER XXI

As Thomas had predicted, no one appeared at the Archbishop's palace to claim his chattels while the archbishop himself sat in his hall; the royal agents were obliged to turn again and go back to the king with empty hands.

King Henry smiled. "There's life in him," he said. The smile came easily because the power that he feared was broken, the threat was gone. Running game does not endanger those who hunt. Next time he passed by Thomas in the crowded court he did not stop but said, in passing, "Has this island grown too narrow to contain us both?" Again he smiled, again denied him permit to cross to the pope in France.

His own ambassadors were busy on that road. Six times in less than three months they made the trip to Sens, asking for papal sanction for the Constitutions. But the pope kept silence. And in this silence Thomas read encouragement to rise and test his strength again.

Watching him, the king made move to tame him with superior power. He asked the pope to give his legatine authority—authority to which all English Churchmen must give obedience—to York. And Alexander, urged by his worldly cardinals on one hand, pestered by conscience on the other, half-obliged. He sent the legatine commission to the king himself with his permission to deliver it to York—provided Canterbury give assent. Henry, insulted, sent it back. In Canterbury new life surged; the Church in England went about its business as before, ignoring those of the Constitutions that lay in its path.

In this way, with move and countermove, with growing anger and frustration, the year 1164 grew old. Henry could wait no longer. He was the king in England, bound to his people by both blood and oath, and he had gone among them ceaselessly since his return—castle to forest-lodge to town—and worn his sacred crown before them on appointed days. But always the Church stood up before him in the person of one man, calling his folk away from him, flouting his laws. Was this man trying to be king himself, this ex-friend and false priest?

Does he expect to play the role of king and not take up its burdens? Henry thought. He knows well enough what I have asked of him. I chose him; doesn't he remember that? I named him chancellor. I made him archbishop. And now he uses these very gains and powers to go against me and escape me.

But I can pull him down as easily as put him up. Is he so vain he doesn't know that? What's in his mind? Does he indeed think he is equal to a king—and on his own, without the king's support? And that forever, not for the period of time the king allots?

He uses power—power that I gave him—to defy me. Well,

let us now remove that power. Can he stand up against me then? He stopped his pacing, smiled. No, I will see him once again as I first saw him, there in the wood. He was the man for me then, what I wanted. I will bring him down to that once more. Then we shall see.

This Henry set himself to do before the eve of Hallowmas which was a sacred day for him, a day for sacrifice. He called a conclave to be held in Northampton, the largest and most solemn he had yet convened. To it he summoned not only every earl and baron, bishop, abbot, officer of Church and court, but also, so the citation read, "all men of every kind who were of any name or standing in the realm." The reason given was to hear the case of John the Marshal who had brought suit against the archbishop for title to a certain holding. So small a matter for which to call so many men! The only person of any dignity at all who was omitted from the list was he who held the highest dignity of all, the archbishop himself. To him peremptory command was issued through the Sheriff of Kent: Appear at Northampton on Tuesday, October sixth, to answer in the case of John the Marshal.

Thomas came riding to Northampton on the appointed day, twenty knights before him, forty clerks behind, flying the Canterbury banner in full dignity. But here beside the river Nene, outside the castle gate, his train was halted by the king's seneschal. "Turn back. There are no lodgings here within the town for the archbishop."

What of the mansion house that was reserved by custom for the archbishop? It was already occupied by courtiers of the king; the archbishop must seek some hospitality elsewhere. As for the king himself? Why, he was hawking up along the Nene, and John the Marshal was delayed in London on urgent business for the exchequer. Did the archbishop expect a royal welcome to this court?

Thomas heard this message and was silent. What answer was there he could give to this crude underling? He turned his head aside and stared a long time at the river where it moved below him here, breathing along the castle wall, licking the slime-green line of water weeds that clung to it. Above him, on the crenelated battlements, the black rooks with their naked faces moved and flapped their wings.

He knew this castle with its courtyards and its poison-fingered yews, its stony halls and many-chambered towers where hung old flags and iron weapons from half-forgotten battlefields. His face was pinched as he swung round, leaving the seneschal, the silent townsmen who had gathered here to see their archbishop, and rode away. That afternoon he found a somber welcome at the monastery of St. Andrew outside the town walls and there took lodging for as long as he was called upon to stay.

The council lasted seven days; for seven days the sun did not come out. Each day his progress from the monastery through the gray streets of the town was watched—with curiosity, with awe, with terror—by the townspeople; his passage through the crowded great hall where the riffraff and the "wild beasts of the court" here gathered was marked by hostile silences and narrow looks.

Each day he went on through the hall into the audience chamber to await the king and there sit—for it was so designed—and stare into the bare stone walls, or at the carved and darkly painted oaken doors that led into the council chamber where the barons gathered, or at the strip of iron sky that showed through deep-embrasured windows at the farther end. Before him where he sat among his clerks upon the benches was a dais with a row of chairs should the king's majesty hold court there, but on the first day Henry did not come at all, and on the second day came late.

He had been hawking once again and Thomas, waiting, heard the horses and the horns outside, and then the old familiar sounds, the shouts and laughter of the hunting party as they came through the hall. He rose, but Henry strode on by and through the oaken doors into the council room and up the turret stairs beyond to his own private chambers on the floor above. He had not given Thomas so much as a glance. And for another hour Thomas and his clerks, and the barons, also, who had gathered for the court, waited while the king attended Mass, while the king breakfasted, while the king lingered in his rooms.

At last he came, lightfooted on the stairs, and entered with his judges and the members of his court about him and took his seat upon the dais. He called for blessing from his chaplain and to business:

Item, the court of the archbishop did not give justice to John the Marshal, and when said John brought his appeal to the king's court the archbishop did not appear in answer to the royal summons.

Thomas rose to state his case: John the Marshal had sworn falsely in the archbishop's court; he had sworn upon a book of songs which he drew from his cloak, not on the Gospels as he claimed.

King Henry interrupted: John the Marshal was not present to give his answer; he was detained in London on king's business. Crux of the matter was, the archbishop had not appeared when the king summoned him . . .

The archbishop had sent a deputation of four knights to answer for him, being himself too ill to travel at that time . . .

The archbishop had not appeared when summoned. This was contempt of the king's majesty. Incontrovertible. And the charge: treason.

Thomas, already standing, took a step forward, but the king rose. He gave his adversary one swift look. The judgment to be given and the penalty to be assessed tomorrow. Then he turned, smiling, speaking lightly to his courtiers, and pushed his chair aside and left the room.

So, as a prisoner is taken to the torture place to see the rack, Thomas was given one swift glimpse of what King Henry had in store for him.

Next day the bishops were called in to sit in judgment on their archbishop but they demurred; they might not judge their spiritual lord; it was a secular crime; the barons must pronounce the sentence when it was agreed upon . . .

But the king cut them short: "He has been judged; you know the sentence; now pronounce it." And he let his eye fall on the aged Henry, Bishop of Winchester, who stared at him a moment, thoughtful, and then stepped forward.

Thomas rose to face him and smiled at him while he spoke, commenting of this new mode—perhaps thought up at Clarendon?—of doing justice.

"The judgment of the court," said Winchester, "is guilty. And being guilty you may give yourself into the mercy of the king."

Thomas caught the smile on the king's face. "I know his mercy," he said quietly.

"Then you must forfeit all your goods, or pay the fine: three hundred pounds," said Winchester.

"The customary fine for failing the king's summons is forty shillings," Thomas said.

"Three hundred pounds," repeated Winchester, his old eyes fixed upon his friend, his tone emotionless, "and I myself shall be the first to put up surety that it be paid."

The king rose, knocking back his chair, and left the room. The barons followed him. The oaken doors were closed. And now the bishops breathed more freely, thinking the matter closed, and all but York and Foliot put up their bonds along with Winchester. "I shall be glad to leave this place," said Bishop Hilary, still whispering, for it was fearful to be caught thus in the perilous castle full in the glare of the king's vengeance on their spiritual father.

But what of John the Marshal? That case was dropped; he was not here. The bishops sighed, looked at each other, made move to ask their sovereign's leave to go. But in the council chamber the king had more to say. There was another sum the archbishop owed to the crown, three hundred pounds again, for revenues he had received from Eye and Berkhampstead.

"I was not called here to answer for my holdings," Thomas said. "But I will answer. I spent the revenues, and more besides, on repairs of those castles and on the Tower of London . . ." Again the aged Winchester caught his eye. "But let it not be said that for my own sake I have thwarted the king's justice or that money has been a bar to peace between us. I only ask a little time." An hour was given him and in an hour he raised securities among his friends for payment.

What was to follow? Only the king knew and the king was laughing. "He thinks he has escaped my justice through this wealth of his. But I shall bring him down to what he was when I first found him. Then we shall see. Tell him 'Return tomorrow,' nothing more." And on the morrow he stretched his victim yet a little farther on the rack:

Five hundred pounds are owed the king upon a loan for the Toulouse campaign, five hundred more owed to a Jew for the same purpose for which the king stood surety. Where are these thousand pounds?

A gift! A gift for the Toulouse campaign . . .

Produce your evidence.

The king himself . . .

In writing.

Given a little time, said Thomas, securities could be produced for these debts too.

The archbishop wants time and time and yet more time. While he takes time, then, let him take time to render his accounts for all the revenues of vacant sees that came into his hands while he was chancellor. By the reckoning of John the Marshal, busy at the exchequer, it comes to thirty thousand pounds.

Ah, here it was. "He means to have me," Thomas thought.

"I was absolved," he cried, "by the young king himself, of all my debts as chancellor when I became archbishop. I was absolved, as is the custom. I have witnesses."

He looked around, but all his witnesses drew back from

him. The king rose, left the room. The barons followed. He stood alone.

Defiantly he raised his head and shouted, "I will not answer to these charges! I refuse! I was not called to answer any but the charge of John the Marshal. I will not be hurried thus into a trial for which I was not called. This is unprecedented and I call upon the law!"

Did his cry carry to the king beyond the doors or in the rooms above? Perhaps. For Henry's voice came, muffled, echo of violence, enraged beyond control: "God's blood, I'll have his tongue out!" And "God's wounds, I will not tolerate delay!" Then sounds of argument, of chairs flung and of tables overturned. Then silence, long drawn out, before the Earl of Leicester came down, crablike, quick upon the stairs, and through the doors, and said to Thomas that the king allowed him one day to comply. Or he could put himself in the king's mercy. No? One day, then, and no more.

All day on Saturday the bishops met in anxious consultation with their archbishop but they could not agree. Gilbert Foliot admonished: "Make yourself more humble for the sake of all! Yield up your office and your properties if they be ten times what the king has asked for, and submit!" Chichester, Lincoln, Exeter all added voice to this. "Give up your see," they said, "and throw yourself upon the mercy of the king. In time he will restore you." But Thomas said as he had said before, "I know his mercy." And his old mentor Winchester blew out his cheeks and asked, "If the archbishop, Primate of England, set us example of bowing to the nod and threat of any angry prince, must it not follow that we all, the whole Church, be confounded by the whims of secular men?" And some agreed that it was evil to urge a bishop to resign his charge of souls while others cried as loud that it was criminal to advise resistance to a king. Roger of York said with some relish: "Your choice is clear; either you lose your office or your life." And thus their time was spent and Thomas, worn with arguing, begged of the Council to ask the king to grant them yet another day, and this was done.

All day on Sunday the earls and barons met in little groups and whispering conferences throughout the castle while Thomas stayed retired in his monastery rooms and messengers came to him from the castle bringing tales of plots against him and of King Henry's rising temper and strange oaths. The words, "He means to kill you" went whispering through his ears. He answered, "He can kill the body, not the soul." But somewhere in the darkness of his memory a young voice echoed: "Did I not tell you I am of the Devil's brood?" And then it was he felt his soul in danger and his strength ran out.

On Monday he lay ill.

The knights who had come with him in his retinue called on him as he lay in bed and bent their knees and asked his understanding that their first allegiance was to the crown, they must withdraw from his protection and his service, and they departed. Even his clerks drew off from him, lest murder prove contagious, for they were sure his death was near. Two only stayed: his chaplain Herbert of Bosham the hotheaded, and the clerk Fitzstephen who was drawn to drama and to danger as a leaf is drawn into the vortex, spinning merrily.

Again the bishops sent a deputation to his chamber telling him that he faced new charges since the day before, charges of treason and of perjury for breach of his feudal duty to the king and of his promise to obey the Constitutions. "Submit, submit!" they begged him, "for you endanger the whole Church!"

Thomas rose up on his elbow and thrust out his hand. "It is you bishops who endanger it!" he said. "You bishops who join with laymen in judging me. I charge you on your obedience to the Church and to myself, do so no longer. And I further charge you"—he shook his hand at them—"if violence is done to me, lay sentence of excommunication on those who do it. This I command you in the name of God." He lay back on the pillows. "As for myself, for my protection and the protection of the Church in England, I have appealed to Rome."

He did not turn his head to see the consternation on their faces but dismissed them and received no other visitors until, late in the darkness of the afternoon, the earls of Cornwall and of Leicester came with a message from the king: Was he indeed so ill? the king asked. Could he not rise and stand upon his feet?

"Tell him, tomorrow I will come," said Thomas, "though I be borne upon my couch."

On Tuesday he rose early and stayed long at prayers. Then when the time came took leave of the silent monks and mounted to ride to the court, with only his two loyal clerks to ride before him. But at the monastery gate he found an escort waiting, a shivering knot of ragged men, the beggars and the hopeless of the town who saw in him salvation and would come with him. Thomas looked down at them and saw himself, an outcast, there among them and compassion moved him and he said, "Yes, come with me, for I go now to face the king. You are my knights and officers, my children and my friends. I have no others. And if God wills that I return again, then shall we dine together and warm each other with our mutual love." And he rode on, at footpace, through the narrow streets, and many people wept as he went by or turned to follow him. But at the castle gate the archbishop alone, with his two clerks, went through. After them the doors were quickly shut against the townsfolk and the key turned in the lock.

Word had gone whistling on ahead of him that he was coming, that he was dressed in full pontificals with the pope's pallium about his shoulders and a gold miter on his head, that he had chosen for his service of that morning, in defiance of the king, the Mass of Stephen, protomartyr, with its Introit "Princes sat and spake against me," that he had clothed himself in rags and came barefooted like a penitent, that he was weeping, that his eyes shot fire.

Thus when he came into the hall men saw him variously as they were prepared to see. But one thing all men saw, because it was a thing no man among them had seen before: a bishop entering the royal court—the way a mutinous knight might enter fully armed—bearing his cross in his own hands. They gasped, they murmured, "Look there how he comes! He bears his cross as though it were a sword against the king!" And some were angry although many more were awed because it was a symbol that they feared.

But it was the bishops who were most affected. They were assembled all together lest one should say about another that he gave secret counsel to the king—or that he had advised the archbishop against the king. And now before their eyes their spiritual lord advanced as though to challenge him who was their secular lord. "Does he court ruin for us all?" breathed Chichester.

Robert of Hereford went quickly through the crowds and said to Thomas, very low, "Oh let me be your crossbearer, my lord, as I was once your master and am now your son." But Thomas did not even turn to look at him. He came on steadily, the silver cross on its long polished shaft catching the light above his head, until the Earl of Cornwall, a peace-loving man, stepped up to Bishop Foliot and asked, "What is the meaning of this, my lord of London, that you allow him to bear his cross himself?"

"My good friend," Foliot turned a sour smile to him, "he always was a fool and always will be."

However, as he watched the cross approach, watched Thomas' face, absorbed as though he marched to war, watched those about him caught between loyalty to peace and order and fear of God, his scorn gave way to irritation and he stepped forward and placed himself in Thomas' path.

"My lord Archbishop, as your dean, it is my privilege to carry . . ." and he put his hands out and tried to take the cross by force.

Thomas stared down at him, his grip firm on the shaft, his lips drawn tight. He did not speak, but there was such a piercing look of scorn in his deep eyes that Foliot's temper cracked. "If the king hears of this," he hissed, "he will regard it as a sword drawn in his presence! Are you so blind that you cannot see this? Give it to me!" He tried to wrench it from him but Thomas held it. "I know what I am doing," he said impatiently. Then, as Foliot still clung, he raised his voice and spoke out so that all could hear: "The king's sword is the sword of war; I know it. Mine is the sword of peace."

"Fool!" whispered Foliot, choked by wrath. "Are you so blinded by your pride you cannot see your folly? The king will blame us all for this!" He jerked and tugged upon the cross as though he were a schoolboy fighting for a rod. But his ascetic way of life had not prepared him for such a job as this, and Thomas, trained in knighthood, taller, stronger, shook him off. He staggered back and caught himself from falling.

Someone, friend to Thomas, whispered, "Fly, my lord, or else you are a dead man. Fly!" But Thomas spoke out in a loud stern voice: "If the king's sword can kill the body, mine can send the soul to hell." And he proceeded, still unhurrying, out of the thickness of the crowd into the empty anteroom.

All these happenings, in every small detail, flew to the royal ear from many eager mouths. Henry was in the council chamber with his barons, for they meant to reach a final judgment on that day. But when these tidings were brought in, he rose and left the court, withdrew himself into his upper room. He called the bishops to attend him there and they came up the spiral stairs in dread lest they be held responsible.

The king was waiting for them, seated on a chest and in an attitude of ease, one leg pulled up, his arm across his knee, but they were shocked to see the look within his eyes. He stared at them a long time and his breath came deep and pulsing so that his tunic rose and fell on his broad chest.

He spoke at last in a high voice, without the customary greeting, saying, "Does the Church hold that I am the oppressor of my people? Am I a traitor to the law? Am I a tyrant, a persecutor of the innocent that he comes to my court full armored, as though against injustice?" He did not say "archbishop" or name the name of his old friend. "Have I usurped the sovereignty that is mine? Am I a despot, ruling without council?" And all the while the bishops murmured, "No, my lord, no and no," and looked with terror at his face. The blood was seeping upward into it, suffusing it, until it seemed to swell up, bloated, like a drunken man's.

"Do you complain against me and my ancestors that you so lightly treat their customs and my laws?" He took his foot down and sat crouching forward with his fists upon his knees and now his voice grew till it smote them on the ears.

"Do you hold counsel with him against me? Have you forgotten that I raised him up this commoner, until he stands so high he puts his foot upon my throne and shakes it? And you, you bishops . . ."

"My lord, if I may speak . . ." said Foliot.

"You follow after him. He comes armed to my court, insults my Council . . ."

"My gracious lord . . ."

"And none among you puts out a hand to stay him . . ."

"I speak for myself that I . . ."

"This insolent hypocrite!"

"My lord."

He stopped, sat panting for a moment, and then said, "What say you, my lord Bishop?"

"I myself with my own hands tried to wrest his cross from him, lest he offend you. And all of us have pleaded with him to show more honor to your majesty. We disavow complicity in this or any other of these strange proceedings against your sovereign court. These are the acts of one man only, one madman who has set upon his headstrong course and spurned our moderate counsel. He will hear nothing but his own words in his ears. He is beyond all reasoning. . . ."

"God's breath, I know that. I know that," growled Henry.

"We have advised him with what words we have, and with our tears, to make submission to you, our gracious lord, for though we know he has offended, we know your mercy and . . ."

"What said he?"

"He will not yield, my lord," said Foliot. "He will not yield."

"So say you all?" asked Henry, looking from one face to the other with his fiery eyes. "So say you every one?" Some nodded and some stared into the corners of the room. They owed obedience of spirit to their archbishop; they saw injustice here; but they were not so ignorant of the world. The king sat here before them in all his power and with a murderous rage within his breast.

"Aye, that is so, my lord," said Foliot speaking for them all. "He has rebuked us for what we do in these proceedings. He has forbidden us to take a further part. He has appealed, my lord. He has appealed to Rome."

Henry leaped up. "It is forbidden!" he yelled at Foliot. "It is forbidden to send petition to the pope without my leave!"

"We know, my lord. We know that well," said Foliot.

The king drew back. "It's death," he breathed. "He asks for death." Again his chest began to rise and fall in that slow, pulsing rhythm. "He has betrayed me. It is treason. He defies my court." His voice was rising. "Call Leicester to me. Call me Cornwall. I shall hear it from his own mouth. Then shall he feel the judgment of my Council . . ."

The Earl of Leicester stood inside the door with Cornwall close behind him, breathing heavily, for they had heard the king's shouts from the council chamber and come quick-footed up the stair.

"He has appealed against me to the pope!" The king swung round from Foliot to the earls. "Go sound him out on this . . . And sound him also if he hold this court in such contempt that he refuses still to answer for his debts." And then, as Leicester bowed, he said, "Then let the lords come to their judgment and let it be pronounced. He has played with my dignity too long!" And as the earls bowed once again he screamed, "Why do you wait so long? Go find him out! Go let him know there is a limit to my patience! Let him prepare himself for justice!"

There was no need for Thomas to wait until the earls came to him in the antechamber to hear these words. He sat, as he had sat all morning long, his cross upright between his knees, his silent clerks beside him, hearing the mutter of growing violence among the barons in the council room and once or twice, though muffled, far away, the high-pitched screaming of the king. These last words he heard clearly, for the door had just been opened, "Let him prepare himself . . ."

Herbert of Bosham whispered quickly, "Father, you must

use your power to excommunicate . . ." But at the door the marshal brought his staff down sharply, calling for silence. They were not allowed to talk. Fitzstephen, with his blood up in excitement, put his finger to his lips, then pointed to the cross. And Thomas, feeling as he sometimes felt in battle, sent him a glowing look. Then the earls entered.

Leicester was struck to see the archbishop, whom he admired and liked, sitting in half-light and in silence here, his cross held up before him as against the world. He himself loved the cross and would have followed it, into the monastery even, had the matter of his birth not kept him in the world.

He spoke more slowly than was his wont, putting the gentlest question first: "The king requires to know," he said, "if you will answer to the charges brought against you in this court?"

So sharp were Thomas' ears attuned to all the king's maneuverings, his tricks, his threats designed to terrify, he thought he saw a legal trap and answered in a lawyer's words: "I was called to this court to answer to the charge concerning John the Marshal. This I have done. I was not summoned to defend myself against these other charges that have been brought up to confound me here."

Leicester nodded and tried once again: "My lord Archbishop, let us speak frankly to each other. I ask you only this: Will you abide the judgment of this court, the king's Grand Council meeting in due solemnity?"

And Thomas answered, "You know, my lords, how long and loyally I served the king in all his worldly doings when I was chancellor. It was for this he thrust me into the office I now hold. I did not ask it; I knew my infirmities. It was for the king's sake I consented to it. And when I did I was acquitted of my responsibilities for all that I had done and spent before. Therefore, I am not bound to answer to these charges. And I will not answer."

Cornwall drew back as if to leave, for this defiance meant an end to him who sat before them and he would have it over with. But Leicester, though he feared the answer, asked again: "The king desires to know from your own mouth, as he has heard it from Gilbert Foliot, if you have sent appeal to Rome."

"I have," said Thomas.

The earl's face twitched as though in pain. "You understand, my lord, that such appeal would violate the oath you took when you swore your allegiance to the king. It breaks your promise to observe the Constitutions. Such an appeal would be an act of treason. I ask you to remember this when I ask once again: Have you appealed against this court to Rome?"

Thomas met his eyes and held them as he answered: "I have appealed against the bishops to the pope. They may not sit in judgment on their spiritual lord. This is my appeal; against the bishops. And I will keep to it. I place myself and all the Church in England in the protection of the pope."

It was a slim distinction, but Leicester could not hope for more from this embattled, stubborn man. He nodded and then he and Cornwall left the room.

Their passage through the council chamber created uproar as the barons crowded them, demanding, "What says the archbishop?" "What said the king?" "Will he abide by our judgment?" "Will he submit?" The Earl of Leicester threaded through, but Cornwall whispered to those closest, "He will not answer to the charges; he has appealed to Rome." He went on after Leicester and the clamor followed them as they wound up the stairs, the barons shouting in their council: "What say you, my lords, is he guilty?" "Guilty of foul contempt!" "What say you?" "Put him in chains!" "Imprisonment!"

The king, on hearing, went forward to the door. "Tell me from his own mouth," he rasped at Leicester. And Leicester, though his own words were quiet, confirmed the shouts below. "He has appealed against the bishops to the papal court."

The king said, "Hah!" as though he had been hit. "He has condemned himself!" He fixed first Leicester and then Cornwall with his eyes, a long time, as though to suck and taste the truth from them. "Is he prepared for death?"

The earls said nothing and Henry turned and walked away. He knew the fear, the superstitious dread men had of the unearthly powers of the Church. Had they not cringed before the cross when Thomas brought it in? And he knew Thomas; that had been his purpose. He might equally have shouted out as he came through the hall, "Beware, for I can excommunicate!" Henry brought his fist down on the chest. "Now he gives warning he has sent appeal to Rome. Another threat: interdict. Who of my cowards can be brought to speak the sentence and face the vengeance of the Church? Who is so . . ." Suddenly he stopped and straightened up. Abruptly he swung round upon the bishops with a red and grinning face and shouted, almost laughing, pointing his finger, "It is against you, my lord Bishops, that he has made appeal. You shall pronounce the judgment on him!"

They stood together and none spoke, not even Foliot. It was forbidden to them to pronounce such judgments. They feared the king, but they feared more the threat of their expulsion from the Church should they proceed against their archbishop who had appealed against them.

Henry's smile was still upon his face as he approached them slowly, saying, "What say you? What say you to your king?" Instinctively he chose the weaker ones. "What say you, Walter? What say you, Hilary?" They gasped and did not answer and he walked along their line. His pace was like an animal's, rhythmic and low-slung on his stocky legs. He stopped at Winchester and breathed into his face. "What say you, Henry?" and he put a finger out and wagged the old man's beard.

Winchester stiffened and said in an old man's voice and with an old man's courage, "We are prohibited from such a judgment. We owe obedience to him. He is our primate and our spiritual lord."

"Hah!" Henry said, as he had said before. He glared a moment longer and his fingers twitched the beard, but then he looked away, along the other faces, and said, not as a threat this time, but as a question: "What say you, Gilbert?"

"My lord," said Foliot smoothly, "if by your gracious leave we ourselves make appeal against the archbishop for perjury, as he swore falsely to observe your Constitutions, we may gain to our side the pope and all the power of the Church. In this way he may be deposed, and none of us in danger from his spiritual wrath. Meanwhile, as we owe him obedience and as he has forbidden us to sit in judgment and as our order is prohibited from passing sentence where a man's life is concerned, we beg that you excuse us from this duty. Let the barons of your Council undertake it, and may our own appeal to Rome protect them as it protects us all."

Henry's hands had dropped down to his sides. One thought consumed his mind: The time is now and I must have him now.

"Go, then, and tell him. You may have my leave to send appeal to Rome. And tell him to prepare himself to hear our judgment, for he shall hear it now."

They looked at one another in uncertainty and some made move to speak, but Henry's rage broke and he leaped upon them shrieking, pushing at them, kicking them toward the door. "God, and God's eyes! God's wounds! I will not listen to you any more!" he yelled. "Get out! Go tell him what you said—that you obey the king, that you owe no obedience to him. Send your appeal to Alexander, for God's sake, and take up no more time!" He struck out, hitting Bishop Walter in the neck, and kicked at Bishop Hilary. Hilary jumped and put his hands behind him.

Abruptly Henry stopped and stood still, laughing. "Chichester, you tell him! Chichester shall speak the words!" He found this comical because he knew the bishop was a coward. But when they paused again he put his head down like a bull and charged at them. "Get out!" he roared. And in a crush, all piled together, they fled through the door and down the spiral stair.

In the council chamber they collected what they could of dignity and called their clerks around them and proceeded in full solemnity, some close to tears, into the antechamber and across it to where their primate sat. Chichester stood before them, trembling, and spoke the words: "My lord of Canterbury, whom we sometime honored, I am come to tell you in the name of all, that we regard you as a perjured man, a violator of your oath, and, therefore, are no longer bound in our obedience to you. We send appeal against you to the papal court."

He stopped and there was silence for a long time, so that the murmurs from the hall beyond, the furtive opening and closing of the council chamber doors seemed very loud. Thomas stared at them, one by one, then turned again to Chichester and said distinctly, so that the words cut, "I hear what you say."

They waited, but he spoke no more, and in confusion they retired to the benches along the farther wall. York only stood a moment longer, then called his chaplain to him and spoke loudly, for the first time that day, "Let us withdraw," he said, "for it is not fit that we should look upon what is to be done here to him of Canterbury." And Thomas, stung as only Roger could sting him, cried out, "Yes, leave me, Judas, and be damned!"

This way he cut off sympathy and many who had wavered hardened against him. Only a few old friends sat weeping to see him, lonely, his cross before him, awaiting judgment. The trumpets sounded and the doors swung open. The earls and barons of the Council entered and the foremost took their seats upon the dais. The king was not among them. He had chosen Leicester to pronounce the sentence. He himself waited up above.

Now this trial was ended and the king's will accomplished, only waiting Leicester's final words. But the earl was slow.

Reluctantly he rose and walked to Thomas, limping slightly and stood before him, waiting for the archbishop to rise. But Thomas, with his cross between his knees, sat rigid, and reluctantly, at last, the hunchback spoke.

"My lord and father," he said softly, as though apologizing for what he was to say, "as the king raised you up . . . and showered benefits upon you and held you dear . . . it should have been that you served him and held his honor up above your own. But you have held his laws and customs in contempt . . . and in this court you have refused to answer the king's charges. This Council has heard your defiance of the king's majesty . . . and from your own mouth that you have appealed . . . against his laws . . . an act of treason . . ." He paused, so long the barons coughed and muttered at his slowness, before he said: "Hear, then, your sentence."

"Nay, my son earl," cried Thomas interrupting. "Do you first hear me!" He rose and towered over Leicester, planting his cross between them, as he said: "A layman may not judge a bishop, nor may the son the father. The king may not judge me, nor may you judge me."

He looked up frowning when he heard the gasp around the room, and he continued louder: "The priesthood is superior to royalty as much as gold to lead! And as much as a man's soul is more precious than his body, so much and more are you, son earl, bound to obey God and your spiritual father than any earthly sovereign. And I forbid you, under anathema, to pronounce your sentence."

The gasp that greeted his first words had grown into a rumbling murmur and he looked around the room. "And under God I will be judged by our lord pope alone," he cried, "for he alone is competent to judge me. And to him, in your presence, I appeal!"

His eyes swept from the barons to the bishops by the wall. "And you, my brothers, since you choose to scorn God and obey an earthly king, I call to that same judgment to which I go . . .

"For I depart now," he said, glancing again at Leicester, "under the protection of the Apostolic See."

He turned and walked deliberately, his cross held high, past all the barons of the Council toward the hall, and he had almost reached the door when a young man sprang out before him crying, "Traitor, you may not leave!" It was the Earl of Hamelin, half-brother to the king. Thomas did not even break his stride. "You are a bastard boy," he said. "Not worth the notice of a man," and walked away from him, out of the chamber.

The tumult in the hall was greater, for here the men of no responsibility had gathered, the household officers and servants and the young knights spoiling for a fight. They called out "Coward!" "Traitor!" when they saw him, and they hissed and hooted at him and some spit in his direction as he walked through. And then when he had passed, they picked up knots of muddy straw and sticks and gnawed bones that had fallen from the tables and flung them after him.

Still he walked on and no one dared to touch him, till he was almost at the door, when suddenly he heard a change of sound behind him, a catch of breath. A lighted torch came flying past him, close to his head. He flinched away, his foot struck on a pile of firewood, he stumbled. At that the yelping of the pack behind him, the hoots, the shouted insults, rose to a shrieking pitch. Before he could recover, while he was half down, the knight Ranulf de Broc thrust forward and laid his hands on him. "Stay, perjurer," he shouted, "and hear your judgment!"

Thomas swung round on him and on the taunting crowd. "Take your hands off me!"

"Coward!" Ranulf yelled.

"Liar! I know you, Ranulf. Hangman's son. Liar. Were I a knight I would prove you lie with my own hand. But I am a priest of God. Stand back from me!"

Even a godless man may have a fear of God, just for a moment. Ranulf hung back. And in that moment's time Thomas turned round again, showing his back to them and reached the door.

The shouting followed after him but he heard no one's foot upon the steps behind him nor in the cobbled court as he strode toward the gate. The porters and the grooms had fled away lest they be held responsible, either for stopping him or not. They watched him from the corners by the stable shed and in the shadows of the yews as he went, walking steadily, unerringly, to his own horse among the many tethered by the gate. They watched him lay his cross upon its withers and then mount, the way an unhorsed knight in battle must sometimes mount, unaided and with lance in hand.

They knew the gate was locked but they said nothing, neither good nor bad, and watched him ride up to it and, without a pause, as though directed by an unseen hand, reach out and take the ring of keys that hung beside the door and with the very first one that he tried, unlock it, push it open, and ride out. They stared with mouths hung open after him and scratched themselves and some among them said it was a miracle and in their hearts became his liegemen after that.

Thomas rode out into the town where, in that twilight hour the multitude were waiting, fearful of the news. They saw him, tall and lean upon his horse and with his silver cross slung on his arm, and a great shout went up. He was alive! They rushed upon him, knelt before him, wept and asked his blessing, and he rode slowly through them, followed by them, giving his benediction as he went through the streets and from the town and, still surrounded, to the monastery of St. Andrew where he left them and took sanctuary in the little cloister church.

That evening when he went to the refectory, the last of those young nobles whom he had nourished, with the young king, in his household, came to him sadly, their lips quivering, full of shame, and asked him to release them from his service for their fathers had demanded it.

Thomas smiled gently at them. "Others have long since gone—your elders, and those learned clerks"—his voice was scornful—"who fed at my table and have fled like swallows when they feel the storm. Go with my blessing. I shall have other company." And when they left he ordered that the poor who stood about the gate should be let in to be his guests at supper as he had promised.

In this strange company he ate, sending down morsels from his own plate to this poor coughing wretch or that blind man. Herbert of Bosham sat upon his right hand, Fitzstephen on his left, for they had fled the castle by devious routes while the confusion there was at its height. The three of them, like soldiers in a lull of battle, were strangely cheerful and they recounted to each other what they had done and thought all through the day and how they felt at each new crisis.

"What is to be done now?" Fitzstephen asked. For he had heard while he yet lingered, inconspicuous, in the dark castle passageways, the barons' threats against the archbishop and the king's ominous command: "Leave him alone. Let no one touch him. For he is mine."

Thomas heard everything Fitzstephen had to tell before he murmured, "It has been written 'When they persecute you in this city, flee ye to another,' " and they understood.

"So go you by another way," he added, "and save yourselves, and we shall meet again, with God's help and in time."

He had a bed made for him between two altars in his sanctuary church and he retired to it but did not sleep. He heard the monks come for their final office of the night and then as they went out he heard, and thanked God for it, the first great drops of rain come pelting on the roof. The deeper darkness that it brought, the permeating sound of it, would cover what he meant to do.

He rose and found the two strong monks with whom he plotted waiting for him at the postern door. Without a word or sound between them they stepped out into the rain and crept along the pathways of the kitchen court to the farm buildings and the stables where, in the deep hay-smelling dark, they took three horses, saddled and bridled them in silence, mounted, and rode into the storm. The sounds of hoof and harness were smothered in the drum of rain; the sight of a tall rider wrapped in a canon's cloak was covered by the dark. No one observed them as they rode, skirting the town, to take the road that led to Lincoln, north. The king would look for them along the roads to Canterbury and the coastal ports.

[illegible] any better way," [illegible] "and [illegible]
[illegible] with God's help and a [illegible]."

Meanwhile, [illegible] made for him between [illegible] his [illegible] church and [illegible] to [illegible] the final office of the [illegible] [illegible] [illegible] out [illegible] [illegible] that came [illegible] on the [illegible] the [illegible] darkness [illegible] [illegible] that he meant to [illegible].

Thomas had found the two young monks [illegible] [illegible] for him at the [illegible] [illegible] stepped out into the [illegible] along the pathway of the kitchen court of the [illegible] buildings and the stables where in the dark [illegible] [illegible] [illegible] horses, [illegible] [illegible] [illegible] and [illegible] [illegible] [illegible] and [illegible] were [illegible] the [illegible] of a [illegible] in a sober cloak [illegible] the dark, [illegible] and [illegible] the [illegible] to [illegible] the road that led to Lincoln, North. The [illegible] would [illegible] the road [illegible] and the [illegible].

BOOK FIVE

THE EXILE

CHAPTER XXII

IT WAS EVENING of All Souls' Day—that day that Henry held so sacred—when on the low-flung, wind-blown dunes near Gravelines on the coast of Flanders three Black Monks went toiling all alone, up from the dark deserted shore where they had beached their little boat and where it lay now with the wavelets lapping at it and the coarse sand hissing underneath.

The three walked heavy-footed, slogging, for their clumsy shoes could not find purchase and their rough wool habits, soaked with spray, dragged in the sand and weighted them. And they were tired. They had left Sandwich secretly, before the dawn. They had escaped from England but they did not know if they were yet beset by enemies. The Count of Boulogne was an enemy they knew. The Count of Flanders? Or King Henry's men come here before them? Plodding, sliding, stooping to lift their heavy skirts, they hurried on. Somewhere ahead must lie a road.

The tall one, Brother Christian—for that was the name that Thomas had adopted when he took on the disguise of a monk—had been thus fleeing, hiding, fleeing by little lonely tracks at night, for three weeks since he left Northampton. The others, brisk young Mass-brothers, had joined him only at Eastry, sent by the prior there to be his boatmen and his guard.

They went on down the final sloping dune. The road ran here, along the line of beach, and they stepped into it.

They could not know the Count of Flanders had received a letter from King Henry: "Be it known to you, and all our friends, that Thomas who was once the Archbishop of Canterbury has taken to lone hiding places and may have fled our realm like a vile traitor. Woe unto anyone who shelters him . . ." They had no way of knowing this, but Thomas, knowing Henry, knew the probability. He looked both ways along the road but saw no guards, no mounted men patrolling up and down. He straightened, then, and sighed, making a little groaning noise within his throat, for he was very weary. Then he took off his heavy outer robe and shook it, slung it round his shoulders, and they turned south along the road toward Gravelines, and walked on.

There was but little traffic here at nightfall: a line of fishermen, their crusty net slung, looping, from one shoulder to the next, who ducked their heads and pulled their caps as they went by; a stooped old man with salt-grass piled upon his shoulders; a whistling boy. They had no fear of these; their whole concern now was to reach shelter, for the sky came closer in a fine and permeating mist.

Behind, they heard the clop of horses and they paused and stood aside. A party of young men in capes and tasseled hats came riding by, and one of them had on his wrist a handsome peregrine. Thomas stared at it for it was a fine young hawk and at another time he might have asked some questions as to its training and its ways. His eyes spoke for him, even in the dust, and one among the party noticed this. He reined his horse and spoke to his companion in an undertone:

"See the tall man there? See how he eyes the bird? He is the Archbishop of Canterbury if I am not wrong."

"Fool," cried the other. "How could he be the Archbishop of Canterbury, dressed like that?"

He laughed and all the others laughed as well and Thomas laughed along with them and said, "Would that I were, that I might take the weight off the episcopal feet." They thought he meant by hanging and they laughed again, but the two brothers cast their eyes down and kept still. And after that, when the young horsemen had gone out of view, they went on faster, scurrying down the road.

Thomas said nothing more; that sally was the last that he could muster. How many times in England had he had to dodge and lie? The time in Lincoln in the fuller's house when he had had to hide beneath the rolls of cloth . . . the time at Eastry when the novice found him in his little hole above the choir stalls . . . the time along the road near Havelor when a passing traveler had asked him outright, "Are you the archbishop?", and he had answered, "Would you expect to find the Primate of England mounted like this?", for he was riding on an ancient mule. But he was mounted, then, at least. Now he could say, "Would an archbishop walk?"

Indeed, the labor of it grew unbearable. The rain had soaked into the clay so that it clung in lumps upon his shoes. To lift his feet and thrust them forward—just to keep upright—took all the strength he had. And they went on an hour thus, plodding and staggering, not speaking, while the night grew black. At last it was too much. One more time Thomas stumbled, caught his balance, wavered, and went down.

"Brothers," he murmured, when they turned back and leaned over him, "you must leave me, for I cannot go on. I cannot rise."

They stooped and raised him in their strong young arms but it was not enough. "No, you must find a horse," he said, "I have not the training for this walking on rough ground." He paused and thought a moment and then raised a little smile. "And I am old to learn." It was the first time he had noticed the slow drag of years upon him. He was forty-six.

They waited by the roadside for the next passerby and sent him—for when he came it was a lad, going to Gravelines on some tomcat errand of his own—on to the nearest inn to hire a horse for them and bring it back, and he should get a silver penny for it, so he went. But what he brought back hardly could be called a horse, so sway-backed, lop-eared, and lame-legged was it, with but a rope of twisted straw for halter and no saddle of any kind.

"Am I to ride on that?" asked Thomas. They nodded and the brothers heaped their cloaks upon it for him to sit on and he came thus to the first inn at Gravelines, feeling sick and weary and ashamed.

The inn was steamy, crowded, and the landlord very busy and his good wife busy too, but not too busy to make note of every guest, for this was what gave color to her life. It was her boast that she saw everything, heard everything, told nothing, but remembered all. She noticed how the three monks sat as equals, side by side, but that the older one had long smooth hands that bore no calluses from field work and that he gave out morsels from his plate in such a manner as betrayed a lord. She knew, as all the world knew now, that the archbishop was hiding from the king and she scanned every traveler to see if it was he, and she had found him.

"Husband," she whispered, going to him and putting her mouth close, "look over there at the far table, the tall monk. Don't tell me I am wrong. It is the Lord of Canterbury. Take a look." And he dropped what he had and walked around the table and stared hard and then turned to his wife and smiled, and she smiled too, triumphantly, and both said, "True enough!"

They were good people, though. They said no more than

that. Only they brought so many delicacies to the table—apples and nuts and cheese—that Thomas had to frown on them and shake his head lest other guests, less friendly, make surmise.

So they gave nothing more and let the monks sleep in the loft with all the other guests without distinction. But in the morning when they took their leave, declining graciously the hire of that horse again, and she watched them as they took the muddy road toward St. Omer, walking stiffly, the tall one limping a little, pity welled in her and she snatched up the stick she used for drying fish within the chimney and ran after them and offered it to Thomas for a walking staff. He took it, greasy, sooty, smelly as it was, as though it were a jeweled crosier, and holding it he blessed her with a look although he dared not raise his hand. The tears popped to her eyes and Thomas smiled. *"Dominus vobiscum,"* he said very softly. Then he turned away.

Now Thomas was aware that every eye was out for him, here as in England, and he shunned all habitation and would not stay even among the monks of Clair-Marais where they came next, but took a little boat by night to the small island in the middle of the marsh where stood a hermit's cell belonging to the abbey of St. Bertin. Here, safely hidden, he rested several days and sent out word through secret channels where his followers might find him, and sometimes spies came to him telling him what transpired in the outer world.

Herbert of Bosham, whom he had left at Northampton, from whom he hoped for funds, arrived on the fourth day. Though they rejoiced to see each other there was disappointment. Herbert had gone, as he was bidden, straight from Northampton to Canterbury to secure such rents as were in process of collection then. But Henry had been quicker, he placed all of the primate's property in custody until he could secure the pope's permission to take it for the crown. Herbert, although in danger, had snatched up a hundred pounds out of the coffer, and such silver plate as he could carry hidden in his cloak, but that was all. Little enough with which to wage a battle against the wealth of kings.

"I must call upon the King of France to help me, though I approach him as a pauper," Thomas said.

"Go to him barefoot," Herbert nodded eagerly, "and in such rags as you have on, and show him what the King of England does to the Church."

But Thomas laughed. "My habit is not rags," he said. "This is an honorable garb. I do not find it shameful. No, you must go before me, Herbert, and take my letters to him and find out how he accepts the embassy King Henry has sent to him, for I have heard the Earl of Arundel and others —Gilbert Foliot, I heard—are on their way to him."

"He is at Compiègne just now, on progress through his northern counties, so I am told," said Herbert, eager for this new role, "so I may reach him there."

"I know what they will ask," said Thomas, nodding. "Find out what he replies. Then send me word. I will make my own move when the time is right."

At Compiègne King Louis, somewhat pale and mild for one who held such royal power—or so it seemed to subjects of the English king who were more used to power boldly shown —walked with his guests within the forest-bound enclosure of his royal park. He had come to this castle to keep the vigil of St. Martin and he wore a black cloak, almost like a monk, but on his head a golden circlet with the fleur-de-lis upstanding on it, which was reminder enough for any prudent man. Thus the Earl of Arundel and Bishop Foliot were guarded in their speech and Bishop Hilary spoke very unctuously to him with many "my gracious lords" and "by your royal leaves."

"My gracious lord," said Hilary, "you have seen the letter from our lord the King of England to you his most beloved overlord to whom he bows the knee . . ." Foliot looked bleakly at him but the king's eyes rested on the forest tops. "And read, my gracious . . . read how this man defied the crown and then refused to answer for his conduct. Why, to my very face, my lord, and on my knees, this man denied all his responsibilities! He was condemned, as you have read, my humble lord . . . I humbly suggest, my lord, a traitor, by the full Council of our realm. And now this man . . ."

"What 'man' is it of whom you speak?" asked Louis looking at the clouds.

"What! Why, when I say 'man' I mean the late archbishop!" cried Bishop Hilary, surprised. What other man could they be speaking of?

"And why do you say 'late'?" continued Louis. "I noted that King Henry used the term. If you say 'late' archbishop, who has deposed him?"

Hilary could utter no more than one quick "Why!" when Louis went on talking in his gentle voice. "I am a king as well as is the King of England, but I should have no power to depose even the meanest clerk in my dominion," and he smiled at Foliot.

"My lord," said Foliot, "the archbishop is now a fugitive within your kingdom—or soon will be, perhaps, if he is not already—and it is our request that you comply with that agreement lately made between King Henry and yourself for mutual surrender of such fugitives from your laws."

"Agreement?" Louis turned his pale blue eyes on him. "No, I remember no such mutual agreement between your king and me."

"My lord . . ."

"And if there were such understanding, which I do not remember, it would not bind me, I should think, to seize or to deliver the archbishop into King Henry's hands, for he is not King Henry's vassal but rather, I should say, his lord and patron. Would you not say so, my lord Bishop?"

The Earl of Arundel broke in. He was a man who had but little fear of kings; he had known many, and the very bed he lay in was a king's bed, for he was wedded to the widow of King Henry I. His years gave him solidity as well, and a long memory. "This man, if I may call him 'man,' my lord, is that same chancellor who laid waste to your kingdom and would have put his hands upon your very person at Toulouse. And it strikes strange to me that you should stand in his defense."

"In this he acted as the faithful servant of his king," said Louis. "It does not strike me so strange, brother Earl, that I should defend loyalty to kings." He smiled again and they walked on in silence along the gravel path, their pages following, King Louis breathing in the cold November air.

The Earl of Arundel looked at Bishop Foliot and Foliot at him. The bishop spoke: "My lord King," and he paused. "Our lord the King of England asks of you one thing above all others, that you write to our lord the Pope at Sens and put our case before him and request of him that he withhold his favor from the archbishop in this, his quarrel with the realm of England and with her king. And with her bishops too. For we stand with our sovereign in this matter, we bishops of the Church in England, and we are her champions more surely than is an archbishop who flees where none pursues, as does a guilty man, and leaves his flock untended . . ."

Louis had led them deftly round the pathways of the park and they came now into the cloistered walk outside his private chambers. Here he stopped.

"My lord," repeated Foliot, "we ask for Christ, as Henry asks for England, that you will give your understanding to our cause in your communications with the papal court. Can we expect it?"

"No," Louis said. "No, that I cannot do." And he turned from them, then, and left them at the door.

Thomas came to Louis at Soissons, where he had moved along his progress through his realm. The king embraced him, and if either man thought back to when they last had met, outside the red walls of Toulouse, they did not speak of it. They spoke of the embattled Church, of Alexander exiled and of Thomas, now a fugitive in exile too. And Louis pledged that Thomas should be "partner in his realm," and furnished him with clerks and servants, knights and horses, chapel, vestments, robes—all that an archbishop might need upon an embassy of great importance to the papal court. Thus in a day did Thomas rise again from pauper to a place beside a king, and set forth—not so many days behind his rival embassy—well clothed, well rested, well supported, and with three hundred horsemen in his train.

As he neared Sens with all this company, pacing along the valley of the placid Yonne, one of King Louis' knights, who rode ahead, returned to him and said, "My lord Archbishop, the Earl of Arundel with all his party have been observed across the river."

Thomas looked quickly down the sloping hill, across the water lying quietly between the fields, but all was empty.

"No, my lord, not that direction," the knight said. "They come from Sens. They travel north. We will soon pass by them. There!" He pointed and Thomas, following his hand, saw on the other road, far, far across the fields, up from the farther river bank, the banners of the Earl of Arundel—Albini colors—and the tiny horsemen moving like a trail of ants.

"So they have seen the pope," he said, and to himself, with a small chill of fear, "and they return to Henry—with what news?"

Thomas had been to Sens before, this famous city on the gentle Yonne, crossroads of France and seat of her archbishop. He had come once from Paris in his student days, once on his way to Auxerre. Then it had seemed a quiet place. Now with the papal court established here, the streets seemed narrower, the buildings jumbled all together, and the cathedral square, the churches and the Churchmen's palaces, even the broad walks on the ramparts were crammed with members of the Curia and their petitioners, with foreign clerks and strange Italian servingmen putting their elbows in the ribs of local folk. To see a cardinal borne in his palanquin come in collision with a bishop's entourage at some sharp angle in the streets was commonplace. Prelates in Sens these days were as the grass that grew along the river bank before.

Nevertheless, when Thomas came there was a stir. The pope sent out a party of his cardinals to meet him as he approached the town and to escort him back. The people cheered as he rode by. And when he came into the papal presence, Alexander rose. Thus he was greeted, welcomed, and acclaimed, he who had stumbled up the dunes at Gravelines two weeks before!

When he was granted formal audience, Thomas went down upon his knees before the pope, bent low, and as though laying some rich gift before him as the custom was, spread on the floor a roll of parchment—the Constitutions which had been forced on him at Clarendon. With his hands upon it and bowed down, a penitent's pose, he said: "My lord and father, my lords and honored members of the Curia, brothers in Christ. It is my fault, my grievous fault, that I should ever have conceded to these sentences against the liberties of the Church. It is through me the Church in England has fallen to her present state. All the calamities of this past year must be traced back to my promotion to the see of Canterbury—not by a free election of holy men, but by the will of one unholy, worldly man who persecutes me now.

"I have long known I was unfit. But, Father, I could not resign this office under the pressure of self-seeking men. I have waited—though the waiting has been dangerous and bitter—until I came into your presence where, with your leave, I lay this burden down."

He drew the archepiscopal ring from off his finger and looked up and gave it to the pope. "Father, I place the see of Canterbury in your hands. Pray you, appoint some other man, more capable and worthy than myself, to guard the interests of the Church in England."

He meant it, oh he meant it, but he knew the impact such a scene would have upon the pope and on the Curia. He knew well what would happen next.

Pope Alexander took the ring and looked at him. "Yes, you did wrong, my son, in ever giving your consent to these restrictive laws, and you are right that that unworthy act —so soon repented—was a renunciation of your priesthood, for it reduced the Church to the condition of a bondmaid to the king. But you have suffered for your error. And your championship of right since that first weakness has atoned for all.

"You may not lay this burden down, but trust in Christ to help you bear it—as I bear mine." He paused. "You and I, my son, are brothers in our banishment. Let us be in fellowship for life." He reached for Thomas' hand and placed the ring upon his finger once again.

Thomas rose, his cheeks still wet—for he, like other men of feeling, had the gift of tears—full of humility and gratitude and, yes, some exultation too. Now he was, once again, this time incontrovertibly the archbishop. Better that he had stopped his thoughts there, with humble thanks to God. But Thomas' mind was of the ever-searching kind, looking for possibilities; it had been trained to this. Therefore, his thought went on: Now that his power was beyond all questioning . . . and with the pope and King of France so strong behind him . . . he could bring all the terrors of the Church to bear on Henry, warn him, chastise him, and lead him to repentance . . . He would need weapons for this struggle; he would need papal sanction to pronounce and interdict if need be, or excommunications against his enemies. If he returned to England with such threats as these . . . with France behind him . . . and the spiritual power of the pope . . .

But Alexander, looking at his face, saw more than sorrow and contrition there. "My son," he said, "until this time you have lived in the midst of luxury and abundance, too close to the world. Now you must learn to be as you should be, the comforter of the poor. This is a lesson that can be studied only from poverty herself, who is the mother of religion. Therefore, my son, do I commit you to the poor in Christ. Go and live awhile in solitude and learn to conquer the temptations of the world among the holy brothers of Pontigny. Our friend in God and well-beloved brother Abbot Guichard will receive you there and be a father to you, even as I would be."

What disappointment Thomas felt he did not speak. Still, it went very hard with him to have to stand back from the battle now. He sought advice, obliquely, from prelates whom he trusted here at Sens, but they were eager to a man that peace should be restored among the factions of the Church. "Go softly for a while," they said. "And trust in God."

Advice like this was not made easier to take when he learned from Herbert Bosham what the king's ambassadors had gotten from the pope. Roger of York had joined them and had given the king's promise that the Peter-pence would henceforth come to Rome not only from each villein chimney that gives forth smoke but from the chimneys of free men and knights as well. "The pope resisted them," said Herbert, still with the jubilation he had felt when he was witness to the scene. "He said that it was clear to him that without cause they persecuted an innocent man. And when they asked that he return you into England he refused. He said, 'For a man to contend on an island against the king of that island is as if a prisoner in his chains were to contend against his jailor!'

"Nevertheless," concluded Herbert, his enthusiasm waning, "he sent two legates back with them to talk with Henry further, and that is ominous."

"And I must go to Pontigny," cried Thomas, "when at this time I should be striking back. It is a wasted opportunity!" But Robert caught his eye.

"With what would you 'strike back' against a king?" he asked him mildly. "Money and arms?"

"The Church has weapons," Thomas countered him. "You do not understand who have not charge of souls upon you as I have."

"I understand," said Robert softly, though his eyes flashed once.

"What else am I to fight with then?" asked Thomas stubbornly.

"If you must fight," said Robert, "then you have no other power to fight with than the power of God. But it is you who do not understand."

They rode to Pontigny on St. Andrew's Day, the last day of November, and Thomas for the first time saw the abbey in the vale, far from all other human habitation, with its wide fields spread around it and the wide pale sky above. The fields were dead this season and the massive abbey church seemed too austere, unwelcoming. It had no towers, no carved facings on its stones, no gilt, no gaudy pennants; all was plain. For Pontigny was one of those retreats built by the strict Cistercian brothers who fled from the world and sought out God away from humankind and all its vain imaginings.

He did not know if he could force himself into the somber life of work and prayer here in this backwater while all the world went by without him, but he tried. He wore the white monastic habit of this brotherhood, he ate the bran and lentils and drank the water of their frugal meals, he helped them with the threshing and the winnowing, the plowing when the fields thawed and the breaking of the clods. He spent much of the night in prayer and penitence and slept upon a pallet on the dorter floor. And when his flesh rebelled he whipped himself and—being so sensitive to cold—stood by the hour in the chilling stream nearby. Soon he fell ill.

Nevertheless he found there were rewards. The silent brothers, so it seemed to him, lived close to God. And in the abbey church—so drab outside, so dull—he felt the glowing presence of the Lord in every pure white line. Where in his own cathedral, so richly decorated by the clever hand of man, he strode in rustling processional or knelt or lay upon the inlaid stones conscious of glory, here he must creep and whisper under the eye of God. The frosty pillars rose above him in a soaring arch and he, so small, knelt as though floating in a luminous cloud and felt his soul washed and his heart made clean.

When he had first arrived, at that first Christmastime, he thought he heard God speak to him again, as though He said "Well done" for these austerities, and he rejoiced in spirit—though his body tortured him—that Christ was born and he was serving Him. He wanted, so he prayed most earnestly, no other life than this.

On that same day that Thomas had arrived at Pontigny, St. Andrew's Day, 1164, the English embassy arrived at Henry's court at Marlborough where he had gone to celebrate the Christmas season and rejoice that, though the traitor still was not within his grasp, he soon would be. The Earl of Arundel made his report without embellishment: King Louis' rancor, so long harbored quietly, was bitter, deep, and he would go all lengths to bring the English down. He had the pope within his pocket, there was no suasion—either by argument or force or bribe—that could bring Alexander to renounce the archbishop or send him back to England or even transfer him to some far see where he could do no harm. The French were hostile and the embassy had made the journey back from Sens in fear of ambush all along the way. The archbishop, by contrast, traveled with a regal train and used the open roads as though they were his own. Thomas would soon be partners with Louis, by the look of it, and if the Frankish king should set upon King Henry's Norman lands, Thomas would stir up trouble behind his back, here in the English kingdom where some traitorous folk still clung to him.

He finished and the king sprang from his chair. "What do

you tell me? What do you tell me, traitors, carriers of lies!"

"It is God's truth," said Foliot boldly.

Henry stood swaying, staring at him, hands working and chest heaving, but he did not speak. His rage had come upon him and his eyes grew bloodshot and he tore the clothing from his throat. At last he burst out cursing, cursing so violently that the spit flew from his mouth, calling upon God's mercy and God's wounds, God's blood and body, God's heart and bowels, while his voice rose until it was a scream.

No one was fool enough to try to stop him and his rage worked on him till he was exhausted by it and fell down upon the floor, pounding the pavement, clutching the rushes, stuffing them in his mouth.

Later, on Christmas Eve, he issued a set of orders to his court. These were not uttered in the cursings and convulsions of his first mad rage; no, that had cooled. They were the products of his studied wrath. He ordered that the properties and revenues of Canterbury be confiscated and that the Peter-pence as well be shunted to the royal treasury. He ordered that all bishops bind themselves by solemn promise not to communicate with Thomas or anyone attached to him, nor with the pope or members of his Curia. He ordered that any person whomsoever found having commerce with the pope should be imprisoned and anyone caught bringing letters into England from the archbishop be hanged or put into a leaky boat and cast adrift. He ordered that no priest or deacon—nor any layman either—might speak the name of Thomas in any public prayer.

And by his order, all Thomas' relatives, dependents, household clerks, those who had helped him in his flight or were in secret sympathy with him, were to be seized and banished from the land—put into open smacks or any boat available and sent to France to show themselves to Thomas that he might look at them, and Louis have the weight of harboring them.

He named the man to execute these orders and have the handling of the Canterbury lands and those who lived upon them: Ranulf de Broc. And after that he set himself to celebrating Christmas as best he might.

* * *

At Barking the nuns' priest was reading from the Scriptures while the senior nuns sat near the fire of their common room, some stitching silver threads into an altar cloth, some making pomanders or cracking nuts, some nodding, for it was a day when all was frozen out of doors, Epiphany, a time of giving and enjoying. "Arise, shine, for thy light is come," the priest read. "And the glory of the Lord . . ."

There was a heavy knocking at the gates. A little novice nun came bursting in, "O Sister Mary . . ."

"Then the time has come." Mary rose, went to the mother abbess, knelt and asked her blessing.

She had been granted warning; there had been messengers; all was as ordered by the king, and lawful; there was no reason for complaint. She kissed the sisters who were her only friends and left what was her only home in perfect dignity—except for one small flurry of delay when she ran back to find her little dog, who sometimes sat upon her lap and gave her what affection she had in her life. She found him, kissed him, slapped him off for licking at her face, then pulled her cloak about her and told the novice to bring her box along, for it was ready—several days it had been ready, standing in her cell.

The king's men grumbled to be kept thus waiting in the cold. The abbess had not asked them in to warm themselves or offered food or drink to them, though she was famous for her hospitality. Therefore, they said to Mary when she stood among them, "Madam, make haste."

"In God's good time," said Mary, "I must have my box with me."

"We have not got all day."

"No? I am ready, then," said Mary. "But you must help me, for I am a woman and not young." She frowned at them; they hesitated. Then:

"Aye, madam." And they helped her mount and she rode off with them without a look behind.

* * *

William Fitzstephen went to the court in Marlborough dressed in the height of fashion, suitable for Christmas, in a tunic and a cloak made of the green cloth of Auxerre. He had taken pains with this. His eyes shone and a little smile played on his freckled face. The more men started when they saw him or stared, or drew away, the more his eyes gleamed and his heart beat very hard.

The king passed and Fitzstephen stepped out boldly and went down upon one knee. He held a parchment out, a poem of his own composing—he had taken even greater pains with this—and begged the king graciously to accept it from a humble man, the least in all his realm.

The king stopped and looked down at him. He took the parchment and, while everyone stood still, he read it. Then he laughed, for it was very curiously rhymed, a charming Latin verse.

"My lord, may I have leave to stay in England?" William asked.

King Henry laughed again, rolled up the parchment and tossed it to a waiting man and laughed again.

"You have my leave," he said.

* * *

The soldiers came to Canterbury in the middle of the night. Osbert, the chamberlain to the archbishop, heard their feet upon the stair and rose up from his cot—he was full dressed—and took the little bundle from the corner: a clean shirt and extra pair of shoes, the gold chain of his office, and some bread and cheese (he had a little jeweled colombe stuck in the middle of the loaf) all wrapped up in a cloth, and lifted up the latch before they knocked. They went downstairs and outside to the Highstreet where he saw many men assembled and all around them horsemen looming in the dark.

The street filled; men came through the darkness from this side and that, for they had been removed from the cathedral precincts some days past and lived wherever they could find a corner for a cot. Some came as quietly as he, some running with the soldiers hustling them, some seemingly elated to be martyred thus, and some with angry faces and their hands bound at their backs. It took four hours till some hundred clerks—two hundred—who could tell?—stood in the Highstreet from the East Bridge to St. Andrew's Church. And yet the city all around lay very quiet, no lights shone. The curfew rules were harsh since the de Brocs had come.

The stars paled and the wind sprang up and still they waited, for Ranulf had it in his mind to clear the villages around of certain people of unwelcome influence. Therefore, at Certeham when the first light of pre-dawn stood at the windows of the little church, Almon was wakened from his sleep behind the altar by a commotion in the road outside. He got up with his eyes wide and went wonderingly to the door.

Soldiers were in the road beyond the gate. The gate was open, but anyway he could see well enough above and through the hedge, for it was thin this time of year. He could see Father Lambert's cottage and its tiny orchard: four small apple trees and one old cherry that bloomed beautifully in springtime but bore sour fruit. The trees were bare now and looked spidery in the dim light.

What was that? Father Lambert on his knees? He wore his old torn cloak, as though he had snatched up the first thing when he leaped from bed. He looked very old. Why, Father Lambert is not old, thought Almon. He even thought this must have been some older relative come to the village with the soldiers after him, someone in need of help, he looked so beaten by the world, so poor. But he knew right away that it was Lambert.

He heard him cry out roughly, "My wife! My wife!"

The soldiers laughed. There were so many there, walking around the orchard, up and down the road, into the house and out again.

They had pulled Lambert to his feet. They took his arms and twisted them behind his back and bound them, and his cloak fell open. It was shameful.

Oh, Almon thought, they have bound up a priest of God! Such shock ran through him that he could not move.

Then he heard Lambert scream, a man's scream, rough around the edges but still piercing, and he saw the soldiers with a woman in their midst. Oh, she was flopping in their hands, her long hair flopping up and down as she lunged forward and then back. And now she bent and they bent over her. Almon could see her rump all white. Her skirts were pulled above her head. Then they went at her just like dogs; she like the bitch, down on all fours. And then there so many crowded round he could no longer see.

But smoke was coming from the cottage now and little flames of red leaped from the edges of the thatch! Lambert was going, stumbling down the road, for they had tied a rope around him and a horseman jerked him on. And more were following. And more got on their horses once again. And they were going. Almon was on his knees in the church door, his arms outstretched. He did not know how this had happened. He cried out . . .

No voice came from his throat.

He ran out to the gate and waved his arms. The soldiers passing, just the last of them, looked at his open mouth. His face was very white; his mouth was open; but there was no sound. They rode on out of sight, not bothering, for they must get to Canterbury with this haul, and then the weary ride down to the coast . . .

Almon ran back into the church. He flung himself before

the altar, a peculiar sight—a thin young man, so very pale and shaken, waving his arms before him, clasping his hands and stretching them out to the cross, then clamping them against his mouth, then stretching out again, and crawling back and forth.

Could I have saved them? Why did I not call out? Should I run now and cut the rope? And tell them, "This is Father Lambert; he has done no wrong?"

From the altar came God's answering voice, so long familiar—could it be truly God's voice, or was it after all his own?—saying: "No, Almon, there was nothing you could do, for you were not prepared for evil."

It was his own! It was his own and always had been! Was it his own?

He jumped up and ran back behind the altar to the safety of his bed, crawled into it—it was no longer warm—jumped up again and ran out of the church and down the empty road, crying out, crying, so that the sleeping people might wake up and see the evil being done and stop it . . .

But who could hear him? No sound came.

In this way, throughout England, were Thomas' followers—men, women, children, babies not yet old enough to talk—seized by the king's men and taken to the sea, in wains on horseback and on foot, thrust from their homeland and told to show themselves to Thomas in their misery—four hundred forty of them by the final count.

CHAPTER XXIII

THOMAS STOOD ABOVE the crowds at Vézelay, and over them his voice rang out as deep and solemn as it had been all this ceremony through.

". . . Wherefore in the name of God, the Father, Son, and Holy Ghost, of the blessed Peter and of all the Saints, in virtue of the power which has been given us of binding and of loosing in heaven and on earth, do we deprive Ranulf de Broc, himself and all his accomplices and all his abettors, of the Communion of the Body and Blood of Our Lord; we separate him from the society of all Christians; we exclude him from the bosom of our holy Mother Church in heaven and on earth; we declare him excommunicated and anathematized; we judge him condemned to eternal fire with Satan and his angels and all the reprobate, so long as he will not do penance and satisfy the Church; and we deliver him to Satan to mortify his body that his soul may be saved on the day of judgment . . ."

He dashed the candle to the floor and watched it splutter and then stamped upon it till the flame was out. He closed the book.

Around him rang the chorus of the priests, as it had done six times before: "Fiat! Fiat! Fiat!" And solemnly the bells were tolled as for a death.

This last name was the easiest. Ranulf de Broc was in the hands of Satan and had long been; it was but just and right that he be cut off from the Church. The others, closer to the king and old friends of his own, had been more difficult. And he had wept and stumbled on the name, Richard de Luci.

Now it was done. The sanctuary doors were closed against them and their names were nailed up on the gates to warn all men to shun them if they held their own salvation dear. Henceforth, until they should repent through suffering, they were as lepers, cast out by their fellow men.

And these first seven, Thomas had made clear, were but the first. All men who acted on the Constitutions, which he anathematized, lay under threat of excommunication, and his long finger pointed at the forehead of the king himself, though he forebore to name him, hearing that he lay ill.

Thus Thomas made his answer to the king—though many months had passed. Henry had used the voice of cruelty to cut across the boundaries of land and water that lay between them, to bridge the abyss of failed friendship turned to hate. Now Thomas used the thunder of a wrathful God. And as two men may hold a conversation in a room, stand eye to eye and speak, make answer, speak again, and never hear, these two called out to one another across their battlefield month after month. Their common ground was open enmity, and yet they spoke across it, muffled shouts and long-drawn echoing calls, each seeking out the other's heart, although they used most devious messages.

In early spring, 1165, the refugees had come to Pontigny —those who were not too weak or not too proud to make the journey from the coast—and Thomas, looking at them with distracted eyes, made oblique answer to the king: he placed them, every one, in castles, monasteries, convents, from the shores of Flanders to the isle of Sicily, there to live on the bounty of their hosts and make of every mouthful that they ate a practical reminder of the treacherous English king.

Hearing no answer, he then appealed to Alexander for papal sanction to excommunicate those who encroached upon his rights and who advised the king toward his own spiritual downfall. And Alexander, feeling his fortunes rising and even then preparing for return to Rome, made answer: "You are my brother and you have my full support."

This Henry heard. For answer he proposed alliance with the German emperor, champion of the anti-pope, and said he only waited a just reason before withdrawing his support from Pope Alexander and his perfidious cardinals.

A thrill of shock went through the Curia to hear this threat. Should England join with Germany against them, then they were lost. Hastily, Alexander sent his second thoughts to Pontigny: "Move cautiously, the days are evil. Venture upon no violent course until the times shall change—at least for one year more."

Now Thomas, thwarted, took his pen and gathered legalistic clerks about him and laid his case against the king and sent long letters, ever more heated, ever more certain of his right, to all his suffragans and other bishops far afield, to all the chapters of the several orders, and to the courts and chancelleries of Europe until the roads from hidden Pontigny were thick with messengers and he, stooped at his desk, lived with his bitter thoughts abroad and saw the quiet life around him with but a passing glance.

Friends saw he grew cantankerous. Robert of Merton, close by his side, and John of Salisbury, writing from St. Rémi, gave warning but he would not heed. He was the cause of right and he would fight for it.

King Henry used his year's reprieve to feel out all the possibilities. He could embrace the anti-pope and make alliance with the German emperor, and this he tentatively tried. But his own people, fearing God, were set against him; the Earl of Leicester with his own hands tore down the altar at which the German prelates had said Mass. Another course was to assure his power through his son; anathema might touch his person but it could not touch his throne if the young king were crowned. Yet who dared to anoint an English king except the Archbishop of Canterbury who claimed the right? Unless Pope Alexander gave such sanction to the Archbishop of York?

The year was up, and Alexander, feeling strong now that

he sat in Peter's seat again, wrote strong words to the king: "Because you turn against the Holy Church in Rome, we must take back from you the legate's office which we offered you before. It seems more fitting that we return where it was: to Canterbury and our beloved brother, Thomas, in order that by our authority as well as by his own he may inflict such penalties as he deem necessary on the enemies of the Church.

"Herewith take notice we refuse to shut his mouth up any longer as we have done until now in your interest; but let him rather, from now on, pronounce the justice and the punishments of God according to the duties of his office. These are our words."

King Henry, holding Easter court in Angers with his queen, received this letter, read it, and kept still. The words were not so frightening as they might have been had he not known, as he knew—for his own exchequer was the lighter for it—that the emperor's army, marching with the anti-pope, was even now near Rome.

The year was up and Thomas was again the papal legate, free to act. But he was moved, before he acted, to warn the king and plead with him. For the first time since they had parted he spoke directly to him across the battlefield: "Long have I wanted to speak to you," he wrote. "For how it is with me, living so far from home and on the charity of strangers you may well understand who know me well, for we are two who once the world called one. God has done so by us that you are rightfully my master and my king, and yet my spiritual son. Therefore, I pray you, my beloved child and revered lord, king as King David was, repent . . ."

Much more he said, all in his own words to the king. He would not let another put his hand to it. And after it was sent the days were long while he sat waiting for the messenger to bring his answer, but there was none.

He wrote again, more sternly, and rebuked him for his silence saying: "Waiting, we have waited to hear if you had turned the manner of your life into the path of right. We have been waiting for a messenger to bring the word, 'The king your son was dead but now he liveth; lost but now is found.' But no word came.

"So we are drawn on to admonish you, because it is the duty of the father to correct the son; it is a bishop's duty to be judge, not to be judged. You are the son of the Church and not her father, and it would be more seemly in you to listen to the words of learned Churchmen rather than try to teach them—for who would think a son in his right mind who bore down upon and beat his father, or a thrall so dealing with his master?

"It does not rest with you to tell bishops whom they may excommunicate, or to force clergy to make answer in secular courts, or to interfere with tithes, or do any of these things which you pretend in the name of Custom.

"And so be pleased, my good lord, to restore the Church her properties, her castles and her towns and villages, which have been taken and distributed, and dissipated and laid waste . . .

"So also let me come again in peace and freedom to my own see and there abide in quiet. For if you grant this I will serve you as best I know how. But if you refuse, consider well what ending you may bring about. Farewell."

Again the messenger to Henry stood by for answer but was given none, although he heard the king's remark—not meant for him—that he had oftentimes before known the archbishop to mistake his own will for the will of God.

For the third time he wrote; the thunder warning of the coming storm: "Now remember how you came into the world and all that God has given you. But low now, lest the shaft of excommunication strike. Forget not that He cometh who is mightier than you, who knows well how to take away from kings—both life and might. Take heed you are not unprepared when that time comes, for even now it is your season. May God grant you health of spirit and good-will. And with these words we make an end to writing."

It was time to act.

Just before Whitsuntide, then, Thomas rode to Vézelay, that elegant and lofty church where Cluniac monks pursued their rounds of offices high up above the soft Burgundian fields. No other shrine in Europe, excepting only Rome itself and Compostela, drew such a stream of penitents or pious travelers—or simply summer wanderers in search of things to see. Therefore, the road was clogged with pilgrims as Thomas came, his banner and his staff before him and his dark face drawn with bitterness, his black brows frowning, as he rode.

It was five days since he left Pontigny with his intention locked within his heart. He had gone north to Soissons and for three days and nights kept vigil at the altar of St. Drausius, patron of duelers and men condemned to trial by battle. Then he had ridden south to Vézelay, his wondering and solemn clerks behind.

Now, as he rode along the valley, he raised his eyes to where the great basilica stood high upon its mound, gray in the distance, hung between earth and sky. A single dark cloud, edged in light, rose up behind it and he saw in this a hand raised up in admonition and he took it as a sign, for he himself had come here to admonish and his hand was raised.

When he had made his long way up the hill, the abbot greeted him beneath the gate and he was given honor in this place. On Whitsunday he celebrated Mass before the multitude of brothers and the pilgrims thronging in beneath the green-gold arches of the mighty church.

He rose and faced the congregation and from the pulpit preached the sermon of Pentecost. The wonder of that monument to God stretched out before him, pillar beyond pillar, arch on arch, so marvelously framed and carved that here the very stones were made flesh and the flesh made spirit. But he did not see. His eyes were inward as he preached and he spoke not about the wind of Pentecost, or tongues of fire, but of the persecution of the Church in England and of King Henry's Constitutions which were the instruments of this persecution and of his struggle to bring the king and all the evil-doers who surrounded him to do the will of God, but they were stubborn in their disobedience. Therefore, their hour had come, for mercy could no longer hold the hand of duty. Here, on this very day on which the Holy Spirit had come to the world of men, would he, Thomas the Archbishop, the primate, papal legate, cut them off from the society of Christian men and cast them from the Church.

"But that the king lies ill," he went on (for this King Henry had given out for all the world to hear, and shut himself up in his castle in Chinon), "would he be punished in like manner till he repent. But let him take warning lest our wrath fall on him—even though death should stalk the closet where he lies.

"Thus in the name of Father, Son, and Holy Ghost do we proceed." He beckoned the twelve priests who would assist him and they preceded him down through the nave, pushing the pilgrims back and making way for him, on through the portals to the narthex, lest he profane with curses the holy sanctuary of the church.

There in the portico he stepped upon the dais and took a candle and the light went flickering across his face as he pronounced in a loud voice, so loud it echoed in the vaulted room and carried out into the open, into the crowded square and steep streets leading up to it: "Now by the power that has been invested in me, do I pronounce the sentence of the Church on John of Oxford who has had damnable traffic with schismatics and schemed against the Church of Rome, to his soul's peril and despite our admonitions, and who has scorned to make acknowledgment of these same crimes but has persisted, in the face of warnings, in his stubborn disobedience.

"Wherefore, in the name of God the Father, Son, and Holy Ghost, of the blessed Peter and of all the Saints . . . do we deprive said John . . ."

The book lay open but he had no need to look at it. He knew the formula. It had been, in the nights of his humiliation, when his power was withheld, a source—no, surely not of comfort, for it caused him pain—but of relief from the frustration of his will.

". . . and we deliver him to Satan to mortify his body so that his soul may be saved on the day of judgment." He cast the candle down and with his foot put out the little flame.

Henry was quick enough to make a reply to this. He let it be known to the Cistercian Brotherhood that should they any longer harbor the archbishop in any of their monasteries anywhere, then would he confiscate all of their properties in his domain. It was a simple choice he gave them: either they expel his enemy from Pontigny or he would expel them all from all his lands. And though some argued at their meetings that a friend of God who had been put into their keeping by the pope himself must not be sacrificed to a king's whim, the worldly truth of it was that there was no choice at all.

They put the matter to their guest, and Thomas, reading the king's words and looking up to see their faces peering at him full of shame and doubt, said he would go. "For who would put so hard a burden on his friends who has already burdened them so long? Be sure that God who feeds the little fowl and clothes the lilies of the field will find a place for me."

They were surprised to find him cheerful as he said these words. They did not know that far worse had befallen him and this new blow was welcomed by him as a further proof that Christ had chosen him to suffer in His name. The truth was that the pope had once more found himself beset, with the emperor's army at the gates of Rome. He wrote to Thomas guardedly: "If matters do not for the moment come off to your satisfaction, wait a more favorable time." And then he let him know he had suspended all the sentences pronounced at Vézelay, withdrawn his legateship, and at the king's request had named two cardinals to come to

France and arbitrate—nay, be the final judges—of the quarrel that was so painful to the Church.

One of these cardinals was an open enemy, the other one blew neither hot nor cold; Thomas gave way to anger and despair. "Ridicule has fallen on me," he cried out, "and shame upon the pope!" He wrote to John of Salisbury: "I am to be obeyed no longer. I am betrayed and given to destruction by my enemies. But let the pope be sure of one thing: I will never while the breath is in my body accept the Cardinal of Pavia for my judge. They whisper that when they are rid of me, he is to have my place at Canterbury. . . ." He put down the pen. So are God's servants made to suffer in this world, he thought.

And it was then that the true meanings of his sufferings had come to him; and it was then that he began to welcome every painful blow. That night he had a vision as he lay asleep. "Thomas, Thomas," a voice called out to him. And for a third time, "Thomas."

"Who art thou, Lord?" cried Thomas starting up.

"I am thy brother, Jesus Christ, and in thy blood shall my Church be glorified."

Thomas was kneeling, transfixed on the bed. "So be it, Lord. In my blood shall thy Church be glorified."

Next morning he described this vision to Prior Robert, but he was disconcerted to see his old friend smile. "I do not think the cup at which you drink accords well with the cup of martyrdom," he said. And Thomas answered stiffly that he knew he was too worldly, and after kept back his thoughts and pondered them alone.

Through Louis' bounty a place was found for him at Sens, and with his little party he moved there on the eve of Michaelmas, 1166.

There he took up his old austerities again. He tried to hide his actions with a smiling face, but it was known to Robert that he wore the hair shirt once more and would not change it though it crawled with vermin, and that he rose at dawn to pray and after Mass went by himself to pray again, and five times every night and day submitted to the scourge and that his food was bread and water, and that he seemed obsessed.

Was this the way to martyrdom? He thought it was. Had not his vision promised that his blood would glorify the Church? More than a year he tried and weakened, tried again. With all his strong determined mind, with all his tortured body, he sought to find his way to God, to vindicate

God's cause. But no more visions came to him—only some nightmare dreams: of spiders once again, of murderers.

Robert, watching, said to him one day: "Are you God's champion?"

"I am," said Thomas.

Then Robert sighed and said, "There are two things you need to know: First, what you are; and then that you are not such of your own self. These are two forms of ignorance. But more than ignorance, you, Thomas, must avoid presumption." He paused, for it was difficult for him to speak these words.

Then he continued. "Presumption leads men deliberately to credit to themselves the things we all know well are God's. This is an arrogance far graver and more perilous than ignorance, in that it sets God's gifts at nought. Pride is indeed," he softly said, "the greatest of all evils, since it leads us to use God's gifts as though they were our own by natural right, and to usurp the glory due to the bestower for what we have received."

"You think that I am proud," said Thomas.

"I think you must beware of pride," said Robert, "for it is a sin that men fall into unawares."

"Do not be soft with me. You think me proud." But in his heart he wondered how he could be proud and meanwhile make himself so humble, mortify his body and deny his wants.

"I think that God is His own champion," said Robert mildly. "Therefore, I questioned you."

From that time, in his meditations, Thomas fought with pride. He craved to be the lowest and the last, who through his lifetime had always sought the highest place. When he went to his chapel he lay down upon his face, and prayed that he might be delivered from the sin of pride, and thus find Glory. Was that what he sought? He groaned and tried again.

Could a man so degrade himself, and hate his body and punish it, and wallow in humility month after month and never see the end? Some men might do it. But it would seem that God loved Thomas, for He made an end.

One day—it was the Christmas season of 1168—when snow was on the ground and he went barefoot across the court into the church and turned into his chapel and knelt down, it struck him suddenly—there was no reason for it—that he was but a man. A little man in all the oceans of humanity. He saw as from a distant height men working in their fields, their tattered tunics drawn up from their knees, the sparrows following their plows; he saw men in their council hall, gesticulating, arguing the law; and bloody men upon a battlefield; and men at sea—so small; and then men laughing all together in a tavern room, eating and drinking, warming each other, comforting, against the darkness closing in. And what was he but one of them, those little creatures capering through their lives? Where in this picture was there room for pride? What was it so concerned him about humility and suffering? Was it not human to be small and suffer? Why should that lead to glory?

He knelt as though he had been turned to stone. All the elaborations of his former thoughts dropped from his mind. And for the first time a dreadful clarity came on him, and in a little voice, full of surprise, dismay, he said aloud: "Why, I am loathsome!"

"Nevertheless, I love."

Whose voice was that?

Thomas spun round upon his knees, his hands flung out, his face turned to the pointed arches up above, to the dim corners where the light was gray. He heard the echo in his heart, "I love." It was the voice that he had heard at Canterbury, at his consecration, that he had not heard since. And he collapsed upon the floor and hid his face and trembled, and from his startled body, from his lips, the words came stuttering, "I love . . . I love . . . I, too, love . . . Oh let me love . . ."

How painful to feel love for the first time.

CHAPTER XXIV

THE KING OF ENGLAND and the King of France arranged a meeting on the borders of their lands, at Montmirail, in January of 1169. Each had his reasons for it though neither felt it necessary to tell the other what those reasons were. There had been skirmishes along their borders, rapine and killing, for several months, and the affair of the archbishop had strained their friendship further.

Nevertheless, they met. And the display was marvelous to see.

King Henry brought his sons to make obeisance to King Louis for the lands he held of him, which he now planned to designate to them, and he began the conference with formal words: "My lord King, on this day of Epiphany, on which the three kings brought their gifts to the King of Kings, do I commend my three sons and their lands into your keeping."

King Louis had not had such ample time for composition as had his vassal king. Nevertheless men noted, smiling inwardly, that he made apt reply: "Since the King to whom the Magi brought those gifts has been the inspiration for your words," he said, "may your sons, as they receive their lands and take their title by our grace, do so in the presence of Our Lord."

King Henry made a graceful bow to this, said nothing, and brought forward his first son, Henry, the "young king," on whom he doted and in whom he saw his hope for immortality. Here was the handsome youth, tall for his fourteen years, full of the grace of all the Poitevins, clear eyed and noble in his bearing, sweet of voice—"a little lower than the angels," as men remarked of him in later years, "he was a man who turned all things to evil." The young count, still unknighted, received the lands he had been promised at his birth, of Normandy, Maine and Anjou, and then he knelt and placed his hands between King Louis' hands—the father of his still child-wife—and did him homage for these provinces. And all the while he kept within his mind, as did his father, that it was time and past time that he be crowned the King of England—and for this do no homage to any man.

The second son, his mother's favorite and her heir, young Richard, then stepped forth. He heard his father grant again the counties of his birthright, Poitou and Aquitaine, and knelt before King Louis as his brother had—and all the while *he* kept his eyes upon his mother, for it was she who guarded his ambitions.

The lands of Brittany were given to the third son, Geoffrey, ten years old, and with them the little countess to be his wife. And all the ceremony went in the high manner, peaceful, and each man in his place, the banners hanging in their ranks, color upon color, stirred by no wind.

Far in the farthest ranks of the French nobles and their assembled allies and of the prelates who had come at Louis' bidding, hung the banner of the English archbishop. He had been loath to show himself on such a field; he had faint hope of reconciliation with King Henry now and it was hurtful to his pride—oh give a man some remnants of his worldly pride—to come into the presence of such kings and princes like a beggar. But Louis wanted it and Alexander wanted it and even Henry said that he would welcome him. The world was tired of this costly quarrel. Louis had sent a decent escort of some clerks and knights to ride with him from Sens, and lent his castle for his entertainment, and gave him heart in many other ways.

Thus Thomas stood and looked across the shoulders of a hundred men and saw, as though four years had dropped away, his friend of old, his king, his wayward son. Surely the winter light dropped first on him, illuminated him, his crown, his burly shoulders in their scarlet cloak, before it spread itself to shine on other men. And in this light his face, his keen gray eyes, his very thoughts were clear to Thomas as they had been when, close together, they had bent above their work and laid their plans.

The young king, foster son whom he had sheltered, nourished, loved, stood forth. How he had grown! Not changed though; Thomas knew his mind. He was as clear to him—all of this pageant was as clear—as if he studied little figures painted in the margins of his psalter, posturing among the brightly colored vines. He did not even have to look at Richard; he saw Queen Eleanor. It was upon her face the light shone now. If the king had meant to tear his whole domain in little shreds and fling them out away from him, he could have done it in no better way than this—unless he meant by this to bind them even closer to himself; to give and yet to keep; to build a broader platform from which to climb. And Thomas then remembered—a little flicker ran across his face—how when the two had shared their secret thoughts, the king had said, lightly enough, "The whole world might be better off under the rule of one just, able man."

And I could help him—under God, he thought. For no man rules, either the world, or just one kingdom, or himself, without the help of God. This I could teach him . . .

What old thoughts were these?

The kings were seated side by side upon their thrones, their treaty drawn and signed, their parley and the ceremonies done. A richly painted canvas lay beneath their feet and at their backs their courtiers made up a milticolored wall of greens and blues and grays and soft-striped robes of wool. The English king was clothed in scarlet and the King of France in gold. They wore their crowns.

Now came a swarm of bishops, prelates, clerks across the trampled grass. They had been sent to bring the archbishop because King Louis and the legates said: Let us have concord and a peaceful ending to all dissension on this field of peace. They pressed him forward toward the thrones, and the kings waited.

Thomas, walking in their midst, saw only Henry. When the escorting bishops halted, he went on alone. He stood a moment staring, then went down upon his knee. King Henry saw the gaunt face and the pallor and the glint of tears —Why, he has truly suffered!—and he sprang up from his throne. He put his hands upon the shoulders of his friend and drew him up.

"My lord, my lord," said Thomas from his heart. "Forgive me. Forgive the pride that led to our dissension. That I have suffered for it you may see. That the Church has suffered, I will take upon myself and bear the blame. The Church has suffered, suffers, even as I do, and is in rags and stands before the world with no protector. Have pity on the Church, my lord, and deal wtih her in justice and in righteousness."

"That will I do," said Henry gently. "I have asked only that the Church allow the throne such dignities as it has always had. No more." He smiled at Thomas questioningly and Thomas nodded. Then, still with his hand upon the other's arm, he turned to those behind him.

"My lord King and you lords and prelates, what I require of the archbishop is no more than that he will observe the laws and customs of my land as they have been observed by archbishops before him. I ask him now, before you all, to give that promise . . ." and he turned again to Thomas and stepped back.

Then Thomas spoke in a strong voice: "My lord King, in the presence of the King of France, the papal legates, and of these princes who are your sons, I here commit the whole case and the issues that have come between us to the mercy and the judgment of your royal will . . ."

Why did a shadow veil the king's eyes now? Where was the light, now, that had made of him a god? He saw that it had shifted in the clouds. It fell elsewhere.

He glanced beyond the crowd to where a barren tree stood in a shaft of sun and saw a lone leaf dangling, held by some spider's web perhaps, from a dead limb. It twirled and caught the light upon itself, spinning against the sky although there was no wind. It had no reason to be there, midwinter, except to catch his eye. He stared at it, then looked again at Henry. ". . . your royal will," he said. "Saving the honor of God."

It was the phrase, new-worded, that he had used at Westminster, that he had foregone at Clarendon to his destruction, that was the root and stem of their dissension: the honor of God and of the men of God against the honor of kings.

Now blackness fell, full shadow, on Henry's face. "Deceiver!" he said very low. "They told me you had promised to leave off these phrases. What is it? Do you think I have no honor for God myself?" He saw the answer in Thomas' eyes and he burst out: "Oh how you pride yourself that you once knew me! But I know you. You think that you can climb upon my shoulders. And at the same time you claim protection of the Church! Is that it?"

Thomas' silence so enraged him that he reached out and grabbed the clothing at his throat. "I knew you had designs upon my throne; I watched your pompous doings even when you were chancellor. And here again, you mock me!" He was beside himself; he had forgotten where he was. Thomas staggered as he shook him by the throat.

King Louis rose, astonished to see this. The bishops started, and a sound of murmuring came from the watching men. King Henry heard. He dropped his hand and stood back, ran his palm across his face. Then self-controlled once more, he turned to Louis: "My lord King, attend me if you please. You see how foolishly and proudly this man—who ran off and left his church, not driven out by me, but running off in secret and by night—how he would now persuade you that he is champion of the Church. But he deceives you all. Whatever this man finds"—he raised a thumb at Thomas—"whatever he shall find displeasing to him in the affairs of government he will declare contrary to the honor of God. Thus will he have the last word with me, always. But I also honor God.

Now he was calm again and spoke with slow deliberation as he said: "Lest I seem in any way to honor God less than do other kings let me propose this to you all. There have been many kings in England before me, some with more and some with less authority than mine; there have been many archbishops of Canterbury, great and holy men. Let this archbishop yield to me only what the greatest and most saintly of his predecessors conceded to the least of mine, and I shall be well satisfied."

The words, so calmly spoken and so reasonable, brought

every man to his side in the quarrel and they nodded. "What could be more just?"

"What say you, Thomas?"

Thomas said nothing, though his silence seemed to pound upon his ears. At last King Louis spoke: "My lord Archbishop, do you desire to be higher than the saints, more strict than Peter's self? Why do you hesitate? The peace that you desire is within your hand."

The bishops nodded to him, urged. The papal legates signaled that the pope would have it so. Even his closest clerks implored him whispering, "Let us have peace now, Father. Let us go home."

But Thomas knew that peace was not at hand. He knew the king. What were his words but a rephrasing of his Constitutions? He knew his deep designs. He looked at those about him, each of them, a long while in the eyes. He shook his head. "Shall I," he asked, "when all our fathers before us have suffered in the name of Christ, forswear the reverence I owe to God in order to regain my temporal state?

"It cannot be, my brothers. All heaven and the saints forbid it. It cannot be."

He was allowed to ride away from Montmirail without a salutation or a single word from king or legate, bishop or anyone. King Louis had abandoned him. He was alone. Even his clerks found fault with him and blamed him for their exile and spoke scornfully behind his back.

He was alone. How was it, then, that on Palm Sunday at Clairvaux he had again the power to take book and candle and send the thunderbolt of his anathema across the earth—at Bishop Foliot as the inciter of King Henry's malice, at the de Brocs again and all the others whom he had cursed at Vézelay and whom the pope had saved? No doing of his own: Henry had turned back from the field of peace and, scarcely taking time to ride into his own domain, broke faith with Louis and murdered with a barbarous cruelty the very men to whom the treaty gave protection. When Louis heard, he hastened down to Sens and threw himself upon his knees before the archbishop. The clerks looked on, astonished. Then he said: "We were all blind but you. King Henry's name is treachery. Forgive me." And again: "From now on my support shall be unwavering."

Thus did the tide turn. And in another month it swelled to lift the archbishop to eminence again. The forces of the anti-pope had conquered Rome the year before and Pope Alexander had for his very life placated Henry, slighted the archbishop. Then plague had taken all the German army, twenty thousand men. God's power manifested the world. And Alexander, on his throne again, gave permit to the archbishop—should peaceful conference with the king be given trial and fail—to loose his wrath upon his enemies. He set a limit to the time the archbishop must wait: Ash Wednesday of 1169.

Ash Wednesday came; the warnings had been sent. And Easter, and the sentences were read. Now again forty days had passed. It was Ascension Day. A young man stood beneath the pulpit, close in the shadow of the pillar and the curved stone stair, in the Cathedral of St. Paul in London, while at the altar, behind the rail, the priest intoned the creed. ". . . *exspecto resurectionem mortuorum . . . vitam venturi saeculi. Amen.*" It was the service of High Mass on this high day, so the long nave was full of people and the young man stood pressed in among them, in the forefront of the crowd.

The priest turned from the altar to the people. *"Dominus vobiscum . . . Oremus."*

Quickly the young man pushed out from the pillar, went and knelt before the rail. He held a packet in his hand and thrust it out as though it were an offering. The priest came forward, and as he took it the young man seized his hand. He held it, firmly closing it upon the packet, while he said, "Father, I charge you in the name of God and of our Holy Father and of the archbishop, read what I here deliver to you and convey it to your bishop without delay. Henceforth leave off celebrating Mass within this church, for it is cut off from the Church of Christ and the communion of all Christian men."

The priest, dumfounded, let the cover of the packet fall; within he saw the letter from the archbishop announcing to the Bishop of London, Gilbert Foliot, that he was excommunicated. The warnings had been given and the sentences pronounced on Easter Day.

Still the young man held him by the wrist. Where had he come from? That which he held within his hand had long been dreaded; every precaution had been taken to keep it from the land—the ports closed and the roads watched night and day and double guards set by the king around the city and even here within the bishop's church. He had no words, but stood, the letter dangling in his hand.

The young man rose, still holding him, and turned to face the congregation. In a loud voice he said, "Know all that

Bishop Foliot is excommunicated and anathematized and every Christian man is warned to shun him if he holds his own salvation dear."

The church was in a turmoil, some men flooding out to be away from danger, others crowding up to see. And through the jostling crowds, the clamor, came the king's guards threading, pushing, shoving with their maces against yielding flesh.

The young man saw it all and with a leap was back within the shadow of the pulpit, sheltered a moment, gone. Someone was there who held a cloak. Men saw the swirl of it. And after that no more than two bewildered Londoners, like all the others, crowding from the church and asking questions: "What did he say?" And, "Is it true the bishop has been excommunicated?"

Then two young travelers upon the road, going on pilgrimage. And two young squires on an errand for a local lord. And two young fishermen in a small boat casting away from Romney before dawn.

To such lengths would a young clerk go to serve the archbishop.

Bishop Foliot cried out against the archbishop. He had received no warning! The whole proceeding was irregular! King Henry pointed out that it was in the pope's own interest—there was the matter of the Peter-pence—to shelter loyal English bishops from such attacks as this.

Pope Alexander was annoyed; the cardinals fumed. This quarrel would surely be the ruin of the Church. Had he not cautioned the archbishop to go carefully? Had he not told the king that mediators even now were on their way? For five years had these two hot, stubborn men disturbed the peace of Europe and by their bickering made the very throne of Peter an unsteady rock. He was sore tempted to translate the archbishop to some far corner of the Holy Land, or else to loose the full wrath of the Church on that most treacherous and mendacious king. But caution counseled him again. He sped the new legation on its way to Henry's court and wrote to Thomas to hold his hand. To Bishop Foliot he sent a letter of absolution, for it was most important to keep the English bishops in allegiance with the Church in Rome.

Five years of single-minded effort and frustration may reduce a man—strip from him as it were the layered teachings of experience and leave him open to unguarded actions like a child. Thus did both Thomas and King Henry act when the pope's words reached them.

Thomas' letter to the papal court was like the outcry of a beaten Cheapside boy: "I know not how it is," he wrote, "that in the court of Rome the Lord's side is in each case sacrificed—that Barabbas escapes and Christ is put to death! With you, the wretched, exiled, innocent are condemned—and for no other reason than they are the poor of Christ, the weak, and will not go back from the righteousness of God.

"Yes, I am poor and weak. But is it not the very spoils that these impenitents and reprobates have robbed from me, or rather from the Church, which the king's emissaries lavish on the cardinals of Rome and pay them to do their bidding? For my own part I am resolved never to trouble the Curia again; let those go there who take pride in iniquity, and let them—after they have triumphed over justice—let them return with boasting, to the confusion of the Church!"

Henry cried out as loud when the pope's emissaries came to him at Rouen to press for reconciliation. When they reminded him he stood in danger of the Church's wrath, he took his cap off from his head and flung it at them, next his belt and next his boots as they backed out the door. And when they pressed again he cried, "I know what you would do, I know it. You would interdict my lands. But if I can take one of the strongest castles every day—which I can do—cannot I take one clerk who threatens interdict?" But he could not—he knew that now. Even the pope could not control the archbishop. Therefore, he found another path: if the young king were crowned and sat upon the throne, then was an interdict less likely.

As soon as the ambassadors had left he took the young king secretly to Caen and left him with his mother. He himself, with all his fleet, set out at midnight in a furious gale and landed on the coast of England all unexpected, like a god who travels on the storm.

No one among his prelates dared to counter him, and some indeed were eager to comply. The Archbishop of York had long contended that it was his right to crown an English king whenever the see of Canterbury should be vacant. Surely to all intents and purposes that see was vacant now? Gladly he prepared himself, and one by one the bishops fell in line. By June all was in readiness and the young king was summoned.

The ceremony of his coronation lacked no single thing—saving the presence of the archbishop. His little wife as well was left behind, lest something lacking in the rite offend her father, but the young husband did not care. Roger of York anointed him; the mighty gathering of lords cried vivat rex; the English bishops bowed before him and outside the people cheered. Afterward, when he presided at the coronation feast, King Henry with his own hands brought the boar's head to the board.

"Not every prince," said Roger, watching, smiling with his lips, "not every prince can be thus served at table by a king!"

"It is but right and proper," said young Henry, smiling back. "And it can be no condescension for the son of a count to be the servant of the son of a king."

The company took note of this remark and let their eyes dart from the son to father and from the father to the son. But Henry let no shadow fall upon this great occasion. Only, when he made ready to depart for Normandy again, he put the young king in the care of loyal men, stern tutors, who might keep an eye on him.

As for himself, his next move must be made before the archbishop could act. He knew that Thomas would attempt to excommunicate him, perhaps induce the pope to nullify the coronation, even proclaim the interdict, unless he could propitiate him and make peace. He went at once to France, to Louis, and by the workings of his charm, his power to make promises seem real, soothed over his offended feelings and appealed to him to help him reconcile himself to Thomas, for "there have been misunderstandings on both sides; for my part I am willing to make redress," and, "when the archbishop shall be restored to Canterbury, then shall we have a second, true and final crowning in which the princess shall share with the king the blessings of the primate and of yourself." He begged that Louis bring the two of them together once again, saying he knew that it had always been the king's desire, out of his goodness, to foster peace.

This time the meeting was at Fréteval, within the French domain; the weather smiling, for it was the feast day of St. Mary Magdalene, July. The conference ground was in a meadow hard by the castle and a giant oak tree gave its shade to the two kings. Thomas had been persuaded to attend by Louis and the Archbishop of Sens; he came, but not as he had come before. This time he wore a stern, uncompromising face because, this time, the power was his. He had new letters of excommunication in his hand. The pope had sanctioned them. Therefore, he rode up to the meeting slowly, as one on whom all others hang.

Louis withdrew, lest it appear he put constraint on either man. Henry had left behind those enemies of Thomas'—Roger and Gilbert and the rest—who might cast sour looks upon their king's submission. There was to be no bar to peace this time.

Thomas rode slowly from the shadow of the castle with the sunlight at his back. The Archbishop of Sens rode at his side, his train of clerks behind. King Henry saw him, black against the sun, upright, unhurrying, his very outline bitter dignity. He saw, and settled in the saddle, watched him approach, and thought, Now we shall see.

What Thomas saw was meadow, sky above, the oak tree with a crowd of horsemen standing by. He saw the shadow of a cloud pass smoothly through the field as though a hand passed over it, and his own shadow, darker, stretching out. The nimble insects shot up from his horse's feet as he moved through the grass and the field flowers, daisies, blood-red poppies, shook their heads. Was this a warning? He looked again and saw the king among his courtiers and reined his horse and stopped.

King Henry, watching, took a breath, then with a plunge broke forward from the crowd and spurred his horse to canter across the field. He doffed his cap as he came up to Thomas. He was the first to give the salutation. And he was smiling, smiling as a man smiles full of joy, untroubled, to see a dear old friend.

"Come, let us ride apart," he said.

They turned their horses and rode side by side till they were out of earshot. Then Henry said, the light of frankness and the shadow of contrition playing on his face: "Thomas, my archbishop. My friend." His voice was earnest. "Let us renew our ancient love for one another; let us smooth over all our differences; let us show each other all the good we can." Thomas sat a long time silent, looking at him, and he continued, but more painfully, more from the heart: "Come, I beseech you, show me honor in the sight of those who watch us from afar."

Still Thomas sat unmoving and Henry once again, as he had done when he first saw him, took a breath. "Thomas, what is it stands between us and the peace we both desire but, after all, a matter that can be cleared away by good faith and good actions on both sides. You have demanded that your properties be restored and that the crown make restitution for all you have lost. That is within my power. That I can do."

"The properties of Canterbury?" Thomas spoke at last. "And of those men whom you have exiled? All that the Church has lost?"

"All this," said Henry.

"And all the revenues from these lands that should have come in to the Church for these five—these nearly six years past?"

"All these."

"What of the depredations of your men, the farms burned and the houses left to ruin, the churches to dilapidation? What of the treasure stolen from the cathedral and the chattels stolen from the huts?"

"Name me the figure and it shall be paid."

"What of the honest men your officers have maimed? What of the widows left to starve? The child left fatherless? Can you pay me for these, my lord?"

"What can I say?" asked Henry patiently. "Only that you must come to them and be their comfort. You must return. You have my promise that you will stand as high with me as ever you did, and help me rule as you once did . . ." He put his hand out tentatively on the other's arm. "Thomas, I have been thinking that I may take the cross and go on pilgrimage, that I might leave my son under your care as I once did, and that you might command my kingdom for me while I am gone . . ."

At what price? Thomas thought. He felt the hand upon his arm and he was not convinced. Indeed, the words of warning he had written to the legates came to his mind: "Beware the king if he perceive he cannot frighten you with threats; then will he change like Proteus. Look with suspicion on him and whatever he may say, whatever shape he may put on . . ."

"You show a lack of caution," he said stiffly, "to speak of the young king, since you have had him crowned in bold defiance of my rights."

King Henry looked surprised. "I had not supposed it to be an invasion of your rights to have my own son crowned by whom I pleased. William the Conqueror was crowned by York. And my grandfather Henry was anointed by the Bishop of Hereford. There was no slight intended to the Canterbury privilege."

Now Thomas smiled a little with his lips turned down. "There was no bishop on the throne of Canterbury when King William was anointed. Archbishop Anselm was in exile when Hereford crowned Henry—and on his return, my lord, if you remember, the king asked that he be crowned again, by Canterbury, as it was Canterbury's ancient right."

King Henry brightened. "And so shall you, when you return! We will have a second, final coronation. You shall anoint your foster son—he asks for you, Tom. He wept that it was not your hand that held the crown before."

Could this be so? It touched his heart to think that it might be.

"You are changed, my lord," said Thomas doubtfully.

"Aye, Thomas, I am changed."

"Then you may prove it." That small smile again.

"What, do you doubt me?"

He waited for an answer but he let the silence pass.

"My lord," said Thomas, "I have the papers with me, and the papal sanction, to excommunicate those bishops who have counseled you against me and who took part in that false coronation. Have I permission to deliver these just punishments?"

Now Henry stiffened. Now would come the truth.

"My lord Archbishop," he said soberly, "how can you punish men who acted on my orders, and yet not punish me?"

"You say you did not know that you were violating Canterbury's rights. They knew. York knew, and London knew, and all the rest. They knew that they usurped my privilege and, more than that, ignored the dictates of the pope. This is a matter for the Church, my lord, for these are Churchmen who have defied the Church."

There was a stubbornness in Henry now. The softly smiling look had gone, and Thomas noted it.

"The pope had sanctioned York . . . some long time past . . ." the king broke off. Again contrition and humility took over. "No. You are right. They played me false, and you have my permission . . . yes. The Church must deal in churchly matters . . . As you say . . ."

Thomas felt a flood of gratitude, and yet he checked himself. "My son," he said, "then tell me that you understand me, truly, in your heart, that it is not for kings to judge in matters of the Church. For kings, as I have written you before, are granted all their power through the Church. They are but laymen, though they be exalted, and they may not judge nor touch God's children of the Church. I speak to you as father to his son, not to admonish but to bring you to the truth. Do you hear me, my son?"

Never a twinge crossed Henry's face, whatever boiled beneath. His voice, though, broke and faltered as he formed the words, "I understand you, Father, what you say."

"So that as father of the Church in England it is my right and duty to punish disobedience to the Church? But as your loyal minister I ask permission to proceed? You understand this?"

"Aye," Henry nodded. He could speak no more.

Thomas looked long and closely at him. Yes, he had changed. Never before had he worn such a look—humility and heartfelt suffering. Thank God who brings an end to strife! Peace and return to home and friendship with the king again, a softened and a chastised king. God's rule in England!

He dismounted and would have gone down on his knees before the king, but Henry jumped down quickly and raised him up.

"No, do not kneel to me, my lord Archbishop. You are my father; I your son. You are my chosen friend, as in old times." He moved to Thomas' horse and held the stirrup as he said, "You shall be king in England now . . ."

What words? What echo of what other words? What act, what sign, was this, to hold the stirrup for him as for a king indeed?

Thomas stopped, frozen, in the field. He means me to stand ready in his place, he thought. He is afraid of his old gods and of the people, should they demand his death. He has learned nothing from me, and he would trick me into this, and hold me to it. How many times has he done this to me—tricked me and held me at his mercy? How many of his traps I have stepped into? But I am older now. Yes, I am old.

He looked away. Far off he saw the courtiers waiting by the tree, saw in his mind's eye those other waiting watchers outside Northampton long ago. Not this time. Not again, he thought.

He looked at Henry stooped before him, waiting so tense to see what he would do. He did not say a word until he put his foot into the stirrup and rose up. Then he looked down at Henry's upturned face. "Not king, my son," he said. "Not king. But archbishop."

The conference was over. Peace was at hand. And yet no word had been said of the Constitutions, no oath exacted. And when the two had ridden back together to the waiting crowd, and some suggested that the king bestow the kiss of peace, binding them both to all that had been said, Henry explained that in a fit of rage he once had sworn never to kiss the archbishop again. He could not go back on his oath.

They could absolve him; there were bishops here who could absolve him of that oath!

But Henry smiled and said he would be willing, eager, to kiss the archbishop—upon his hand, his foot, his mouth, a hundred times—only that now it might appear coerced; let it be done in England, in his own domain, where it would have the grace of being voluntary. That he would do.

Thomas, listening, nodded wordlessly. He had no strength left for another fight.

They met once more. Thomas had taken leave of Louis, and of the home that he had made at Sens and gone into his chapel for the last time and prayed soberly. He did not hope to hear again that he was loved, and he did not. Then with his few clerks he rode into Normandy, seeking a meeting with the king, perhaps the kiss of peace to reassure against the doubts that weighed on him. But Henry was elusive, for five months avoided him. And when at last was trapped into a confrontation, explained that though he hoped—had even promised? had he promised?—to return to England with the archbishop and show the world that they were of one heart again, he could not do it. He was obliged to go to Auvergne where there was trouble among his underlords. He would send someone else to escort Thomas. He had already sent instructions to the young king to make the restitutions he had promised. They would see each other later; all would be well.

He looked at Thomas quickly, looked away. This man before him, grown so gaunt, so dull, what was he to him now? Even his eyes were dull. Old Thomas, all the fire gone. I cannot use him, Henry thought. He is not what I took him for. He is too stubborn. He has been selfish with me. Though I gave him my heart, he never offered to lay down his life for me, although my lowest page would do as much. He knew I wanted this of him but he would never understand me—although he understood me well enough. He knows.

And here he comes to ask me to raise him up once more and go with him to England as though he were my friend. Doesn't he know he's nothing to me now? Let him go back to England if he wants to, and be quiet there. He can do me no harm as long as he's away from Louis and the pope. And if he tries, why he will be there in my own domain where I can handle him.

He would have said goodbye then, but Thomas standing somberly before him made no move.

"Why are you sad?" he burst out nervously.

"My heart tells me," said Thomas, "that I shall see you no more in this life."

Then Henry flushed. "You take me for a traitor?"

But Thomas shook his head. He dared not stir the embers of their quarrel any more. "That thought is far from me, my lord. Absit."

He did not look into his eyes again, though, and he did not smile. And Henry, searching in his mind for words, found none. He coughed and then he turned away, and Thomas likewise turned away, and in a little while the distance grew between them and they had parted.

CHAPTER XXV

THOMAS EMBARKED FROM Witsand on December first —not, as the king had promised, as a partner in his realm, not with a noble escort. He went alone in a small boat, a handful of his clerks beside him, and for his sole protection the primatial cross raised on the figurehead.

The man whom Henry had sent to escort him was John of Oxford—a man whom he had excommunicated twice, who twice mocked at his sentence and the Church, twice was absolved. The money that the king had promised him to pay his debts and to provide a fleet had not arrived. Even more ominous was the news that while he waited, hesitating, at Witsand, the bishops of York and London were preparing to embark for Normandy to claim the king's protection against the threatened censures. And furthermore—so said the messenger—he saw the cliffs near Dover studded with armed men.

"Then I shall go to Sandwich," Thomas said.

He could not turn back now. To what? Again to lean on Louis? Again to plead before the Curia? He would go on. But he would send his thunderbolts before; then should he fall into the hands of soldiers, they would not find his instruments of power. So, as before, he gave the letters to a bold messenger and as before they were delivered and the bearer disappeared. The prelates raised an outcry and the soldiers searched the town. But as before, no trace of him was found, and word came safely back to Thomas that the deed was done.

So he embarked, and set his eyes for England. It was six years since he had crossed these waters in his flight. And though he had fought bitterly, with all his strength, he did not know if he would come again to his home land as he had left it, destitute. And though he had the king's word for his safety, he did not know, he did not know, if that would hold.

The little boat came sliding on the waves as they came round the wide chalk wings that formed the bay and saw the marshy lowland of Sandwich landing place. What was that crowd upon the shore? The little figures moving in the mist. Why were those horsemen on the rise behind? Who waited for him there?

Thomas stood in the boat. He saw the people run along the beach. He saw, as he came gliding forward, that some waded in the surf. The foremost came on toward him, arms held high, the water rising, splashing at their belts. They reached him, hands upon the gunwales, faces raised. He heard their shouting: "He has come!" "It is the archbishop!" And from the beach the cry of those who waited. "Blessed is he!"

The boat ran forward with the waves, came grating to a pause. Thomas leaped out. He felt the land of England hard and wet beneath his feet and saw his people kneel before him where the waves washed in, down on their knees in the dark pebbly sand. He blessed them as he walked among them and they reached out to touch his robe. The women crawled upon their knees after his footsteps, crying, "Blessed is he who cometh in the name of the Lord!"

The horsemen stood apart, upon the rise before the Sandwich gates. With narrow eyes they watched the crowd below, they heard the shrill cries, "Blessed is he!" Ranulf de Broc's hand twitched upon the rein. The others cautioned him. They had come up from Dover in time to witness this, but not to clear the place and shut the people up within their homes. They were not armed, and here in the archbishop's town, among his folk, they did not feel so certain of their strength as they had felt at Dover and they waited, frowning at the scene.

When Thomas reached them, Ranulf moved his horse. He blocked his path. The mob pressed up around them and spread out. They numbered in the hundreds. Ranulf paused.

The Sheriff of Kent moved forward and bid Thomas welcome in a grudging voice. He asked, then, if there were any foreign clerks among the primate's train, for they must take the oath of fealty while they were in the realm. But Thomas answered, just as grudging, that there were none, and furthermore a Churchman owed no oath.

The sheriff grunted and then asked him what his meaning was in excommunicating the king's prelates without the king's consent. Was it that he defied the king?

"Not so," said Thomas, "I have the king's consent."

The barons stared at one another. Should they laugh? What answer was there to so monstrous a lie? But Thomas, looking up at them, said that he did not wish to hold a further parley here. If they would speak to him, they might come to his palace when he had settled there.

Again they looked at one another, looked at Thomas, at the silent crowd. Then Ranulf wheeled his horse. "That we shall see!" he said. They rode away.

Thomas spent the night in Sandwich and the next day said Mass at dawn and blessed the people and then left the town. The sky had cleared. The fields were blurred with frost. The road to Canterbury dipped and rose, dipped and rose, across the little hills, the fields. On every hill there stood a village and a church. At every church the people waited and knelt for his blessing, spread their cloaks before him and brought winter leaves and strewed them in his way.

The little journey took him all day long and it was dusk when he rode up St. Martin's hill and saw the city and the dark bulk of his cathedral. Here he dismounted and thanked God and went on foot down through the city gates and through the shouting multitudes. On every church the bells were clamoring, and in the flare of torches, banners and green garlands flickered in the light. The trumpets blared to greet him at the monastery gates; in the cathedral the monks' choir chanted hymns of praise.

The brothers met him at the western door. They turned and went before him down the nave, triumphant progress through the glow of candles, scent of incense, sound of plainsong filling all the church. Thomas walked on, uplifted, till he mounted to the altar and lay flat upon his face. He kissed the stones. Then he rose up and went to his primatial throne and there the monks came to him one by one to ask his blessing and to receive the kiss of peace. And only then did he observe that Prior Odo was not there, and only then remembered that he had got but small and grudging help from Christchurch through all his years of paupery in France.

He looked more closely at the brothers in the stalls and saw that though some wept to see him and displayed their love, others sat silent with closed faces. They were the prior's men.

That night he feasted in the cellarer's hall and after that the people were let in to the cathedral and he preached to them and spoke to them upon the text, "Here we have no continuing city but seek one to come." Hearing the words they made a noise of sighing, as though a wind blew through a tree. For theirs had been a city of desolation for six years and they were crushed by Satan's hoof. They dreamed now of that City and of one who would go on before them and prepare the way.

At last he left them and went from the church, across the windy courtyard, to his palace. It was bare. The hall was cold and dirty straw lay scuffled on the floor. No stores had been laid in, no candles put into the sconces, no fires laid. His inner room had been ransacked. His books, his plate were gone. He went from room to barren room and outside once again. The barns and byres were empty and the gardens desolate. Ranulf de Broc had left behind him ruin and bare fields.

For six years the land had been harried and the people fatherless. On little manor farms and in the villages the villeins feared their lord, for he demanded all their livelihood and sent his soldiers down upon them, and in his court their voices were not heard. And should an old man plead to go into the forest for winter fuel, then he was mocked, his house set fire that he might warm himself. Or should a young man curse them, then his tongue was cut out so he could curse no more. Or should a young girl, running furtively along the path, be caught, then she was seen no more until they found her face down in the waterweeds—or never found, although the mother went on calling down the lanes.

There was no solace. There was no warming fire in the cold. Only the wind made answer to the trembling prayer. In Harbledown the priest dreamed of a horned man. In Burgate Church a worm was found coiled like a serpent in the sacred host. The priest at Godmersham took up his scrying bowl and polished it, anointed it, saying the secret words, and called the boy in so that he might scry, and asked him what the future showed him, what he saw. The shadows in the bowl, the moving shapes, were clear. He saw a crown, a tree, a knife. What was to come?

At Certeham there was no priest. The church doors stood ajar, the leaves blew in. The mice made nests behind the altar and birds roosted in the beams. Almon had gone to Hortone, still with his lips sealed up. The villeins thought that God was with him, for his fame was known, and asked him what these portents meant, what was to come? He eyed them mildly and put his fingers on his lips. He could not say.

The reeve was gone from Hortone, dead. Five others had run off. They lived as outlaws in the forest now, hunting the king's deer, hunted in their turn. Old men, old women, children, worked the Hortone fields. Wulviva worked beside them like ten men. But though she hid the grain beneath the flooring of the barn and drove the cow into the thicket and hid the pig behind the curtains of her bed, the soldiers found all she had hidden, and the winter came on cold. She took her son and barred the door, driving the nails in fast, and turned her back upon the manor and went down the road, taking her son to Canterbury to live there.

In Elured's house Hawisa's demon took up half the room. He was not large—no larger than a cat, a small dog, or a hyena say. More like a toad. He did not run about. He squatted in the corner, waiting, yet he filled half the room. Hawisa made them move the washing tub and all the crocks, and put the bench that Viel slept on next to the door.

Hawisa watched him from her bed, transfixed him with her eyes, and kept him down. And if someone went near him, forgetting he was there, Hawisa screamed, for then he smiled and drew his lids across his eyes and squatted lower, shifting, making ready for his spring.

Walter tried to comfort her: the archbishop had come home, would bring them God's protection once again, would bless them all, would exorcise her demon . . .

Hawisa screamed. Her demon moved. His toes clicked on the floor. He shivered, prancing in his place, then he crouched down again. He squatted, smiling, swallowing, working his swelling throat until he brought up something dark. He licked it down again. He grinned and watched Hawisa with attentive stony eyes. Then he sat up, sat back, and strained, and pursed his lips. And suddenly the blood came spouting from his pointed mouth.

Some people who read portents thought they knew what was to come. The scrying boy had seen a knife, the moon had worn a crown, the archbishop had stumbled when he reached the altar stone, and now the housewife, Hawisa—sh of the fairy strain—had seen the black blood dripping and falling on the ground.

* * *

Ranulf de Broc, the sheriff, clerks from the excommunicated bishops, came to the palace to see the archbishop. He met them in his devastated hall so that they all might see how the king's promises of restitution had been carried out, but they were blind to everything except their cause. The clerks spoke out reprovingly, quoting their bishops, saying how they had waited to receive him back with honor, and in return he covered them with shame; how he had come with fire and sword, inflicting censures without cause or warning, when all they longed for in their hearts, all that they sought, was peace.

"I know your masters," Thomas said. "I know what's in their hearts. When has it been that Roger has not thirsted for my blood?"

"Is it a thirst for blood, my lord, to crown the young king at the king's command? Is it bloodthirsty to be loyal to the king?"

"They know the reason for their sentences."

"What reason, my lord Archbishop? What reason can there be to punish men who carry out the wishes of the king, who honor the young king, do no disservice to the Church? We ask you to remove these censures and cease your plotting . . ."

"I do not plot," roared Thomas. "Nor is it in my power to absolve, when it was by the order of the pope himself that they are excommunicate. Let them seek absolution from the pope—unless they dare not go against the 'customs of the land' to seek their peace with God."

"You sneer, my lord. But all your words are written in our hearts."

"Let them be written! I do not fear your threats. It is no disloyalty to the king to punish men who break the pope's command. Nay, I go farther. Because I love the young king as my son, and honor him, and say no word against his coronation except that it was basely and not honorably done, I will myself suspend the sentences provided that the guilty ones swear to obey the pope's commands in all they do, and bind themselves by oath."

"This can they not do. You know well that such oaths would go against the custom!"

"Then can I not absolve them, and go against the Church."

"Then you shall suffer for it."

"You do not know the meaning of the word as I have felt it! Go tell my brothers that I do not fear their threats."

"Aye, we will tell them, all that you have said. And the young king, as well, that you proclaim him basely crowned!"

"Then you will lie!"

"We heard your words."

"Get out!"

"Why heap such fuel upon the fire when it is smoldering at your own door?" The voice was dry, and Thomas turned and saw John standing next to him, as he stood throughout. "Calm words would have done better," he went on. "If they came seeking peace, then you were foolish to deny them. If they came to provoke, they have succeeded."

Thomas closed his eyes a moment, let out a breath, and nodded. "I know, I know," he said.

"Contrition will not help you. They will go to the young king now."

"I know," said Thomas once again. He looked at John, his calm returning. "So will I also go."

The journey toward the young king's court in Winchester took a strange character. At every crossroads, at every hamlet, church or hospital the people ran to kneel before him and thrust their children out. He halted and dismounted every time, to bless them and confirm the children, and when he started on always a few more followed him along the open road.

At Rochester the townfolk cheered him and crowded in the streets and rang their bells and hung bright blankets out their windows and strewed winter greens. Bishop Walter, his old friend, wept when he saw him and knelt down and asked his blessing and rose up and kissed him and bid him welcome always in this town. No other man of rank appeared, however, and the castle gates were shut, and as he went on northward he observed that every stronghold, every great manor house, was closed and barred.

Still his procession swelled and lengthened. As he passed by, men dropped what they were doing and ran after it, crying hosanna, weeping as they ran. At London he was met three miles outside the gates. A great procession gathered there, three thousand clerks and scholars from the London schools, who gave a great shout when they saw him and turned and went before him toward the town, chanting the *Te Deum* all the way.

Thus he came into Southwark, with music in the streets. But not one man of dignity or any rank came out to welcome him—only old fearless Henry, Bishop of Winchester, came forward and showed him honor and took him to his palace and brought him in.

The young king's guardians read rebellion into this. Thomas had sent an embassy to the court to ask permission to come himself and bring his dear son gifts and kneel before him and explain such matters as might trouble him, but they were turned away. Now came the word to Southwark, stern command, that as the archbishop had broken the king's peace he should proceed no farther, nor enter any of the royal towns or castles, but return to his own diocese without delay and there restrain himself from further curses on the king's lords or further rioting among his folk.

Thomas stared hard into the faces of the messengers. "Who speaks thus?" he demanded. "Is it my Henry who would drive the shepherd off so that the wolf may tear the flock? Is it indeed my son?"

But for an answer he was told that they had come here to deliver the commands, not to dispute them, and they left.

Then Thomas said to Bishop Henry, "I will not go. Until I hear the king's commands in his own words, with his own voice, they shall not drive me off." And he sent secretly to the Earl of Cornwall begging him to speak for him at the court. But Cornwall answered him in cryptic words: "Look to yourself. I see wild work in England before the new year comes."

Then Thomas sought another path. He went to Harrow and there called the Abbot of St. Albans and that venerable man himself went to the court. But he was turned away with threats and came to Thomas hastily, saying, "My lord, take warning, for their bows are bent."

Circling in the narrowing circle, Thomas turned again and went to London, but he did not venture through the gates. He met the people flocking to him in the ward of Farringdon Without, there by the Church of St. Bartholomew where in his boyhood he had thought God lived. The people cheered him and their shouting raised the birds. But all the while a madwoman cried out, her shrieking voice above all other voices: "Archbishop, beware the knife! Beware, beware, the knife!" And Thomas shuddered, for he knew that madness cloaks the truth.

He turned, then, from his circling and rode home.

He came to Christchurch on the eve of Christmas and again learned how the de Brocs had kept King Henry's promise to restore his lands: they robbed the ships that brought him wine from France and seized the sailors and imprisoned them; they ambushed his supply trains on the roads; they mutilated sumpter horses, stole his hounds, hunted within his forest lands and killed his deer; and in the lanes and on the highways, everywhere, they sought his people out and threatened them, and beat them, and spread terror where they went.

On Christmas Day he preached a sermon. "Peace on earth, to men of good-will . . ." but as for others, for them was no peace. For those who steal the Church's goods, usurp the Church's rights, for those who murder—and there have been murderers of archbishops before—there is the wrath of God. Then once again he cursed the bishops who crowned the young king, cursed the barons and the courtiers who were his enemies, and for the third time excommunicated Ranulf de Broc.

When afterward his sane advisers, Robert and John, reproved him for inflammatory words, he shook his head. "If they encompass me about, to kill me, then will I stand and fight," he said. "I have not acquiesced."

On that same day that Thomas rode from London toward Christchurch, the bishops Roger and Gilbert Foliot, straight from a secret visit to the young king's court, set sail for Normandy to seek King Henry and make report. They met him on the road, on Christmas Eve, as he came riding, weary from the rebellion in Auvergne to make his winter court in Bures. Stories had reached him of the censures, of what transpired in England, but they were sketchy: hasty messages delivered in the field. Now came the full blow while he sat, cold, unprepared, upon his horse.

They did not need to speak. He saw them and he knew what they would say. Therefore, he told them he would hear them later, and they rode on. The harness jingled and the early stars blinked through the winter twigs; the horses' hoofs struck sparks when they rode, grimly silent, into the castle court.

The hall was blazing. Green boughs decked the walls. The smell of fir, the smell of spices and of scented women's silks hung warm upon the air. The parti-colored robes of courtiers flashed by. Queen Eleanor had summoned her trouvères and there was singing to the lute, and laughter—till the king came in. He walked among them, glowering, spoke to those barons whom he wanted, then walked out again. He left a wake of cold resentment and some silent smiles among the courtiers around the queen.

In the small hall above, his private chamber, the king sat and the bishops stood beside him. The barons squatted on the floor or leaned against the walls. Some crowded in the doorway and peered in. Sir Reginald Fitz Urse stood thus in the door. He had come up from Auvergne with the king. He knew what was to come.

King Henry spoke: "Now, my lord Bishops, tell us what you know."

"My lord King and my lords," said Foliot, "we have been censured by the archbishop because we took part in the crowning of the young king."

Henry said nothing and the barons nodded. This was known to them.

"My lords," persisted Foliot. "All men who took part in the coronation—not only Churchmen, but all men—fall under his anathema. He threatens all."

"Aye," Henry flashed a bitter smile. "That we have also heard." The barons watched their king and waited.

Then Roger spoke. "My lord King, this you have not heard. He goes about your kingdom with armed men, a rabble army following. Three thousand marched with him on London, and only through God's grace, and by the foresight of your loyal wardens, was he stopped. Three times he sent ambassadors to Winchester to threaten the young king, and would have ridden there himself, up to the very throne, had not his armies clashed with yours and he fell back."

"God's wounds!" said Henry, jerking his head up. "Would he be king?" He pictured in his mind the scene as Roger told it and saw Thomas riding through his lands as he had seen him in Toulouse, thirsting for power and with devastation in his wake. Was this the truth? Or was it something else. He saw again the broken Thomas as he had seen him last, and heard the parting words, "I shall not see you any more in life." What was he after, martyrdom? Did the people think the time was now and was he making his processional before them?

"What does he wear? Does he go crowned?" he asked.

But Foliot mistook him. "He seeks the young king's crown," he said, "because he claims the privilege of crowning for himself."

"What do the people say who follow him?"

Gilbert was silent, bringing his thoughts around. But Roger moved in closer to the king. He stood behind his shoulder and spoke softly, for his ear. "They cry hosanna, and say 'Blessed is he . . .' "

"They do?" cried Henry, twisting round and staring up at him. "They do?" But Roger turned his eyes away. This was uneasy ground.

"My lord, he tried to bribe the Earl of Cornwall to join him and he has made alliance with powerful Churchmen; Winchester and the Abbot of St. Albans. Rochester is on his side . . ."

It is rebellion, then, thought Henry. Why should I ever think that he would be on my side, act in my interests, follow my will? A common villein, base born, treacherous.

Aloud he said. "It is rebellion! What shall we do with him, my lords?"

Then some cried that the young king should arrest him, that he should be put in chains, some that he should be brought to Normandy, some shouted exile, some answered that the Tower was the safest place, till all were arguing, drowning each other out. Fitz Urse stood in the doorway, watching the king.

Bishop Foliot put his hands up and pled for silence, saying, "My lords, my lords, do not take this upon yourselves. He is your archbishop. Appeal once more to Rome. The pope will see him now, at last, for what he really is. He will relieve us of him without violence."

Henry leaned forward in his chair, his fist upon the arms. He turned his face around to Foliot. "So say you, Gilbert." Then he turned farther, crouching, twisting round. "You, Roger, what do you advise?"

Seeing him turn from them, the barons paused, and Roger's answer, soft and smooth, lay on their silence like a film of oil. "Such things are not for me to say, my lord. Ask of your barons. But I know this: that there will be no peace within your kingdom so long as Thomas lives."

Henry sprang up and stood hunched forward, legs far apart, fists working, and his face grown red. "I shall have peace. I shall have peace," he growled, "despite him."

He looked with fury at his barons, one by one. "Who will bring the traitor back to me, for I shall have him!"

They saw his rage had come upon him and were silent. "Who will rid me of him?" He glared at them. Then savagely he burst out: "What kind of cowards have I all about me? What kind of men, who live upon my bread, who lean on me—and who stand silent while a villein comes into my court and climbs upon my throne?"

Roger stood behind him and looked out upon the crowd.

His eye caught Reginald Fitz Urse' and he nodded. Fitz Urse looked at him steadily a moment. Then he drew back from the door. Three others turned and slipped out, following him, and made their way down the dark passage to the turret stair.

They heard the king's voice, rising, echoing, the words distorted as they hit against the walls: "He came into my court on a lame sumpter mule. All that he had he carried on his back. I raised him up. I made him what he is. And he grew fat on all my favors and would now be king . . ."

They paused upon the stair and held their breath. They heard the growling of the barons' answers, heard Henry's voice: "Is there no man among you?" echoing. "Is there no man? Is there no one who will deliver me from this foul priest?"

Silent, they pushed against each other and hurried down. The light poured from the hall, the music, laughter. They crept along the wall and found the dungeon stairs and went on down. They found their armor and their swords; they roused the guard. And to the jingling of his keys, the grate of hinge, they stepped outside. The night was black, the frost crunched under foot, and from above they heard the muffled voices in the upper room. Their scabbards clanked against their shields as they ran heavily, clutching their armor, to the stable shed.

They separated at the coast, Fitz Urse and Richard Brito found a merchant ship bound for the port of Dover. Hugh de Morville and William Tracy embarked for Winchelsea.

"Where shall we meet?" they asked.

"At Saltwood," Fitz Urse said. "Ranulf de Broc still holds the castle there and he has soldiers. God give you speed."

They nodded.

A cold wind blew against their hearts. The decks were wet. The earth was wet when they stepped onto land. The sky was low. They rode to Saltwood in a rising wind and saw the castle crouched against its hill, blurred in the first dark drops of rain.

De Broc was hearty but they had few words for him. They sat together in the dimness of the hall, around a barren table, while the darkness fell. It was the night of Holy Innocents.

A single candle lit their faces and threw shadows in their eyes.

Fitz Urse said, "If he will not answer all the king's demands . . ."

But Hugh de Morville broke in saying, "We will shed no blood."

Then Tracy said, "If there is blood, it is upon his head."

And Brito laughed. It was a high, queer note, and Ranulf, hearing it, moved up to them and brought them wine, and clapped the Breton on the shoulder and kept his hand there, heavy on his neck.

Fitz Urse said, "We will give him warning. He will have the choice." He saw the agony in Morville's eyes. He reached his hand and cupped it on the candle and the light was quenched. Then in the darkness he continued: "Let the choice be his. He may absolve the bishops and lift his threats, he may go down upon his knees, and come with us to Bures Castle and let the king decide. Or he may feel the royal power as we deal it. Let him decide."

Morville's heavy voice said, "He is archbishop."

Fitz Urse's voice answered, "But he would be king."

Thomas stood by the window of his inner room. The wind swept winter leaves across the garden, rose, and broke against the Christchurch walls. He watched a swirl of birds fly out around the turrets and sweep the sky and circle, struggling to come back again.

He had sent Herbert Bosham to King Louis but he knew there was not time. "How long, do you suppose," he said, "would it take me, this weather, to ride to the coast?"

John stood behind him. Robert was also in the room. He did not wait to hear them answer but turned to them, smiling, and said, "No, I will not go."

Still he stood by the window, and he could hear the ivy twigs that clung beside it flutter and tap in agitation against the stones. He felt their agitation in his breast, as he had felt it, mounting, all month long. He knew what was expected of him. "What was to come?" they asked.

What was to come? The year was dying and the world grew dark. How build the fires up and bring the warmth, the sun, to the cold hearth? Wherewith to build it while the hunters' dogs ran with their jaws hung open along the forest edge? The old year dying, and the broken fields lay trampled, without seed. How give it life to bloom again when all the bins were empty and the field mouse starved within the crib? With what to nourish it and give it life?

What was to come, they asked. More of the chase, the starving poacher racing in the open field, the yelping and the shouts behind? More of the hiding in the millhouse, trapped, the sound of grinding stopped, the footsteps close?

More of the demon, squatting, waiting by the bed? More of the fear of dying? More of the fear of death?

What was there could bring life again, and light, and the seed sprouting, and the hope that death would die? Who was to come?

He knew what was expected of him; he knew King Henry's thoughts.

"I will not go," he said. "This is my place and I will not desert my church again."

"You know," John's voice was dry, "that four knights came to Saltwood yesterday?"

"I know."

"And do you know," asked Robert quietly, "that evil stalks you—far more dangerous than four armed men? That your God is a jealous God? That no man come unto the Father but by Christ?"

Thomas went to him and said, "Yes, I know."

"And you will not be tempted?" Robert asked. He raised his face. "You see the suffering and hear their cries and you will not be tempted to take their sins on you?"

"No," Thomas said. He paused. "They are my sheep and I will guard them. I left them for too long. But I will not desert my God."

"He will protect you," Robert said.

It was a wonder, though, thought Thomas wearily, that God gave him no sign, no comfort, did not speak.

"Nevertheless," said Robert, reading him, "not our will, but His will be done."

Two men stood in the doorway, peering to see if they were welcome, and Thomas turned and saw that they were Osbert his chamberlain with the monk Edward Grim of Cambridge, come on a visit to the archbishop's court. It was his habit to receive such visitors, with his own chosen clerks, for conversation after dinner, and he welcomed them.

"What was the noise within the hall?" asked John.

"Some knights have come, and though the servingmen are finishing their meal, I bid them stay and eat. Have I done right?" asked Osbert.

"Aye, make them welcome," Thomas said.

Now yet another clerk stood in the door, William Fitzstephen who had returned to Thomas when he came to London and stayed with him though he smelled the danger in the air. "My lord, four knights of Henry's court have come. They will not stop to eat. They ask for you."

"I have said that they are welcome," Thomas said. "Come in and let us talk."

He sat upon the bed, by Robert, and the others grouped around. "Robert has said to me," he said, " 'Not my will but Thy will be done.' Let us concern ourselves with this. How shall we know the will of God?"

"Through faith," said the monk Grim. "For therein is the righteousness of God revealed, from faith to faith: as it is written, The just shall live by faith."

The four knights came into the room, said nothing, but scooped up the straw that lay upon the floor and sat down on it and fixed their eyes on Thomas. He did not look at them.

"How, then, does faith reveal His will to us?" he asked.

Osbert answered that he spoke to us out of the mouths of his holy prophets, but the monk answered that "the invisible things of God . . . His will . . ." He turned around to glance across his shoulder, some several times, as he continued, hesitating, ". . . are clearly seen, and understood by us through the things that are made . . ."

Now Thomas turned and looked at the four knights. "Benedicite," he said quietly.

They did not answer and Thomas spoke their names. All but the Breton had been his sworn men when he was chancellor. "Hugh de Morville, William . . ." He would have gone on but Fitz Urse broke in.

"God help you."

Thomas said no more. They stared a long time at each other until Fitz Urse spoke again. He was their spokesman and his speech was well prepared. "We come from the court of the king," he said, "beyond the sea. We bring you word from him. Listen to what the king says. When peace was made he put aside all his complaints against you. He let you come back to your see as you desired, a free man. Now you have broken the treaty. You have added contempt to your other crimes. You censure those who crowned the young king, though it was done at the king's own command. You make it plain that if you could you would take the young king's crown from him."

Now Thomas rose. Fitz Urse went on: "Your plots and scheming are notorious to all. Say then"—he put his hand up—"will you go with us to the king and there defend yourself—if you can do it?"

"How can you say it?" Thomas cried. "I love the young king and never wished him any hurt."

"You go about the country with great troops of men . . ."

"Not troops! The people come. And if my followers rejoice to see me after so long an absence, there is no harm in that. What does the king complain of here? As for the bishops, if they wish absolution they must ask the pope. It was on the pope's authority that they were excommunicated, not on mine. They know that. And the king knows too. He gave me leave to punish them."

"Say that again, what you are saying," Fitz Urse growled. "Do you call the king a traitor? Do you charge him with such monstrous treachery as to allow you to excommunicate the men who crowned his son? Is that what you are saying, treachery?"

"Reginald," breathed Thomas. "Do not slander me. I did not charge the king with treachery. But many prelates, nobles, monks—hundreds of watchers—heard us make agreement. You yourself were there."

"I was not there! I never heard so false agreement made."

"God knows. I know I saw you there."

Fitz Urse sprang up. "You call me liar and the king a traitor! How much are we to bear? Will you come with us now and make submission to the king for all your crimes?"

"I will not come with you."

"The king commands it!"

"That I doubt!"

John stood beside him murmuring, "Go carefully! You tempt them. Ask to speak privately with each one in turn." But Thomas would not stop.

"And even if the king commands it, I will not go. I will not put the sea between myself and my defenseless people ever again. Unless you drag me by the feet, I will not go!"

Fitz Urse had taken off his gloves and flung them on the floor. There was such roaring in the room—the barons shouting and the sharp exclamations of the clerks—that no one heard his words.

Morville, slow to anger, still squatted heavily upon the straw. He put his hand on Fitz Urse's knee, and Reginald stopped, looked down. The others paused. Morville spoke deliberately, calm in the midst of quarrel. "I do not speak of crimes and accusations. My lord, I speak of fealty. Do you not hold your offices, all that you are and have, at the king's pleasure, from the king? Are you not sworn to him?"

Thomas stared at him, straight into his eyes. "The temporalities, yes. The temporalities of my office I hold from the king." He knew that Robert watched him from behind. "The spiritualities I hold from God."

Now Morville rose, and Tracy also, and Brito, watching, got slowly to his feet. It was Fitz Urse who spoke. "Do you not own that you hold everything from the king? He chose you and he raised you up from nothing and made you what you are, and you are his?"

"I do not," Thomas said. "I owe my fealty and may be judged by God alone and by the pope, God's representative."

"Thomas, I hear you. You defy the king. And you will suffer . . ."

"Do not threaten me . . ."

"We will do more than threaten!"

"You owe me fealty. You are my vassal . . ."

"Then I renounce it, in the king's name. I owe you nothing. I am no more your man!" Fitz Urse swung around. "Guard him!" he shouted at the clerks. "Guard him, I charge you. Guard this man."

They stared at him as he moved slowly, backing toward the door. Morville and Tracy were already in the threshold and Brito in the hall.

"Do you think I would fly?" cried Thomas. "You will find me here!" He followed them and called out after them. "If you are ready, so am I, and I will fight you foot to foot in the Lord's battle. Come back here! Hugh, Hugh de Morville!" But they did not turn.

He dropped back, panting, and John came to him. "Why will you never be advised?" His smile was small. "What need was there for you, an archbishop, to get up from your seat and trade hot words with them? These men are lawless . . ."

Thomas shook his head. "I know what lies before me. I need no advice."

"Perhaps," said John. "God grant it turn out well."

Thomas said nothing more. He went back to his seat. The others all stood silent and the room grew dimmer as the daylight drained away. They heard the wind blow, and the crack of thunder, heavy rain upon the leaden roof. They heard the portal of the hall slam shut. Then they heard shouts outside. A monk rushed in.

"My lord, my lord, the knights are arming!"

"Let them arm."

"My lord, they have brought soldiers to the courtyard! The de Brocs are there! They have forced Brother Ernold to lace their hauberks! They took a hammer from the carpenter . . ."

"What matter, let them," Thomas said.

But now his clerks came round him, urging, "You cannot stay here. These men are drunk and lawless. Come into the church!"

"I said I would not flee."

"Come with us. They are murderers!" "Come to the sanctuary." "Make haste to the church."

He did not listen to them until Robert said, "It is the time for Vespers." And indeed they heard the bell. "It is your duty to attend the service of Our Lord. So come." And Thomas rose.

They went into the antechamber and out through the little window that served as a door. They heard a banging on the portals as they filed out. By a back way they came into the cloister, but here Thomas paused. "I cannot go without my crosier. It has been left behind."

"No. Hurry!" Someone pushed him. But he stood fast.

The monk, Grim, ran back to the inner room, snatched up the crosier and ran out again. Now they could hear a hammer against a boarded door.

"They have found a passage," Osbert breathed.

Fitzstephen nodded. "The de Brocs have learned the palace well!"

"For God's sake, hurry!"

Grim ran up. He walked in front of Thomas with the crosier and Thomas followed, slowly, as in processional. He heard the chanting of the monks come from the choir, and he tuned himself to that. The storm had come into the cloister; rain slanted in; a wind scooped down beneath the eaves and wet their faces and blew their garments wildly in the dark. The chanting faded and then rose again.

Voices behind them, and the splintering of wood.

"They found a ladder! They are through!"

They passed the chapter house. "This way, this way," hissed Osbert, and he ran ahead and pushed the transept door. Grim entered it and stumbled on the sill. Thomas stepped through. Then the procession, hastening, pushing, scrambled after him and Osbert closed the door.

The church was dark. Only the altar lights glowed in the choir, far away. Thomas, with Robert, crossed the transept and started up the steps. But then he heard the door close and the sound the bolt made sliding into place. He stopped.

"This is the house of God," he called. "Let all come in who will." And he went back again. The clerks stood huddled in the darkness, barring his way. "Out of the way, you cowards." He pushed them aside. "The church is not a fortress. Open the door."

He wrenched the bolt back and the door swung in. Some of his followers who had come, panting, late, pressed in the doorway and he pulled them through. Now he heard heavy running and he saw, as they came past the chapter house, the glint of mail. Four heavy figures. Four armed men.

The clerks pressed around him, pushing, whispering. "Hide in the darkness . . ." "Come into the crypt . . ." "Across the nave and out . . ."

He thrust them off him saying, "No! Where is my crosier?"

Grim stepped out.

"Then lead me to the altar, for we will serve God."

Again he crossed the transept, had his foot upon the stair.

A shout: "Where is the traitor!" Fitz Urse was through the door.

The clerks had fled. The monks had left their service and there was silence in the wavering dark.

"Where is the archbishop?"

Now Thomas turned. "Here am I. Not a traitor, but a priest of God. If you seek me, you find me here. What would you have?"

Morville called out into the darkness, "Flee! You are a dead man!"

"No, I will not flee." He came back down the steps toward them and facing them he put his back against the pillar and stood still. "I do not fear you. If you bring death, then in the Lord's name do I welcome it!"

They closed in toward him, groping in the dark. Behind them, Ranulf swung round to the open door. Some monks peered in. One scuttled past him, fleeing from the scene. Ranulf brought down his hammer and the man groaned and fell. Ranulf turned from him. "Guard all the doors!" he bellowed. "Guard the doors!"

Morville took his sword in hand and crossed the nave toward the south transept to keep the people back.

The three came on and Thomas saw the bulk of shoulders in the dark, a glimmer on the mail, the pointed helmets and the blur of white—their faces, cloven by the nasal guards. Robert stood by him, and the stranger, Grim, holding the crosier out and crying, "This is the house of God!"

They came on, crouching, arms held wide.

"This is your archbishop!"

"We know the man."

And Fitz Urse, very close, said, "Do not move. You are our prisoner."

And Tracy: "Come with us."

"I will not go. You can do here what you have come to do."

Fitz Urse sprang at him and clutched the pallium around his neck, and Tracy, crowding Grim, reached for his body to lift him off his feet. The monk cried once again, "This is a church!" But Thomas stood against the pillar and fought back. They would not drag him like a villein where they liked. He would not run behind their horses. He would not kneel to them.

He swore at Fitz Urse. "Take your hands off me! You are my vassal!" And he flung him back. He turned on Tracy, grappled, shook him with such force he fell back on the floor.

Fitz Urse came on again, not speaking, growling in his throat, and Thomas grated, "Reginald, you pimp, don't touch me. Take your hands off me!"

Fitz Urse crouched back and drew his sword: "Then have it! Strike!" he screamed. He swung his sword. It arched and whistled in the darkness, grazing Thomas' head, knocking his cap off, leaving his tonsure bare.

Tracy was up again, sword in both hands held high. "Then strike!" he shouted, and brought it down.

Grim held the crosier up to ward it off. It glanced along the shaft, sliced through his arm. Then bloodstained it descended on the tonsured head.

Thomas stood wounded, blood upon his face. He felt Grim drop beside him, felt him roll away. He heard the voice of Robert: "Father . . . Son . . ." And then no more.

This was his moment; he had chosen it. Not Henry. And he died for God. For God alone. No other way. He crossed his hands and bowed his wounded head. "Now am I ready to die for Christ, and for the Blessed Virgin, and for the Church . . ."

He saw the bloody sword come up again. Now was the time. "Into thy hands, O Lord . . ."

Fitz Urse struck first and Tracy after. He faltered to his knees. Brito ran up and struck him, struck him as he fell, a blow so savage that the iron sword broke off against the stones. "King's men!" he cried out. "Take that for the king!"

The others stood back panting. Now de Broc pushed through. He looked down at the body and nudged it with his foot. He put his heel upon the neck and thrust his sword point into the broken skull and scooped the brains out.

"He will not rise again!"

He swaggered as he walked away. He was so sure.

But when the knights had gone away, when all the church was still, the people came in, crowding at the doors, and crept up to the fallen body and knelt down. They kissed the feet. They wept. And while they wept they reached their hands out and touched the body, dipping their fingers into the healing blood.

EPILOGUE

THOMAS WAS MURDERED on December 29, 1170. Hawisa was the first to make his blood into a potion and drink it and get well. But many others knew the value of his death. They waited for it, and although he did not die for them, they profited. They put their faith in him. And if their faith was strong enough there happened to them something they could not explain. It was a miracle.

Such is the caprice of miracles that sometimes evil men experienced this flash of light, this change, this lifting of their sorrows or release from pain, while better men came to the tomb and prayed and went away again as they had come. It was a matter of belief, of purpose, of self-seeking maybe—the ability to concentrate upon one's self until the self is lost. Almon, for instance, who lived close to God, was never cured, just as St. Paul was not. Perhaps he had no need. Perhaps his faith had taken him on past the tomb and it was not important to him any more whether a miracle was worked for him. You will be glad to know he went back to his church and lived there happily and was much loved.

Thomas was murdered as the old year died. The new year came, the days grew lighter. Prior Odo watched from his retreat and saw the miracles increase and grow respectable. The Church was watching what the people did. Whenever in the years of man had those in power followed the common people's will? There was a miracle!

Just two years later and a little more—in Lent, 1173—Pope Alexander from his throne in Rome pronounced the canonization of St. Thomas, holy martyr of the Church.

Meanwhile, of course, the world went on much as it always had. Bishop Foliot fell ill (some people said that Thomas did it) but he got well again (it was a miracle) and in the summer of 1171 he was absolved. Roger's absolution came a little later, in December of that year. The four knights went to Knaresborough where Hugh de Morville had his castle and stayed hidden there a while. They were excommunicated but soon absolved and in a year or two they drifted back and took their place at court. Morville was reinstated as justiciary of Northumberland, and Tracy named that of Normandy. Fitz Urse went with the king to Ireland and stayed on there after he left, and founded a great family. They did not seem to suffer for their crime.

Henry it was who suffered. When he heard of Thomas' death he fell down on the floor and wept. He would not eat for several days and shut himself into his room for five long crucial weeks. His enemies made profit of the murder and of this time. King Louis was sincerely shocked. The young king raised his hands and cast his eyes to heaven and cried, "Oh, alas!" and then, "Thank God, it was not any of *my* men who had a share in it." An interdict was laid on all King Henry's continental lands, and when his emissaries at the papal court pronounced his name, the cardinals recoiled in horror, saying, "Forbear! forbear!"

In August he withdrew himself and went to Ireland, pausing in England long enough to go to Winchester to ask advice. Old Bishop Henry, down at last, was on his deathbed there.

In May, next year, he was recalled. The pope would hear him now. He met the cardinals at Avranches and there gave solemn oath for his perpetual obedience to Rome; promised to send two hundred knights into the Holy Land and go himself for three years if the pope should so command; renounced those of the Constitutions the pope objected to; and with his hand upon the Gospels swore that he had not desired Thomas' death, did not command it, and was grieved by it as if he had been his own son. On these conditions Henry was absolved.

And yet the world went hard against him. Louis was unappeased. All his old enemies arose. Queen Eleanor made plots against him and his sons rebelled. They circled him, attacking, nipping, drawing back. The King of Scots came down across his border and the young king, crying vengeance for the martyr saint, massed a great warfleet on the Flemish coast.

Midsummer of 1174, Henry came back to England. He went from Southampton straight to the lepers' church at Harbledown and there put off his clothes and put on sackcloth and a pilgrim's cloak and went barefooted down the hill to Christchurch. He followed Thomas' footsteps, through the cloister, through the transept door. He knelt down by the pillar and kissed the stones. He went into the crypt, went to the place where Thomas lay, and there he flung himself upon the ground and wept. All the community was watching him. He rose and flung his cloak off and knelt down and leaned his head upon the tomb, and every prelate of the crowd around him took up a scourge and whipped him five times on the back, and then each of the eighty monks of Christchurch filed behind him and struck him three times more. And after that he took his cloak again and sat upon the floor and there remained all through the day, all night, till morning came. What he said then to Thomas, I do not know.

Thomas was dead, and many people profited. Brother Benedict fared well; while still quite young he was elected Abbot of Peterborough. Odo fared not so well; the pope accused him of complicity in murder, but he cleared himself and afterward was Abbot of Battle. William Fitzstephen fared best of all: the king made him the Sheriff of Gloucester and an itinerant justice and thus he traveled round observing many interesting things. He wrote a life of Thomas, with some miracles, and it was well received.

Edward Grim, the monk of Cambridge, also wrote a life of the archbishop, and so did John—a very short one, in a letter. He made no attempt to profit by his friend's posthumous glory. He went back to his books, and afterward became Bishop of Chartres. Many others wrote their versions of Thomas' story—his life, his passion, and a record of his miracles. Benedict did this. And a French poet visited Christchurch and also Barking, where sister Mary was now abbess, and wrote down all he learned in verse and then recited it beside the tomb and was rewarded by his listeners. Herbert of Bosham took too long with his biography and, as the years of composition dragged, added too many words and thus—as he complained—was slighted when at last his book appeared.

Richard de Luci was surprised at first by all the miracles. "A man so worldly?" But he came round. He built the Abbey of Lesnes in Kent in honor of the Blessed Virgin and of the Blessed Martyr, St. Thomas, and he retired there after his long years as justiciar and died in the black habit of a monk.

In a few years the pilgrims came so thick and fast to Canterbury that the town grew rich. So many inns sprang up to house them—here, there, an extra room built on to every house—the aldermen were forced to pass a law: no host or keeper of an inn could run outside his door to cry up his own hostelry, solicit patronage of passing strangers, or snatch the bridles of their horses and bring them in. Wulviva suffered from this law; they had a room built on. But after that she went out selling tokens of the saint—the little flattened images that Walter cast in lead. He also made tin bottles—fit to hang around the neck—in which the monks dispensed the water of St. Thomas. Thus they all prospered.

The Thomas water was not sold; it was a holy thing. But if a pilgrim at the tomb asked for a little to take home, or if he felt the need to show his gratitude for any other thing, the monks were willing to accept a gift. And thus the offerings at the tomb piled up. First came the crutches and the bandages, the worms that children had coughed out (sometimes a yard in length), the little gifts of treasures—silver pennies in a cup, a carved wood bowl, a pair of gloves. Then lengths of woolen cloth and silver broaches, embroidered chasubles. The wedges of pure gold King Henry brought, the heavy silks.

A votive candle always made a proper offering. There was a custom, when a miracle took place, of measuring the succored part—the arm, the head, full body length—and giving a candle of that height as thanks. "Measure me for St. Thomas!" became a common cry. And thus a candle-forest grew, below ground, in the crypt.

Above, behind the choir, they built a better place: a chapel with a golden shrine with pearls and precious stones, with painted screens and brocade curtains over a marble tomb. It was completed in 1220 and they moved Thomas there—with trumpets blaring, choirs singing, and such festival as never had been seen in England, and all the great men of all nations walking in his train. Few of them had seen Thomas when he was alive. Henry was dead a long time, and all his sons. The boy king, Henry III, knelt at the tomb for England.

More than three centuries St. Thomas' shrine gave glory to the world, solace to pilgrims, legends and tales to tell. It was a meeting place of strangers, a spectacle of wealth, source of a thousand miracles in Thomas' name. More than three hundred years—until another king sat on the throne, another Henry, rougher than the first. He pulled the shrine down, carted the treasures off, rifled the tomb and took the rotted body out, scattered the bones.

So all is gone now, all the wonder gone, the spirit vanished, the miracles stopped up. The bones are gone and scattered, lost in dust.

Nobody knows where they lie now.

SIGNET Biographies You Will Enjoy

Other Outstanding Novels in SIGNET Editions

HURRY SUNDOWN **by K. B. Gilden**

The sensational bestselling novel in which a group of intensely human characters become involved in every kind of conflict when the rival forces of tradition and progress make a battlefield of their Southern community. (#W2860—$1.50)

THE PRIZE **by Irving Wallace**

The skillfully woven background of Nobel Prize history and the dramatic reconstruction of the lives of six Nobel Prize winners, have made this novel an international bestseller. (#Q2305—95¢)

WANDERERS EASTWARD, WANDERERS WEST

Ranging across the continent, this is a shocking novel of bold men and women, from the rugged mining camps of Montana to the ruthless business of Wall Street, the people who shaped America. Slated for movie production by MGM. (#Y2822—$1.25)

THE LOCKWOOD CONCERN **by John O'Hara**

A national bestseller, the century-spanning saga of a family in pursuit of money, power, status, and sex, set in the "O'Hara" country of eastern Pennsylvania. (#Q2876—95¢)

TOMORROW'S HIDDEN SEASON **by George Byram**

The highly-acclaimed novel of a young Mexican's struggle toward manhood in the horse country of Colorado—and of the sensual woman who helps him. (#T2657—75¢)

YOUNGBLOOD HAWKE **by Herman Wouk**

The massive bestseller about a young novelist from the Kentucky hills—a man of great talent who rockets to success and piles up and loses fortunes in a dazzling career. By the author of *The Caine Mutiny* and *Marjorie Morningstar*. (#Y2325—$1.25)

FLOOD **by Robert Penn Warren**

Old crimes and forgotten indiscretions haunt the citizens of a Tennessee town on the brink of disaster. (#Q2611—95¢)

To Our Readers: If your dealer does not have the Signet and Mentor books you want, you may order them by mail enclosing the list price plus 10¢ a copy to cover mailing. (New York City residents add 5% Sales Tax. Other New York State residents add 2% plus any local sales or use taxes.) If you would like our free catalog, please request it by postcard. The New American Library, Inc., P.O. Box 2310, Grand Central Station, New York, N. Y. 10017.